# Connected.

NICK APUZZO

PUBLISHED BY:
LULU.COM

Connected.



nickapuzzo.com

ISBN 978-0-557-50867-9

*To my family,*
*who had more faith in me*
*than I had in myself.*

ACKNOWLEGMENTS

My deepest and heartfelt thanks to Robert *Big Guns* Gundersen, Ryan *Ry Diggity* Mull, Michael *Mobile Boyz* Riddell, and to my older brother Joe.

Words cannot express the gratitude I feel to my Jedi Master of "*Keep Moving Forward....*" Scott Schweitzer. He never lost faith in me.

Finally, for the sheer audacity to try this, I'd also like to thank Jonathan Palmer and Barry Grieder.

*Chi troppo vuole nulla stringe.*
*(One who wants too much, holds on to nothing.)*
*— Italian Proverb*

# Chapter 1
# *Last Words*

*The Bronx, New York City*

Angelo Cento sat at his usual table in the back of the social club, a dark brown maduro in his shirt pocket and a demitasse of pungent black espresso laced with Anisette on the table in front of him. He had gray hair and black thick-framed glasses and from a distance he looked like the typical senior citizen; when you got close though, you saw something else. His shoulders and arms were fairly large and muscled, and his eyes were inquisitive and intense. Angelo didn't speak much and when he did it was with a minimum of expression; in fact, no one had ever heard him raise his voice in anger. His serious and contemplative nature made him a man both respected and feared.

The dimly lit interior of the club smelled of cigars; the windows had long ago been painted-over with the exception of a wide rectangular one high on the wall across from the scuffed wooden bar. The sun was setting and its golden rays spilled in through that one window, glinting off of the brass plating of the old espresso machine. The club was nearly empty at the moment; a small group of men were there reading the sports section and watching ESPN. 'Pin' stood behind the wooden bar making a cappuccino. Primo Pinelli was called 'Pin' because of his last name and his needle-thin physique, and was the oldest guy in the room; in fact he was probably the oldest guy in the room back in the days when Victor Forza, one of Angelo's predecessors, was running things. Pin usually had a smile on his face and barely said three words all day; he'd been there and done that. Wiseguys spend a lot of their time talking about nothing in particular: sports, women, the next scam and many of them had a talent for spinning thirty seconds of nothing into thirty minutes of bullshit. Pin had done it for so long he'd run out of bullshit, so now he was content in his old age to listen to everyone else's.

Jimmy 'Knievel' Leonardo sat at the bar in a black suit custom tailored by Gino Fiore, a local tailor of legendary skill and with an equally legendary clientele. Jimmy had a white cloth napkin across his lap as he ate his usual salsiccia e peperoni from Nino's Deli, located just a few doors down from the social club. Jimmy was a dapper man, even by mob standards; on his left hand he wore an enormous pinky ring made of white gold and set with a large blue star sapphire encircled by diamonds and on his wrist a vintage Patek Philippe. He'd earned the nickname 'Knievel' many years ago in front of this very building.

A local couldn't pay Jimmy the money he owed on a gambling debt, so Jimmy took the man's customized '58 Harley-Davidson Sportster as payment. The motorcycle was parked in front of the club that day as Jimmy looked for a buyer and everyone going in and out of the club noticed the bad-ass wheels. That evening Jimmy mounted the chopper to find a place to store it; he'd gone a total of ten feet when the front wheel hit the curb and took on a strange angle. As the motorcycle's extended forks cocked, it began to tip over and Jimmy was not prepared for the Harley's considerable weight. When the heavy frame was just inches from the asphalt, Jimmy's ankle broke its fall. The shattered ankle called for a plaster cast and to his consternation and despite the threats he issued, from then on everyone called him Jimmy 'Knievel'.

At the moment, Angelo was waiting for a visit from Eddie Ferrara. He looked up and almost imperceptibly raised an eyebrow at Jimmy, an unspoken 'Where is he?' Jimmy answered the gesture with an equally subtle shrug 'He should be here.' Angelo returned to staring into his cup, lost in thought.

Angelo didn't survive this long in 'the life' by taking anything for granted. He was slow to trust anyone, slow to trust even for a wiseguy, and wiseguys trust nobody; it's their defining characteristic. The life had taught him to be dispassionate about continuously evaluating the people around him, analyzing their strengths and weaknesses, their habits and volatility. You had to use your brains and adapt to survive, that was the reason humans were at the top of the food chain. It was especially true in the jungle Angelo thought; everyone knew that in the jungle you needed strength to survive, but even more important, you had to have a plan. Everyone in ‘the life’ was brutal by necessity and most by nature as well, however some were also intelligent. Of course, intelligence itself was also not enough. If you expected to survive in his environment you had to think ahead, had to have a plan; the intelligent and prepared outlived the strong and careless.

The people that surround you in the life are people who don’t have much in the way of a moral compass. Angelo smirked as he considered all that popular culture about the mob having a moral code and honor and all of that horseshit in the movies. Whatever it may or may not have been back in the days of Charley Lucky and Joe 'The Boss' Masseria, the family was a business, and it operated successfully because it had rules and organization.

The rules were brutally enforced; the only reason people in the family didn’t lie, cheat and steal from each other more than they already did, was that it would cost them their money or their heads.

Organization and stability were the characteristics that most differentiated the Italians from other ethnic crime enterprises. Brutality, determination and ambition were qualities that every ethnic crime organization displayed on a regular basis. Within Cosa Nostra, emphasis was placed on each member knowing his place within their borgata, and this allowed the organization to maintain its integrity even when key members were sent to prison or killed. It was a successful system of government for thieves and murderers and for it to work, it had to be simple and it had to be certain.

A family’s structure is paramilitary and commanding it is the Capofamiglia, commonly referred to as simply 'the Boss', absolute ruler with unquestioned life or death authority over everyone in the organization. At his side is his Consigliere, an advisor chosen for his loyalty, knowledge of the family business, and political strength internal to the family's alliances and factions.

The boss's second-in-command, the Sotto Capo or 'Underboss', has powers that vary depending on the man holding the position. The underboss more closely runs the day to day activities of the organization and acts as a buffer between the boss, who gives the orders, and the people responsible for carrying them out. The underboss is the successor to the boss in the event of his death, or his representative on the street if the boss is imprisoned and chooses to run the organization from his cell.

The underboss directly controls a group of Capo régimes usually referred to as Capos or Captains; these are the family's middle level managers who run 'crews' (groups) of soldiers. Since only the Boss, Underboss and Consigliere are above the rank of capo, it's a powerful position; a soldier at odds with his capo is a soldier with a severely limited life expectancy.

Finally, the people who rely on a soldier's protection and power to conduct their business, yet are not members of the organization, are known as 'connected' guys. To a connected guy, a made guy is his boss, his agent and his police, all rolled into one; of course in some cases he may also turn out to be his judge, jury and executioner.

Eddie Ferrara was thirty years old and commanded a lot of respect in the family for someone his age, he lived in a world that usually equated respect with the number of contracted hits a guy had under his belt. Eddie's rise wasn't related to those qualities and in this way he stood apart. He wasn't 'straightened out', which is to say, Eddie was not a full-fledged member of the family, yet he was entrusted with responsibilities beyond those of some 'made' men and that was truly unprecedented. The fact that Eddie's 'made man' was Angelo, a capo, made his situation even more unique.

Eddie had, on a two occasions, declined to carry out an action against someone. To Angelo, for business purposes, the reasons were less important than the fact that he needed to be able to count on his orders being followed without question. A soldier carries out the orders of his capo without question, or risks being whacked. This hadn't backfired on Eddie because of his reputation and because he had a way of handling it deftly and with respect. In all but these two incidents where he declined to act, the job was always handled well. He was a stand up guy and a good 'earner'; he just didn't exactly fit the mold of a soldier that Cosa Nostra had relied upon since its beginnings. Eddie, in his subtle but effective way, had positioned himself to remain connected only; Angelo's ability to read people was incomparable, and he trusted Eddie, so others in the organization did too.

Angelo mused that in another life Eddie would definitely have been a civilian, an academic or something… anything but a wiseguy. But this wasn't another life and everyone had to play the cards they'd been dealt. He heard the door open and looked up to see Eddie coming into the club.

As he approached Angelo's table, Eddie stole a glance at Jimmy Knievel who had finished his sandwich and was now reading the paper; Jimmy returned the glance over the top of page 6 of the Daily News and wordlessly returned to his reading, a sign that Angelo might not be in the best of moods. As Eddie reached the table Angelo sat back in his chair and took a sip of his espresso, then gestured to Pin to bring a cappuccino for Eddie.

"So?" Angelo asked.

"For once he wasn't full of shit...unfortunately." Eddie replied.

Angelo leaned forward, and fixed his eyes on the small black pool of espresso in front of him and grunted softly. Just then Pin arrived at the table and placed a steaming cappuccino in front of Eddie, who nodded his wordless thanks.

"We really don't need this bullshit right now." Angelo said to his cup, then looked up at Eddie "The FBI will be grandstanding all over this, and in the end it's even money they fuck it up."

This prompts a nod from Eddie and after a minute of silence he says "And you can also lay odds that if the Feds can pin some kind of bullshit story to us about being connected with whoever these fanatics are, they'll do it."

"Did you get what we needed?" Angelo asked, his casual tone betraying none of the anxiety he felt.

"Yeah. I think so." Eddie said.

"Where is he?"

"He was tired of living…what can ya do?" Eddie shrugged.

"Yeah, that's a real fuckin' shame." Angelo said sarcastically. "Well, we need to finish this thing before they mobilize a task force the size of a small army." Angelo said, referring to the FBI.

Eddie smiled and said "As it turns out, it probably wouldn't matter if they did." prompting a quizzical look from Angelo. "They'll get what they're after…just not what they want." Eddie finished.

Angelo looked back down as his cup again, and after a long and contemplative silence said "The only way I can see that working is if there are two of them." he looked up at Eddie "There are two of them?"

Eddie's expression remained neutral, but only due to years of practice; Angelo had figured out the situation and his strategy that quickly; the man had skills.

"Exactly. The man gave up the plan. If you give me the OK we'll be wired up and waiting for his friends, but first we'll take a drive over do a dry run."

"Something this size…take Jimmy and a couple of his guys."

"You want my opinion?"

Angelo nodded.

"Less is more. These guys have gotta be lookin' over both shoulders." Eddie said reasonably "If they spot anyone they'll call it a day and its more time for the Feds to assemble their troops." Eddie took a long sip of his cappuccino and continued "Even if they see some pedestrian walking behind them and think they spotted someone…I figure the best approach is to minimize the risk."

"That fuckin' thing goes off, they'll be a lot of people askin' questions." Angelo said, prompting Eddie to think about the consequences of failure, within the family. "A catastrophe like that…the Old Man…and Carbone too…" Angelo shrugged, indicating that once the boss or the underboss got involved, he would have little influence over what the fallout was.

"Not the issue…" Eddie said "…it's whatever gives us the best chances. Fra il due mali scegli il minore…yeah?"

"Broad shoulders you got." Angelo said with the beginnings of a smile "OK. You need anything, get word to me; I'll talk to Jimmy, he'll be ready just in case."

Connected.

◆ ◆ ◆ ◆ ◆

As I leave the club I'm feeling like someone took a baseball bat and went to work on my skull. This was a busy day. We find out that some scumbag group is planning to explode a bomb in a container at the Brooklyn Piers and its sheer luck we find out ahead of time. We don't know if it's nuclear, biological or just the old-school kind that goes BOOM, but we're searching for some way to pin down who's going to do the work. The obvious problem is that there are thousands of containers at the Red Hook piers and the one that contains the bomb is a needle in a hay stack.

All of the five families have a combined financial interest in the smooth operation of that port, and the last thing anybody needs is a fucking bomb blast and all the resulting homeland security news and political grandstanding. The FBI would be giving out free colonoscopies to every wiseguy in the northern hemisphere, and that would disrupt our business, maybe permanently.

Yesterday, a pair of FBI men come strolling into the club, Special Agents Spina and Woods, and they tell Angelo that they know he's in possession of some information regarding a possible terrorist attack on one of the major ports. They lay out the basic bullshit to Angelo: we have a common interest in seeing the threat neutralized; the security at the ports would become a matter of public interest and would spark an outcry for far more stringent security measures, so we should work together. They even waved the flag a little bit. Wisely, he tells them he has to think it over and make some inquiries.

The guy involved in our finding out about this whole thing in the first place is a small time smack dealer and street hustler named Benny, and this guy has an uncanny ability to pick the losing team in nearly any major sporting event…and bet heavily on them. It's this special talent that has landed Benny in debt to Angelo for a pile of cash, and he tells me he'll put us on to one of the guys involved if we reason with Angelo to forgive some of his debt. Considering how much pain we're going to go through if the bomb goes off, Angelo agrees.

Benny fingers the mutt for us and we pay the guy a visit. After a few hours of stimulating conversation, he rolls over and gives us details. Sadly, they turn out to be his last words. Life is cruel.

# Chapter 2
# *Chase At The Piers*

The black Lexus sedan accelerated into a left turn onto east 176th street, its tires squealing slightly in mild protest. It stopped in front of a three story apartment building in the middle of the block then slowly continued on, stalking westward and coming to a stop at the corner in front of Sal's Pizza #1. The heavily tinted driver's window slipped silently into the door, revealing a wide face and broad shoulders.

"Get in."

"What's up?"

The reply was silence, and of course 'the stare'.

'That fucking dead-eyes stare.' Mike Zirella lamented as he got into the car. They pulled away from the curb and turned left onto Jerome Avenue. Unnerved by this surprise visit, Zirella commanded himself to relax.

"I have somewhere I'm supposed to be." he said with more calm than he felt.

More silence. Richie Scala wasn't much of a conversationalist.

They had merged onto the Cross Bronx Expressway toward the George Washington Bridge, when Richie finally spoke.

"I'd like to have a piece of every fuckin' Duracell the FBI buys to keep their bugs working."

Zirella's eyes flashed toward the dashboard.

"Fuckin' miniaturization.. parabolics… GPS… they have all that shit working for them." Richie said in his gravely voice "Smarten up!"

A few more minutes of silence passed. Richie was scary to be around; even while driving he looked menacing. His chest, shoulders and arms were disproportionately large, and the jacket he wore strained at the seams; his neck looked like the trunk of a redwood. His body language had always radiated complete confidence and Zirella had no doubt that the Richie saw him simply as a pack mule, someone to do some heavy lifting.

"All due respect, how long we gonna be? I have to be somewhere."

No response.

"Can you just…"

"Managgia…" Richie cut him off with irritation in his voice "You are somewhere, and you'll be done when you're done." The tone and the wave of his hand said it all; 'Conversation over.'

'Well…' Zirella thought, '…at least we're heading towards where I needed to be.'

They took the ramp for 9A, the highway that ran down western shoreline of Manhattan. Traffic was dense, as it nearly always was, but moving none the less. Zirella glanced over at the driver's large muscled hands gripping the steering wheel, a tattoo peeking out from under the cuff of his right sleeve. He sighed softly and resigned himself to the situation; in a practical sense there was nothing he could do but wait to see what this was all about.

Fifteen minutes later they took a left at 26th street, and suddenly Zirella knew where they were headed, yet still had no idea why. Another left onto 8th Avenue and the car came to a stop a few doors down from Spice, an fairly popular gay sex club that in fact, Mike Zirella owned.

"You came to drive me to work?"

Richie ignored him "Come on, let's go." He got out of the car and headed off toward the club.

Instead of entering through the front door, Zirella led Richie down an alley beside the club and around through the rear door.

The first thing that one noticed upon entering was the muffled music, heavy on the subwoofer; it caused rhythmic 'thudding' in the center of the chest. Then came the odor, pleasant and vaguely citrus; incense. The corridor they were standing in was unlit, and they walked slowly waiting for their eyes to adapt. They reached a door and Zirella opened it to reveal a cramped office, but Richie grabbed him by the upper arm before he could enter.

"Not in there."

"Huh?"

“I don’t like the way it looks. No good.” he said shaking his head as he peered inside the tiny room “This place has a basement?”

Zirella nodded thinking ‘Christ what a paranoid pain in the ass.’

“Show me.” Richie commanded.

Zirella led the way to a door a few feet away, and halfway down the narrow staircase, became aware that someone else was already there.

“Who’s down here?” he asked in an authoritative voice as he negotiated the last few steps down.

No one answered and as he turned the corner he saw two men, younger than the he or Richie. Both clean cut; one was dressed in a navy blue Adidas warm up suit, the other was wearing jeans and a black nylon windbreaker with a BMW logo.

“Th’fuck are you? How’d you get down here?” Zirella asked, feeling real irritation that two guys from the gay ‘clientele’ upstairs decided to go exploring, thought it wasn't the first time it had happened. He also knew that for all the fear his burly associate inspired in him, Richie was also completely capable of dealing with any conceivable threat.

Zirella hadn’t put it together yet.

In the blink of an eye the man in the Adidas warm up suit reached out and grabbed Zirella savagely by his hair; the top of Mike's head instantly felt like it was on fire as he was yanked down into a wooden chair.

“Arrrrgggghhh what the fuck!”

Richie didn’t move, he just stood there and waited.

“Shut your fuckin' yap and pay attention!” Adidas suit growled, as he released his grip on Zirella’s hair.

The man in the BMW windbreaker produced a large roll of duct tape and with practiced speed the two bound Zirella's arms and legs securely to the chair. When they'd finished they stepped back and for a few seconds Zirella strained to free himself, then resigned himself to the fact that it was hopeless.

“What the fuck is this?” Zirella protested.

He’d barely completed the sentence when Adidas guy grabbed his throat, the tips of the fingers of his big right hand mercilessly squeezing Zirella's throat in a grip of steel; the attacker's left hand held his head immobile by the hair on the back of his head. Zirella tried desperately to shake his head and dislodge the hand that was nearly crushing his windpipe, but to no avail, the man was just too strong.

The pain was excruciating and he couldn't breathe as he stared into the eyes of the source if his torment, finding no hint of emotion. As Zirella felt his face begin to swell from the lack of oxygen and circulation, Richie stepped forward and bent over to stare directly into his eyes.

"I'm going to ask you some questions. If you lie to me, it's all over for you. Capisci?"

Zirella couldn't speak and he strained to nod despite the hand crushing his wind pipe.

"Now don't make a fuckin' jerk outta me! You understand?" Richie snarled as he waved a thick finger a fraction of an inch from Zirella's now reddened face.

Again, a strained nod.

"OK." Richie nodded to the man at Zirella's throat, who released his grip.

Zirella sputtered and gasped for air as his face began to return to its normal color.

The question-and-answer session lasted half an hour. The essential information Mike Zirella gave took no more than perhaps five minutes to tell, however Richie changed the wording of the questions a few times to ensure he was getting the whole picture. When he was satisfied, his questions ceased and he seemed to relax; the room became quiet and the heavy thumping beat of the music from upstairs was suddenly noticeable again. Richie stood silently, looking at the floor and carefully sifting through the information he'd received.

"OK." he muttered, more to himself than anyone else "I guess it all adds up."

"I'm not stupid enough to lie to you! Don't you know that?" Zirella said, shaking in his chair as rivulets of sweat continued to make their way from his hairline down his cheeks and soaking into the collar of his shirt.

Richie turned quickly to face him "The fuck do I know who's lying to me? Who am I Mento the fuckin' Magician!"

"You think I was holding out on you?" Zirella shot back in a plaintive voice.

"I didn't say that!"

"Then what the fuck was this?"

"There's what I think I know, and there's what I know." Richie said.

A long silence followed.

"Can I go now?" Zirella asked, his voice cracking and his fear only just beginning to subside. His body started to shake involuntarily as he came down from his adrenaline rush. He was convinced in that first instant he couldn't breathe that his life was coming to an end, but now he was feeling the full force of relief that Richie wasn't going to kill him.

"Yeah, you can go." Richie said casually, turning his back on Zirella.

The man in the Adidas suit approached Zirella slowly and looked down at him with a bored expression for a moment and then placed a thick clear plastic bag with an elastic band, over his head; the band was tight enough to form a seal around his perspiration slicked neck. Panic gripped Zirella and he tried to thrash about and shake his head free, but it was a futile effort, the two had done a thorough job with the tape. The bag made a crinkling sound as it expanded and contracted with the owner's desperate gasps for air. His lungs started to burn as he looked wide eyed through the now fogging plastic at the blank expression on Richie's face. He felt his panic start to subside as the strength slowly left his limbs; spots appeared in his field of vision as his consciousness ebbed.

He saw Richie turn and make his way toward the stairs, and the last thing he heard before he passed out was Richie's gravely voice saying "Finish it. Don't fuck it up."

*Brooklyn, New York City*

Eddie Ferrara took a long pull on his Grande Cappuccino; his eyes stared expressionless over the rim of the white paper cup, through the glass storefront and down Dean Street, just another New Yorker overcoming his 'brain-fry' with a little chemical assistance. He heard a voice in his head say “Couple of those chocolate glazes and a coffee regular.” which nearly prompted a smirk. He caught it in time though. For ten minutes Eddie sat, sipped and listened unhappily to the sounds from the tiny wireless surveillance earpiece buried in his right ear canal: the slurping of coffee, the rustling of thin wax paper as it cradled a doughnut; ‘This is really fucking annoying…’ he thought ‘I’d go crazy if I had to listen to this shit all day’.

Suddenly, sound burst painfully into his ear, loud enough to make him wince "He's moving. South."

Eddie was leaning back in his chair, his legs stretched out and his feet under the empty chair that faced him. His forearms rested on the little wooden table as he stared lazily at his smart phone, tapping at the screen slowly. He looked like the majority of the population these days, just another guy on a break from work, but not really a break, leashed as he was…as they all were, to their mobile devices. The casual movement of his eyes was barely perceptible as he glanced at the slight reflection from the glass pastry case to his left and slightly behind him. Still there.

“West on Livingston.” the disembodied voice said. "Dark blue collared shirt, pants and work jacket… a few more cannoli and he'd be a dead-ringer for Ralph Kramden."

Eddie would have to make a decision soon, within two minutes at most. He tapped at the screen of his smart phone again; anyone would have guessed he was checking email, or perhaps exchanging text messages. He wasn't. He hit the refresh button on its screen, and the noticed with satisfaction that tiny red dot on the map hadn’t moved, it was still on Hicks Street between Pacific and Amity. The seconds ticked by and the voice in his head, Tony D.’s voice, was as quiet as a tomb. ‘Patience…’ Eddie told himself ‘…sometimes doing nothing IS doing something.’

A little more than a quarter mile to his north, Tony carefully shadowed the guy dressed in blue.

Eddie stole another quick glance at the pastry case and saw movement. He went back to his ‘email’ and commanded himself to do nothing. He remained seated a full thirty seconds after the ‘reflection’ had left the coffee shop, then stood, tossed his empty cup in the trash can and left the shop looking like someone in no particular hurry. When his feet hit the sidewalk he restrained himself from taking a look around, and instead immediately turned to his right and headed south on Court Street. He moved along, his eyes focused on the 'middle distance' that people in any big city gaze into when going about their normal routine. Not in a hurry, but not sightseeing. After just half a minute he followed his subject onto Amity Street, toward the shoreline just a half mile to the west.

The sun was particularly bright today, but he snatched a glance down the street without squinting. Bingo. His target was perhaps two hundred feet ahead of him, on the opposite side of the street. Faded green hooded sweatshirt, black jeans with tan work boots, medium height and build, olive colored skin. He was walking at a normal pace, hands empty.

“West on State.” Tony crackled loudly in his ear.

Eddie fished the phone out of his pocket; the red dot was still in place. So far, so good. The target had picked up his pace a little and Eddie did not match it, allowing himself to fall a bit farther behind. Patience.

Discipline played the most significant role in this game, tailing a target without being noticed was difficult if that target was trained, but not impossible. Of course, you stood a better chance of remaining undetected if you had a crew of trained people since you could set up zones, leapfrog, waterfall and generally avoid being recognized. If you didn’t have that kind of resource, than you relied on discipline, technology… and of course, luck.

They crossed Clinton Street and were halfway to Henry, when Tony spoke again; "West on Atlantic from Henry. Getting close." Tony’s subject was moving more quickly than Eddie’s.

Eddie’s target was about twenty feet from the next intersection, and he’d probably take the opportunity to look behind him when he reached the corner. When and if that happened, Eddie didn’t want to be seen; he might be forced by circumstance to be seen by the target later, and didn’t want to be recognized.

Tony’s voice again "Feds.” then he added “Black Suburban."; indicating that he had 'eyes-on' the red dot displayed on the map on Eddie’s phone.

When his target reached the corner Eddie squatted down between two parked cars, and in the space between their bumpers saw the target glance backward for an instant, then make a left onto Henry Street. Eddie continued his pursuit and upon reaching Henry he turned to follow him. He immediately spotted a homeless man twenty feet ahead, coming out of a doorway, undoubtedly to ask him for change, so he crossed over to the opposite side of the street and resisted the urge to look directly at his target.

“Turning south on Columbia.” Tony reported.

Eddie followed his target down Congress Street and over the noisy and crowded 'BQE', the Brooklyn-Queens Expressway. The target was walking quickly now, a little too quickly Eddie thought. "His nerves are beginning to get to him. That could work for or against me." he told himself "No big deal, just continue to be invisible."

“I can see the park.” Tony said, his tone remaining neutral and detached.

Eddie casually fished the phone from his pocket and glanced at the screen. The red dot had finally moved and it was his turn to speak to Tony for the first time since the pursuit began.

"Take a walk."

A quarter of a mile to Eddie's north, Tony slowed his pace and crossed the street, breaking off his pursuit and heading westward toward the shoreline.

Eddie tapped at the refresh button on his phone's display, this time however there was a delay. The GPS unit that was tracking its location and sending that location back to Eddie's phone as a red dot, didn't 'see the sky' on this particular cycle, which triggered its automatic backup system. Instead of determining its position relative to the constellation of satellites in geosynchronous earth orbit, it resorted to triangulating its position relative to the nearest three cellular phone towers. The red dot appeared on Columbia Street just south of Atlantic; it was approaching the man in the blue work clothes.

The 'red dot' was actually a black Chevy Suburban with heavily tinted windows, a NightHawk NoProfile light and siren package hidden behind the grill, and unknown to its occupants, a real-time GPS/CDMA sending unit held in place with a magnet on the undercarriage of the vehicle. As the Chevy moved slowly and silently down Columbia Street, a dark blue mini-van, also with heavily tinted windows, turned onto Columbia from an adjacent street and took up position behind the Suburban. Their target, the man in the blue work clothes, was ten yards ahead of them.

At that moment, two hundred and fifty yards to the south, the man in the faded green sweatshirt had crossed Columbia Street and was entering the parking lot of the New York Port Authority administration building at the Red Hook Container Terminal; more commonly known as the Brooklyn Piers. Eddie slowed his pace and then stopped at the corner of Warren and Columbia, waiting for his target to get completely across the wide flat expanse of Columbia Street. When the faded green sweatshirt had disappeared between two tall rows of cargo containers on the north side of the parking lot, Eddie quickly crossed Columbia in pursuit.

To the north, the man in the blue work clothes had just crossed the street that served as the 'Exit 27-Atlantic Avenue' off-ramp from the expressway. As he stepped up onto the sidewalk his eyes warily scanned the public park ahead and to his left. There was a game of four-on-four on the single basketball court, but both tennis courts were empty. A slight smile appeared on his lips. A line of trees stood further to his left and he quickly stole a glance in their direction, his satisfaction increasing as he found it deserted.

Just as his head was returning forward a wall of moving black metal appeared from nowhere, barely an arm's length in front of him. He stopped dead in his tracks as his heart nearly leapt from his chest. He opened his mouth and closed it again without making a sound, his disorientation lasting only a few seconds, but that was long enough. The moment his brain caught up to his surroundings, there was a thunderously loud voice from just a foot or two behind him.

"DON'T FUCKING MOVE!"

Another voice overlapped the first "FBI!"

The Red Hook port facilities are spread over 80 acres of shoreline and comprise a significant part of the largest seaport complex on the east coast of North America. As Eddie approached the wall of containers he reflected on the fact that the man in the faded green sweat shirt had just disappeared into one of the largest mazes of stacked cargo containers on the planet.

As Eddie followed him into the maze, a tall and hugely muscled man in a black leather jacket got out of a bronze colored Cadillac Seville parked in the rear of the administration building. He saw Eddie disappear into the space between the containers and stared for a long moment at the point where he'd lost sight of him. As he took a moment to completely survey the entire parking lot, he quietly closed the car door and used his key, rather than the remote control, to silently lock the doors. He turned and headed west, into a different section of the container area.

Eddie carefully made his way through the first rows of containers in pursuit of his target, when he heard Tony's voice in his ear again.

"They grabbed him. I'm at the south east corner of pier 8."

Eddie reached to the transceiver hooked to his belt at the base of his spine and pushed the small 'manual transmit' button once, silently signaling that he'd received the message. He carefully stalked around stacks of containers toward the south and was still in the cargo area, but now between piers 8 and 9A. He was about to cross a large gap between rows of containers when a new voice came through his earpiece.

"Wait one."

His anxiety rose a notch. He stood as still as a statue for fifteen seconds, although it seemed more like fifteen minutes, before hearing "Head directly south, then into the first row east."

Again he reached back under his jacket and keyed the transmitter without uttering a sound. Twenty seconds of cautious and silent movement later, he was in position. He waited for the update he knew would come.

"Big man's south of you thirty yards, and the mutt's almost exactly between the two of you. Hold up a minute." After a pause of thirty seconds "Yeah. I think this is it. Grey container. Looks like this is it. You're clear."

Connected.

Eddie didn't acknowledge the message; he was totally focused on getting as close as he could to the target without being spotted. Creeping between a row of containers adjacent to his target, he made his way silently to the north end of the row, peered ever so slowly around the corner and saw the shoulder of faded green sweatshirt a mere ten feet away. He again reached for the transceiver on his belt and pushed the manual transmit button three times in a row. He took a deep breath and dashed around the corner. The man in the faded green sweatshirt was caught totally by surprise and looked up from a kneeling position in front of a grey cargo container. His right hand began to reach for something buried under his bulky sweatshirt, but never made it there. He was startled by a deep voice from behind him.

"Hello asshole."

Suddenly his right hand was caught in a crushing grip of steel. Unable to move his arm, he strained to get a look at the source of his pain and immobility. A huge man in a black leather jacket smiled menacingly at him and incredibly, the agonizing grip became even tighter. His hand was already becoming numb.

Eddie spoke, but not to either of the men in front of him.

"How’s it look?"

Two hundred feet to the northwest, Vin carefully surveyed the surrounding area through a pair of Kowa High Lander binoculars. Perched atop the huge Liebher sixty-ton loading crane, one hundred feet in the air over pier 9A, his arms were beginning to ache. There was no convenient place to rest his elbows as he scanned the Red Hook facility, and the high-end binoculars were nearly a foot and a half long and weighed fourteen pounds.

"You're alone." Vin said.

"Clear to the car?" Eddie asked.

"Aspetta…" and then after a short pause "Yeah."

With his free hand, the hulking Philly grabbed the man in the green sweatshirt by the back of his neck and lifted him to his feet. No words were necessary; he shoved him back towards his Seville parked behind the building.

The man in the green sweatshirt had been carefully trained to say nothing if he were caught. He knew the questioning would start at some point, and he was fully prepared to be as silent as a painting. Eddie removed a big piece of chalk from his pocket and drew a large 'X' with a circle around it, two feet tall and at eye level, on the side of the grey metal container. He turned and hurried after Philly and his charge.

Eddie caught up with them just as they came to the parking lot where the stacks of containers ended; there was no concealment between where they stood and the car. Philly tossed the keys to Eddie as he hurried by. Eddie walked briskly to the car and opened the trunk. He jumped in the driver's seat and started the car. Philly shoved the man in the green sweatshirt forward, quickly covering the distance to the opened trunk. Pushing the man against the sill of the trunk, Philly took a quick look around then pushed the man down so that the top half of his body was inside.

"I got nothing to say." said the man in the faded green sweatshirt.

"Yeah, I know." replied Philly, as he reached inside of his jacket retrieving a small .22 caliber pistol fitted with a silencer and fired two rounds into the back of the man's head. He threw the pistol into the trunk, lifted the lower half of the corpse into it as well, and slammed it shut. Philly quickly jumped into the passenger seat and Eddie drove slowly toward the exit.

Vin's voice came to life in Eddie's ear.

"Can I get the fuck down from here now? I'm freezing my nuts off."

Eddie didn't respond immediately, waiting until he'd exited the facility and made a left onto Degraw Street, before he spoke.

"Let me know when he's on the ground and you're clear."

"OK." Tony replied.

About ten minutes later, Eddie received word that Tony and Vin were both safely away from the piers. As he continued to drive he gestured to the glove compartment. Philly popped it open and found it empty except for a cell phone and its battery; he fished them out, attached the battery, depressed the power button to turn it on and handed it to Eddie who pressed a speed dial button.

"Spina." a voice answered on the second ring.

"Behind the Red Hook admin building, grey container chalk marked with a big 'X' in a circle. Bring help 'cause it might be rigged…who the fuck knows."

"Who is this?"

"Go. You can thank me later." Eddie said.

"I can't…"

"Merry Christmas." Eddie cut him off and ended the call. He handed the phone to Philly who removed the battery. They made their way south on Hicks street toward the entrance to the expressway and Eddie slowed as they passed by a corner sewer grate. Philly flicked the phone into the sewer and a minute later tossed the battery out the window as they merged onto the BQE heading north.

Eddie and Philly followed the BQE, proceeding on through the Brooklyn Battery Tunnel which deposited them at the southern tip of Manhattan. They continued northward on the Westside Highway and then the Henry Hudson, exiting at 125th Street. They turned north onto Broadway and found a parking spot three blocks later. They were still two blocks from their destination, but the walk felt good after the car ride.

They turned the corner onto West 134th Street, and could see the white brick front of the five story apartment building on the south side of the street. Eddie led the way, their pace casual as they entered the front door, passed the elevator and entered a cramped stairwell that smelled of paint. The elevator bell chimed its arrival at the ground floor as the door to the stairwell was about to close, but Philly heard it in time and stopped, peering through the crack in the door to see who was getting off. Only one person emerged from the elevator, a man in jeans and a leather bomber jacket.

“Madonna! Check this.” Philly said under his breath.

“What?”

“We almost missed our appointment.”

“Oh yeah?”

“He headed out the front.” whispered Philly.

“Let’s see where’s he’s going.”

They waited half a minute and then left the building. Benny, the man they’d come to see, was not quite half a block east heading toward Amsterdam Avenue. They followed him from a distance of half a city block, and tailed him unnoticed through the City College campus and into the dense trees of St. Nicholas Park to the east. Once inside the park they allowed themselves to fall a bit farther behind Benny; there were fewer people in the park than on the streets at this time of day. They lost sight of him for a moment, but upon rounding a stand of trees they spotted him again as he approached a man near the line of trees that bordered the eastern edge of the park. Benny walked up with his hand out to greet another man who was leaning against a tree, but the gesture wasn't returned; the body language was pretty easy to read and clearly the man leaning against the tree was no friend. Benny and the unidentified man walked quickly to the sidewalk and got into a taxi that was double parked. The unidentified man drove, pulling away from the curb very quickly, speeding off northward on Edgecombe Avenue.

"I got it." Philly said, scratching down the license plate number of the cab on the edge of a dollar bill.

"Well, I guess we'll have to see what's what." Eddie said, looking at his watch as he turned back toward where their car was parked.

As they walked Eddie held his hand out and Philly put the folded dollar bill into it.

"Now you owe me money." Philly said deadpan.

"Minchia, I'm shitting my pants." Eddie returned with a smile.

# Chapter 3
# *The Neighborhood*

*The Bronx, New York City*

***15 years ago…***

It was not as much the neighborhood I grew up in, as the friends I had at the time, or rather the fathers of those friends that lead me into the life. It wasn't as though there were groups of kids from mob-connected families who socialized exclusively; in fact, a consequence of growing up in a huge city like New York was that you had several groups of friends simply due to the number and density of people. Eventually you establish hundreds of casual acquaintances before reaching adulthood, and yet in spite of this a universal truth about growing up is that whether you live in a metropolis like NYC or a small town in the mid-west, close friends are always few and far between.

Two such close friends from my early teens were Victor Forza, Jr., known as 'Junior' for obvious reasons, and Carmine Ruzzi who we called 'Buddy'. The three of us were the same age and we were part of a fairly large group that congregated each night on Vincent Avenue in the Bronx. My father had died of a heart attack when I was twelve, and Junior's father, Victor Sr., kept an eye on me, exerting a little fatherly influence from time to time. Victor Sr. had a rock-like physique and sometimes when I'd been invited to eat dinner at Junior's house, his father would flex his forearms at the table as we all made small talk. It was like he had tree trunks growing out of his sleeves. He also had 'the stare'; if he was pissed at you that stare would immobilize you.

I remember one day we broke into a vacant house that was for sale on Junior's street. It had been on the market for months and we'd never seen anyone near it, so boredom took over and in we went through an unlocked window. After we'd been in the house for about ten minutes, wandering from room to room and bullshitting about nothing in particular, we turned a corner into the living room and found ourselves face to face with Victor Sr. He looked at Junior and me with that stare and suddenly I needed a change of underwear. You get the picture.

I saw much less of Buddy Ruzzi's father, Mario. He 'worked nights' and was always sleeping in the day. We had to be quiet if we were bullshitting in front of Buddy's house so we wouldn't wake up his father. Mario always looked like he was on his way to something important. He dressed in expensive suits, big pinky rings, wafer-thin watches and always drove a new, washed and waxed Cadillac. It was hard not to notice him once you caught the smell of his expensive cologne or the reflection of the sunset off of his jewelry as he was heading out to 'work'.

Junior's father, Victor Sr., dressed like most of the other guys his age in the neighborhood; you could call it Bronx-middle-class casual. You definitely got the impression Victor was trying not to attract attention, to appear as just another average Joe. It didn't work. He had a magnetism about him. Some people just seem to have that inexplicable charisma that draws attention in their direction…Victor Sr. had that in spades. With that aura around him it was a futile effort on his part to try and 'blend in'; he stood out to anyone who glanced in his direction.

In my early-to-mid teens I'd see Victor on a daily basis; he was friendly and fatherly to me, and always encouraging. I can remember only one time that he unloaded on me; I was sixteen and got into some trouble in high school. I attended an all-boys Catholic high school that was run by the Jesuits. These guys were all dedicated, educated and I speak the truth…tough. Occasionally some clown would take a swing at one of them and all I can say is that what resulted was always fun to watch.

By way of example, I recall a day I received after-school detention for being late to first period. The ritual consisted of standing outside of the principal's office for a couple of hours, your back touching the wall; in fact if you received detention it was known as getting 'the wall'. On this particular day I was standing there against the wall when a senior named De Luca, roughly the size and shape of a soda machine, knocked on the door and entered the office of the principal, Brother Mark Curran; De Luca barely fit through the doorway. He was a few inches over six feet and his shoulders looked every bit as wide; he played on the school's defensive line. He closed the door after he entered, and within a few short minutes it was becoming clear that they were arguing; their voices becoming louder still as the seconds ticked away. I'd never heard anyone yell at the Principal.

Brother Curran was of only average height, and all of the Brothers wore loose black robes so you really didn't get a sense of their musculature. In Brother Curran's case, the power he projected was not a result of his physical size, nor did his authority come from his position as principal. His power lie in the way he carried himself, he had a serious and focused bearing. He radiated confidence; he had no doubt that he was in charge and would take no bullshit.

There I was mouth open in shock after hearing De Luca yell "FUCK YOU!" to Brother Curran.

After a second or two of stunned silence, Brother Curran yelled "Get out of here!"

I was amazed that De Luca wasn't picking his teeth up off the floor. Big as he was, I'd never had any doubts about Brother Curran's ability to deal out a little 'attitude adjustment' when needed. At that moment I'd imagined that in a rare display of tolerance, the little voice inside of Brother Curran's brain said '*I shall allow him to live.*'

As De Luca walked out of the office and into the hallway, every eyeball of those on 'the wall' was glued to him. Brother Curran followed close behind, saying nothing. Then without warning De Luca spun around and sucker punched the unsuspecting principal square on the jaw.

What happened next, happened so fast, that the re-telling of it later by each of us on 'the wall' that day took on widely differing versions. The punch knocked Brother Curran against his office door frame, stunning him for a moment. He rubbed his jaw and shook his head as if to clear it; then without putting more than his shoulder into it, his right fist lashed out and smashed into De Luca's beefy chin. The punch was so hard that it sent the De Luca's huge frame sailing backward and almost on top of me; instinctively I leaned slightly to my left and avoided the impact.

De Luca hit the wall hard, his legs folded under him and his body slid down the surface of the wall landing on his ass. It was only when he continued to fall over onto his side that we discovered he was out cold. It was pretty impressive. Brother Curran still didn't say a word; instead he simply dragged the unconscious De Luca back into his office by the collar and closed the door. The way it worked out, his loss was our gain because when De Luca's father arrived, Brother Curran sent us all home.

Back to Victor's fatherly influence; a teacher was riding me and I got angry and told him off. I didn't curse at him, but basically did everything but curse at him. I was sent to the principal's office where I refused to back down, and though I didn't have words with Brother Curran, I did refuse to relent. As a result I received a suspension and somehow that very day Victor found out. Junior came looking for me to tell me that his dad wanted to have a word. I didn't think much about it as I was sure he couldn't possibly have known about the suspension yet.

We went to Junior's house and found Victor in the garage.

"Are you a fuckin' baby?" he asked in an irritated tone "I thought you were a man." He had the stare on, and it felt as though his eyes bore through my own and out the back of my skull.

"What are you talking about?" I said with my best 'Who me?' face on.

He reached out and slapped me, hard. It was so sudden that I felt disoriented and my ears were ringing. Victor had a big beefy hand, it felt like a brick.

"Well? We going to play fuckin' games here Eddie, or are you going to act like a man?"

I thought about running, but sometimes you have to face the music.

"I'm going to act like a man."

"Good. Now, tell me."

"Brother Brendon was riding my ass, even more than usual. The guy's got a hard-on for me Victor and I got fed up; I have my limits like anyone else does. I refused to apologize so they suspended me. That's all of it."

“Ohhh I see.” Victor said, clearly not really agreeing with me. In fact I got the feeling that he saw something that I missed.

He continued “So, let me understand this. Maybe it’s me, ya know? Maybe I’m fuckin' stunad.” he said, his anger growing.

“Your father dies, so your mother is raising you alone. She’s waiting tables five nights a week to keep a roof over your head, put food on the table and clothes on your back. She probably doesn’t ask you to do more than drag the fuckin’ garbage cans a few feet to the curb and cut the grass, and I’ll lay odds that even that gets her an argument. Your sister’s getting married soon, no?”

I nodded.

“Your older brother Peter dropped out of school and is living with a girl up by Fordham Road, right?”

Another nod.

“OK, now let's add it up. Your mother has no husband; she’s alone, with no one to share that house with but you. She works her ass off to provide for you and doesn’t ask for anything in return. We up to date here?”

A nod dumbly; I was feeling pretty idiotic at that point.

“So let me ask you something genius; why do you think this is about your teacher riding you? Your mother doesn’t have enough on her plate? She doesn’t have enough heartache? She lost her husband! Her oldest son dropped out of school and left home! Her daughter is married and gone in a month… now her youngest son is suspended from school.”

I didn't have a snappy answer, and the look on my face probably mirrored exactly how moronic I felt at that moment. Victor wasn't finished though.

“Your mother deserves better. After what she’s done for you, she deserves a lot more from you. You owe it to her! I have to point this out to you? YOU OWE IT TO HER! I mean when is this woman going to catch a break?”

Then in a tone that put the final nail in the coffin, he took a step backward and said in a soft voice “You should be ashamed of yourself. I thought you were smarter than this. This isn’t what a man would do, this is what a selfish little punk would do, now get outta my sight.”

I opened my mouth to tell him I understood, and that I'd make it right, but he cut me off.

"Now!" a tree trunk extending from his sleeve, pointing to the street.

Junior followed me out to the street. He was a good friend; he knew not to say anything and just sat next to me on the curb.

Finally he asked "What are you going to do?"

I said "I feel like shit. I know what to do though."

Victor wasn't interested in explanations or excuses. He wanted results.

Things were strained between Victor and I after that, until the end of the semester. When I received my report card I took the bus to one of Victor's businesses, a private cab company over by Morris Park, and saw his car parked outside. I waited an hour for him to emerge from the office and caught up with him as he was getting into his car. I handed my report card to him without saying a word; I had gotten one B+, the five A's. He studied it in silence for a long time, and then a slight smile slowly crept across his face. He grabbed the back of my neck with his big hand and gave it a hard squeeze, nodding his approval. He got into his car and drove off without a word. I could hold my head up in front of Victor again.

# Chapter 4
# *Loss*

Even at this stage of our lives, we didn't know that Victor and Mario were in the life. When we asked about what they did for a living, there was an answer of course. Ostensibly, Victor was "a businessman"; he owned a cab company and part of a construction company. Buddy's father Mario I was told, owned a nightclub, which is why he worked nights.

There were others in the neighborhood that we did know were wiseguys of some kind. They were more obvious (or more stupid depending on how you chose to look at it), than Victor and Mario. They always had hot stuff available to sell, if they didn't have it they could get you whatever you wanted the next time it 'fell off the truck'. They were flashy and wore their money more visibly, when they had some. In comparison, Buddy's father Mario, dressed well but was an understated sort of guy. He wasn't as loud or talkative as most of the fathers of our friends in the neighborhood…truth be told, you were lucky if you heard Mario say more than 'Hello.'

I had tried to bring another friend of mine, Tony Donato, who we called 'Tony D.', into the group of friends on Vincent Avenue but it didn't work out. He gravitated toward the crowd over by the cemetery, near the Brukner Expressway. I tended to spend more time than most running here and there, keeping tabs on groups of friends from several different areas. We didn't use the word 'networking' back then, but that's what it was. Looking back, it was that characteristic that landed me, unintentionally, my first paying gig as a connected guy although I didn't recognize it at the time.

When Junior, Buddy and I were seventeen, we did some work for Buddy's father, Mario. He'd drop us off at a little warehouse off of Pelham Parkway and we would sort through piles of merchandise. Steel belted radial tires, cases of razor blades, clothes of every type, shoes, watches, pen and pencil sets, televisions, radios, motor oil, tooth paste, light bulbs, sun glasses. You get the picture. He told us that these were goods he'd brokered, purchased from stores that were going out of business. Our job was to separate it, create an inventory list of everything, and package it up in boxes for sale on the street. The pay waspretty good and it was easy work. The topic of whether the stuff was, as Mario had told us, close-out merchandise, or in fact stolen goods, never came up. We just did our jobs as we traded bullshit for hours and hours as only teenagers can.

Some of the items would pile up and sit unsold for a long time, and since I knew and saw so many people each week I would find people to buy the unsold goods. At first I'd give their names to Mario and he'd have one of his people take care of it from there, but that didn't last long. Within a couple of months I was the point man for any business I was able to create and I took to it like a duck to water. I'd make the rounds to friends all over the Bronx, mention what I had 'on special' that week and find out anything they were looking for specifically. Mario told me a million times, not to carry anything written, not to write down requests or carry a copy of our inventory list with me when I went out. I followed his advice and found out that I had a talent for remembering a lot of detail, who was looking for what and so forth.

The following year Junior, Buddy and I graduated High School, which meant that the decision point had arrived for us, the one that we had been avoiding all of our senior year…do we continue on to college? By this time we were making great money with Mario and getting more involved week by week. I had moved up and was now responsible for everything sold out of the warehouse. It was during the summer after graduation that I noticed my mother was not looking well and when I asked about it she said that she was feeling tired all the time and wasn't sleeping well. I took her to the hospital and a week later she was diagnosed with breast cancer.

In light of the situation I postponed any deliberations about college and focused on taking care of my mother and paying all of the bills. I stepped up my pace with the warehouse and started to bank some serious cash. I was able to make up for some luxuries that her medical insurance didn't cover, and to cheer her up I bought her a new car; it was a month before she gave up telling me to take the car back.

One day I went to collect a payment for a half-truckload of watches, and after I'd gotten the cash, four guys were lying in wait for me. Three were in their early twenties, tattoos, T-shirts and so on. The fourth guy, the one in charge was much older; maybe mid forties, tall and thin, with a face like a ferret. The older guy didn't look like he was mobbed up, he was dressed like shit and needed a shave; he had this wild longish silver gray hair that made him look like a madman…like one of those guys who has his wife neatly packed in mason jars on a shelf in his basement. They took the money, twelve grand, and while two of them held me, the third guy did a little art work on me with a big rusty pipe wrench as the older guy watched. They knocked out a couple of my teeth and cracked two ribs, but in all it wasn't that big a deal. To be honest, the cracked ribs I could have avoided had I just kept my mouth shut, instead of telling the guy swinging it where he could put the wrench when he was done. Some people have no sense of humor.

I drove myself to the hospital and of course, had to sit in the emergency room bleeding for the better part of two hours before they called my name. The doctor patched me up and asked a lot of questions, none of which I answered. After I was bandaged up, he left the room for while and I took the opportunity to get out of there before the police showed up to ask me more questions.

I arrived home about nine o'clock that evening and noticed that none of the lights were on in the house, yet my mother's car was in the driveway. I found her inside; she had passed away lying on the sofa watching television. I was overwhelmed; I shut off the television and sat in a chair across from the sofa just staring at her, memories from my childhood streaming through my mind. I remembered my third birthday party, the earliest one I could recall, a gold cardboard crown, a cake with white frosting, a loud room crowded with relatives, and my father taking pictures. Curiously, I don't remember opening the presents but I can clearly recall my mother holding me up to blow out the candles and helping me to do it.

I sat there and wept, missing her already, feeling guilty that I wasn't there to hold her hand, to comfort her while she died. She was truly an unselfish woman; for as long as I could remember Margret Ferrara was never motivated by material things, she had always been about the family. She had worked as a waitress. It was a hard job and she worked a ten hour night shift in a busy diner in New Rochelle, a suburb of New York City that required a forty five minute commute each way for her. She normally worked only Friday and Saturday nights, however when my father died, she went to work five nights a week to pay the bills. For a woman in her late forties, five long night shifts a week in a very busy environment took their physical toll on her. She denied it of course, she wasn't the complaining type, but it was evident. Between the strain of work and missing my father as she did, I entertained a notion that there was a merciful dimension to her passing. It was a tenuous thought, but it was something to grab on to. For nearly an hour I sat there in the dark, bathed in silence. I searched my mind for some sense of reason, for some rationale that I could apply to live with losing her. When it finally came to me, it didn't relive the pain; in fact it tended to intensify it while somehow comforting me at the same time. I had been lucky to know her at all. To have been fortunate enough to be her son, to receive all the love and support she had selflessly given me was the most beautiful thing I had in my life. I knew I would always miss her, but I also knew that what she did for me would always be with me.

Three days later, on the first night of the wake, Tony D. had come to pay his respects. Our paths had not crossed for a few months, and he took one look at me and said "You look great!" Although my bruises had faded a bit and most of the swelling had disappeared, I still looked like a guy who'd been in a car accident. Naturally, I was telling everyone that I had been in a car accident, but Tony D. didn't buy it. After some prodding, I was telling him what had happened and an idea came to me. We were making decent money, and there was enough to go around, so I asked him if he wanted to come in with us, working for Mario's father. He agreed, I think mostly out of friendship, but I knew that he'd soon discover what a good thing we had going.

Mario would have to agree if Tony were to come in with us, so after the wake that night I grabbed him before he drove off and asked if we could talk; as it turned out, he wanted to talk to me as well. He said that after I'd taken care of my mother's funeral service we'd talk, and also mentioned that the cost of the services was 'taken care of', and I thanked him.

There was another wake the following night, and the funeral mass and gathering afterward happened the day after that, on Sunday. It was good to see my older brother and sister, Peter and Carmella, and we spent a lot of time hugging, sharing stories about our mother and some about our father as well. Each of us tried to be strong for the other two and the result was that none of us really had a chance to grieve openly, that would happen when each of us was alone. A girl that I liked, Antonia, came by and spent some time with me, holding my hand and doing her best to comfort me. Before she left we took a walk around the block, and I think she was trying to prompt me, in her gentile way, to open up and face the loss. I'd done some of that on the night I'd found my mother on the couch and it felt good to tell someone about that. When we'd completed the trip around the block, she kissed me on the cheek and said her goodbyes. After the drive to the cemetery and the burial service, we had everyone over to Belio's Trattoria for some good food and wine. To my surprise and delight, Antonia was there waiting for me. My brother and sister each spent some time talking to her amid the incredible din of conversation, and each at some point during the event, flashed me an approving smile. I spent a little time with Junior, Buddy and Tony D. as well, but with all the relatives and friends, there wasn't much free time to be with my closest friends. I spent a half hour with Victor Sr., and I had to admit to myself, it felt good to be around him at a time like this; he was like a rock to lean on. Before he left, as did Mario with the funeral arrangements, he told me that the check was 'taken care of'. To refuse him would be ungrateful so I thanked him, we hugged and he went off to spend some time with my family and mingle with friends from the neighborhood. When the gathering was over, I said my goodbyes, drove home and slept for twelve hours straight.

At eleven the next morning I was awaked by the phone, Mario called to tell me he'd pick me up at my place at ten that night. He also told me to knock off for the day, read the paper and relax. That night I had Tony D. come by an hour before Mario, thinking that I'd introduce him and get the ball rolling. Mario showed up right on time and when he saw Tony D. his expression betrayed some irritation. I tossed it out there: who he was, how long I'd known him, and my idea about how he could fit in. I could tell as I was speaking to him that he was inclined to say no, however I kept giving him reasons. Tony was smart enough to keep his mouth shut. Finally, a look came over him that was hard to pin down; an enigmatic smirk that came to rest on Tony. Clearly his wheels were spinning, but spinning where…who could tell? With a slight nod he told Tony D. to get in and take a ride with us.

Half an hour later we were on Gun Hill Road approaching White Plains Road when Mario turned into an alley between a shoe store and Gun Hill Electrical Supply. We all got out and Mario who led us to the rear door of the electrical supply place. It was pitch black and quiet for this neighborhood, even at this time of night. He rapped loudly on the big steel door and it opened immediately; someone must have seen us pulling into the alley. The three of us stepped inside and the door closed behind us with a fairly loud clang. Once inside I could see that we were in a cramped little vestibule, the only illumination came from behind us, a dim yellow light bulb flush mounted over the top of the doorway we had just walked through. When we were all inside, with the steel door closed, the guy who had let us in opened another door that lead to the back-room area of the building.

Our eyes were suddenly assaulted by harsh white fluorescent light coming from inside. We stepped into the room and surveyed the scene, and then as if on cue, Tony and I looked at each other. The room was obviously a back office, but the desk, file cabinet and everything else had been pushed against the far left wall. In the center of the floor sat four guys, and it was obvious that they'd recently taken a beating. Their faces were swollen and blood smeared, their hands were bound behind their backs and they were sitting up on the floor in a line facing the far right wall. Three of the four were the guys who did the tune-up on me with the pipe wrench, and the fourth, I was surprised to see, was the guy who I'd sold the half truckload of watches to. In those first few seconds, as I continued to take it all in, another of my senses catching up to the surroundings; someone had pissed himself.

Standing around the guys on the floor were two huge guys who, I assumed, worked for Mario. I'd never seen these guys before but each was as big as a mountain. I looked at the line of mutts sitting on the floor and followed their gaze over to the right wall. Crumpled and sitting on the floor with his back against the wall, was the crazy-looking deadbeat with the long silver hair. He looked to be in the worst shape of any of them.

"Get up." Mario said to him "On your fuckin' feet Tommy.".

The guy struggled to his feet, using the wall to support himself. Mario studied Tony D.'s face for a few seconds and then looked at me as if he were waiting for me to say something. I didn't speak right away. I surveyed all of their faces as my mind wrapped itself around the situation.

"A setup." I said, not making a question of it.

Mario simply nodded and I looked them all over again. The guy who bought the watches worked for Tommy, the silver haired guy. The scheme was obvious, take the watches and then have Larry, Mo and Curly snatch the envelope full of cash back, and protest innocence if I did put two and two together. What they hadn't counted on was my relationship with Mario. In Mario's eyes, their not knowing made no difference at all; they stole from him. End of story. If they didn't know, that was too fucking bad for them; it was the price of their ignorance.

"This jadrool… he's the architect…" Mario said "…Tommy Fornaio."

I looked at the guy; he snatched just a glimpse at me, keeping his head and his gaze otherwise locked onto the floor. He was scared, his face said it all; he was shitting his pants. A third guy of Mario's, just as big as the other two, stood next to the very unlucky silver haired Tommy Fornaio. He held a two foot length of pipe in his hand that he had undoubtedly recently put to good use. Mario took the pipe from him and held it out to me.

"Good as a wrench…" he said to me, gesturing to the pipe with his eyes; he was inviting me to deal out a little payment to this guy if I was so inclined.

"Did we get our money back?" I asked.

Mario nodded.

I carefully turned the situation over in my mind "And the watches?"

He nodded again.

It had been barely a week since the work had been done on me by these mutts, my gums still hurt from the missing teeth and my ribs would take at least a month to stop aching when I coughed. In the moment though, and quite unexpectedly, I felt no strong emotion; instead my mind was focused and analytical. I think I sort of surprised myself with this reaction.

I heard Tony D.'s voice for the first time since leaving my house.

"Which one was swinging the wrench?" he asked me.

I pointed to the one closest to him. In one motion he grabbed the pipe and smashed the guy hard across his teeth. It had to hurt more than a little. The guy whimpered but didn't really make that big a fuss, I think because he was already lumped up. He spit out a fragment of a broken tooth.

"Big fuckin' mistake you made." Tony growled threateningly, his anger clear to everyone.

He got within an inch of the guy's face and said "I hope you're gonna come after us, 'cause I'd like to finish this." and hit him a second time, this time bringing the pipe down savagely on the bridge of the guy's nose, breaking it. The mutt started to sob.

I had to admit to myself that if it were Tony D. who'd gotten jumped instead of me, I would be exacting a little revenge with that length of pipe now instead of him. It's just like that with friends; it's easier to handle adversity yourself than it is to watch the people you love go through it.

Tony threw the pipe on the floor.

Now Mario spoke to the four of them, but kept his stare locked onto Tommy.

"These guys are with me. When you spit in their face, you spit in mine." he shot a look to his guy standing next to the deadbeat "When you steal from them, you steal from me…"

Tommy was propped up against the wall and Mario's guy moved with lightening speed; he pinned Tommy's hand to the wall by the wrist and in his other hand magically produced a large switchblade that opened with a loud click. He slammed the point of the blade into the wall between Tommy's ring and pinky fingers, and quickly brought the handle of the knife down like a paper cutter across Tommy's pinky, severing it completely. It dropped onto the floor and blood immediately started to run from Tommy's hand as he let out a wail so loud that I thought I'd go deaf.

Mario stepped closer to him.

"Look at me!" he commanded, and Tommy tried to control himself and meet Mario's stare. "Consider this your lucky day, I'm letting you off with a warning." then pointing his thick finger into Tommy's face, his voice became all the more menacing for it's softness "Keep your fuckin' hands out of my pockets." Then he turned to Tony and I and said "Let's go."

On the ride home, Mario was silent, and considering that it was Mario, was nothing new.

Turning onto my street he broke the silence "First lesson, never show weakness. They take from you, you take it back with interest, and you hurt them so bad they won't think about it a second time. If you don't, you invite other mutts to do the same thing to you. Word gets around."

As Tony D. and I got out of the car, Mario asked him "You still want in?"

"Definitely." Tony answered.

"OK. Eddie'll show ya the ropes." Mario said, and as he put the car in gear he added "You handled yourself well tonight."

Tony nodded.

Mario waved and drove away, and Tony D. and I went inside and had a few beers while we watched The Honeymooners on the little black and white TV in the kitchen. We didn't exchange a word about the night's activities.

So there it was; Buddy, Junior, Tony D. and I, making decent money, more than most of the working stiffs we knew and more swag was coming in each month. Mario was there to collect his end and to take care of any big problems that came up like paying off the cops, collection problems, etc. Even though Buddy was his son, Mario dealt with us pretty much through me, and Buddy, the most amiable guy in the world, never showed the slightest sign of caring; maybe because we were together so much of the time that we were like brothers. It was too easy for all of us to keep going, to not even seriously consider changing paths and going legit, to college and onto a career as a civilian.

One night, during the week between Christmas and the New Year, Buddy was closing up the warehouse when somebody got the drop on him. They tied him up and took about fifty thousand in jewelry and furs, and as they were leaving, shot Buddy in the head.

He'd gotten the nickname 'Buddy' at an early age, not from his parents but from us, his friends. People usually speak uncharacteristically kindly of the recently deceased so we don't really take it at face value, in Buddy's case though it was no exaggeration. He always seemed 'above' the bullshit that consumed the rest of us at that age, the rivalries and petty jealousies; he just went with the flow. I cannot recall him ever bitching about anything or anyone; he just didn't make issues of things. He was one of those people who are universally liked and he'd always be there to lend you a hand; we would say the phrase so often "Thanks Buddy…." that it just stuck from sheer repetition.

# Chapter 5
# *Commitments*

If there were a range of possible reactions that Junior, Tony D. and I could have had, the fact that Buddy was tied up when they shot him pretty much limited them to a single one. We were going to find who did it and even it up. None of us had grown up employing muscle to make a buck; true we were a product of the Bronx streets, but none of us had ever come close to killing anyone. We hadn't stolen things for money's sake either, much less with the threat of a beating. None of the people who knew us would ever have described us as potential 'enforcers'.

There had been times that we had gotten into trouble, joy riding in a stolen car and even a city bus that Tony D. and I road tested once upon a time. On another occasion we stole this enormous five foot diameter plastic and metal clown head from the drive-in lane of Happy's, a burger joint over by Westchester Square, and bolted it securely atop Jerry Havik's father's yellow taxi cab. I took a file and went at the threads of the bolts in a few places so he couldn't just unscrew the bolts. Jerry was a friend or ours from the neighborhood and his father was a mean drunk. When he'd come home loaded he would beat him up pretty good sometimes, so I guess we saw it as a little payback. Two nights later we saw Jerry's father come home from his cab shift and he still had that enormous silly fucking clown head bolted to his roof; we almost pissed ourselves we laughed so hard. The way it was, none of us was a 'problem child' and on the way to becoming public enemy number one.

The one thing that could have happened to harden us, did happen; Buddy's death. We loved him; he was our brother. We had a very short meeting at the warehouse late the next night as we waited for Mario. Whoever did this had to go. There would be no explanations, no searching for reasons; that ship had sailed.

There was no discussion of who would do what, or how it would be done, and there was no posturing or bragging about what would happen when we found the mutts who did it either. There was simply unanimous agreement that it would be done, and we would do it ourselves.

Mario showed up, understandably looking like shit. As bad as we felt, he had to feel worse. He didn't say anything for a while, he just stood there trying to collect himself.

"The wake is tomorrow night. You can call Gina and ask her about the arrangements." his voice barely a whisper. He was struggling to maintain control, and suddenly turned and left. I knew it had to be at Spiro's Funeral Home and I would call there to find out the arrangements. Gina was Mario's wife, and there was no way I was going to call Buddy's mother to ask her about her son's funeral.

The wake and funeral happened pretty quickly. The entire extended family was there of course, but outnumbering them three to one was a vast sea of wiseguys. The line of men in expensive suits, quaffed hair and cologne, and many of their wives, offered their condolences to the Ruzzi family. Junior, Tony and I kept to ourselves pretty much as we talked about our times with Buddy, it made us all miss him twice as much.

On the second night of the wake, Mario motioned us to follow him. He led us downstairs and into the room where they work on the bodies. It definitely looked just as it should, cold and barren. The overpowering smell of formaldehyde was sickening. The rubber tile on the floor was nearly worn through on either side of the cadaver table, which had a ceramic top with a shallow channel that ran around the edges; I suppose to collect the bodily fluids. I didn't know, and I didn't want to know. I wondered if the cold temperature of the room was intentional, so the bodies wouldn't decay quickly while they were being worked on by the mortician.

Mario faced us and said in a gravely voice "You got anything?"

"No." I answered.

"If you hear anything, anything at all, come see me right away. Even if you think it's nothing. Capisci?"

I knew that no matter how I put it, if I tried to express our sympathy it would just sound hollow, so I said nothing. After what seemed like an eternity of silence, I decided that it was a good a time as any to let him know how things were.

"Mario, we're going to handle this." I looked at him, a hard determined ball of ice in my stomach.

He looked surprised, and just stared at us, looking from face to face, and settling back on mine.

"Pfft. Handle what?" he said, showing a little smirk "You guys don't know what you're talking about. You want some advice? Don't stick your fucking beak where it doesn't belong."

"Doesn't belong? All due respect, what are you talking about Mario?" I said, keeping my voice steady and my tone emotionless "He was your son, we understand, but we loved him too. He was like a brother to all of us. Christ he was our brother, more even than my own brother!" my tone becoming more intense, my voice almost cracking with the emotion I was barely controlling.

I locked my eyes onto Mario's. In the moment, I couldn't continue to speak about Buddy in the past tense to his father, so I said nothing.

"Stay the fuck out of it! You hear me?" He said, in an even but threatening voice.

"I'm sorry Mario, but we can't." I said, looking down at the floor, my chin tucked into my chest, shaking my head side to side "Can't do it. Anyone here disagree with me, any of you able to leave it to Mario I have no problem with that. Say your piece now. I can't leave it alone, and I'm not going to lie to Mario about that."

Junior and Tony D. were as still as statues, and just as quiet. They just stared at Mario along with me, taking their chances as I was.

Mario looked at us, from face to face, and said "You boys have done well with me, but you'll do what I goddamn say or you know what'll happen. Don't make me do something you're going to regret." I'd never seen 'the stare' from Mario, we'd never given him cause, but I saw it now. No doubt, he could be a scary fucking guy.

This was one of those moments where you make a choice and many other things later on in your life result from it, though you rarely recognize it at the time. I felt so angry about Buddy, such a sense of loss as it sank into me that I'd never see him again, that the only thing I cared about, even more than my own survival, was seeing whoever killed him, dead.

"We know you're gonna do what you have to do Mario, and so are we. Whoever did this is going to pay, and there's no fucking way we're going to leave that to someone else." I softened my voice. "We loved him too much. We won't hold it against you, whatever you have to do, but we're not going to lie to you like two-faced rats. We're going to find out who did it…" I said, gesturing toward the floor between Mario and I, my hand in the shape of a pistol "…and the three of us are going to end it."

If the room seemed quiet already, it became even more so. There was a loud hum from an electric light-up Bertoli Bros. Mortuary Supply wall clock. It struck me that now it sounded unusually loud as I waited for Mario's next move. He exhaled and then slumped a bit, walking past my shoulder. Suddenly his hand came up and grabbed me by the throat, his grip was solid steel, cutting off my air and hurting like a motherfucker. I forced myself to hold his stare, not to show even a wince of the pain I was feeling. He held on for a while, I couldn't breathe but I was determined to stare him down.

Squeezing the words out of my constricted throat, I croaked "Don't treat me like a punk Mario."

"Punk? You fuck with me and I'll end you." He said in a soft voice, more deadly for its comforting tone.

"Whatever." I croaked as I held his stare.

He let go of me and turned to leave, but stopped in the doorway with his back to us, and said "We'll do this my way. Either you'll take orders from me and we'll do this my way, or I'll put you all in the hospital for a few months and you'll be out of it altogether. Hai capito?"

"Yeah." I answered for all of us.

As he slowly climbed the stairs, he looked like the weight of the world was on his shoulders.

The next day I made my rounds as usual, only a few people knew what happened and I was careful to say nothing. I kept my ears open for anything at all about goods for sale that could have come from us, but heard nothing about it. Keeping our motives secret required patience and if anything was going to turn up, I knew it would be fairly soon. Swag is evidence; it's sold as quickly as possible. So long as someone is holding it unsold, it's a potential bust.

The following day as I was making the rounds I went to see a guy I knew down by The Bronx Zoo named Armando Navas. We met on the corner of 182 St. and Prospect Avenue and the wind was fucking arctic. We walked back up Prospect and got into my car and I set the heater on 'tropical'.I gave him a price on 30 cases of red wine, when it seemed as an afterthought he turns and says "Hey, have an outlet for some nice fur coats?"

Everything stopped.

I heard my own voice, even as my head felt as if I'd been hit with a brick "What, like winter coats?"

"No, I think they're fur coats, like mink and shit."

"Depends on the price." I said, trying my best to sound bored. "Can you get one for me to take a look at?" I didn't even ask how many he had to sell, I didn't want to do anything to risk anyone connecting me to Buddy.

"I don't know these guys really, so they won't just trust me with one. We'd have to go see them. That OK?"

"Sure. But I can't make any promises unless the price is good. OK?"

"Yeah."

"Good. You know these guys? You vouch for them?"

"I'm not vouching for anybody Eddie, I just said I don't know them well. But I wouldn't have suggested it if I thought I was going to get burned too."

"I hear you. OK so call me and let me know." I said.

"This fucking cold; my dick is an icicle!" he put his hand on the door handle looking out at the freezing cold as he mentally prepared himself for the miserable egress.

"Hey, your people should have stayed in that warm and sunny paradise!" I said, pulling his Puerto Rican chain.

"Yeah, well yours too!" he shot right back.

"I guess your right at that." I chuckled as I'd never really considered that thought.

He bolted out of the car and into the freezing wind.

Upon returning to the warehouse, Junior and Tony D. were eating a large pie with onions and anchovies from Frank's Original down the block. I grabbed a slice and wolfed it down in three bites. I just stared at them and said nothing.

Tony was the first one to pick it up and said "You found something."

"Yeah. A guy I know." I said.

"So what is it?"

"He has a source for some furs."

"Did you set up a meeting yet?"

"I asked for one. I figure I'll go and try to find out if they're the mutts, or just middling them."

"Not without me you won't." Tony D. said.

"I don't want to spook anybody."

"You're not listening Eddie. When you walk in there, I'm going to be covering your ass, so don't waste your fucking breath."

Tony didn't sound worried, it was more like determination in his voice. He might be right.

"OK."

We gave Mario our word that we'd do things his way so I called him and let him know our plans. He said that he had someone, whom I took to mean someone in the NYPD, checking to see if they could connect the theft with others of similar profile. We agreed that I'd go to the meeting with Tony D., but that Junior wouldn't go. I knew that Victor being Junior's father had something to do with Mario telling me not to bring Junior, but I also knew that understanding the relationship between the two was beyond me right now.

# Chapter 6
# *The Two Rickys*

In anticipation of the meeting, Tony and I paid a visit to "the two Ricky's", Ricky Montez and Ricky Johnson. Ricky Johnson's first name was really Jimmy but he was dubbed 'Ricky' due to his resemblance to Ricky Ricardo from the TV show I Love Lucy; the Cuban accent he had inherited from his mother had cemented the nickname. The two Ricky's were the right guys to see about getting an untraceable piece. They ran a shop that did custom motorcycle work and we occasionally had racing parts and accessories that we sold to them. Tony and I knew next to nothing about guns, but they knew a lot about them and did a small business selling some out of the back room of their shop.

Their shop, by the way, was an absolute pig sty. There were big rough welded pieces of motorcycle frames lying on the floor, cardboard boxes stacked one atop the other full of gauges, cables, nuts and bolts, chains, brackets, and the like. Nearly everything had grease or oil on it. Newspaper was laid out here and there, some with recently painted gas tanks and frame parts drying in the thick air of the shop; some newspaper had only an outline of some part or other that had been painted. You really couldn't get the short distance from the door to the back room in under a minute or two, and it wasn't because the place was big, it just took that long to carefully step around all the shit on the floor without tripping and breaking your neck. Jesus, if you did fall, what would you hit? It was anybody's guess, but it would be metal and it would be sharp.

Tony and I walked into the front door and saw little Ricky, meaning the physically smaller of the two, Ricky Montez, on the phone by the cash register. We made our way over to him as he finished his call.

"I feel like fuckin' Magellan, navigating my way here from the front door." I said.

"Eddie! How we doing today chief?" Little Ricky called everybody 'chief'.

"No bad, no bad. How's business?"

"We're under water man, it's been ridiculous. I need a fucking vacation." Ricky said, rubbing his forehead with a grease stained hand "Hey, I'm going to be looking for another welding station. You gonna to have anything for me?"

"Yeah, I'll keep my eyes open. Give me a couple of weeks to do some looking." I was almost getting high from the pungent smell of paint, gasoline and oil that hung in the air. The scent was so thick I'd swear you could almost see it.

"OK, don't forget though, huh?"

He reached down behind the glass counter and picked up a greasy old cardboard box filled with motorcycle chains. It had to weigh fifty pounds and he dropped it onto the counter top which was already cracked and taped back together with silver duct tape. I took a step back in anticipation of the sound of shattering glass from the collapsing counter, and when it didn't come it prompted me to verbalize a thought that had run through my brain since the first time that I set foot in the place.

"Christ Ricky! Clean this fucking place up will you!"

He just laughed at the earnest frustration on my face. I continued.

"You need another welding station? Jesus there's something else missing here that you need more than a fuckin' welding station….." I said more to myself than anyone else.

I was looking around the floor and really noticing for the first time how long it might take just to pick all this shit up, never mind organize and store it. Then I noticed the silence and looked up. Ricky and Tony are looking at me, waiting for me to complete my thought.

"Pride of ownership!" I said in a southern twang.

They both cracked up at that, I'm sure it was as much my reaction as my wit.

"I'm serious, look at all this crap." I tore a piece of paint streaked newspaper stuck to the bottom of my shoe and read in mock surprise "Holy shit, the Japanese bombed Pearl Harbor!"

Ricky continued laughing, but struggled to come to his own defense “Who are you? Mr. Clean? You don’t like it here chief, there’s the door.”

“Where's the door?" I shot back "What makes you think anyone could even find the door! This is fuckin’ shangad!” I said with a sour expression on my face.

“Blow me Eddie.” he said, his face still red from laughing “You come here just to break my balls, or you have something I need?”

“Neither.”

We went into the back room of the shop and discussed what we were looking for. I was careful to avoid any talk that might prompt him to think that a particular event was behind our request. Tony and I just represented the situation that we’re in a cash business and it seemed smart to prepare before something bad might happen.

Ricky put several types of pistols in our hands and explained the merits and drawbacks of each. I needed something easy to conceal and I was worried about the thing jamming, so he suggested a .38 snub revolver instead of a semi-automatic. He added that if I did have to pull the trigger, it would be up close and personal, so my weapon didn’t have to be accurate from any sort of distance. I told him that Tony often went with me on collections to watch my back, so something bigger might make someone think twice before getting cute. Also, at times Tony would hang back by the car while I had a one-on-one with a guy, so he might need to use it from farther away. He recommended a .357, saying it was more accurate at a distance than my snub nose revolver and added that it looked more menacing as well. I was hoping we wouldn’t have to use either during this meeting, I wondered about Tony though.

He took an extra 15 minutes showing Tony and I how to clean and load each weapon. The tab for both pistols came to seven hundred since these were untraceable so I stuffed eight yards into his shirt pocket, thanked him and promised to keep my eyes open for a welding station.

In the car on the way back to the warehouse Tony D. seemed a little pensive. Finally he turned to me and said "If we use our heads we won't have to use these, agreed?"

I almost laughed; he was thinking the same thing I was. I didn't say anything though, I kept a straight face and may have even displayed a trace of a scowl.

Breaking balls, it's not just a job, it's a lifestyle.

Junior had to make a trip to New Rochelle for his father that day, so we agreed to meet him at the Thruway Diner off I-95. We barely finished ordering when he spat out "You went to see the two Ricky's?"

"Yeah." I said.

"Why didn't you tell me?"

"Mario said to leave you out of that part. I figured you knew."

"Yeah well I didn't." He looked as though he was ready to take a swing at me.

"OK. OK. Hey it's not like we were trying to hide anything." which wasn't entirely true.

"Yeah well don't assume. We're in this together right? My father and Mario.... whatever... you know? That's their business. We're doing our business. Together I thought." he said sarcastically.

He was angry, but it was just because he wanted to be sure that it wasn't the start of him being left out of some things because his father may want to protect him in some way. It was smart and I could appreciate it.

"I swear Jun', it's not like that. No matter what they tell me I'm not going to hide anything from you or Tony." I said.

Tony nodded "Same goes for me."

Junior seemed satisfied with that, and we talked about our plans as we ate.

The following day I got a call from Armando, the meeting was set for three o'clock. I called Mario and he told me how he wanted me to handle it: Don't do anything. The purpose of the meeting was to collect information; nothing more. I assured him that it would be OK.

Tony D. and I picked up Armando on Laconia Avenue and we headed over to Yankee stadium. There was a white unmarked box truck parked across the way from the Stadium, it wasn't as big as a semi, more like a medium sized moving van. Just as we pulled in behind them, the door to the back of the truck rolled up in front of us. We could see that there was another guy deeper inside the truck in addition to the one who opened the door. Tony and I had been through this; we didn't want them to see Tony as any sort of deterrent, but instead as just one of two guys interested in some quality furs if the price was right. To further this end, Tony was wearing a dirty and frayed 'Pep Boys' orange ball cap; it had miniature 'Manny, Moe and Jack' faces on the brim. He'd chosen wisely, the hat was in need of a garbage can and it definitely 'softened' his look.

As we were getting out of the car I said to him under my breath "You look like a complete douche-bag in that hat." struggling to suppress the smirk coming to my face.

"That's the point, ass-head." he shot back under his breath.

The one near the door offered his hand and helped the three of us up into the truck and closed the door. They had the dome light on, but it didn't cast much light. Introductions were made by Armando. The one by the door Armando called 'Val' and the other one he called 'Pira'. I don't know what there real full names were and in this type of situation you don't ask.

I got right to it; I wanted to keep the initiative "The light in here is too dim, we'll have to open the door so I can get a good look."

Pira had a couple of spotlights rigged up and with a click the entire inside of the truck was instantly bathed in harsh blue-white light.

"OK." then looking around I said "Let's see 'em." rubbing my hands together.

Pira pulled a clean painter's canvas tarp off a rolling clothes rack, revealing five mink coats. We had so much stocked in the warehouse I couldn't tell if these were our minks or not.

I spent several minutes inspecting the furs, putting my all into convincing them that my only concern was the quality of garment. After a while I started the questions; it had to be handled patiently.

"I'm not a furrier, but these look like quality. Is there anything I should know about them? Are they defective in any way that I need to know about up front?"

Pira said "They're top quality furs man, if you have an outlet for them. Armando says you do a good business and you can be trusted. You think you have a home for these?"

"Well, that depends. What were you looking for?"

"Two thousand a piece."

"Yeah, well they're homeless fuckin' orphans for two grand each."

"These go for anywhere from six to ten grand retail."

"Retail? Listen, you and I both know anyone who walks into a retail store to buy one of these is looking to impress his wife…or his girlfriend." I snorted "A guy who's buying from me is too fuckin' cheap to bring her to the store. That's my bread and butter."

Pira exchanged looks with Val, but neither said anything.

"I'll give you eight hundred each, that's four thousand for all five." I said.

"Fifteen hundred each."

"Can't do it. Something like this I have to move fast and to do that the price has got to be right." I shook my head and held my hands up as if to say 'give me a break'.

'Patience' I thought to myself. In my mind I psychically willed him to say it. The voice in my head egged him on 'Come on, you know you want to say it. Just say it.' I kept my mouth shut and waited.

"Can you take more than five?" He said.

Bingo.

I exhaled and glanced at Tony D., then slowly turned to Pira and asked "Depends. How many are we talking? If I take them all at least I can control the turn. How many you got?"

He hesitated for a moment "I've got twelve."

And the clouds part. We had fourteen lifted from our warehouse; I didn't need to see the two missing coats on their girlfriends to know these were the coats.

"Listen, no disrespect, but I don't want to get jerked-off here, if you're telling me that's all of them, it has to be all of them. I don't want to have to compete with anyone else offering your furs at the same time."

"You don't have to worry, that's all there is." He said.

I looked at them again, and then said to Tony D. "What do you think?" Tony and I had discussed this, it was his turn to look bored and play his part.

He looked at me and said "What do I think? I think the furs look alright, but how would they know if the people who scored these did split some off for another buy? Maybe those guys sold some themselves."

"Maybe those guys sold some themselves." I repeated to Pira. Breaking balls, it's a gift.

"I don't think so." was all he said.

"Yeah well there were some coats in Queens that a guy offered me, I never got back to him so I don't know if they were furs or just winter coats. See? We can't be sure they're not from the same score." I said, trying to sound as if I was thinking out loud.

"These aren't from Queens. I don't know nothing about anything in Queens. I know where these came from, and it wasn't Queens." He said with a little hostility. He was getting annoyed, which was my hope.

"I'm not fuckin' with you, I think I can take the coats, but how can you be sure?"

"I'm as sure as anyone can be. I'm certain, I'm not guessing."

I took a breath trying to look as though I was in the throws of making a decision and finally said "OK. Here's what we'll do. I'll give you eight hundred for one of these and I'll take it with me. I'll show it around…take me a day or so. If nothing goes against what you said about the twelve being all of them, I'll buy the rest for a thousand each."

"Twelve hundred each." he said.

"Eleven hundred, take it or leave it."

"Done." he said.

"How will I get in touch?"

"Armando can reach me." Pira said.

We shook hands and I almost wiped my hand off on my pant leg right in front of him, catching myself just in time. I peeled the bills off the roll in my pocket while he took a new black plastic trash bag from a box on the floor and punched a hole in the center of its bottom. He threaded the coat's hanger thru the hole, transforming the plastic trash bag into a makeshift garment bag.

On the way back to drop Armando off, Tony D. made small talk and kept the mood casual. I was glad he came along after all because I was so pissed off that I wouldn't have been able to casually bullshit with Armando; he'd have sensed something was wrong. We dropped him off and headed back to the neighborhood and to Rudy's, a neighborhood bar for a beer with Junior.

# Chapter 7
# *Turning at Locus Point*

Later that night, Mario picked the three of us up and took us out to dinner at Gates Harbor, a seafood joint by the Whitestone Bridge. When we got to the table Victor was waiting for us. Tony D. and Junior were both surprised and showed it more than they should have. I wasn't surprised at all; I had a feeling Victor wasn't going to be a bystander, and not just because of his son.

We talked as we ate. I spoke for us and told Mario and Victor everything. I suspected the two we met were the scumbags we were looking for. Victor said he needed a couple of days to see what he could find out about them, and that it wouldn't be hard to get them to talk. He meant to get them to say whether they were the only two, or if there were more involved. Mario and Victor were going back and forth about Armando, and while I knew they expected me to keep my mouth shut, I had to stick my nose in.

"Armando doesn't run with these guys, he's just middling some swag."

"It's a risk Eddie, why take a risk?" Mario said.

"Because if it weren't for him we wouldn't have dick."

"Yeah, well suppose he puts two and two together and later he gets pinched, and decides to use you two for collateral?"

"He can be trusted, especially if he doesn't know more than he knows already. In a way, we owe him; I'm asking you to just let that be. I'll take that chance. He's never met Junior so it doesn't apply to him. I can't speak for Tony though.

"I think it'll be OK." Tony said, and nothing more.

Mario looked at each of us "You're vouching for him, so if it goes bad, it's tough shit for you. You keep your mouth shut and take whatever time you've got coming." it wasn't a question. The three of us understood what he meant.

Mario looked at Victor, who seemed to be lost in thought for a minute. Finally, Victor nodded ever so slightly. We set our plans over espresso. For the first time I felt certain that Mario was a made guy not just a half-assed wiseguy, and that Victor was his capo. For all those years living down the same street from each other I'd never seen them socialize and I believed it was due to Victor's careful nature with appearances.

The following Monday, Mario summoned us to the Shore Inn by Schley Avenue in the Bronx. He was sitting in the kitchen bullshitting with the owner Pete Oh'Alin. Pete was a Golden Gloves boxer in his youth, and now in his mid-forties he still has the physique of a boxer, but the gray at his temples and the lines on his face betrayed his age.

As we walked in, Pete was saying to Mario "He who hesitates, right?" Pete had this habit of stopping in the middle of an adage. It wasn't as though you didn't understand him, it just had a peculiar sound to it.

"Definitely Pete." Mario said "Hey grab a smoke will ya, I need a minute with the young Turks here."

We all said hello to Pete on his way out, then Mario turned to us "It checked out, they're the ones we're looking for, but there was one more with them."

"He have a name?" It was bold of me to ask, this was more of a 'shut up and listen' kind of situation, but I was feeling angry and spoke before I thought. To my surprise, Mario didn't react to my impertinence; he just gave me a straight answer.

"No name. Couldn't get it. They work the Bronx and they have a third guy we need to find." Mario said "What does Armando look like?"

"Five Ten, heavy set, maybe 230, brown hair and eyes. His skin's on the dark side, he's Puerto Rican, no accent." I say.

"OK. It's not him. The guy we're looking for is skinny, white guy, maybe six one, has tattoos all down his forearms. Long brown hair in a ponytail and brown eyes. He's a doper. These guys work together, he would definitely be with them. Forty three square miles and ten bridges…he'll show up."

"Snakes." I said.

They all looked at me.

"On his forearms, they're snakes. I've seen this guy around. He hangs here and there, but I know I've seen him in this joint next to Carl's Chop House, it's that bar across from the Nathan's, I don't remember the name." I said.

"In Yonkers?" Mario said.

"Yeah, on Central Avenue. We've got to grab him right away, before he can go anywhere."

"He's not going anywhere. His friends are still healthy and this Armando doesn't know anything right?" Mario asked, still needling me about Armando.

"Right. Not a word."

"Alright then, you three go out there and hang around, have a few drinks and keep your eyes open. When he shows, go outside and wait for him, then make the grab in the parking lot." Mario said.

"Questions?" Mario asked. There were none.

"OK. When you have him, you bring him over to the jetty. You know the one I mean, in the marina down from Hoffman's?"

"Yeah. Into that shack out on the jetty?" Tony D. says.

"Exactly. That's the place. When you have him there, one of you peel off and come get me. Then we'll go get the other two."

"We'll have to set the buy meeting though, through Armando." Tony D. said.

"Naa. I know about these guys now. I know how to find them. We'll go grab them when we have that fucking Snakes guy under wraps." Mario said. For the first time I saw him smile, just a little one, but clearly he was looking forward to this.

The name of the bar turned out to be The Track, it's not far from Yonkers Raceway. On the second night the mutt shows up. He's impossible to miss because the silly fuck is wearing one black sneaker and on the other foot, a yellow one. We grab him when he's leaving, in the parking lot on the way out to his car just as we'd planned. Junior, who's as wide in the shoulder as his old man, pushed him into the car. Tony D. is at the wheel, and Snakes is in the back, sandwiched between Junior and me. The light at the corner turns red and we have to stop because there's a Police car facing us on the other side of the intersection, a couple of cars back. Snakes sees the cop car and starts yelling his head off and trying to get to the passenger door. The cop would see us if we blew the red light, but he can't see us from where are at the moment.

Snakes is on my right, so as his arms are reaching for the door I slam my elbow into the soft spot in the middle of his bony chest, the air whistles out of him and he doubles over. The light is still red so there's time for another shot. I bring the heel of my right boot down on the instep of that yellow fucking sneaker he's wearing. I couldn't tell if I broke something, but he's not able to inhale yet from the shot to his chest. His mouth is wide open but nothing's coming out.

"Now shut the fuck up or I'll smack you." I say, irritated.

He gave us no trouble for the rest of the ride. It takes us a little less than half an hour to get him to the jetty. Tony takes off to get Mario while I handcuff Snakes to a pipe running low along the west wall of the shack. He's in pain because of his foot.

"What the fuck is this? Whoever you're looking for, you got the wrong guy." he said in a nasty tone, trying to sound unafraid but coming up short by about a mile and a half.

I pointed to a rusty axe lying on the floor under an old workbench "You see that axe?"

He looked over and saw it, and looked back to me.

"Open your yap again…I'm gonna' take that axe and chop off that ridiculous fuckin' yellow sneaker." I said, in a calm and but intense tone."One more word outta' you and I'm Paul fuckin' Bunion."

He didn't make a sound from that point on.

After only fifteen minutes or so, Mario came in with Tony D. in tow. It's the only time I've ever seen him dressed in anything but a suit, and seeing him in that sweat suit and deck shoes made me a little nervous.

"Junior, keep an eye on him. We'll be back." Mario said.

We followed him out to a white van that said "Best Cleaning and Upholstery Service" on the sides. We hopped in and Mario drove. Nobody spoke. He made a quick stop at a pay phone, less than a minute, then got back in and started driving faster. We stopped in an alley behind some retail stores, got out and approached the windowless rear door to one of the stores. When we were within a few feet of the door, it opened suddenly and Pira stepped out with a cigarette and lighter in hand. He saw me first and wore a puzzled expression as Mario reached out and hit him over the head with something that it sounded like a wooden club; was hard to see in the darkness.

After Pira dropped Mario said “Tony, tape his hands, feet and mouth and dump his ass in the back of the truck.” then looked to me and said “Let’s go.”

We entered the place and went through another doorway just inside and to the left. The place was well lit and there was music at a low volume coming from inside. We turned a corner and I saw the other guy from the truck that day, Val. He was sitting with his back to us, in front of a big folding table covered with pot; there were screens and bags and so forth scattered on the table. Our boys were doing a little marijuana distribution between heists and murders. I motioned for Mario to stay put, and took the club from his hand. I stepped up behind Val and clocked him good in the side of the head, right on the temple. Boom, down he goes, dazed but not out. I grabbed a handful of his hair and put my all into a punch at the bridge of his nose; it was enough to put his lights out. We moved him to the van and Tony D., as he had done with Pira, used a roll of duct tape to bind Val’s hands and feet, and to cover his mouth. We headed back to the marina; the two 'passengers' saw that it was useless to struggle and we didn’t hear a peep out of them for the entire ride.

*Eastchester Bay, One Mile Northeast of Locus Point*

Eastchester Bay is really a Sound, because it joins larger bodies of water at its ends. You have Pelham Bay and the Hutchinson River to the north, and the East River, Little Neck Bay and Long Island Sound to the south. In the daytime the Bay is pretty crowded, mostly with sailboats and outboard pleasure boats, but there's also some commercial shipping since it feeds into Long Island Sound which is a major channel to some large New York harbors. At the moment though, against this possible traffic, it's winter, so most pleasure boats are up on blocks. Also, the night is pitch black and it's almost low tide which probably means no barge traffic heading in or out of the Hutchinson.

The engines make a low throaty rumble as we move slowly through the waters away from shore. Forty minutes ago Mario led us down to a cabin cruiser moored near the tip of the jetty; perhaps thirty feet long, whoever owned it had named it cleverly after their children… "Three Gulls and a Buoy" was stenciled across its stern. The jetty has disappeared in the darkness behind us twenty minutes ago and the lights from City Island are off our port side; the harsh winter wind coming straight at us from the direction of Sands Point is killing my eyes and freezing my extremities. I was sure my ears would freeze and fall off. Mario is not taking us out into Long Island Sound proper, instead when we neared the midpoint between Locus and King's Points, he cut the throttle back and has us slowly trolling along at a couple of knots. The three amigos are stowed inside the cabin where Tony D. is keeping an eye on them. I climb up a few steps to the bridge of the small cabin cruiser and stand beside Mario.

After a while he breaks the silence. “How you guys doing?”

“Good.” I say.

“Listen to me for a second…being here, it’s different from thinking about it or talking about it. Capisci?”

“It’s not like that.” I say quickly.

“Oh? What's it like?”

“We’re ready. You want to leave it to us, we’ll handle it.”

Mario studied my face for a minute, like he was trying to decide if I was secretly pissing my pants. I wasn't.

“Junior, take the wheel. You see that light?” he asked, pointing forward. Junior nodded. “Just keep the bow pointed towards it and call me if anybody comes anywhere near us. Don't get distracted, OK?”

"I got it Mario." Junior said earnestly, taking the wheel and continuously scanning the waters around us.

I followed Mario down and into the cabin with the three stooges, and while it wasn't heated, simply being out of the freezing wind made a big difference. We had laid some plastic tarps down before we brought them aboard. They were still bound with their hands behind their backs.

“Take the tape off his mouth.” Mario said to Tony, motioning his head toward Pira.

Mario went to the little forward closet and hauled out some chain and one cinderblock. When the tape came off Pira's mouth, he was smart enough to remain silent.

"One of you is taking a swim tonight." Mario said in a very matter-of-fact tone "and that'll be the scumbag who shot my guy at the warehouse. Whoever tied him up don't concern me, it's who pulled the trigger."

For just an instant Pira's eyes darted toward Snakes, it was so fleeting that I wasn't sure Mario had caught it. Mario nodded toward Pira.

"I don't know what you've been told, but you've been told wrong." then he looked at me continuing "What the fuck is this anyway? The furs were a setup?" back to Mario "I don't know what these guys are telling you, but it's bullshit. You're being played."

Mario's hand came up with a .22 out of nowhere and shot Pira in the kneecap. It exploded all over his pants leg. He screamed his head off for a few minutes, Mario just waited for his screams to die down to whimpers and moans. He stepped forward and put the muzzle to the other knee.

"Now. Are we all done with the bullshit?"

Pira's just moaning "Please… please… please…" over and over.

"I guess not." Mario said in a calm tone and then pulled the trigger and blasted the other kneecap.

It was a real mess. Veins looked like they were going to pop out of Pira's head as he writhed in pain on the deck.

"Right now it's looking to me like you did it yourself you fucking mutt." Mario said.

Pira whined "No! Oh Christ I didn't fucking shoot him!"

"Who then?"

"Him!"

For some reason, as angry as I was up until this point, hearing him say something of an admission produced a feeling deep inside me as if a switch had been thrown and a wave of anger swept over me that far surpassed any I had ever experienced. I stepped on what was left of his kneecap.

"Who am I, a fucking mind reader? 'Him' who?" I growled.

"Bobbyyyyyyy!" He screamed in a tortured wailing, sounding more like an animal caught in a trap than any sound a human could make.

It was pretty common for people doing business on the street not to use their real names, so he was saying it was one of the two others, Snakes or Val.

Mario turned his back and said "Bobby, how do I know if your friend here is lying to me to save his own ass."

Nothing.

"Answer me God damn it!" Mario shouted.

Snakes tried to say something through his tape, of course it was unintelligible since his mouth was taped. 'Val' didn't make a sound. That along with that quick glance before…at least we knew who Bobby was.

"We don't need these other two anymore." Mario said and shot them both in the chest. Two shots each.

"Chain them up with the blocks and put 'em over the side."

They weren't dead, but were fast on their way, and I'm sure his leaving them alive to experience the drowning in addition to the chest wounds was intentional. While we chained them up and put them over the side, Mario went to check with Junior on the bridge. I heard the motors stop and suddenly it was very quiet, the only sound was the wind against the hull; the boat started to pitch more noticeably in the swells.

Tony and I ducked back into the cabin and the sound of Snakes' frantic breathing through his nose filled the cramped space. Understandably, he really looked like he was going to have a heart attack before Mario did whatever Mario was gonna' do.

Mario entered with Junior behind him, and got down nose to nose with Snakes "Hey scumbag, that wasn't just 'my guy' you shot. That was my son."

Mario slowly pulled away a few inches and his face and demeanor changed instantly, speaking in an almost sympathetic voice seemingly devoid of any anger. "You've got to be the stupidest fuck that ever walked the earth. Kill the son of a wiseguy?" He paused a beat, and looked at me "It's just plain unlucky is what it is."

It freaked me out a little bit, the instantaneous and dramatic change in his demeanor, it was like he was a madman. Mario never said much, so seeing him emotional like this was scary.

Then his tone changed yet again, this time to apathy, as if he was discussing the weather, with no trace of hostility or threat. "Both of your friends are gone. You're gonna' wish you could've traded places with 'em."

He turned to Junior "Take him out to the back of the boat, make a slip knot, like a noose ya' know? Put it around his neck. Leave about 10 feet of line and then tie the other end to one of those cleats on the stern."

Snakes kicked and screamed and flopped around as Junior dragged him through the door. Even though his legs were taped together, he tried to wrap them around one of the sides of the ladder that lead to the bridge. Junior dropped him to the deck and stomped on his balls. The guy folded up and stopped his fuss. We followed Junior out but didn't help him with Snakes, feeling that Junior wanted to play his part in the thing.

A couple of minutes later Mario came out of the cabin with a big revolver, a .44 magnum which had an obscenely long barrel; it looked as big as a fucking cannon. It was the biggest hand gun I'd ever seen. Snakes laid eyes on it and began freaking out all over again, which had to be Mario's intention.

"Turn him over. Turn him so he's on his knees and his forehead." Mario said.

We turned him over, his knees and face were on the deck, and his ass was sticking up in the air. Mario put the barrel up to the guy's ass, right where his asshole would be, and held it there. Snakes was trying to thrash about, muted screams sounding urgently from under the tape.

"You had him tied up you fucking punk. You could have just taken the swag and left it at that. No, you had to shoot him like he was a piece of shit. He couldn't even defend himself and he had to take it. WELL NOW YOU'RE GONNA TAKE IT, RIGHT UP YOUR FUCKIN' ASS YOU COCKSUCKER!"

He fired one round, and the sound that cannon made was enough to wake the dead. My ears rang from the boom, and the air stank with spent powder. Snakes didn't let out a scream as I had expected, in fact it appeared to me that the shot had killed him instantly. Mario motioned for us to stay put. We waited, and after a short time, Snakes started to come around, moaning and whimpering.

"Yeah. Now have a nice fuckin' swim." Mario said, stood up and spit on him.

We picked him up and threw him over the stern as Mario started the engines up; the line was short enough so that he couldn't fall completely under water while the boat was moving even slowly. We trolled with him behind the boat at slow speed, dragging him by his neck through the frigid water for a little while. Mario pulled him in close a couple of times to see if he was still alive. Maybe ten minutes later, Snakes was still breathing, but barely so. We chained him with some cinder blocks and cut the stern line. Down he went.

I had never seen or taken part in anything remotely like this before. But as brutal as this had been, having lost Buddy for essentially no reason other than he was some bizarre entertainment for this bastard, I didn't feel guilty. I also didn't feel better. I just felt…numb.

# Chapter 8
# *Dinner with Michelangelo*

*The Bronx, New York City*

***Present Day…***

I had to go see Angelo to wrap up the work at the piers, and let him know about Benny what's-his-name. Jimmy Knievel called me and said that Angelo was waiting for me, so I go down to the club and he's sitting at his table. He's not reading the papers when I walk in, just staring into his espresso. When you see Angelo staring into his cup, there are two possibilities. One, he's got a problem that he's thinking through; or two, he's irritated. I figure I'm a 'category-two' visitor. I'm not complaining because if he ordered someone clipped, he'd be reading the paper and completely relaxed. You couldn't read Angelo when it came to 'reorganizations'. He thought about every angle when it came to that, and then he'd decide, and that was that. No second guessing; very analytical and decisive. I respected him for that.

"Angelo." I stood back from the table a couple of feet and waited to be invited to sit down.

"I hear the last part of that thing didn't work out." He said, not looking up but nodding toward the empty chair.

"You're right, it didn't." I said and sat.

"I don't have to be told I'm right, I know I'm right." he said calmly "What happened?"

"We finished at the piers and went directly to the guy's place, Benny… what's his last name… I'm drawing a blank."

"Fuhgetaboutit." Angelo said.

"So, as we're heading up the stairs, who comes out of the elevator?" Eddie arched his eyebrows to indicate it was the very person they were there to see. "He leaves the building, so I decide to follow him. He leads us a few blocks away in that park next to City College, and meets with a guy."

"Meets with who? Who's he meeting?" Angelo repeated, which considering Angelo's normal stone like demeanor, almost qualifies as an emotional outburst.

"Whoever it was, it didn't look friendly." I said "He headed off in a cab with the guy." Then I added "The guy was driving."

"A cab driver." Angelo said monotone, meaning that it might be a cop.

"A cab driver." I repeated.

"You got the plate?"

"Yeah."

"Give it to Jimmy."

"OK."

Angelo didn't say anything for a couple of minutes, then he asked "You sure the FBI didn't know you were there?"

"Sure? All due respect Ange, I'm not sure about anything." I paused and thought it through all over again while he waited "They didn't know we were there."

More quiet. How I enjoy these moments.

Finally, "The phone call, any chance there?"

"No."

"Let me talk to someone and see if there's any noise about this Benny right now. Maybe they have hooks in him too." He said.

"Well…he could be playing both sides of the street."

"First we see what we can see. Then, if there's any doubt, there's no doubt." meaning that Benny would have reached the age of mandatory retirement.

"Anything else?" I asked.

"No sense in going anywhere near his place until we know something." then he added "What about the other strunz?"

"Taken care of." meaning the body of the late green sweatshirt.

"OK, shove off." he said with a slight wave of his hand.

Our meeting ends and I get about 3 steps away from the table when a thought occurs to me, I turn back to face him.

"If it was a setup, and they wanted to pin some terrorist national security bullshit story to us, they'd need him to corroborate. They'd only get what they want if he agreed to lie for them."

"Maybe." Angelo said with the slightest smirk.

"Well that, or he lied to them and they believe it, or at least it suits their purpose to believe it." I said.

He didn't say anything; he just gave me an enigmatic stare. He's already there five minutes ago. Angelo…he's a cagey bastard.

"What about the rest he owes?" I ask.

"Fuhgetaboutit for now…one thing at a time. Let him stew."

The following night there was nothing in particular going on so Vin, Philly and Tony D. and I meet for dinner at Endico's and then some cards later at Louie's on Tremont Avenue. I'm sitting in front of a plate of scaloppini when Philly get's this look on his face. He's staring at me like I have food in my teeth. We haven't said a word about the pervious day's events, but I know what's on his mind. Philly is built like an ox and because of that people tend to underestimate his smarts. He's a very sharp guy.

"Angelo's looking into it." I say.

He goes back to his rigatoni Bolognese with a satisfied grunt.

I look over and notice that Vin's frowning. What the else is new. I'm watching him as I eat; he's poking at his pasta with his fork, moving it around on the plate, flicking at it and then the slight shake of his head. I've seen this movie about ten thousand times, and it's one of the few things that get's under my skin. This man is the most critical sonovabitch I've ever met when it comes to food and when he gets that look it means the show's about to begin.

"Don't fucking start." I warn him.

"I didn't say anything." he says defensively.

"Good." I continue eating.

We know what's coming. After only two more minutes of watching his ugly frowning fucking face, the miserable bastard just can't help himself.

"There's no basil in this sauce."

"Vaffanculo!" I slammed my fist on the table, rattling the dishes and silverware "I fucking knew it! Jesus Christ, every god damn time!"

"What the hell are you pissed about? I'm the one eating it and I'm just saying it's not made right."

"I just want to have one fucking meal without you whining about what they didn't do right!" I plead.

It's been a tough day, and I'm just not up to watching another rerun of Vinny Finds Something Wrong With His Food.

Tony D. reaches over and spears a few penne from Vin's plate which prompts a disapproving look from Vin. Tony chews and says bluntly "The sauce is fine. Shut the fuck up and eat your food Vinny."

"Yeah well you don't know good sauce then." He turns to Philly, because he knows better than to turn to me, and says "He doesn't know good sauce."

Tony stops chewing, exhales and looks up at Vin for a few seconds as he considers the futility of responding, then wordlessly returns to his dinner.

I offer "Maybe it's just you…maybe you like too much basil. Ever think of that genius?"

He shrugs and goes back to his dinner. Another minute passes and my irritation is just starting to subside when he says "The pasta's over-cooked a little too."

"I'll carve your fucking eye out if you don't stop!" I glare at him, picking up my steak knife and pointing it at him.

Tony interrupts me, saying scornfully "Why do you let him get to you? Just ignore him!"

"I have to listen to Wolfgang Fuck-face over here every time we eat. If you don't like the food, don't eat. But stop the bitching and let me eat a crust of bread in peace!"

Half a minute of silence follows as I use my fork to take out my aggression on my food…stab, chew, breath, stab, chew, breath.

"I had no idea you were so… emotional." Vin chuckles; they all join in.

"Yeah, you can't keep it all bottled up inside Eddie." Philly says, motioning at the sides of his massive torso "You gotta let it out or it could cause an ulcer."

"Yeah? Well Vin's an ulcer-artist." I glare at Vin and use my steak knife to emphasize my point "You work in aggravation the way Picasso worked in paint. You're the fucking Michelangelo of ulcers!"

We bullshit our way through coffee and desert, without critique by Vin to my relief, and drive over to Louie's Tavolo da Pranzo on Tremont Avenue. Louie's pushing 80 and is a sweet old guy, soft spoken and serious, not unlike Angelo. He's not in the life, not a connected guy at all, but he's Angelo's first cousin so he allows the card game in his place. Everyone loves Louie.

As we walk in we hear some raised voices, something you never hear in Louie's. I look over to the right and see the only customers in the place; two girls sitting at a four-top laughing, along with their boyfriends, who are half out of their seats slapping at each other and generally being a problem. Mid-twenties, open shirts, gold chains…real cugines. They're laughing and swinging at each other, having a slap fight right in the middle of the place. The waitress is standing back from the table, clearly frightened, and Louie is pleading with them to stop, in his quiet way. All of a sudden, one of them slaps Louie, and this sends the two pricks and their girlfriends into hysterics.

I turn to Philly and say "Let me handle this okay?"

A nod and a scowl from Philly, he knows my old grade school is two blocks from here, and that I used to work here after school busing tables when I was in eighth grade. Louie was like a grandfather to me back then. I nudge Tony D. and we make our way over to the table.

I put myself between Louie and the two mutts and say to him "Louie, it's okay. Go on into the kitchen; let me talk to these guys." The waitress disappears into the kitchen before I'm even done saying it.

Louie pauses, and says in his thick Italian accent "It's OK Eddie. They no understand. They customers."

"Not anymore. It'll be OK Lou, go ahead."

As I'm saying this to Louie, the guy closest to me grabs my shoulder, so I reach up grab his pinkie and twist it in a half circle as I turn to face him, hearing a snap. Before he can yell, I give it an extra tug. Louie sees where this is going, frowns and slowly heads into the kitchen.

"Arrrgggghhh" the bastard moans, and I backhand him across the face sending him reeling backward.

"Shut up you whining prick." I say in a soft voice.

The other guy begins to move, but Tony D. grabs a salt shaker off the table and rams it full force into his solar plexus, knocking the wind out of him; it sounds like a hammer on a coconut. The mutt goes down in a fetal position, not yet able to snatch a breath. My face betrays a little surprise as I'd never seen a salt shaker used in quite that way.

"I'm surgical with this fuckin' thing." he says earnestly, emphasizing his words by brandishing the salt shaker at me as if it were a knife.

One of the girls tries to throw a glass of water at Tony. None of them looked that bright to begin with, and he knocks it out of her hand and slaps her hard enough to knock her out of her chair and onto the carpet. The other girl opens her mouth, but has a sudden attack of brain, and closes it.

'Pinkie' is cradling his broken finger and grunting. To his disbelief, I reach out and grab his broken finger again. His knees give way under the pain, and he goes down on his knees, his pain-contorted face looking up at me.

I squeeze the broken bones and say "Show me your license."

He wails in pain and says "What?"

"Your driver's license." I say calmly.

He takes out his wallet with his other hand and offers it to me.

"That's your wallet. Are you fuckin' deaf?" I ask softly, squeezing harder.

He flips through his wallet with his one free hand and holds his license up for me to see, it's hard to see as his good hand is shaking like crazy. I study it for a few seconds.

"I see you here again, you're all done. Go ahead and run to the cops. They'll call me. Understand what I'm saying?"

He nods violently, his face drained of color now.

"I didn't hear you." I scowl.

"Yes…I understand." he grunts.

"Good. Now take your life-partner here and your putana, and take a walk."

He struggles to his feet and they all follow him toward the door. 'Pinkie' almost pisses himself trying to get around Philly, expecting to get another beating, but Philly just stares at him. The other three follow.

Philly looks at me arching his eyebrows and says "You're a people-person Eddie, ya know that?" turning to Tony he says "He's like an Italian Mother Teresa, isn't he?"

"What can I say?" I reply with a sympathetic shrug "I care."

We head into the back room but I stop in the kitchen for a moment, to tell Louie that the 'customers' decided to leave and everything is all right.

I join the others in the back room, Tony D. has a seat for me next to him. Tony and I have been friends since his family moved from Brooklyn into the neighborhood near the Throgg's Neck Bridge in the Bronx. The neighborhood was decidedly blue collar, predominately Italian and Irish, but with a substantial population of German, Polish, Puerto Rican and some Spanish. There were so many 'Tonys' in our neighborhood that we had to use the first letter of the last name of some of them to keep it straight. Tony's last name was Donato, hence, Tony D.Tony and I were both fourteen when he moved in, and we first bonded because we were die-hard New York Rangers hockey fans. Dale Rolfe, Pete Stemkowski, Rod Gilbert, Eddie Giacomin; we idolized them all. We played roller hockey together in the P.S. 181 schoolyard. Saturdays during late spring, summer and early fall, before the snow came, we skated the two miles through city streets in full equipment to the schoolyard. We played pickup games for three or four hours and then skated back home exhausted and satisfied. For a while we were inseparable.

One Sunday afternoon in September, Tony and I are hanging out in front of Franco's candy store. As happened a thousand times before, the city bus pulled up devoid of passengers and parked across the street. This spot was the last stop on the number twenty three bus route.

In the winter, we used to 'hitch' on its bumper; we would run up behind it as it left the first stop and grab onto the bumper and hold on for dear life as we slid through the snow in our slick-bottomed winter boots at thirty miles per hour or more. It was our inner-city version of snow-boarding. Sometimes, when the snow was fresh and still falling, we would hitch for the entire route, miles and miles. Other times we would get several miles away and hit a bare patch of street, maybe one where a city snow plow had salted the street, and go tumbling while hoping the cars behind the bus didn't run over us. It's a miracle we survived.

As we stood there in front of Franco's, the driver got out, walked around to the driver's side window, reached inside and hit the switch to close the doors. He crossed the street, entered the store and sat down at the counter to order lunch. I'd watched this ritual so many times that I never gave it a second thought; the bus drivers had always done this as far back as I could remember. Tony D., who'd only lived here for a couple of years, got an idea.

He thought it would be fun to take the bus for a little spin and I put up only token resistance. After making sure no one was looking, I boosted him into the driver's side window, he opens the doors and off we go. Since Tony and I have a similar sense of humor, we drove the bus along its route, laughing as we drove past people waiting at the stops. They'd wave as we passed, looking confused and then angry when they realized that bus wasn't going to stop for them. We'd flip them the bird and laugh our asses off. We even stopped in front of an apartment building that was one of our hangouts. 'Chunky', a friend of ours, was leaning against the telephone pole in front of the building. He was called 'Chunky' both because he was…well…chunky in shape, and because he was always eating those Chunky chocolate squares that came in the silver wrapper. As we pulled up and stopped, he's looking at the bus, wondering what's going on. The door opens and he sees Tony D. in the driver's seat smiling at him.

"Your lucky I'm a good driver Chunky, I might have run this bus into that mobile home you call an ass." Tony said.

"I'd lose weight but your mother's so into it." Chunky replied deadpan.

I break out with a cackle.

"Alright. C'mon let's take a ride…" Tony says with a smirk knowing he'd lost the exchange.

“Seriously…” Chunky cut him off “…your mom likes me to smother her with my balls…”

“ALRIGHT ALREADY!” Now it was Tony's turn to cut Chunky off .

Tears are forming in my eyes I’m laughing so hard.

“C’mon. We’re taking a ride.” I say when my laughing fit had subsided.

“Naaa. If we get caught the old man will kick my ass.”

“We’re not gonna get caught.” Tony says in a condescending tone.

“Naaa. I’m on his shit-list as it is. It’s tough enough living in that house lately, he’d fucking lose it. Don’t get caught.” He waved and turned, heading down the block.

“Well, at least we don’t have to stick to the lower gears now.” Tony chuckled as he closed the doors.

Tony took us onto I-95 and just like that, bang, a cop is following us with his lights on. It couldn’t have been even ten minutes since we took off.

“Fuck!” we both say simultaneously.

Tony pulls over and I head out the door first. When I’m on the bottom step, he kicks me square on the ass, causing me to fall face first onto the grass on the side of the highway. The cop is still in his car on the radio.

I hear the doors shut behind me, and turn around completely shocked. He’s leaving me to the cops! Jesus H. Christ! He puts the bus in gear and floors the thing, which really, is not that impressive a show from an old city bus. He takes off, and to my amazement, on comes the siren and the cop takes off after him. Light begins to dawn…Tony’s saving my ass. He kicked me out and took the bus so that he’d be followed and I’d get away. I spring to my feet and bolt from the highway. In one smooth motion I scale the tall chain-link fence that separates the highway from the service road and without breaking stride I beat a path back to the neighborhood.

Tony took the heat. The cop saw me get up and run in the rear view mirror, but was never able to get Tony to give up my name. Because of that, the Judge wasn’t inclined to show leniency and Tony spent some time in Spofford Juvenile Center.

When he got out, all he said was "One of us was going to get caught. There was no reason for both of us to get caught." And that was it. He never mentioned it again.

I took the seat next to Tony and brought my attention to the game. I've heard it said that when you sit at a poker table, if you look at your competition and can't tell which one at the table is the sucker…it's you. I also once heard, and thought it more to the point, that poker is a game about people that's played with cards. It entertains me to watch a mix of players, some I've known for a long time and some that are strangers, go about their strategies and try to 'psych' each other out.

Take Vin for example, all things being equal, he's an odds player. You can usually count on him to show the strength of his hand by the amount he bets. I've also noticed a 'tell' he has, that I'll take with me to the grave. Vin's image conscious, always dressed nicely, neat, groomed and organized. Christ, the glove compartment in Vin's car is neater than some four star hotel rooms. He stacks his chips the same way, neat and organized. If he's not done stacking his chips, but he stops to place chips in the pot, you can be pretty sure he's holding something good…good enough to interrupt his favorite pastime: anal-retentive precision chip stacking.

Philly's very calm and cool. Since Philly has all the expressiveness of a tombstone, there's not much in the way of tells. He's not easy to read, but the truth is most of the time it doesn't matter because he isn't a big risk taker at the poker table. If Philly's got an ace high flush, he's as likely to bet some minor amount. It's just his nature.

Tony D. is good company to play with, and a real pain in the ass to win money from. He's good at reading people and doesn't get emotional about the pot. If there is anything I can use, it's his hatred of whistling, humming, tapping my fingers on the table top, little physical repetitive tics and so on…using the same phrase over and over even works. One night I remember saying "Well…there ya go." after nearly every hand; inside of half an hour he was ready to choke me. You have to show restraint because if he thinks your doing it intentionally, he won't react at all. If you're subtle enough about it, he'll become irritated and red faced, and stay that way. If you do it superbly, you'll even get a lecture about why it's rude to do so. It's hilarious to watch.

It adds some kick knowing that I'm being watched too. Essentially, being watched watching them. It's hard not to at least smirk when I notice someone watching me. I'll throw in some bullshit body language to establish some false 'tells', a deep breath or a slight shake of the head,bet on a weak hand or two that'll establish me as a loose cannon and generally try to irritate and confuse.

Of course, at the end of the night, sometimes the guy with the best cards wins.

# Chapter 9
# *A Walk In The Park*

We're playing for about an hour and I'm ahead. The guy from the linens company who delivers the table cloths and napkins for Louie is in the game now, as well as Dom the locksmith, a friend of Vin's. I'm, of course, drumming my fingers absent-mindedly as I consider my bet.

Finally, Tony nearly shouts at me "Hey! Ringo! Have you ever had someone play Babaloo on your ass with his fuckin' shoe?"

"Scusa." I say holding my hands in mock surrender, while exerting maximum effort to not smile.

I get a call, it's Jimmy Knievel.

"I heard about that guy."

"Yeah?" I ask.

"There's no doubt about that guy. He's taking a trip." meaning Benny.

I guess Angelo's contacts were able to confirm that he's double-crossing us, and his ticket needs to be punched.

"What about his tab?" meaning the money he owes Angelo.

"Show's over. Fuhgetaboutit"

"Well I'll let him know." Meaning I'll take care of it.

And that was it. The order was given.

I cash myself out while saying to the guys "C'mon, let's take a ride."

I catch Philly's eye for an instant, and in return he nods almost imperceptibly. On the way out as we pass through the deserted kitchen, Philly grabs an expensive looking ice pick off of the magnetic rack near the broiler and squirrels it away inside his jacket.

We're near Webster Avenue and we pull over so I can use a pay phone. I get back in the car and tell Vin to head over to the Cross-Bronx, we need to make a stop in Manhattan. The stupidity of people never ceases to amaze me. No doubt a degenerate gambler like this Benny whatever-his-last-name-is had been told many times in his life, ‘Bet with your head, not over it.’, and he hadn’t taken that advice to heart. Of course if he’d won, he wouldn’t have expected a song and dance from the bookie, he’d have expected to get paid. And he would have gotten paid. So you would think it would be obvious to him, you lose some money and owe a guy like Angelo money, you don’t try to be cute, you pay him. Such deceit. It’s an imperfect world.

So we get to a place that's one of Benny's hangouts, we met him here the night he made his proposition, a restaurant-bar called Camile’s in mid-town. Parking is a cast-iron bitch of course, so Vin pulls out the Daily News and stays with the car, double parked a half block away. Tony D., Philly and I sit at the bar and have a drink, hoping that this mutt will show up.We’re on our second round when...BINGO...the star of Raging Bullshit himself comes waltzing in, looking like he doesn’t have a care in the world. He looks over and notices us at the bar, and his face turns about thirty shades of white.

He starts in with “Just the guy I wanted to see, I need to talk to you about the rest I owe.” blah blah fucking blah.

He’s making this easy. I buy him a drink, and we wind up having more than a few and really work the bullshit. We yap about the Jets, the Yankees, the Rangers, the barmaid’s tits, and before long he’s all lubed up and ready for a ride.

Finally, it’s last call and I say “I'm hungry, let's take a ride and get some eggs.”

We’re all a little buzzed at this point, but we made sure Benny was tanked; it makes things easier on all of us. Philly grabs Benny what’s-his-face and we head out the door.

Before we get in the car, I turn and ask him “Benny, what the fuck is your last name anyway?”

“Guomondussonur.”

“You’re shitting me.” I say in wide-eyed disbelief.

“My father’s half of the family is from Iceland.” he slurred.

I look at Philly dumbfounded “Jeez. How did I ever miss that one?”

We get him in the back seat between Tony D. who is chatting away to keep him happy, and Philly, who’s not big on conversation. The mutt is nodding off every few minutes, and by the time he notices where we are, Vin's got us on the Taconic parkway and almost to the spot. I give him some bullshit about stopping at Philly's goumada in Briarcliff.

As soon as we're on the exit ramp, Philly says "Find somewhere for me to piss or grab your snorkel."

Vin pulls into a densely wooded section of a park just off the Taconic.

*Graham Hills Park, Pleasantville, New York*

We pull over at the spot and we all get out and start watering the plants. Vin takes a walk into the woods surrounding us, making sure there isn't an unexpected audience. Finally, needle-dick gets out and starts to take a leak. Philly finishes and zips up, walks behind him and pulls out the ice pick. He basically has two choices here, spear him through the back of his skull and up into his brain, which will be quick and essentially painless since you check out almost instantly. In this case however, since Benny was trying to play both ends against the middle, Philly gives him a good hard shot right between his shoulder blades and pulls the pick back out. Boom, he goes down faster than Paris Hilton in front of a camcorder. It had to hurt.

Philly figures he'd watch him squirm a bit, and he does, but after a few seconds he starts screaming bloody murder, which is understandable since just then he's literally the victim of one. I mean this guy sounds like a fucking air raid siren…that warbling kind of screech. I'm looking around and you can't see shit because it's so dark, but I can just imagine some nosy fucking cop parked somewhere nearby in the trees catching a nap in his cruiser, or some teenage kid feeling up his girlfriend.

Philly realizes this too, and starts stabbing him in the chest and he's really going at it, but Benny's hands are getting in the way of Philly getting him directly in the throat, which would shut him the fuck up.

He's rasping to Philly"No…no…"

Philly's grunting "Die you rat fuck."

Finally Philly winds up and puts all of his enormous weight into one last stab, which sinks into Benny's chest and impales the pick at least a few inches into the dirt beneath him; with a ‘snap’, the handle breaks off of the ice pick. Philly's instantly flustered and after a moment he looks over at Tony and I, then back at the wooden handle he's holding. Benny is weakly waving his arms around, but Philly’s kneeling on his chest and Benny’s pretty much done. It was an awkward moment. He's leaning over Quai Chang Pain with a piece of wood in his hand, and looking totally clueless.

He looks back toward Tony and me and asks "What the fuck do I do now?"

Tony and I answer in unison "Wait'll he melts."

On the way back, Tony D. and I are recreating for Vin, the moment when the ice pick broke; our keen senses telling us that Philly probably needed to live through it again.

“You really ought to get a better ice pick next time Phil.” Vin says “Don’t be so fucking cheap! For chrissakes, buy quality.”

Tony D. adds “Hey, write them a letter and explain exactly what happened. Maybe they’ll mail you a new one.”

To his credit, Philly realizes that silence is the best option at times like this.

# Chapter 10
# *Investigation*

*The Bronx, New York City*

I had a cappuccino with Angelo after the walk in the woods.

"So…how's the man on civilian patrol?"

"He caught a cold, you won't see him no more."

He didn't even nod, and we just sat sipping our coffee. There was something else here and I needed to wait until he was ready.

"There's something I need you to straighten out." He said.

I waited as he took another sip.

"There's a guy who we're lining up some things with, a Jewish fella, over in lower Manhattan. They make software for the computer. We were working on a thing with him, Mikey was working with the guy."

Mikey Zirella owned a couple of whore houses, a gay leather-bar and sex-club, and an adult bookstore. He'd recently been found dead, dressed up in a leather outfit in the basement of his gay joint. He'd somehow been smothered to death and it looked like a case of auto-erotic asphyxiation. No one had yet determined who his playmate had been.

He wasn't a made guy and was only an average 'earner' for a connected guy, so while it was being looked into, it wasn't red-hot.

"What kind of software?" I asked.

"It's not my thing, it has to do with the internet. I don't pretend to know about that stuff. I'll leave it up to the guy to tell you about it. I've heard you talk about computers and the internet, you know about that stuff right?"

"I know a little Ange." I said, shaking my head.

"Come on, I mean who do I have here?" Angelo said, holding his hands out palms up "Mikey met this guy so he was cultivating it from our side, but ya know, he wasn't the right guy from the start." quickly adding "May he rest in peace." and made a subtle sign of the cross with his right hand.

"Well yeah, compared to our crew I guess." I say.

"This is what I'm saying." Angelo said, "OK so go see the guy, Jimmy will give you a number. Keep me up to date on this thing."

"OK."

It was understood that Angelo, being Angelo, knew much more about what was in the works than he let on. He pretended to be completely computer illiterate for two reasons. First, he wanted my attention on the matter and his feigning ignorance was meant to motivate me to look into it carefully. Second, he'd made a habit of misrepresenting how much he knew. In most situations it was to his advantage to have people underestimate him, it allowed him to see agendas people had that they would otherwise do a better job of hiding, keeping in mind that these 'people' were murderers and thieves. It was a great survival skill and he was a Zen master at it. He knew that I knew that he was feigning ignorance, we had spoken of it on occasion, but he did it anyway; think of it as one of those 'best business practices', for wiseguys.

"Heard anything?" meaning was I aware of anything relating to Mike Zirella's death.

"No, nothing, but it's only been a couple days."

"Yeah, well keep your ears open. Whatever happened, one way or another we're going to find out. I don't want to drag my feet on this thing."

"OK. I'll take a ride over there and take a look."

"Good." Angelo picked up his paper, signaling the end of the discussion.

I saw Jimmy Knievel before I left the club and he gave me the information on Jacob Seiden at Seventeen O Three Associates. I stepped out to a pay phone and arranged to meet him at the Capri in mid-town to learn about the internet thing.

I grabbed Vin on the way out of the club.

"Where we heading?"

"I need to start looking into this Mikey Zirella thing. Let's pick up Philly and Tony D."

When we'd rounded up Philly and Tony, I said "OK, take a ride over to that joint on Morris Avenue…"

"They found him in the place over in Manhattan though..." Vin shot back "Finocchio Central." meaning Mike Zirella's gay bar.

"The cops have scrubbed that place already. From what I know, he spent more time at the joint on Morris Avenue. I want to take a look over there first."

"Mikey never came across like a fag." Vin said shaking his head "I guess a guy can hide that kind of thing, but still…"

"Mmm?"

"I don't know. I don't know if it adds up; that's all I'm saying." Vin said.

"Yeah. I don't know either. If I had to guess I'd say it's bullshit." I said.

"Made to look like he was a finocchio?" Vin asked.

I shrugged.

"Like he was doing that…what the fuck is that thing they do? With the choking… that thing….?"

"What thing? What are we talking about here?" Tony D. asked from the back seat.

"Where they choke themselves when they're about to shoot their wad."

"Auto-erotic asphyxiation." I say.

"Bingo! Ass-ification." Vin exclaimed "So maybe its made to look like he was into that shit, to cover up the job?"

"Maybe." I say "Who knows? Let's get over there and see if anything shakes loose."

"Hard to figure, Mikey I mean. Doesn't seem like a guy who had enemies, and even if he had some, not those kind of enemies." Vin said, pulling away from the curb.

"Yeah, I know." I agreed "If it turns out it wasn't an enemy, then it could have been a friend, you know?"

"Can of fucking worms that would be." Vin said.

If it was a friend, that is someone connected or even a made guy, then it gets sticky since protocol was broken by whacking him without approval of his sponsor, Angelo. Added to that, there is protocol involved in what can be done in retaliation, if you can find out what happened in the first place. If it were just some ambitious but unlucky civilian, it would make this a lot simpler.

We arrive in front of a non-descript brick building that's painted completely black, a dull and dusty black. On the metal door in letters too small to be read from more than a few feet away, is stenciled in red Hi-Class. This was one of Zirella's straight-sex places, as opposed to the gay joint they found him in. Philly pounds on the door and it opens after a few seconds; it's pitch black inside, and in the doorway the outline of a man's huge bulk is barely visible, his skin as black as night. The only thing clearly visible is the Nike swoop on the shoulder of his shirt; it seems to be floating in air.

"Yeah?"

"Let's have a talk." I say and walk past him into the blackness.

He reaches for my shoulder but Philly grabs him and brings him along with us. When the door closes behind us, I can see that in fact the entrance is lit, in a dim red lighting. I stand still for a full minute, letting my eyes adjust to the light. The doorman is standing in front of Philly who has his hand on the guy's shoulder, and I'm certain he's making no fuss because the muzzle of Philly's nine millimeter is poking him in the kidney.

After a minute, we proceed through a few hallways and doors, and wind up in larger room, also dimly bathed in red light. There are leather sofas to our left and right, and a guy, who could be a twin of the guy we have with us, sitting in a chair next to a door. He's got a black ball cap on that has a white 'X' on the front of it. He senses that something's wrong the moment we enter the room and makes for the door, but Tony D. persuades him to retake his seat with the wave of a very large pistol.

"OK. I think we're long overdue for a company meeting, don't you?" I say.

"What the fuck is this about?" From 'X' cap.

"If he opens his yap again, unless he's answering my questions, put one in his kneecap." I say.

"Why can't I just shoot him now?" Tony says plaintively.

He looks at me, but I just keep my eyes on 'X' cap.

Tony says "You're getting soft on me, you know that?"

I send Vin to round up everybody in the place, knowing that it'll be near empty at this hour. He comes back with six girls, another arm-breaker tattooed and shirtless with a dazzling array of gold chains around his neck, and a guy who is pulling up his pants and looks like he's about to shit them.

"Let him put his shoes on and then show this gentleman out." I say motioning to the half dressed guy.

The john picks up his shoes and heads for the door, Vin trailing an arm-length behind him.

"OK. So. I know I didn't see any of you at Mikey's wake, so let's have our own eulogy right here." I say slowly, smiling at the nine of them.

After a long silence, one of the girls says "We don't know anything about his…death, if that's what you want to know."

"I'll be the judge of whether you know anything." I say to her. "And I'll say this right now, right at the beginning, if I have to leave here with no information at all, then this experience will be…unpleasant." I look at Nike shirt "You. Who have you seen Mike talking to in here, aside from people who work here?"

"He wasn't out here with the customers. He spent his time in the back."

"The office you mean?"

"Yeah."

"Who have you seen in the office with him then?" I asked.

"It wasn't like he introduced us to people he had with him."

"You're here, you hear things, we all know this." I say to 'X' cap. "Who's handling the money now?"

"Gio handles the money, Mikey came in to collect and do the books. But Gio handled things day to day." he said.

"Gio?"

"Giovanni."

"Last name? I asked.

They all just shook their heads.

Looking at all of them I ask "So? Where is he today?"

One of the girls, the one who was the first to speak, said "I saw him an hour ago, but he took off, I don't know where."

"Did anyone else come around in the past few days looking for Mike?"

"He was dead, man." Gold chains said, with a definite condescending tone.

I walked over to him, and gave him a hard stare "That's not what I asked. You trying to give me a hard time?"

Silence. After half a minute "There was a guy that came to see Gio yesterday. In the office." It was another of the girls, a young skinny blonde with shoulder length hair. Her hairstyle and lingerie gave her the appearance of a school girl, maybe 17 or so. Even though she was unquestionably pretty, her face said twenty five, and her accent said Midwest.

"You are?" I say to her.

"Honey." she says.

"You in the office a lot, Honey?"

"No, but I was yesterday for a little while."

"Why was that?"

"Gio called me in, he had a friend with him. He told me to be nice to him."

"So?"

"I gave him head." she said.

"Think Honey. His name? What did he look like?"

"Well… he was a little shorter than you, muscular, well dressed. Italian maybe?" she said.

"Name?" I said "Take your time."

She sat trying to remember, her eyes darting this way and that. The expression on her face said that she couldn't remember, then her eyes darted to the left and stayed there for a moment, and it was clear she had it "Richie I think. Or Ronnie." she paused a moment more "Yeah, I think I heard Gio call him Richie."

"Clean-shaven, mustache, beard, hair color, tattoos?"

"Brown hair, short and neat. No beard or mustache or anything like that. He was wearing a suit jacket.

"Come on Honey, gimme something here. Think." I said.

"He had a tattoo, I could see it under his shirt cuff." She said.

"Which arm?"

She thought a moment "Hand. It was on the back of his right hand."

"Young guy?" I asked.

"He was maybe 40?" Honey shrugged.

"OK." Then to 'X' cap "When this Gio comes in, tell him Eddie is looking for him, I want to talk to him, here's a number where he can reach me. Tell him not to make me go looking for him. Understand?"

"Yeah man, I'll tell him." he said.

Once we're back in the car "Well."

Philly says "Yeah."

I let out a breath "That fucking Richie Scala, if there's anyone I'd love to fuckin' smack, he's the gold medal winner."

Vin says "He's got to have the pole position for most beefs and sitdowns, that guy's everyone's pain in the ass. He ought to have his own brand of hemorrhoid cream. Just look for the douche bag on the bottle!"

"The one ass he kisses is the one I wish he'd mouth-off to." Philly says.

"Pfft. Are you kidding? Richie's a psychopath and a prick, but Nicky's utterly ruthless. There's a difference. I mean, Richie knows that Nicky would punch his ticket and not think twice about it." from Tony D.

"Nicky Trosa is a stand up guy, that's true. I feel bad for the guy, having to defend Richie's bullshit." I say "Of course, if Nicky wanted to be cute, he could use that to his advantage too…all warfare is based on deception."

"What?"

"Sun Tzu…"

Vin stares at me and just gives me a little shake of his head.

"Jesus… crack a book once in a while." I smile at him "I have to talk to the Old Man before we go any further. Head back to the club."

I let Angelo know about what I'd learned at Hi-Class.

"What do you think?" Angelo says to me.

"I only have a theory, I don't have any proof."

"Alright."

"Maybe Mr. Aggravation was pushing his way into Mikey's business, and decided to take a short-cut." I say.

Angelo leaned forward, looking into his coffee cup, silently contemplating for a minute. Finally he looked up at me again"And?"

"And, he's going to use that 'I didn't know he was with you, he reached out to me.' bullshit routine of his."

Angelo picked up his espresso cup and took a leisurely sip, slowly returning the cup to the table. "So?"

"Yeah, well he'll say that Mikey was into him for some gambling losses. I mean that's what he'd do." I say "He's no brain surgeon but he is a conniving fuck. He'll cover himself and there's no proof."

A shrug.

Angelo was the quickest guy on the uptake that I'd ever met. There was no way he didn't see what was coming; he was feeling me out. I know what I want to say, but it's out of line for me to say it, so I bite my tongue.

Half a minute later he says "Out with it."

"I don't want to stick my nose where it doesn't belong." I say, looking at the table top. "I'm not a member."

"It's OK. I'm saying it's OK."

"Well, it's just that this guy has been a fucking thorn in our side, and not just us."

"Yeah. I know this, everybody knows this."

"Well, maybe if he was too fucking smart for his own good."

"Yeah but if you miss something…" he shot back in his quiet voice, the rapidity of his response was his way of telling me that this was something that had been considered at some point.

"Then I better not miss anything."

He sat contemplating, fingers interlaced loosely in front of him, as still as a statue.

After a long silence he says "Yeah, alright, take look at it, but don't do anything."

Angelo was giving me the go-ahead to come up with a way to set up Richie Scala so that he got whacked either by his own people, or by someone else not connected to us. The Old Man was also telling me that if I missed some detail and my involvement was uncovered he'd say I was a maverick, that I set up Richie because I had some beef with him personally. In other words I'd be dead. Since I came to him with the suggestion, I had to back it up. He'd most likely sit down with Jimmy Knievel and go over every angle before approving any action.

Why stick my neck out, break the rules and look for a way to whack out Richie when I had no immediate monetary befit? Because I hated the cafone. Everybody hated him.

# Chapter 11
# Confirmation

*Mid-town Manhattan, New York City*

The sun was setting as I walked into the Capri to meet Seiden. I was having a hard time shaking the annoyance I felt since finding out about Richie Scala's involvement. It was a big pain in the ass. As I walked into the Capri though, I was hit square in the face with the smell of good food; sweet basil, roasted garlic and the best bread on the planet. I stood there for a moment, breathing in that great smell and letting my agita fade; with my irritation displaced, I saw a guy sitting at the bar with a black yarmulke.

"Mr. Seiden?"

"Yes?"

"Eddie." I said.

"Eddieeee" he said, drawing out my first name, prompting me to tell him my last name.

"That's right." I smiled; all information will be given on a need-to-know basis.

Jacob Seiden stood up and took my hand. In his forties, about five-nine, black hair and brown eyes, heavy set and sporting a full beard; he had a broad face with a genial and intelligent look. His grey Joseph Abboud was too tight around his middle and his eyes had that 'overworked' look.

"Jacob, we have business to discuss."

"A terrible thing, what happened to Mr. Zirella." he said as his smile disappeared.

"Terrible." I agreed.

"I must confess Eddie, it worries me about my own safety." he said in a soft concerned tone "I hope you can understand my feelings and my inexperience in these matters." he said in an accent that was New York City with the Yiddish inflection.

"I understand completely."

I motioned for him to retake his seat, and leaned against the bar next to him and ordered drinks.

“I need to ask you a question Jacob, and it’s important for you to search your memory carefully.”

He nodded and looked at me earnestly.

“Have you spoken with anyone else about the project you were working on with Mr. Zirella?” I asked.

He started shaking his head halfway through the question “No one else. Keeping information contained about the ‘project’ as you put it, is in my interest as well, no?”

"How did you get involved with this in the first place then?" I asked.

"It was through Mr. Zirella."

Seiden didn't elaborate, so it was a safe bet that it had to do with a call girl, or something like that. Since this was our first meeting I decided not to embarrass him if he didn't want to provide the detail.

"And how did Zirella know who you were, ya know…what you did for a living?" I asked.

"He wouldn't say. I did ask him, but he always spoke around the point. It was clear that he didn't want me to know." he said, then after a short contemplative pause "It would have to be someone connected to the companies involved. The project involves some specific technical details that anyone on the outside of the business would not know about."

"So someone on the inside then?" I asked.

"Yes, that is my guess."

“Was anyone ever with him, when you two met?” I asked.

“Last week as a matter of fact. There was another man with him when we met.”

“Where did you meet last week?”

"In front of a bookstore a few blocks from my office. He wanted an update on how things were proceeding.” he said “He got out of his car to talk with me, but behind him I could see a man in the car at the wheel.”

“Did you get a look at him?”

“Yes, a little. The passenger window was down and he was only a few feet away.” he said “I can tell you he was a very stocky…very muscular looking. Brown hair. Eyes I can’t say.”

“Any facial hair? Tattoos?”

“Not that I recall, but I didn't really have a reason to pay attention to him.” he said “I think he was wearing a jacket… but no tie.” He paused “I do remember he was holding a cigarette in his hand, let me see… his right hand.” he said, then with more confidence he said “Yes. On his right hand, on the back of it, there was something on it. I couldn’t really see it that well but I remember thinking that maybe he had injured his hand, burned it perhaps?”

“Could it have been a tattoo?”

“Oh.” he paused “Yes, that didn’t occur to me at that time, yes it could have been a tattoo I suppose.”

“Did either of them use any names?”

“Well the fellow in the car never spoke, he just sat there watching us.” he said “Mr. Zirella didn’t use any names, no.”

“You’re sure Jacob?” I pressed.

“I’m positive.” he said; he was telling the truth.

“A week ago you say?”

“Yes. Exactly one week.” he said slowly, the shadow passing over his face as he realized that it was very close indeed to the day Mikey Zirella had drawn his last breath.

“OK. Good enough.” I said “So, why don’t you bring me up to speed on this work we’re going to do.”

Over the next fifteen minutes, Seiden laid out the plans that were in place. I was impressed. Not to speak unkindly of the deceased, but there was no way Mikey Zirella had the skills to manage this if things got complicated. He was a knock-around guy, but definitely more inclined to be doing Junior Jumble than Sudoku; which is to say he was industrious but not sharp. This thing was going to be complicated, technical, and if it succeeded, profitable. I’d have to come up to speed on some of the technology, to have a comfort level I could live with, representing Angelo’s interests as I was. I shook hands with Seiden and told him I’d be in touch.

There was enough to convince me that the driver that Seiden had described was in fact Richie The Prick, I’d have to keep digging. I told Seiden to call me if anyone paid him a visit.

Why would Mike be with Richie? It didn't make sense with the facts as I knew them; there was no benefit as far as I could see. Angelo had a piece of the project, so that's money out of Zirella's pocket, and Angelo provided the means and protection. Involving Richie would only wind up reducing Mikey's end, why would he choose to do that…unless of course he had no choice? Knowing Richie, it's plausible.

# Chapter 12
# *The Brothers Bello*

Richie Scala wasn't as tall as much as he was wide. His two hundred pounds was mostly comprised of muscle and thick bones. For a guy who never set foot in a gym, he had awesome upper body strength; his genetics did nothing to discourage him from becoming a predator both physically and by temperament. From a young age, Richie had been nothing but a loudmouth bully and his brutish ways remained unchecked throughout his teens; he had never lost a fight during those years so he'd never received a dose of humility. As a result, he was like a five foot ten inch tall, fifty two inch wide, two hundred pound…bad tempered two-year-old. The only distinguishing feature, aside of course from his imposing physique, was a tattoo on his right arm that began at his elbow and ended at the back of his right hand, depicting a dragon with its mouth open and eyes flaming, descending on its prey, a perfect metaphor for its owner. For the most part, Richie had to have what he wanted, had to have it now, and anyone who stood in his way was 'a fucking rat'. His unchecked ego and inability to see beyond his own desires drove him with boldness and confidence, while his natural physical strength gave him the means. The confluence of both made him useful.

On his twentieth birthday Richie had been out drinking all night with associates; in truth he had no friends although he was unaware of the distinction. He stopped at the Three Stars Diner on the way home for eggs and coffee. Seated two tables away from him was a young couple who had stopped in for a quick bite before heading home from a wedding reception. The woman was blonde, young and very shapely. While she exuded undeniable sex appeal, her eyes didn't wander from her companions. Richie, in his skin tight silk short sleeved shirt and gold rope chain, was an impressive display of muscle. The sleeves of his shirt strained around his bulging biceps and his dragon tattoo looked particularly ominous on his big forearm. As Richie stared at her she lifted her coffee cup to take a sip and he noticed a wedding ring. Richie smiled and glanced at her husband, a fellow of average height and build.

'What a strunz.' he thought sarcastically 'That fuckin' weakling gets to go home and fuck her?'

His gaze returned to the young woman. She was wearing a white blouse of some thin material and a short black skirt. Her breasts were large, heavy and perfectly shaped; and her cleavage bulged a bit when she pressed against the table top to take a bite of her food. Under the table she shifted her legs a bit; the thin materiel of the skirt clung to her perfectly rounded hips, and to Richie her legs looked about a mile long. They were not too skinny nor too full for Richie's tastes, they were perfectly shaped. Curvy, smooth and sexy. Although she was dressed typically for a wedding, she had on a minimum of makeup and her only jewelry was a little gold heart on a thin gold chain around her neck, and of course, her wedding band.

Richie kept staring at her, fantasizing about her charms as he felt the gradual presence of his erection, growing with each passing minute. Eventually she expressed her discomfort at being the object of Richie's leering, but her husband was not the confrontational sort and decided not to make this more than a drunk misbehaving.

After they were done eating, the couple paid their bill and as they rose and turned to leave, Richie could contain himself no longer.

"C'mere and sit on my lap."

The woman ignored him and the slight slur of Richie's words allowed her husband to ignore the comment too.

"Why the fuck would you go home with that?" Richie said, waving his massive arm dismissively at her husband.

Twenty feet away, at the cash register, the manager looked up and instantly sized up the situation. He realized he had only seconds and started moving immediately.

"C'mon honey, c'mere and sit on my lap."

"Go sleep it off buddy." her husband said, gently interposing his body between Richie's table and his wife.

Richie just stared at him, no anger in evidence, no emotion at all, then returned his gaze to the woman.

The couple started to move towards the door again.

"C'mon, don't go. C'mere and sit that fuckin' ass of yours on my face."

The husband spun around and was about to dive on Richie when he felt a pair of arms grip him in a bear hug.

"I'LL FUCKIN' KILL YOU COCKSUCKER!." he screamed as the manager held him back.

"Yeah yeah. I'd swat you like a fly. It's your wife I want to fuck, so stay out of it." Richie said with only a little irritation, still seated in front of his mostly uneaten food.

The manager struggled and strained but was able to drag the husband out of the diner. It didn't take long to persuade the husband to leave the drunk to his hangover and just end the episode.

Two minutes later, as the couple drove north on the service road next to I-95, they noticed headlights growing quickly in their rear view mirror. They continued to grow until they were practically on the rear bumper of their car. The husband could see Richie's face in the car behind them, and against his wife's wishes, pulled over to the curb. The two men got out of their cars and met between them. Richie just stared at the husband who demanded in an irritated tone that they be left alone. Before exiting his car, Richie had taken a small wooden club from under his front seat and held it along the underside of his forearm. He let the club slide down into his hand and without warning Richie swung the club in a tight arc with all of the considerable strength he could muster, bringing the man down with one merciless stroke to his skull.

As his victim lay dazed and barely conscious on the road, his young wife emerged from the passenger side of the car, screaming and running toward him with rage in her eyes. He stiff-armed her by the front of her blouse as she approached, and tore it and her bra from her body in one savage motion. She tried to grab at his face but he grabbed her in a bear hug and forced his mouth upon hers, holding her head by a fistful blonde hair. Richie groped one of her large breasts, squeezing it hard, and that gave her the opening she needed. She reached up and carved four scratches with the nails of her right hand that ran from his forehead to his jaw. The unexpected pain he felt caused two reactions; it sobered him instantly, and it enraged him. He took a half step backward and delivered a brutal right hook to the side of her face, dropping her to the pavement like a rag doll.

His head cleared for the moment, Richie considered the situation; his two victims were lying on the road between the cars, in the harsh pallor of his headlights. He took a deep breath and considered the vulnerability of being discovered here on the side of the road by a passing car. Richie reached down and retrieved his club from the pavement. Thirty seconds later, with all the emotional involvement of a carpenter pounding a nail, Richie Scala had made certain that there would be no survivors.

He got back into his car, and stared for a moment at the bodies in his headlights. The woman's head was a mass of red pulp, her blonde hair scattered in wide pattern on the asphalt. Her naked breasts were full even as she lay on her back, and her skirt had ridden up exposing her panties as she lay dead in the roadway. Gazing at her, Richie felt a sense of loss in the pit of his stomach, but not at all in the sense that any civilized person would feel. The loss he felt was his thwarted desire for a sexual encounter, his regrets were limited to the fact that he wasn't going to be able to sate his own needs. These were the first three lives that Richie had ever taken; the autopsy later revealed that the young wife was pregnant. No one who knew him would find it surprising that he felt absolutely no remorse about taking their lives.

No one had seen the incident, and to his relief, no one had ever come forward from the Three Stars Diner.

Richie worked on the periphery of organized crime for most of his late teens and early twenties, he had served time in prison for burglary and assault, and as he approached his thirtieth birthday his association with organized crime became far more substantial. After the slaying of the young married couple, Richie had killed twelve more times, ten of them contracted hits for the mob. His string of hits added to his street image but also to his bad disposition. Richie was more effective than most wiseguys at scaring the shit out of people who the family needed to scare the shit out of. Anyone in his path easily picked up on the fact that he was a true sociopath and wildly unpredictable. These characteristics enabled Richie to be outstanding at 'muscling in' on businesses and eliciting protection money.

When Richie was thirty eight years old he was 'straightened out' and became a full fledged wiseguy. He'd been given a contract to eliminate two brothers who ran a drug and prostitution ring near Jerome Avenue, adjacent to Yankee Stadium. The Bello brothers, Hector and 'Spook', had a street reputation that struck fear into the hearts of area residents, civilians and some underworld people alike. They were fierce and brutal to anyone who offended them or was unfortunate enough to be in their way. They treated people they did business with only slightly better. Some of the girls in the neighborhood who fell prey to the lure of heroin or cocaine, ended up as indentured sex servants and prostitutes for the Bellos. Over the years, some would turn up in dumpsters, dead from an overdose or murdered. There were also stories of entire families killed whose fathers and brothers tried to exact revenge for the death of a daughter or sister.

One late afternoon near the corner of east 163rd street and Grant Avenue, Hector and Spook Bello were in a car and on the way to pay a visit to a small-time smack dealer who needed to be 'absorbed' into their expanding empire, accompanying them were two of their minions who would deliver the actual beating. As they approached the corner, the driver, riding the last waves of a fix from late the night before and now feeling the low coming on, failed to stop in time and rear ended the car in front of him. The driver of the car he rear ended was alone, and looked hurt.

The reaction of the Bello's, keyed up as they were for their mission, was annoyance, and in a span of seconds, annoyance turned to anger. The four men sprang from their car and descended upon the injured driver, a young man of college age. Without a word, they peeled him out of his car and pummeled him into a bloody mess right there in the middle of the road. As a parting shot, Spook Bello placed the driver's head in the car's door jam and slammed it twice, cracking his skull and nearly killing him. The young man was unconscious when they left, which spared him the irony of hearing Hector Bello scream at him to watch where he was going.

In this case, as badly as the driver had been beaten, it was ultimately the Bellos whose luck had run out. The driver, Anthony Parisi, was a student at New York University and although he was nearly beaten to death, he survived. Anthony's uncle, his father's brother, Salvatore 'Big Sal' Parisi, was a made man; unknown to Hector and Spook, the moment they'd pulled Anthony out of his car, they'd sealed their fates. The order was given and Richie was the one it was given to. Revenge aside, it was also noted that the Bello drug and prostitution business had to be dealt with anyway since it was a maverick operation and attracted far too much attention for the Italians who liked to keep a low profile where income steams were concerned. Richie's capo, Nicky Trosa, said it succinctly if not elegantly "Wackin' these guys…we kill two fuckin' birds with one shoe."

The Bello's we're abducted at three fifteen in the morning as they were heading from a night club in Manhattan to an after-hours club just a mile away. Their car was found, still running, at a traffic light, with two dead men in the front seat. Ballistics determined that both were shot at close range from the window closest to each. Witnesses confirmed that the victims were accompanied that night by the Bello brothers, but as of yet, the Bellos had not been located.

The Bellos were taken to a defunct discount tile and carpet warehouse a quarter mile from the Whitestone Bridge by Richie and two of his leg breakers, Genaro Benvenuto, called 'Pipe', and 'Little Mike' Sullivan. The bravado and threats from the Bellos lasted only mid-way into the second hour. When fingers and toes were being pulverized with a six pound short handled sledge, they turned a corner psychologically and began to offer money and plea in earnest for mercy. The torture was gruesome enough, but Richie, never missing an opportunity to enhance suffering, had Hector and Spook lashed, in their underwear, to adjacent columns that supported the roof of the warehouse. Facing each other, separated by fifteen feet, the brothers had to watch each other being mutilated and in agony. Richie laughed and made jokes the entire time, robbing the two of any dignity they might summon in the face of their suffering.

By the halfway point, about twelve hours into the ordeal, they were pleading and begging pathetically for death. Richie, wanting to take away any hope either brother held for an end to the suffering, told the brothers to save their strength, there were at least a few days more to endure before he'd consider killing them. Richie made a show of looking at his watch and then looked at 'Pipe'.

"Pipe… I must be slipping" Richie said with mock concern.

Pipe didn't say anything; he just shrugged his shoulders as if to say 'What?'

"It's twelve hours we been at this." Richie said.

"Yeah?"

"This is hard fuckin' work. Let's get some food in here."

"Want me to go, or Little Mike?"

"Send Mikey-boy."

Half an hour later, Sullivan was laying out three hero sandwiches wrapped in foil on a card table about ten feet from the Bellos. He placed two cold six packs of beer in the center of the table, and then the three sat down and began to peel the foil from the hot sandwiches.

"Hey, sausage and eggs!" Richie said with glee, looking at Hector Bello who stared at him in agony.

Hector's chest moved rapidly in short shallow breaths. He couldn't take a deep breath without his broken ribs causing him a stabbing pain that set his entire torso on fire.

"Maybe we'll cut off your sausage later." Richie said "Would you like that?"

Richie looked at Pipe, who shrugged and said "He don't feel like talking I guess."

"I like that. Who needs all that talk." Richie said, taking a big bite of the hero "That begging you two did before…you fuckin' babies." Richie taunted with a mouthful of his sandwich "You two are supposed to be tough guys. Crying like that, like a pair of silly fuckin' broads, you should be ashamed of yourselves."

Richie swallowed his food and took another huge bite "OK. Anyone who doesn't want their sausage cut off… raise your hand."

Pipe, smiling, raised his hand. Richie and Little Mike follow suit.

After a few seconds, Richie said "Well, I guess now we know where everyone stands."

The three burst out in laughter, as they finished their sandwiches and beer. Richie stood up, stretched and let out a monstrous belch.

"OK, time for surgery!" he turned to Little Mike "Nurse?"

Little Mike fished around inside a big box on the floor and came out with a large set of shears, they looked like huge oversized scissors and were used for cutting sheet metal. He passed them to Richie.

"Alright." Richie said, nodding his head toward Hector.

Pipe stepped up with a box knife and slashed off Hector's underwear, and some of his skin in the process.

"Grab a hold of him so I can get this fuckin' thing around him."

Pipe reached out, his large and brawny hands encircled Hector Bello's penis and scrotum. He pulled back so that one line of cutting would sever both.

For the first time in hours, Hector spoke, and when he did his voice was a horse rasp.

Over and over he pleaded in a barely audible rasp "No no no no. No no no no." slightly shaking his head.

Richie's loud voice boomed over Hector's "OK. You're right." He turned to Pipe and Little Mike in resignation "He's right fellas. He's right."

He got close to Hector's face and said in a low voice "OK?"

Hector summoned the strength to nod his head.

"Hey, when you're right, you're right." Richie turned to Little Mike "If we do this, they'll bleed to death right away. Can't have that." he said, shaking his head emphatically "Can't have it."

Richie's face looked contemplative; finally he said "You got that torch with you?"

Sullivan already had it in hand, held it up and smiled as he lit the blow torch.

"OK. Back to work!" Richie said in a comical tone, and then looking at Pipe he held up the big shears and said "I hope these are sterile." which prompted all three again to burst out again in laughter.

When Richie had composed himself, he placed the jaws of the shears around Hector's organs. Hector became a bit more animated, summoning all the strength he had left, which was not much. He rasped loudly, drool dripping from his mouth. Behind them, Spook also started to become more agitated, but his voice was totally gone and all he could do was breathe out while trying to voice his protests. Richie squeezed slowly, the razor sharp blades cutting through Hector's genitals; as soon as the dark red blood started to flow from Hector's groin in earnest, Little Mike carefully aimed the blow torch at the exposed tissues, scorching the blood vessels closed. When Richie had completely severed Hector's organs, he flashed a look at Pipe, who then held them up to Hector's face.

"Excuse me Miss, are these yours?" Pipe asked smiling.

Hector passed out.

Richie turned to Spook and shouted "Next!" snipping at the air menacingly and chuckling.

Richie repeated the 'operation' on Spook and then let them both pass out for a while. They hung from the columns, bloodied, beaten and where their genitals had been, now were only large black and red burns.

Finally, when the twenty four hours of unimaginable pain, terror and humiliation had been delivered as ordered, Richie had Pipe inject the two with enough methamphetamine to bring them out of their near comatose state. The two brothers started to moan and squirm, becoming more and more animated.

Reaching into a paper bag, Richie removed two very large syringes that looked as though they were more suited for cattle than humans. As Pipe held a huge syringe in each hand, Richie filled them from a brown plastic bottle labeled "Plumber's Professional Drain-Unclogger". Once loaded with the clear yellowish goop, he fitted the syringes with long thick hypodermic needles, inserted the plungers, and expelled the air from each. Richie stepped up to Hector Bello and slapped him across the face several times until Hector came out of his stupor and his eyes focused. Hector's eyes widened as they moved from Richie's face to the large menacing needle he was holding.

"This should take the edge off the meth…" Richie said, then breaking into a smile he added "…and unclog your arteries."

He stabbed the thick needle into a vein in Hectors neck as if it were a knife, depressing the plunger with his thumb and emptying the syringe into Hector's bloodstream. He left the syringe in place. Richie quickly spun around and repeated the action on Spook. The burning pain and nausea they felt as the acid-toxin coursed through their veins to their hearts, brains and remaining limbs, finally drove them completely insane as they died.

Richie didn't dispose of the bodies; he was ordered to leave them to be discovered as obvious victims of the brutal torture and murder. Though the killings were prompted by the attack on Big Sal Parisi's nephew, the organization wanted to take the opportunity to send a message to other freelance dealers in the area. The infamy of the Bellos ensured that there would be minimal backlash from the police and community leaders; no one would miss them.

Erasing the Bello brothers with no loose-ends for the family to worry about and exhibiting a talent for cruelty towards the two offenders, earned Richie the final notch he needed for full membership. Once he had the full rights of a made guy however, he became even more aggressive and ambitious, eventually landing him in hot water with other members due to his unwillingness to recognize boundaries and existing relationships of other crews. Richie was forty two years old, and had been the cause of a few 'sit-downs' despite having been a full member for only four years.

# Chapter 13
# *Italia!*

The four of us had dinner at Italia!, a joint near Fordham Road that had a decent southern Italian menu. The place was packed and on the way out we stopped at the bar to say hello to Ruairi Oh'Alin, his father Pete was a long time friend and owned the Shore Inn, a bar in the Bronx neighborhood where I grew up. Over the din of a full dining room, the television over the bar set to blast level, and these two annoying fucking guys to our left arguing about the Knicks, who's big mouth do I hear but Richie Scala's. Talk about coincidences. He's yapping at the hostess, I've never seen Richie actually talk with anyone, and he's all smiley. He looked like a fucking game-show-host with that fake 'please fuck me' smile, black blazer with a loud print polyester shirt opened three buttons to show a bale of chest hair. It was accessorized of course by the obligatory gold chain around his tree trunk neck. And people in our line of work wonder why we're stereotyped.

We get up, throw some cash on the bar and head out. I make sure to slow down as we approach him, why not give him time to get both gerbils on that little wheel in his head so he can come up with some brilliant remark.

"Well, look who it is, Mr. Ed." He sneers.

"Mr. Ed? Has your mother been bragging to you about the size of my cock again?" I ask in a friendly tone.

"That's funny. You always were a funny cocksucker."

"Ron Jeremy called; he wants his shirt back." I say deadpan.

Philly, Vin and Tony crack up. Annoyance is starting to show in Richie's face. Six seconds. He's a real tough nut to crack.

"Out for a night on the town huh… what are you and your girls doing in this joint Eddie, the gay bar is down the block."

"Yeah we were just there..." I cut him off "Hey I saw they named a drink after you!"

His face darkens and his eyes fix on mine now, steady as a cat's gaze locked onto its prey "You know, I think all that cazzo you're sucking must be affecting your brain."

"That a fact?" I ask, baiting him.

"I dunno'... I mean it's just what everyone's saying Eddie, don't take it out on me." he says, smiling at the hostess.

"Yeah, well you heard wrong." I say, pretending to be pissed off for a moment.

Then I turn my back to him as if to walk away pissed and in defeat, but instead I stop and look at him over my shoulder.

"Remember Richie, when you're having sex you're facing away from your boyfriend and it's harder to hear what he's saying over the sound of his balls smacking against your ass." The three amigos behind me lose it,

I'm watching his hand, if he goes for his piece he'll never make it.

"Take a fuckin' walk already." all pretense of humor gone from his voice; he had that 'give me one more reason cocksucker' look plastered on his face and no doubt irritated that it didn't work on me.

After a few seconds of staring, I say under my breath as I pass him towards the door "I'm telling you Richie..."

He grabs me by my upper arm and he's putting some muscle into it "Yeah? You're telling me? Telling me what smart guy?" and now that I'm this close to him, the sickening smell of his cologne prompts me to stop breathing.

"I don't give a shit if she has to go back to that homeless shelter; I want your mother out of my house tonight!"

He winds up to plant one on me, but Philly grabs his arm in mock-peacemaker fashion and starts in with "Come on guys, take it easy. Take it easy..."

Vin, Tony D. and I walk out. Philly follows us a few seconds later while Richie, red-faced, just stares a hole in my back.

When we're in the car Vin says "I think Richie's mellowing."

We all laugh at that.

"You'd better watch your back now Eddie…" Vin continues as he starts the car "…that strunz forgets nothing." his hands more in the air than on the wheel "Still… right in front of that girl he's chasing, that's classic."

"You think he knows we know?" Tony D. asks.

"Hey, either way he knows that it's only a matter of time before he's discovered. I don't give a shit if he knows or not. Sooner or later that bastard's gonna catch that needle dick of his in his own zipper."

"The only people crying on that day will be the ones who didn't get a chance to do the job on him." Vin says.

"You gotta wonder if it would be easier to put one in his ear and just be done with it." Tony D. says.

I took a deep breath and tried to purge the remainder of Richie's cologne from my lungs "Won't work. There's a way to do it, but it's a hell of a lot more complicated than that. Fuhgetaboutit, let's go."

# Chapter 14
# *Source Code*

*Campbell, California*

Scott slews his Lotus Esprit into the parking lot at terrifying speed, deftly maneuvering his way around stray shopping carts and streaking like a cruise missile toward The Coffee Terrorists, his regular morning stop on the way into work. As the car screeches to a halt, he smiles as he feels the deceleration pull him toward the windshield, the seat belt biting into him. Most enthusiasts pay attention to a car's acceleration, neglecting stopping distance, but to Scott that made no sense.

He steps into the shop and nods hello to Andy, the owner, who always works mornings.

"The usual?" Andy asks.

Scott nods and Andy turns to the new barista in training at the espresso machine, a kid of nineteen who had about as many piercings.

"Hey Martin, give me a grande Osama Bin Latte". The new guy grins and shakes his head. It's obvious that he's new since the regular staff has long ago gotten over Andy's bizarre sense of humor in evidence on the menu.

"Hey Andy, I was doing some work in here on Friday and the connection was slower that shit… and I got disconnected a couple times." Scott said.

"Yeah, Saturday the router died, I had to go get a new one. Everything's working again."

"Cool. Want me to take a look at it?"

"Nah, it's working fine now. Thanks though."

"No prob."

Since most of the coffee shops in California were 'hot spots' providing wireless access to the internet, many people worked from a coffee shop for part of their day. Scott's position in the company made him a central contact point for several departments, and as such the opportunity to work remotely, from the coffee shop or from home, was limited. Even so he made a concerted effort to work remotely on Fridays.

Back in his car and feeling fully awake now with the promise of caffeine, he merges into the Silicon Valley commuter traffic on 17/880, drinking his coffee and listening to NPR. His mind shifting to work-mode, he begins to prioritize his time for the coming workday at ExchangeVault, the high-tech start-up that consumes his days and most of his nights. His days are bounded by meetings; each morning starts with an engineering status meeting with the molecule and microscope guys, where the progress of the development team is covered in merciless detail. Each evening is concluded with a new product release meeting where news is presented, both good and bad, that determines the ExchangeVault's 'Go Live' date.

Scott always found some amusement in the way people under pressure acted in meetings, based upon the degree of their acquaintance. If you knew someone well and had socialized with them outside of work, then in a meeting you would get the truth with a minimum of bullshit. Even some of the executives, who were perpetually covering their asses on some level, would be much more direct if they knew you.

If on the other hand, your relationship with someone was based solely on the time you spent with them in the office, then it was more likely you would get the usual posturing and justification. Scott often thought that technology companies ought to make every new group of employees go through an orientation consisting of an air-drop somewhere in the Sierra-Nevada Mountains a hundred miles from anywhere, with nothing but a knife, a compass and a map. Do it survival style! That would get everyone up-close and personal, and weed out the NO-OPs pretty quickly. A 'NO-OP' was technology slang derived from the programming instruction for a microprocessor chip to do 'No-Operation', essentially to waste time.

Scott's Bluetooth earpiece began to chirp frantically; he groaned and answered it.

"It's a great day at South Valley Tire and Muffler! This is Heather, how may I direct your call?"

"Hey Scottie." He recognized the voice, and glancing at the clock, the time, as belonging to Doug, the manager of the debug team.

"Mornin' Doug. Wasabi?"

"Did we get an answer from the contractor?" Doug asked; 'the contractor' was Seventeen O Three Associates, a consulting firm in New York who was providing some critical computer programming modules that would be incorporated into ExchangeVault's product. Since Seventeen O Three used parts of these modules in other products for other clients, they provide their customers with 'compiled' program modules only.

Computer programs are written in a variety of languages, and while these may be somewhat incomprehensible to an untrained eye, they are every bit as readable to a programmer who knows that language, as is their native speaking language. These 'high level' languages can perform complex operations with just a few commands, just as a few words of spoken language can convey complex meaning. However, from the simple to the complex, against all of the immense sophistication of computer programming and software architecture, it's ironic that the actual 'processing' on the computer chip itself, is simple arithmetic. The language that the processor chip understands, sometimes referred to as machine language is actually a simple and low level set of instructions that tell the processor chip what to add or subtract and where to store the result.

Consequently, a high level programming language must be translated into lower-level machine language in order for the processor chip to do the 'computing'. This translation from the high level language that human programmers deal with, into the low level one that actually operates the processor chip is called compiling.

If the high level program is viewed side-by-side with its compiled version, in a practical sense there will be no resemblance between them, and the difference is startling when you consider that they are different expressions of the very same program and perform the very same functions. The compiled program looks utterly alien; a seemingly indecipherable block of letters and numbers that represent the millions of simple instructions the computer processor chip must perform to carry out the human programmer's intentions. It's a little bit like looking a long printed list of the brush stokes, widths and colors required to replicate the Mona Lisa, having never seen the painting. Even experts in machine language have very limited ability to interpret how a compiled program as a whole is designed to do what it does, and companies like Seventeen O Three Associates, as a security measure, provide their programs in compiled versions only. Programs can be decompiled, however the effort involved to do it, and the risk of legal difficulties over intellectual property rights, tend to make this an option rarely chosen.

What Doug wanted from Seventeen O Three, was not just the compiled computer code, but the high level language program that was behind it, the source code.

"They said no." Scott said.

"Come on Scott, that's bogus! Ride their asses like Zorro, they'll cave…" Doug pleaded.

"Zorro?.. Where do you get this stuff?" Scott chuckled "Dude, you knew the deal when you agreed to the architecture. They provide the module and you integrate it. If there's a problem they'll fix whatever the problem is with their piece." Scott reminded him.

"Yeah, well I could shed some code on my side if I had access to their stuff."

Doug could ostensibly dove-tail some of his programming into some of that already written by the contractor, in order to save precious computer memory space that stored the program.

"Yeah, and when it doesn't work, their guys have to spend a week in debug just to find out how you fucked it up. That's one of the reasons they won't agree to giving us their source code, they don't want to have to fix the bugs introduced by caffeine crazed psychopaths like you."

"Caffeine crazed?" Doug challenged "I'll bet your hand is resting on one of those terrorist drinks you get every morning…friggin Soy-Milk Hussain or whatever they call it."

Scott smiled as he glanced down to his cup holder "Yeah, let me bring you up to date. I'm not the one who should be at

Twinkies-and-Mountain-Dew Anonymous." he teased "How's that going by the way? Been to a meeting lately?"

"That's original."

"Anyway, they said no dice, so let's move on."

"How do we know that there isn't a security breach in their code?"

"They're reputable; they've done work for major companies." Scott had gone over this with Doug before.

Silence. Scott could almost hear the bits flying around in Doug's brain.

"I guess there's nothing we can do at this point in the development schedule if there was an exposure, not if we're going to launch on time." the resignation just creeping into Doug's voice.

"Yeah, that's a good point." Why not be magnanimous in victory? Scott thought.

"Well… to be continued. I'll see you at the meeting."

"Later." He hung up and decided to take the Bluetooth out of his ear for the few minutes remaining in his commute.

# Chapter 15
# *ValleyWorld*

*San Jose, California*

Situated in an industrial park and surrounded by neatly manicured hedges, grass and assorted flora, ExchangeVault's architectural motif was decidedly 'industrial undistinguished'. Startup companies by the score inhabited industrial complexes like these throughout the valley. A glass and metal front lobby whose center-piece was an arc shaped reception desk, a three bay loading dock in the rear, wide open areas inside for cubicles, plenty of cable-drops with power and computer connection ports, and of course easy access to a local highway. The architecture and facilities were born out of the particular set of needs presented by small business. Employees parked in the lot at the rear of the building, and the best parking spot, the one closest to the door, was a prize given to some deserving member of the company for contribution above and beyond the norm. Lately, that coveted spot was painted with a bright image of Bart Simpson's face, and painted under his mischievous visage "Reserved for Scott Monson".

A few minutes after eight o'clock, Scott parked his car on Bart's face and worked at retrieving his overstuffed and worn black nylon computer bag containing his laptop and a thick sheaf of papers. He grabbed his cell-phone-slash-organizer-slash-leash, and a very thick and worn three ring binder, all without sharing his coffee with the ground or his shirt. ExchangeVault's security lock on the door consisted of a badge reader that unlocked the door when it sensed an authorized credit-card sized badge within a few inches of a small plastic panel beside the door. Scott, with his hands full, mumbled something about 'rectum recognition software' as he turned and waved his ass at the panel, which detected the security badge in the wallet in his back pocket. He heard the ‘click’ of the door being unlocked and struggled to open the large metal door with the pinkie of the hand holding his coffee. Unexpectedly, a hand appeared from behind and grabbed the door handle from him, it was accompanied by a woman’s playful voice “Excuse me, do you have a match?” He tuned to see the CEO’s secretary, Diane West smiling at his predicament.

“If I reach for a match, I’m going to have to reveal my awesome, but as of yet secret, juggling skills.” Scott said earnestly “Is that your game Diane? Stalking me everywhere I go, until the perfect opportunity presents itself, forcing me to expose to the world what some would surely call ‘the most impressive juggling talent in modern times’?”

“Well.” She paused. “When you put it like that you make it sound so… negative.”

Scott chuckled “And how does the day find us Diane?” as he moves through the door, Diane trailing behind.

“Fine. Just fine. And you sir?”

“Oh I have a feeling Diane, today could be the day.” Scott said with inspiration.

“And what day might that be?”

“You know, the day. The big one. The day we come up with something that’ll change the face of the planet.” he said in a grandiose tone as they snaked their way through the maze of cubicles.

“Ooohhh, that day. Of course. Where was my head?” she said, sarcasm dripping from her voice.

“Think nothing of it, we all make mistakes.” he said magnanimously, then drawing himself erect, he thrust out his chin and peered down his nose at her “We shall not speak of this again.”

“May I ask a question Dr. Einstein, or is it Dr. P. T. Barnum?”

“I’ll allow it.” he said, arching one eyebrow and thrusting his chin out farther still.

“What do you plan to do today if it doesn’t turn out to be the day, ya know, hypothetically speaking?”

Arriving at his desk, he began to unburden himself “Well, I’m glad you asked that, because I have a contingency plan.”

“And that would be?”

"It's a biggie." he narrowed his eyes and scanned the room as though looking for a spy and then whispered in a conspiratorial tone "Are you sure you want to be saddled with the knowledge of such a plan? I mean, not everyone wanted the responsibility of knowing the plans for D-Day."

She waited for her answer, hands on her hips, statue-like.

"OK then, here it is. In the unlikely event that the big breakthrough doesn't happen today" he leaned his head closer to hers and reiterated "and between you and me, I think we're due, but, if it doesn't happen I plan to get a little further in my quest to make the product we've already invented, invested money into and advertised… actually work!" He leaned back, eyes wide, with a look on his face as if he'd just discovered electricity.

Diane laughed "That's a bold plan." she said "Are you sure you're not biting off more than you can chew?"

"Too late." he threw his arms up "We burned the ships we came in andthere's no turning back! We've sold the sucker, and now it has to work!" Scott said "But that's just a contingency plan. Just parlor talk. I think the big one's coming today."

He started up his laptop, sat down at his desk and said with his back to her as she was walking away "Oh Diane?"

"Yes?"

"Not a word."

"I hear ya."

"I mean it, this was on the down-low. I read about this tomorrow in the New York Times, CNN calls me for a quote, Bill Gates' email makes it past my spam filter, whatever… I'll deny it. Are we clear?"

"We're clear." She said

In his best Jack Nicholson slash Col. Nathan R. Jessep he repeated with more intensity "I said, are we clear?"

Diane in a respectable Tom Cruise slash Lt. Daniel Kaffee fashion "Crystal."

Diane turned away laughing, heading toward her desk. Scott loved her laugh; it was kind of a high fluttering sound, very feminine. In truth, Scott had yet to discover anything about Diane West that he even had a second thought about. She was certainly attractive, five feet six inches tall, with brown hair and eyes and an athletic build. As pleasing as she was to the eye though, it was her personality that he found most attractive. The woman had style and a sense of humor, but also an intelligent and serious mind. She was resourceful, kind and easy to talk to. But the very first thing that sparked his interest was her ability to remain calm and courteous under pressure.

Scott remembered when Diane was hired at ExchangeVault. On her first day of work, Barry Peale, the sales VP (who was known inside the company as 'BTB', which stood for "Barry The Bastard"), got up into her grill about a laundry list of things that BTB knew she couldn't possibly have a handle on in her first four hours at her desk. It was an obvious and petty attempt at psychological manipulation aimed at putting her under his thumb. Diane didn't get the least bit flustered, not a single drop of perspiration was in evidence on her beautiful face. Poised, she simply let BTB talk himself out, and when he turned to storm-off having failed to shake her, she held up a dish of Jolly Ranchers and offered him one. It was classic. He's red-faced because he can't get a rise out of the new person who controls the CEO's calendar, and she's standing there, calm and cool, holding a friggin candy dish as if he were a two year old being placated. Just classic. The woman was no frail flower; she knew what she was about and what her position was about. Of course, she smelled nice too and wasn't bad to look at either.

ExchangeVault had not yet officially come 'online' yet, although the product schedule that the marketing thugs were imposing on everyone who would listen, would have you believe that the 'product launch' date was imminent. In fact, the product schedule was the universal focal point of derision within the company.

The software engineers and programmers had to create the product from scratch and take responsibility for a lot of unknowns. They knew this, and they knew that the other departments knew this, so the programmers tended to be a group not easily pressured from the outside, and not easily impressed. If a software guy was working 80 hours a week and you started to see things on his desk like a toothbrush, shaving cream and dirty laundry, it might in fact be related to a schedule deadline. However, it was just as likely that he had run into an interesting approach to a problem that had possessed him to a degree that can only be seen in the 'Director's Cut' version of The Exorcist, complete with rotating head.

The sales crew, generally commanding zero respect from anyone technical, had to share the schedule with the prospective customers they were trying to engage, even though they had no product yet. They saw the schedule as a well-coordinated fiction they had to create to get the customers to see the value they were going to offer when the product did launch.

Experienced sales people know that prospective customers are going to talk to each other, and compare the schedule information they've told each of them, to see if it's consistent. Hence, successful sales people developed good working relationships with key technical people inside their own companies, so they could limit the bullshit they were charged with slinging, at least to a degree that would prevent losing the account when there was an outbreak of reality. The technical people didn't deal as much in propaganda as marketing and the executive teams did; in fact they were usually pessimistic and feisty. Ultimately, the sales folks knew that no matter what assurances they received from the marketing or technical people, they'd have to apologize for not being able to provide something they were told to promise. Delivery date, features of the software, pricing, supply, there was always something. If that something caused enough turmoil that they didn't get the business, the marketing folks still got paid, as did the technical people, the administrative folks, even the janitor got paid. The sales folks, for the most part, didn't. Thus, they were for 'whatever works', pragmatists by necessity if not always by nature.

Even though the marketing crew at ExchangeVault were the creators of the schedule, that didn't mean that they actually believed it to be a reflection of reality. When you started from a blank canvas you had to make some assumptions. You also had to have a compelling product, that is, there have to be reasons for people to choose your product over existing competition, and you can often do that by taking some risks and by innovating to some degree.

The marketing people were alone in their responsibility for the bottom line, the "P&L" as it is referred to, the Profit and Loss of the product. Some tough choices have to be made if you're responsible for P&L, and the spectator's view from engineering or sales, is sometimes narrow since they're not charged with making the whole enchilada actually generate profit.

The schedule, beyond serving as fertile ground for humor and bitching, was a focal point for all parts of ExchangeVault to coordinate and communicate. It was ethereal in the beginning and almost believable near 'launch' time, and its metamorphosis from the abstract to the concrete was indeed a metaphor for the organization itself.

The marketing people had to shape it. The technical people had to make it.The sales people had to sell it. It was an intricate dance that required a beat to coordinate everyone's movements.

Connected.

# Chapter 16
# *Vigilance*

"It's a stupid fucking way to do it, that's why!"

"We go through this every time. You mock what you don't understand."

"I mock stupid ways of doing things, and yeah we do go through this every time. And we've made changes."

"True but we've kept a lot more than we've changed."

The antagonist was Vincent Ko, a sleep deprived rebellious programmer of Korean descent. Vincent was notoriously disdainful of large or bloated software design; he liked his computer code the way he liked his sugar engorged Frosted Cherry Pop-Tarts, in small manageable bites. Despite his confrontational style, he was genuinely liked for his honesty and respected for his talents. Today's recipient of Vincent's subtleties was Carlos Vega, 'Chuck' to his friends. He was an alumnus of U. C. Davis where he graduated with honors in computer science three years ago. Chuck's stocky six foot tall frame could not be more different from Vincent's five foot seven wire-thin physique.

"Why don't we have more Asian programmers? We need to get some Asians in here…" Vincent said, his normally slight Asian accent becoming suspiciously thick all of a sudden as he spread his arms expansively "you Mexican's write your code too big. It's all that cheese and beans you eat." he said trying to keep a straight face while popping open a Mountain Dew.

"Hey, you know what you have without Mexicans in this state? A parking lot. We are this state, so go back to China." Chuck said, the veiled and futile jibe being that all Asians looked alike since Vincent was of Korean descent, but he knew Vincent wouldn't bite.

"A billion people and only three Taco Bells, you wouldn't like it there Chuck." said the Los Angeles born and raised Vincent "Combining these segments just makes the job of debug that much harder. In the future we're gonna be building on this stuff and completely replacing some pieces of it. You gotta keep it organized." Vincent said.

It was a hard perspective for an experienced programmer to argue with, but Chuck had a bone to pick as well.

"Look, if your idea is taken to the extreme then every friggin' line of code could be kept separately. There is such a thing as having too many modules too ya know. Having too many separate ones makes it unwieldy too. I'm all in favor of keeping it simple, but there's a limit to that methodology." Chuck countered.

Computer applications as sophisticated as the ones that ExchangeVault was creating are massive and complex, and it was inevitable that errors and problems would crop up. Programmers use a variety of tools and expend great amounts of effort to structure a program so that, in most cases, errors are found relatively quickly. Modifications and upgrades to an application is also easier with well organized programming.

The essence of the dispute between Chuck and Vincent was really about vigilance. In this case, Chuck wanted to add a small piece of programming to the tail end of a much larger one, instead of keeping it separate. While this would reduce the number separate pieces, it could make tracking down an error in either piece difficult. Reducing the number of separate subroutines was an easy temptation to surrender to, but Vincent had more experience than Chuck and it made him vigilant in his guard against things that would make finding errors harder.

"Yeah yeah" Vincent nodded impatiently "but in this case Chuck, the pieces you want to combine do different things. When there's a problem later, the symptom's not going to point clearly to the section of the code that's the problem because you've combined them."

"The reason I combined them in the first place is that they're the only two branch points to 'check_metadata_for_zeros'. So ya know…"

Vincent just stared at him for a few seconds, as did the rest of the people around the table.

Finally Vincent said "So I know…what?"

Chuck saw the bullet coming in slow motion, but he wasn't Neo and this wasn't The Matrix, and he wasn't going to be able to dodge it "So ya know…it's six of one, half a dozen of the other." he said nonchalantly, doing his best to avoid eye contact.

"Six of one, half a…" he looked around the room as if searching for Chuck's point "What the fuck is THAT?...half a dozen of the… What the fuck IS that!" Vincent said in an exasperated tone that was all the more comical for the condemnation that sprang from each word.

Everyone in the room cracked up, it was pretty funny watching someone get nailed if the 'someone' wasn't you.

"Yeah yeah yeah… alright already." Chuck said, keeping his eyes fixed on the open notebook in front of him, a smirk forming at the corners of his mouth; Vincent had won on merit.

"Say my name." Vincent said straight-faced.

Somebody near the door spit out a half mouthful of Red Bull, caught off-guard by Vincent's impromptu sexual zinger, which was not part of his usual repertoire.

"Asshole?" Chuck answered quizzically, which triggered an even more riotous outbreak of laughter.

With that, the meeting came to a close, and as they filed out of the conference room, Chuck turned to Vincent "Sushi?"

"Yeah, give me ten minutes though."

# Chapter 17
# *Death at the Opera*

*Mid-town Manhattan, New York City*

It felt as though her heel was coming loose, so she lifted her leg, as much as a woman can in a tight dress, and craned her neck to scrutinize the simple black pump. Behind her, a pair of eyes locked onto her shapely figure as the fabric of her dress pulled at her hips. Apparently satisfied that her high heel would hold up for the night, she stood up scanned the sparse group of faces milling about in front of Lincoln Center. She strolled over to the fountain and gazed at the streaming water. Her erect posture, long neck and high cheek bones gave her an aristocratic air. She had a gentle and natural beauty, from her blonde hair arranged in a French braid, to the tips of her elegant shoes.

The eyes that had locked onto this prize belonged to a man whose predatory mindset, manipulative skills and handsome features had enabled him to victimize some of the women he met; coworkers, dates, and in one case, a neighbor. His cunning had so far allowed him to escape retaliation, and this had been accomplished most frequently by psychological manipulation of his victim, creating enough emotional confusion to cloud their certainty about what 'signals' they'd communicated to him. On occasion he'd used a drug to assist him in his conquest.

Lately he'd been entertaining the idea of a more forceful and straightforward approach, and the prospect excited him. As he approached her, he'd decided to strike up a conversation and see where that led and to sense vulnerabilities that he might exploit. He waited until she had wandered toward the less populated area on east side of the fountain and then more out of habit than conscious decision, approached her from behind.

“It’s beautiful, isn’t it?” He said, his hands in his pockets, gesturing toward the fountain with a tilt of his head.

"Yes, it is." Like any typical New Yorker, her reaction to someone who she didn't know walking up and talking to her on the street was to acknowledge the person and discourage further conversation. It was an unconscious defense mechanism for an unescorted woman living in a large city.

After a few seconds he continued "You're date is late I take it."

"He should be here any minute." smiling politely as she ambled away from him slowly, so as not to seem as though she was moving anywhere in particular.

He was happy to notice that even though she was not responsive, at least she was moving slowly toward the least populated section of the large open plaza.

"I guess my date is late as well." he said "Your name isn't Janice by any chance, is it?" displaying a smile that was both charming and disarming.

"No it isn't. Sorry."

"So am I." he chucked politely, and affected a convincing embarrassed expression "I'm sorry, I just mean you know how these things can turn out sometimes."

She gave a polite smile and continued looking at the fountain. It was obvious to her that he was trying to meet her, but her heart had belonged to another man for almost as long as she could remember. She'd met him when they were in their teens, and their relationship had always been… unusual and decidedly wonderful. Her love for him had not paled over the years, and she was certain that he felt the same.

The man appraised her face, which showed not a trace of makeup and had a natural glow and a simple beauty. The urgency he felt in his desire to entrap and dominate this woman was growing by the minute, and the less cooperative she seemed the more gratifying would be the conquest. For him, sex was the means to an end.

Subconsciously, whenever he gained a woman's submission, it scratched an itch, the cause of which lay outside of his conscious awareness. That itch was his feeling of inadequacy and helplessness when it came to women, an association implanted in him by his domineering mother during his formative years of life. His sexual predatory drives stemmed from his unresolved feelings of inadequacy and he was driven to dominate women in order to prove he was not a victim. He had no idea why he was driven to do the things he'd done; he only knew that he felt the compulsion and that he felt pleasure when he satisfied it. He had had other values instilled in him during his life, some in direct conflict with the drives he felt to dominate and this other benevolent morality was in constant tension with the predatory one. The one that was most supported by circumstance or most present in his mind in any given situation is the one that dictated his behavior; and this particular evening, his single-minded focus on the lovely woman before him completely nullified his better nature.

He moved closer to her and felt a growing tightness in his groin, and that spurred him to abandon any subtle approach and persuade her to come with him to his car at the point of the knife concealed in the inside pocket of his Armani blazer. He reasoned that the longer he delayed in making his move, the better the chance of her date showing up. He turned his back on the woman, drew the knife from his pocket and concealed inside of the right hand sleeve of his blazer.

The opera crowd had largely entered the building to their north, however there were still a few people scattered about the huge open plaza. He'd need to do something to prevent her from calling for help. One last glimpse toward the building and his decision was made.

He moved so that it would appear as though he was walking away from the fountain area, in a direction that would take him behind the woman perhaps twenty feet from her at it's closest approach; so as not to give her a reason to turn with him. When he was beyond her peripheral vision, he angled left and walked directly toward her. He placed his right arm around her waist, with the knife in his hand and his hand pulled into his sleeve effectively hiding the weapon. He pressed the tip of the knife into her ribs with enough force to cause her intense and shocking pain. Her instinctive reaction was to try to pull away, even before crying out, but he had a firm hold on her, sandwiched as she was between his body and the right arm around her holding the knife. He brought his mouth so that his lips were brushing her ear as he spoke. If someone was watching, they would simply look like two lovers standing together, exchanging amorous whispers.

“Don’t scream.” he said, pushing the knife tip harder. The pain she felt was surprising in its intensity, and his grip felt like a vice around her.

“You’re going to walk with me. If you scream or try to pull away, I’ll drive this through your lung, and then I’ll carve your fuckin’ face up in case you live.” his voice sounding evil and powerful in her ear.

He started to lead her slowly westward but she was stumbling a little under the pain in her side and the fear she tasted in her mouth. His thoughts were already forming about the nights activities, the binding of this gorgeous specimen, then several ‘sessions’ with brief periods of recuperation in between. Some photography, some other humiliations he would inflict upon her, all the while enjoying intense arousal. Then…an exit strategy. As usual he’d come up with effective intimidation, perhaps coupled with some debilitating psychology in an attempt to thwart commitment on her part to go to the police. Of course he assumed she would probably go to the police, and so he had a hood and bindings in his trunk. She would know his face of course, but she'd have no idea where to find him and neither would the police.

As they began slowly moving away from the fountain, there was not a single sign that anyone had seen the abduction, then from the man’s left side he heard a voice surprisingly close.

“Did you drop this?”

Turning to see who the voice belonged to was instinctive, as the speaker knew it would be. In a split second, a terrible stabbing pain became a horrific crushing one, as Eddie drove the first three fingers of his right hand savagely into the throat of the man abducting his girlfriend. The strike was delivered with lightning speed and almost no observable physical motion. The pain from the blow was so great and so unexpected, and the throat such a reflexively protected area, that the assailant immediately let go of the knife and reached for his throat and the crushed trachea within it.

The strike caused severe trauma and the tissues inside the throat started swelling immediately. It was clear from the barely audible croaking sounds, that in a moment no air at all would be able to make its way into his lungs. Instead of reaching for his girlfriend, Eddie grabbed the man under his arms, as if to help him to sit down, and guided him the few steps back to the fountain. The man was so shocked he didn't resist, and sat on the edge of the fountain still grasping at his throat and not able to utter a sound. Half a minute later his face was already turning a bright red. He tried to stand, perhaps to run to the door of the opera house, but Eddie simply held him in his place with a hand on his shoulder as he struggled for a breath. After a short while had passed, Eddie took a quick and look all around, and satisfied that no one was watching, gave him a shove backward into the fountain. He didn't struggle much in the water as his strength was nearly gone; he was fixated on his inability to draw a single breath, still manically grasping at his throat.

Still not having said a word, and as the predator went through his death throes in the water, Eddie casually put his hand around her waist and walked her calmly toward the main entrance of Lincoln Center, blending into the opera crowd. He could feel her shaking, her body felt hot with panic. He paused a dozen yards from the doors, turned and looked for a full twenty seconds pretending to search his pockets for the tickets. He scanned for any indication that they'd been seen, and finding none he presented their tickets and guided her into the theater.

# Chapter 18
# Office Visit

*The Bronx, New York City*

Inside what passed for an office for the brothel Hi-Class, Giovanni sat across from a dangerous man who could charitably be called his 'sponsor'. In a practical sense, he was still alive and his former boss dead, because this man decided that it made business sense. In the first place, he'd not warned Mike because he'd been ordered not to, having no doubt about how brutal his 'sponsor' was inclined to be if he disobeyed. In the second place… fuck him…it was Mike's tough luck, not his. If he could put some more coin in his pocket because Mike was too stupid to see what this man had intended for him from the start… well it wasn't his problem, he had to make a living.

Gio handed a thick white envelope over to Richie, who dipped thumbs and forefingers in to do a quick count of the hundred dollar bills inside. When he was satisfied with the count, he sealed the envelope and slipped it into a breast pocket inside his blazer and looked up with a neutral expression. To someone doing business with Richie Scala, a neutral expression was the same as a happy one; in fact, any expression other than 'pissed off' was something to be happy about.

"Same time next week." Richie said monotone; it wasn't a question.

"OK."

"Remember, keep your mouth shut…" Richie said "…and make yourself scarce but keep this place under control."

As if those two instructions did not conflict, Gio thought. He couldn't keep an eye on things here if he wasn't here. Well, he told himself he didn't have much choice, so he'd cope.

"The guy, Eddie, left word for me, he said not to make him come looking." Gio said "Should I go see him, just to take some heat off? Throw some bullshit at him?"

"What did I just say?" said Richie, his irritation spontaneous.

"I heard you. I was just thinking that if he comes here…"

"Just do what I tell you. Don't think." Richie interrupted "That guy looking for you, he's my problem not yours. Where's that sexy little fuckin' broad who was in here last time?"

"Honey? She's here. Want me to get her?" Gio asked, happy at the prospect of somebody, anybody else occupying Richie's attention other than himself.

Richie didn't respond right away, he sat and looked at Gio with a neutral expression, then finally said "No, that's OK. I got nothing better to do with my time than keep tabs on whores." As Gio got up and made his way around the desk to retrieve the girl, Richie continued "It's a hobby. I just like to follow them around, ya know, cause I have so much fucking free time on my hands." he said, ending in a heavy sarcastic growl.

Honey walked into the office dressed in a cotton powder blue bra and bikini panty set, her long thin legs seeming all the more so for the high heels she wore. She stood in front of Richie, cocking one spindly leg against the other, and biting her lower lip in her usual seductive pose. Richie stood and reached out to her, taking her hand in his as she got on her knees. She looked up and into his eyes, with her best innocent but naughty, "I'm a bad girl" expression as she went to unzip his fly. His big muscular right hand covered hers, the skin of his hand felt calloused. He was squeezing her hand, looking down at her, when she noticed her hand starting to ache. The pressure from his grasp kept increasing but she was accustomed to men inflicting pain on her. She looked up and showed him a pained expression, but did not cry out. Just when the pain had reached her limit of self-control, he spoke.

"A guy came here after Mike Zirella died. What did he want?"

The pressure on her hand increased for just an instant, his grip was like a pair of pliers squeezing her fingers; he was letting her know that he could crush her hand if she didn't tell him what he wanted to know.

"He wanted to know if we knew anything about Mike." She said, her voice cracking from the pain that she didn't allow her face to show.

"Who spoke to him?"

She spoke quickly, revealing the pain she felt, but not fear that accompanied it "We all did. None of us knew anything. Mike didn't tell us about his business, we told him that. He believed us."

"What else? Anyone mention any names?" His expression was constant, his voice calm and measured; he sounded more like someone ordering breakfast than someone wanting information.. To Honey, he was a machine; merciless and powerful. Emotionless.

"Someone told him to talk to Gio. It wasn't me, but that's all." Tears were starting down her face.

"Gio? That's all? That's not what I heard." he said, then with his free hand he slapped her across the face "Don't lie to me you little bitch. If you lie to me I'll cut your fuckin' tits off."

His voice was so menacing that she had no doubt he was telling the truth. She couldn't comply of course, she knew that if she told him that she'd described him, he'd lose it and she'd be dead. She'd even told them his name! No. She would have to trust her instincts and say as little as possible.

"I swear. That's all that happened, he seemed like he was in a hurry. He wasn't even here but a few minutes." she pleaded, grabbing her wrist just under her tortured hand.

He looked down at her, still expressionless, for a bit, then released her hand. She drew it, beet red and swollen, into her chest and cradled it, as a wave of relief swept over her. Though she could not remember where, she'd once heard someone quip 'The good thing about getting pounded on the head with a hammer is that when it stops, it feels soooo good.'

"Now do your fuckin' job." Richie commanded.

Having been on the receiving end of his displeasure a moment before, she didn't hesitate. She might not be able to get herself into her 'girl next door' role in spirit, but it didn't seem to matter to 'the machine' in any case. By her own perception she gave a mechanical performance, and as she'd expected, he didn't show any sign of noticing.

After he had gone, she stood at a sink in the bathroom running cold water over her still-reddened hand. As the swelling began to subside, she stared absently at her reflection in the dimly lit washroom and felt foolish about volunteering the information that day. If I'd stayed silent…why didn't I just keep my mouth shut! What am I going to do now?" She felt as though a large weight was sitting squarely on her chest, as she got cleaned up and erased any trace of tears from her face. Honey had been at this long enough to know that being an attractive 'object' of desire centered around just that… being an 'object'. Genuine emotional intimacy and reality didn't have a place in the business of prostitution. That's what relationships were for.

Connected.

# Chapter 19
# *Antonia*

The Upper West Side of Manhattan, New York City

"I was so…I had no time to think! He seemed so… so 'normal'."

A few delicate tears rested on Antonia Stellini's high cheekbones; she was understandably upset, in a state of mild shock in fact, but not to the point of hysteria. Considering her origins she was decidedly cultured, but appearances to the contrary, she was not fragile. She had an inner strength, a resolve that saw her through some tough times growing up in the Bronx. In point of fact, it was that strength that allowed her to retain her gentle nature despite the turmoil and diversity that were part of the environment. Eddie Ferrara had spotted this quality in her from the beginning; it was her gentility and kindness, her altruistic nature that attracted him most. In 'the life' you came across altruism about as often as you came across honesty, it just wasn't part of the culture.

She had been fourteen and he fifteen when they first met, hanging with the same crowd of friends. Although they were attracted to each other at first sight, teen protocol being what it was, feigning disinterest was always the first move if you really liked someone. Their relationship didn't bloom until three years later when they began to take frequent walks along the waterfront. Talking about nothing and everything, they'd each come to appreciate the simple pleasure of listening to the sound of the other's voice, the intimacy of really understanding the private thoughts of a potential lover. On a mild August night they made love for the first time in a field of tall grass near the Whitestone Bridge. The surroundings could be charitably described as 'not exactly picturesque', but to the two of them, the experience was as ethereal as it was intense.

"He's dead." she looked at him through bloodshot eyes, not really wanting to comprehend, trying desperately to erase the ordeal of just an hour ago from her mind.

Eddie had insisted that they stay at the opera for half an hour, both oblivious to Puccini's La Bohème. Afterward at a nearby restaurant they sat in silence for the most part, trying to return to some feeling of normalcy.

"You've always trusted me." Eddie said in a steady voice, just above a whisper. He looked at her with compassion and understanding, but also with a seriousness that lifted her out of her fear and grabbed her full attention. "Have I ever caused you to regret it?"

She slowly shook her head, looking intently into his eyes, desperate to make her way back to safety.

"Then trust me now." he said softly "Everything will be OK. I promise."

She was silent, but her look said that she would always trust him, and he knew that.

"He put a knife to your side, he was taking you with him, there was no way that…." he paused, his face darkening. "He got what he deserved." Eddie was being careful to walk the line between making her see the attacker's intent, how close he came to succeeding, and yet not inflating the fear she already felt. "I'll bet my life on this Antonia, you're just the lucky one, the one who got away. How many other women didn't, do you think? Search your feelings and tell me, do you believe that he hadn't victimized anyone else before this?"

She shook her head again "No, I understand."

"Do you?" he asked gently. "Let me ask you this too sweetheart, what are the chances that he'd beat the rap in court, or that he may have before? That's assuming he wasn't planning on killing you."

Antonia's father had been a New York City cop for thirty years and she had heard her share of stories over the years about violent perpetrators who posted bail and were out on the street, even before the arresting officer had finished filing the required paperwork. Many of them were never convicted. She admitted to herself that Eddie was making sense, and started to feel differently about what had happened.

“Baby, I need you to look at what happened objectively, I know it’s difficult, but try. If you hadn’t been at knifepoint, if it was a purse snatching or someone stole your car, well… that’s one thing. This wasn’t that.”

She nodded and without realizing it crossed her arms, subconsciously protecting the spot on her ribs that still ached a bit from the pressure of the knife point.

“As much as I want to reassure you and see you through this, I can’t do it until you come to some…” his eyes scanned the table top for the right word “…decision…about what happened. What the consequences would have been for you and probably for others down the line."

He watched her eyes darting this way and that, as she considered what he’d said. At least she was listening, that was a good sign. Eddie was pressing her to reframe the meaning that she’d taken away from the experience. He got a sense that it was working, but it was not easy for her to let go of her initial emotions. Her ability to cope with what she had been though depended more on her being able to recall the incident with some detachment and confidence; it was an emotional exercise as opposed to an intellectual one.

“I understand.” she said in a quiet voice “I need some time.”

“Of course.” he said as he reached across the table and took her hand “Take a breath, you’re alive and safe. The bad guy lost and you won.”

They had more wine, and then he took her home and spent the night at her apartment since she was understandably upset, holding her in his arms and reassuring her that it was all in the past. Mercifully, she drifted off to sleep, continuing to hold onto the brawny arms wrapped around her. He watched her as she slept, her chest rising and falling slowly with each breath. The moonlight that filtered through the sheer bedroom curtains cast a subtle and creamy light upon her beautifully delicate face and her skin looked like an ethereal silk.

Eddie loved this woman completely, and had never really loved another. He was very disturbed by the night's events since, had he arrived a minute later, the night would have ended much differently. He prided himself on his ability to remain two steps ahead, as he told himself on occasion, but in this case an act of random violence…it was… random. Unpredictable. His inability to protect Antonia from a random event made him feel helpless, a feeling to which he was unaccustomed. As far as the killing was concerned, as always, he'd made his decision and acted decisively. There were other men he'd killed that had caused him a lot of soul searching both before and after the act. Not this one.

It was ironic indeed that the impression he made on associates in 'the life' did not reflect his true inclination. It was a façade he wore that was borne of practicality. Survival on the streets required that you be respected and a large part of that street credibility was based upon the perception that you were capable of bringing sudden violence or death upon a rival without hesitation or remorse. He was not a violent man by nature but more than in any other occupation, people didn't survive unless they were able to accept the realities involved. Those who didn't survive were neither pitied nor shown mercy for their weaknesses and failings; they were crushed.

# Chapter 20
# *The Fish*

*The Bronx, New York City*

***8 Years Ago…***

By the time we were in our early twenties, Junior had left our group at the warehouse and became his father's driver. He'd drive him to his appointments every day, and as time went on Victor allowed him to observe some of the meetings. On this particular Wednesday night in September, his father had a ten o'clock meeting in the Bronx, and he arrived at his parent's house at a quarter of ten.

"Where to Pop?"

"Go to Louie's down the street."

Junior grinned. To his father, the Great Wall of China was 'down the street.' He seemed to see everything in terms of it being part of his neighborhood; he'd always spoken that way.

"You got it."

Junior pulled his copper colored Caddie away from the curb while tuning his radio to the all-news-all-the-time station that Victor preferred. When he started driving for his father he'd try to listen to the pop music played by the top-forty stations that are so numerous in New York City. Victor would change the station every time, commenting in his characteristic low tones "Who wants to listen to that fuckin' noise." It wasn't a question. Junior saw the futility in pointing out that there was a reason that so many stations played "that fuckin' noise", and quickly capitulated. He did make one further attempt to manipulate the situation by playing some music that his father did like, however on the second track of the Jimmy Roselli compilation album, Victor still reached over and put on the news, saying "Mind if we listen to the news?" Well, at least he was civil about it, Junior told himself.

They parked in front of the restaurant, Louie's Tavolo da Pranzo, and Victor said "Come on." which was Junior's cue that he'd be allowed to accompany him this evening.

Junior flipped the driver's-side sun visor down and grabbed the special PBA card tucked into the flap, placing it on the dashboard just above the place where the car's VIN number was. He was parked in a 'Loading Only' zone, and if a cop went to ticket him, he'd see the card and most likely decide he had 'friends' on the force since these particular cards could only be issued by people near the very top of the law enforcement food chain.

Upon entering, Louie himself ushered them directly to the private 'banquet room' in the basement, in reality it was more of a private dining room that seated sixteen if you didn't need much elbow room. The spotless white table cloths and napkins stood out against the dark plush carpeting, deep wine colored wall paper and subdued lighting given off by the ornate wall sconces. The room's décor communicated a very 'private' feeling. On the east wall hung a large and striking oil painting of a seaside Italian village. Mounted on the wall directly opposite the painting, hung a large framed black and white photograph of the restaurant when it first opened, over two decades before. The slightly faded photograph showed a young and proud Louie in chef's-whites, with his wife and children by his side; they were all smiles. Louie's brother, Angelo Cento was in Victor's crew and his main business was dealing with the unions. He also managed the 'pad', the extensive distribution of cash payoffs to the police in the area on behalf of the family.

Victor and Junior were the last to arrive, and the air was already thick with cigar smoke and conversation. Victor took his seat at one end of the table and fished a thick Toscano from the inside of his jacket. Junior sat at an adjacent table, his back to the wall; he was to listen and maintain a low profile, which is to say, try not to be seen and never heard. Sitting opposite Victor was Mike 'the Fish' Moretti, an extremely large man, even by mob standards. His love of food had added a foot or so to his waistline and considerable girth to his already ox-like shoulders, prompting more than one of his peers to ask the question Why not Mike 'the Whale'? He owed his nickname to an unfortunate event from his youth; he'd never learned to swim and once had nearly drowned after being forced off a pier and into the water by pursuing police. As the joke went "Anything that big ain't never gonna fuckin' float anyway."

After the wine and antipasto, the small talk died away, and attention was on the business at hand. Victor would let Moretti start the conversation, and was certain he would since Moretti liked the sound of his own voice. Truth be told, he didn't respect Moretti. In spite of the large organization that Victor ran and the dozens of conversations he had with people each week, he kept his opinions to himself about the people involved. He was a disciplined man in a business frequently populated by wild men. Moretti could be fairly characterized as the Victor's opposite; loud and imposing. His bluster had worked in his favor when dealing with underlings and people in a weaker position than he. When in the company of equals, his abrasive ways were 'tolerated' as part of the cost of doing business. Despite his loud and unrefined persona, Moretti was intelligent, ambitious and a born schemer. He owed his success and position as a capo to these last three qualities since they had enabled him to establish himself as a reliable 'earner' for the family.

Sitting to Moretti's right were two of his crew, Joe Cuomo and Pat Vinci, younger wiseguys that Victor knew only by name. They seemed a little stiff for young guys, but it was understandable; being invited to a 'sit-down' between two capos was not an everyday occurrence. To Moretti's left was Tony Bianco, an old timer and confidante of the boss. Where the Fish was round, Tony was angular; tall and thin with long arms and thin fingers, his cheekbones protruded from his thin face giving him a somewhat reptilian visage. Tony's opinions were given consideration by the head of the family, and although he didn't formally hold the position of consigliere, he occasionally fulfilled that role in certain situations.

Tony was artful in his ability to present a noncommittal, essentially neutral appearance. He was insightful enough to strictly maintain this reputation in order to avoid the rat's-nest of positioning that the capos went through to gain favor, or even the appearance of favor, with the boss. Under normal circumstances, Tony would not be involved in this level of disagreement between capos, normally the two parties would have a 'sit down' with the underboss, and come to some arrangement. However, the family's underboss was serving three to five for fraud. Unrest within the management levels of the family was something that could carry an exorbitant price, a price that no one up the food chain wanted to pay. Mindful of Moretti's unreasonable nature, Victor asked Tony Bianco to mediate, and Tony agreed out of respect for him.

Moretti didn't disappoint Victor, and started in with his usual aplomb.

"So. This guy, this friend of yours. You understand what's in the works, what we need from him." Moretti said in his gravelly voice.

Victor didn't respond, he had a natural poker-face, he just continued to stare at Moretti, then slightly arched his eyebrows as if to say 'Your point?'

"You need to have a conversation with this guy. He's a friend of yours, all well and good, but business is business and he's being a prick."

"That so?" Victor said in a reasonable tone.

"Did you hear me just say it? I'm not talking to hear myself talk." for just an instant Victor's eyes shifted to Tony Bianco's, however Tony didn't compound the mistake by smiling. Moretti continued.

"It's business…" he said to Victor in a condescending tone "…and it's not like he won't make out, I've offered him more than what's fair. But the fuck won't budge. You better go explain a few things to him 'cause I don't think he understands, your friend." Moretti's voice was gradually taking on a menacing tone.

"He understands." Victor said simply.

"Yeah well it don't look that way to me." the hand gestures were getting more pronounced "I'm only here as a favor to you, if it wasn't for you he'd be gone."

Well, Victor thought, it didn’t take him long to arrive at that destination; he’d always believed it was a careless decision to make him a captain, the guy had too much 'loose-cannon' in him.

“What does he think, he’s immortal this guy? I gotta do what I gotta do, and in the end he’s gonna be with us or he’s not. Ya know?” Moretti looked at Tony “I mean what’s right is right Tony. I gotta make a fuckin’ living too.”

Moretti looked back to Victor and spoke as if the decision was made “I came down here tonight as a favor to you. If this guy…this Mendoza don’t wanna play ball, then fuck him, he's not gonna' stand in my way.” he said, holding his hands up as if he had no other choice, while trying his best to leer frighteningly at Victor.

Carmine Mendoza was one of Victor’s oldest friends; they’d grown up in the same neighborhood and gone to the same schools. Carmine had some challenging times in the neighborhood, being half-Italian half-Mexican, there were a few members in each of those communities, but a vocal few they were, who were compelled to test him. Victor admired the way Carmine had stood up to those people, alone, facing them head-on when necessary even when it resulted in a beating from one or more of his instigators. Carmine had integrity, a quality that Victor prized, and as they grew to manhood they remained friends. Carmine knew what Victor did for a living and had no desire to be involved; in fact he’d never even brought it up in conversation. Carmine was a straight-arrow and worked hard to build a business; and though he started with nothing, his drive to succeed and willingness to work hard paid off. Several years ago he took all of his savings and started up a courier service, Andiamo Deliveries, Inc., and his vision and drive were responsible for its success. Now all of that was in jeopardy.

Moretti’s guy, Pat Vinci, had done some business with Carmine, Pat owned a small company that did phone and computer installation, of course it also provided him with a pay stub that he could submit to his parole officer. Pat had gotten to know Carmine, and more significantly his business, while setting up his office. The installation company was really just a 'front', Pat’s income substantially came from two other, more lucrative and illicit sources; one of them was the distribution of marijuana and cocaine. He would receive bulk shipments of both, dilute the cocaine to normal street-level potency, divide the coke and weed into parcels that street level dealers and smaller distributors could afford, and then carry out the exchanges.

Since he had a criminal record, he had to take precautions, sometimes expensive and time consuming precautions, to avoid any sort of 'sting'. The feds were everywhere. Since drug crimes had such stiff penalties, it was hard to find people with 'clean' police records to 'front' for his operation, and even harder to ensure someone charged with 'intention to distribute' would decline a deal to reduce their harsh sentence. Currently he could manage twenty to thirty small deliveries in a week; of course the demand knew no limits and the profit to be made was staggering. In the face of huge profit margins and consumer demand that knew no end, the resultant greed was responsible for so many in the drug trade having their lodging provided courtesy of the U.S. government penal system. Pat recognized this dichotomy, and only time would tell if the constant temptation to expand carelessly weakened his vigilance.

Pat's other income came from extorting 'protection money' from local businesses. Essentially, the proposition to the business owner was simple as it was effective; you pay each week and your place of business won't be burnt to the ground, your legs will remain intact and your family will be spared any trauma. There were various ways of approaching businesses. Sometimes property might be destroyed first, perhaps an armed robbery as well, some employees or the owners themselves terrorized, followed by a visit afterward proposing entry into a local merchants association. The association membership would ensure safety and protection of property and employees. Alternately, a business owner might find himself the recipient of a nasty beating by people who had the demeanor, capability, and just as essential, the physical bearing that struck fear into the heart and the logic of cooperation into the mind. Since the world was becoming more corporate, the huge retail chains supplanted the individual business owner, and this was making street-level extortion a less viable business for organized crime.

Here was the rub, when Pat met Carmine and saw the dispatcher sending couriers to all corners of the city, it was the just the kind of business opportunity that his predator mind was constantly stalking. Pat immediately planned to shakedown the owner for protection money; however he also saw a way to make the occasional delivery under the legitimate guise of the courier service. Of course the courier would be one of his people in an Andiamo Deliveries uniform, but there were situations where the legitimacy of the company would be very useful. There would be some opportunity to launder some of the cash he took in as well, once Carmine was under his thumb. Carmine's value to Pat was protection income and the cover of legitimacy. He was a completely untainted civilian with a good reputation in the community. He'd have to strong-arm Carmine's cooperation first, but the guy would either cooperate or get hit so hard he'd forget his own name. He'd begun that first step when he learned of Victor's request for a meeting.

For his part, Carmine had no intention of getting involved with anything illegal, and had politely resisted Pat's appeals, and while Pat didn't disclose the entire scheme, Carmine had grown up in the environment and was capable of filling in the blanks. A week ago he'd decided that the situation was serious enough to impose on an old friendship, and called on Victor, explaining that there was no chance that he'd satisfy Pat Vinci's request. Victor promised his friend he'd do all he could to help him. While a reliable truism about people in 'the life' is that business comes before everything, such was not the case with Victor, not when the friend was a close and respected one. Although Victor was a careful man, he was also absolutely fearless. He'd do what he had to, in order to protect his friend.

Tony Bianco remained as he had been so far in the conversation, his gaze fixed on the table in front of him, his long boney fingers with perfectly manicured nails tapping softly on his silver cigar cutter that set beside his wine glass. His demeanor communicated 'I'm listening.' He didn't cue Victor, didn't break his noncommittal body language. This was in itself a statement, one that Victor recognized and Moretti, feeling pleased with the 'show' he as putting on, laying-down-the-law as it were, didn't. Victor had more length on the leash yet.

"That sounds a little drastic." Victor said, he shifted his eyes to Pat Vinci "Pasquale, you have some problems building your business?"

Pat nodded.

"With all due respect, your problems are not my friend's problems. He has his own problems."

Pat was no dummy, he remained silent and just looked attentive. To show disrespect to anybody at this table would be…unhealthy. Disrespect aside, if you got into a debate with a captain, and you're not one yourself, you're wrong. Even if you're right, you're wrong. He wasn't going to step into that trap.

Victor was mildly disappointed that Pat didn't take the bait and shifted his gaze back to Moretti.

"Yeah well he just got one more problem, you're friend…" said Moretti with remarkable calm "…he's in my way. That's it, either you talk with this guy, make him smarten up, or he's out of the picture."

The meeting had taken place at Victors request to Tony, and Moretti talking as if he his opinion was the only one that counted, it was the opening that Victor was waiting for.

He cleared his throat and rested his cigar in the large glass ashtray in the center of the table. He looked Moretti in the eye and said what he'd intended to say from the moment Carmine explained his predicament. His voice was barely above a whisper and all the more commanding because of it.

He held up the first three fingers of his right hand together,

"Number one" he folded his thick index finger down into his palm, "don't tell me what I have to do. Don't ever do that." He was holding the remaining two, the middle and ring fingers up.

"Number two" he folded his ring finger into his palm "this man is a dear, dear friend of mine. He was godfather to my daughter. You wanna build your business? Fine. You have the right. But this man is a dear friend of mine and you want to get to where you want to go on his back. Ain't gonna happen." Having folded his index and ring fingers into his palm, only his middle finger was left sticking up. "Which leaves us with this." he said, staring into Moretti's eyes, his gaze directly over the tip of the bird he was flipping him.

Moretti winced, clearly not expecting such a direct confrontation from Victor, who did not have a reputation for the 'strong arm' approach.

"This guy kicking up?" Moretti said "Am I missing something here? Because if he's not, he doesn't belong to you, he's not on record and he isn't entitled."

"He's not kicking up, and he's not going to kick up." said Victor.

"Hey, you want to give us what we need to do this thing, we're all ears."

Victor didn't respond, he just took a puff of his cigar and returned it to the ash tray. And waited.

"It's like talking to a fuckin' wall." Moretti said in mock resignation "I don't give a fuck whose cock this guy is sucking, I'm running my business."

Junior bolted up from of his chair at that, ready to slap the Fish out of his chair for the veiled insult to his father; he'd never seen anyone talk that way to his father. Victor immediately put his hand out toward Junior.

"Sit down, sit down. Relax." then turning to Moretti "Whatever. My friend is not gonna be touched. That's it, that's all I gotta say."

With that he casually rose, said his goodbyes to Tony and nudged his son toward the stairs.

The moment they were in the car, Junior exploded "THAT FAT FUCK! You should have let me put my fuckin' foot up that battleship he calls an ass for talking to you that way! That motherfucking blimp!" he smacked the steering wheel.

Victor smiled, he knew he'd have to talk to his son, again, about his lack of self control, but just then he was enjoying his son's fierce loyalty and respect for him.

"Take it easy will you? Watch the road for Christ-sake." he said in a calm voice "He's a captain. You should know better. That's never an option, what you were gonna do." he paused a moment "I appreciate the sentiment, but there's ways of doing things, and that wasn't the way to handle it."

"Yeah? Well what he said to you…fuckin' Shamu was out of line!" Junior said as his anger began to dissipate "That fat bastard would need a search party to even find his dick and he's making a crack about you?"

"Alright already. Put it to bed." Victor said in exasperation "Shut up and drive."

He reached over and flipped on the radio; they listened in silence to the news for the entire ride home.

After Victor and Junior left, Tony knew that he'd have to endure some whining from Moretti, he just wanted to get on with it and be on his way. Moretti for his part, had just completed a string of very lucrative hijackings that came to him without much foreknowledge. With his inflated sense of self importance, he'd been stewing over every dollar in tribute he kicked up the chain, and of course, he always reported less then he actually took in. It was the classic lottery winner's regret, you're earning forty thousand a year and one day you hit the lottery for ten million dollars, a week later you're whining to everyone that will listen, how much tax you have to pay. The Fish believed that he kicked up more than the others, and so he was valued, needed, in fact a necessity for the family. In reality it was the height of arrogance, the only necessity in the family was the organization itself, the structure, the rules and their enforcement. It's the essence of what had allowed it to survive against the determined efforts of law enforcement to obliterate it. Even the corruption that the family induced in law enforcement itself was a product of a systematic approach.

After Victor had gone, Moretti filled Tony's ear. Tony listened in his noncommittal way, neither endorsing nor disapproving, and left ten minutes later. The Fish's ambition and arrogance were emboldening him to make a move, and a risky one to be sure. He left the restaurant with Pat and Joe, and was uncharacteristically quiet on the drive home. Both of the underlings wondered what decision would be handed down, since the meeting didn't provide a resolution.

Connected.

# Chapter 21
# *Politics*

"Carmine Mendoza."

"From Wilcox Avenue Carmine Mendoza?"

"Yeah Carmine. I need you to watch his back for a while."

Victor and Mario Ruzzi had just finished eggs, toast and coffee at the Parkway Diner. It was a small and constantly crowded place, twenty four hours a day, seven days a week; the strong smell of pancakes coming from the kitchen seemed to hang in the somewhat stuffy air. Victor was dressed casual in dark brown loafers, tan pants and a maroon short sleeved shirt, gold watch and wedding band, immaculately groomed, eyes alert and looking well rested. He blended. Mario Ruzzi on the other hand, was rarely up this early since most of his business was transacted at night, and this explained his pallor; pale with lines around his eyes, eyes that were decidedly not fully awake yet. In contrast to his physical condition at the moment, he was wearing a black wool suit, custom tailored of course, a white shirt and 'power red' tie, gold initial cuff links, wafer thin gold Patek on his wrist and wedding band. Against Victor's blue-to-white collar 'blend in' appearance, Mario looked like a corporate executive or a lawyer.

The waitress came by, a coffee pot in each hand, one with a brown rim, the other had an orange rim, leaded and unleaded. She refilled both their cups with high octane and Mario waited for her to leave.

"What's the story?"

Victor gave Mario the details, and a recap of the meeting the night before.

"Tony say anything?"

"No. This is petty bullshit, I'm sorry I had to ask him to be there." Victor said, taking a sip of coffee.

"Yeah but the Fish…"

"Yeah. The Fish." he paused "Well, we didn't come to agreement. He said what he was gonna do, and I said don't do it." he shrugged.

"He's a little crazy." Mario said "You think he'd cut off his nose to spite his face?"

"I think he'd do that, yeah." Victor said without hesitation "Until he actually does something though, there's nothing we can do. He knows that."

"All due respect, Carmine's a nice guy and all, but you sure about this?"

Victor nodded.

"OK I'll go say hello."

Later that afternoon, in an industrial area densely populated with warehouses that bordered a large cemetery, a shiny black Mercedes Benz pulled up to the curb in front of Andiamo Deliveries. The well dressed duo, Pat Vinci and Joe Cuomo, got out of the car and entered the building; a minute later Pat stepped out of the access door into the alley beside the building, then Carmine appeared, shoved out into the alley, followed by Joe. Pat stood close to Carmine, his nose a few inches from Carmine's and as he spoke he poked Carmine in the chest; Joe stood back a few feet, behind him. Out in front of the building, a white Lincoln pulled up from the wrong direction, and parked nose to nose with the Mercedes. Mario stepped out and was approaching Andiamo's front door when he glanced to his left and saw the trio in the alleyway. As he watched, Pat slapped Carmine hard across the face, and a few seconds later, slapped him again even harder. Carmine nearly fell over from the force of the blow, but righted himself and didn't make any move to run. Pat stepped even closer to Carmine, their noses were almost touching, and said something, but Mario was too far away to hear any of the conversation. Carmine shook his head as if to say 'no', and Joe grabbed his arms from behind and held them as Carmine finally began to struggle against the attack.

Pat fished something out of his pocket and held it in his fist, he cocked his arm to begin 'the negotiation' in earnest, when a shot rang out and a car alarm started wailing. Startled, Pat's head whipped around toward the street end of the alley, and there stood Mario Ruzzi looking directly at him, the pistol in his hand however was pointed at Pat's Mercedes. Keeping his stare on Pat, Mario fired again and Pat and Joe clearly heard the sound of glass breaking.

"What the fuck!" Pat said, forgetting about Carmine. He returned whatever it was in his fist to his pocket, and he and Joe walked quickly to the street, stopping ten feet from Mario. "What the fuck Mario?"

Mario said nothing, waiting for the light bulb to go on over Pat's head. If they reached for a weapon, of any type, he'd kill them both without hesitation. For the most part, if you're not sitting at a card table, bluffing is a bad idea.

"Pasquale." Mario said simply, still holding the pistol towards the car.

Pat wasn't sure what to do, and after a pause said "You're gonna pay for this."

"No I'm not. You were told once; this guy is not to be bothered." Joe opened his mouth to speak but Mario cut him off "This is boring, you gonna do something? I'm right here."

Mario was well known in the family. Respected and experienced, he'd done a lot of things. To Pat and Joe, making a move on Mario wasn't about bravery versus fear; it was about smart versus stupid. They knew that. And they knew that Mario knew that they knew that. Halfway up the alley was as far as Carmine came, and his impression was that the confrontation was about who was going to show fear. He was wrong. It was about politics. Violence was seen by wiseguys as a tool to get what you want and only occasionally to vent your anger. It was not seen as a plus or a minus, it was just part of the landscape.

Pat and Joe turned to leave. Pat opened the driver side door, and swept the broken glass from the bullet hole in his windshield, off of his seat. The Mercedes peeled away from the curb, leaving tire tracks, and the smell of burning rubber in the air.

"There's a phone inside?" Mario asked Carmine as he headed for the front door while watching the Mercedes disappear from sight.

Connected.

# Chapter 22
# *Surrogate Provocateur*

*Brooklyn, New York City*

The My Way Lounge, a corner bar in Brooklyn, is flanked on each of its sides by two story apartments. As watering holes go, it's about as out-of-the-way as it gets, which suited the Fish's purposes perfectly.

"Standing in the shadow, ya know. I'm not saying anything, he's a great man, but it's like I got a sign on my fuckin' back that says 'IGNORE'."

Chick took a sip of his seven and seven before going on.

"I could be doing a lot more for him is all I'm saying. I'm family. Instead I'm out there, breakin' my ass like some jamoke trying to turn a buck."

Another sip.

"I'm married to his daughter for fuck's sake! How close do I have to be to get some consideration here? I mean, what's right is right."

"Well that's what I've been saying, if it means anything to you. It's not my business so I don't want to stick my nose in, but that's what I've been saying." Mike Moretti shrugged his huge shoulders and reached for his Chivas "It's a fuckin' shame." he took a sip and said "Ah well, there's no use in stewing on it Chick…stewing on things you can't change."

John Fusco, 'Chick' to his friends, was 'small-time' in every way that mattered; he possessed neither the intelligence nor the ambition to stand out from the crowd, with the possible exception of his capacity for complaint. Chick had always felt the world owed him a living, and against that he was a very handsome guy, six feet two inches, broad in the shoulder and narrow in the waist, with a movie star smile and movie star hair. The boss of the family had one child, a daughter, Francesca; from the moment she saw Chick's good looks and blinding smile she was love-struck. Chick for his part, truly cared for Francesca, but the possibility for advancement in the family business was never far behind. When the reality set in that he'd have to earn his way, it was a huge disappointment. He never entertained the possibility that to the boss, no one would ever really be 'good enough' for his daughter.

Chick nursed his drink, brooding over the Fish's last comment.

"Everything's relative kid." Moretti said "You got some people in this family can't find their ass with both hands and a mirror. You should see some of the shit I see… it's ridiculous."

"I'll bet."

"And if anything…it's getting worse. Take that guy over by the Neck. There's issues there that cost us real money, and there's just no leadership. None. Zero." He mustered his most sincere look. "This stays between us. I have no doubt you and I could work together if you headed that half-assed crew. Instead, I'm forced to put up with that fucking egomaniac and his half-wit son."

Chick just shook his head in sympathy.

"And the fuck of it is, when he retires, who's going to move into his spot?" a slow sip, to let Chick catch up "The idiot-son, who by the way has no balls. The other night I was gonna smack him in the mouth, you should have seen it, it was embarrassing, he almost shit his pants. Seriously, he was shaking. Tough guy… yeah right!"

"What happened?"

"I can't go into it. I had to be on 'the table' about an issue with the guy. I'm telling you, little Lord Fauntleroy; his father raises him like a little fuckin' prince. Never been on the street, doesn't know the business. And this is who's going to take over when daddy's gone? It makes me fuckin' sick."

"I guess that's the difference between being a son in law, and being 'blood'."

"Fuckin' A." Moretti said.

They sat in silence for a minute, on the jukebox Frank Sinatra was wondering what spring is like on Jupiter and Mars. Each was somewhat alone in his thoughts; Chick miserable about the respect he deserved but didn't get, Moretti careful not to overplay his hand. The Fish judged it was time to plant the seed.

"Hey Chick, you're not the first guy to feel unappreciated in 'our thing'. The lines' longer than my cock." he said "I've been through it."

"What did you do?" Chick said

"I did what I had to. I had to take a risk and it paid off, for me anyway." the Fish said "The real question is what are you gonna do about it?"

"What can I do?"

"I don't know Chick, I don't know." Moretti said, shaking his head and feigning a philosophical perspective "All I can tell ya kid, is as long as you play someone else's game, you play by their rules. Capisci?"

Chick just grunted his understanding, but his eyes were boring into Moretti's, he was starting to really consider doing something to get himself some attention, some respect.

"Your father-in-law makes the decisions, ya know, who gets what. Maybe 'The Little Prince' shouldn't have it handed to him, maybe your father-in-law should see that you have the strength to run his business the way he wants it run. Maybe he should see that the son's weak, you know, for his own good he should know." Moretti coughed, his enormous girth convulsed and seemed to come to life "Hey, it's you're business not mine, I'm just saying."

"I appreciate it Mike.'

"I gotta run kid." Moretti said, grunting as he got himself to his feet "Don't do anything stupid, alright?"

"Fuhgetaboutit." Chick said.

They hugged and the Fish waddled out the door.

"Gimme another one Bobby." Chick said to the bartender as he sat back down and considered what he'd heard.

Two phone calls and as many hours later, Chick entered Steel Pier Seafood, a seafood restaurant on Central Avenue in Yonkers. Steel Pier was a five minute drive from the track, the place he'd first learned to gamble on horses. His eyes scanned the crowded bar, and settled on Junior. 'Victor Forza, Jr.' Moretti's voice echoed in Chick's head, the little prince. Chick couldn't help but smirk. The alcohol in his blood emboldened Chick, and his two inch height advantage on Junior only intensified the feeling. Junior was with a friend and they had dates with them. He recognized the friend, Eddie Ferrara. He didn't know either of the girls, and the four were standing at the bar, chatting away. 'The prince and his little fucking court.' he though.

Chick squeezed in to a single open barstool a few feet away from them, and ordered a Jack Daniel's. He sipped at his drink as he immersed himself in resentment for someone he barely knew, but someone who he believed stood in his way. He stood up straight, looking down on Junior out of the corner of his eye. When the couple between he and Junior's got up and moved to a table, Chick relocated himself at the barstool next to them. Eddie said something to Junior, who turned and noticed Chick for the first time.

"Chick."

Chick turned and looked for a minute "Junior right?"

"Yeah." shaking hands with Chick "You know Eddie right?" Chick nodded "Vicky and Antonia." he motioned to each woman "this is Chick Fusco."

They exchanged polite hellos.

"You girls the bodyguards?" Chick said, flashing that blinding movie star smile.

The four genuinely chuckled, though each of them sensed something a little 'off' about the Chick's demeanor; he seemed… tense.

"It was Vicky, wasn't it?" Chick said, she nodded "You look familiar. Have we met before?" he said, furrowing his brow as if trying to remember.

"Really where?" Vicky asked.

"I'm not sure, you just look familiar. Confetti maybe?" Chick asked, looking innocent.

Confetti was a famous, or rather infamous, bar in Queens that was uniquely a strip club during the week, and a conventional bar on weekends. They advertised on local radio stations quite a bit. The place was a total dump, and it prompted the four to consider whether Chick meant it as an insult.

"No, I don't think so." Vicky said, maintaining a straight face.

"Hmmmm." he said, making a show of trying to recall "I could have sworn I saw you there. Was like a Wednesday or Thursday maybe? No?" he asked. By suggesting the weekdays, he was inferring that she was in the place when it was filled with strippers, horny single men, and the occasional woman.

"No. Sorry." she said with a little bit of resentment.

Chick looked from Vicky, to Junior, then back to Vicky "Oh. Yeah. Sorry, my mistake, I was thinking of someone else." shaking his head and smiling, inferring that she didn't want Junior to know she was there.

"What's so funny?" Junior said.

"Nothing. Nothing's funny." Chick said, and mumbled something under his breath.

"I didn't catch that." Junior said, still in a neutral tone.

"Some people have to put on airs." Chick said "No offense."

"She said she wasn't there Chick." Junior said, which prompted a smirk from Chick who faced forward and took a sip of his drink.

Junior didn't take offense easily, but when he did he went from zero to sixty in about three seconds.

"Maybe you should get your fuckin' ears checked."

Chick mumbled into his glass "Yeah, maybe." took a sip and returned the glass to the bar with some force.

He turned to Vicky and said "My mistake. I'm sorry, I must have been thinking of someone else." his tone made it clear that he meant it sarcastically.

Junior judging it best to drop it, turned back to his friends, his temper simmering.

Chick said nothing for about a minute, then without turning "It's just that she looks like this broad who works there, picks up quarters from the bar with her snatch."

Junior's fist was in the air before he finished saying it, but Chick was obviously ready, dodging the punch; in a flash the bartender was yelling "Take it outside… fellas… take it outside or I call the cops!"

There was no way that the bartender was going to stop this, and the two squared off as people around them, crowded as the bar area was, shoved and pushed to make a hole and get clear of the two.

Within all of fifteen seconds, Chick discovered to his dismay and surprise, that Junior was not exactly the pussy that Moretti had made him out to be. In less than a minute one of his teeth had been knocked out, and his face was a fast becoming a bloody mess. Junior had spent his time on the streets of the Bronx, and while he didn't try to project a 'tough guy' image to anyone, he'd learned some lessons. Lesson One: In most cases it's all going to be over in a minute, so go full throttle and don't give the other guy a chance to breathe. Another thing Chick had failed to notice was that although he had a good two inches on Junior in height, Junior was quite a bit wider in the shoulders; he hit like a bull.

During this time, Eddie stood back, scanning the crowd to make sure no one interfered on behalf of Chick, and stealing occasional glances at the pair to be certain neither pulled any sort of weapon. Neither did. Before anyone in the crowd could intervene, it was over. Chick lie on the floor breathing heavily, he looked as though he'd lost a fight to three guys instead of one. Eddie looked over to the bartender who had the phone in his hand, a guy in a suit stood next to him, probably the manager. The bartender wasn't talking; he looked like he was on hold. Eddie stepped behind the bar and approached the two; he spoke for barely a minute, then reached into his pocket and took out a money clip and peeled off a wad of cash, stuffing it into the bartender's shirt pocket. When the man put the phone down, Eddie patted him on the back and returned to his friends; the bartender turned and began to calm some of the customers.

"Let's go." Eddie said.

They grabbed their coats and left.

Chick got back on his feet and slowly stepped up to the bar. He downed the remainder of his drink and accepted a clean wet bar towel from the bartender, wiping his face clean and ignoring the stares of the crowd around him. He pressed the cold wet towel against his left eye, which was nearly swollen shut, and then threw the towel on the bar and left. Surprisingly, Chick didn't feel anger towards Junior; he was certainly embarrassed, but his disappointment was focused inward. Overall, he felt overwhelmed and confused, wondering if he had what it took to get noticed and gain respect as a powerful player. He did not look forward to the spin he was going to have to put on what happened, to save face. Maybe there was something he could do to salvage the situation, he thought, but what? Ten seconds after he pulled out of the parking lot, a black Mercedes exited the lot in the same direction.

# Chapter 23
# *Terminal Velocity*

*Manhattan, New York City*

It was late for a lunch meeting, but that also meant that there were fewer ears to worry about. Victor had a lunch meeting twice a month with his guy who ran numbers in this part of the Bronx. Junior got to sit in on these, again to listen and learn. They went about their business as they ate, and half an hour later headed out to Junior's big copper colored Cadillac.

"Home Pop?"

"Go by the Club down the street, I gotta' see Angelo about a thing."

Junior tuned the key; seven tenths of a second later and three blocks away the heads of a group of three at a hot dog vendor cart snapped in unison in the direction of the sound of a hollow 'boom' and the feeling of a soft 'thud' in their chests. There was a row of large windows that faced the parking lot of the restaurant that Victor and Junior were just leaving; they shattered into a cloud of razor-like shards moving at nearly the speed of sound into the restaurant, enveloping the people at the closest tables. Screams erupted as pieces of the flaming car started to descend upon the street and sidewalk, dropping from the sky as if it were raining scorched scrap metal. The car frame, or what was left of it, was not a blazing ball of fire as seen in so many movies. The roof had been blown off completely, and the 'convertible' that was left was a smoking pit of charred debris in the blink of an eye. Small licks of flame appeared here and there, as the small bits of flammable materials that survived the initial blast continued to burn.

Victor was a guy who did his best to maintain a low profile, but ironically had a larger-than-life charisma that he was never successful at hiding. His son was devoted to him, and was growing up unspoiled by a father who believed that he had to earn his way in the life, with a seriousness and discipline that in time, earned you respect. Victor or Junior had underestimated somebody, and it was a cautionary tale; in their business second chances are pretty rare.

*The Bronx, New York City*

Mario was waiting for Angelo at the social club, he didn't have to wait long. He was pacing, there was nothing frantic or nervous about it, but he had to keep moving physically to avoid fixating on the anger he was feeling. He needed to be analytical, to think clearly, especially at this moment. He saw Angelo enter the club, he had a calm but purposeful stride as he approached Mario, and clearly he was doing his best to effect a calm exterior.

"Any doubt?" asked Angelo.

"No." said Mario.

"You have any orders for me?"

"No one does anything unless and until I say so."

"OK." Angelo nodded "The loss of our friend is bad enough, but this situation…"

"No shit." Mario agreed "If someone does something stupid, it could get a lot worse. Make sure no one does anything; I don't want to hear any fuckin' excuses from anybody. Make sure everyone knows."

"I'll handle it."

"OK. I gotta go see our friend; we'll see what he says." Mario said, meaning Tony Bianco.

"OK Let me send somebody with you. We don't know what we're dealing with here. Jimmy K's here, he can drive you."

"I'll be alright. Let Jimmy handle the phones." Mario said, his face darkening "Send someone over to his house; I don't want Marie to be surprised by the cops." Mario's somber face was matched by his despondent tone.

Mario left the social club and drove into Manhattan using evasive maneuvers and doubling the time it took to make the trip. The delay was necessary, a highly visible hit like this one, with all of the associated collateral damage, it was a reasonable bet that the cops would put a tail on as many of ‘the usual suspects’ as their manpower permitted.

“What do you know?” Tony Bianco asked Mario.

Mario shook his head “Our friend and his son were in that car. It went up and they’re gone.”

“Did anyone actually see it.”

“Yeah. Ronnie, ‘numbers’ Ronnie, Victor’s guy, he actually saw it. They had their meet, business as usual, I checked it out. Anyway, they were in the parking lot, and as he’s getting into his car he looks over and sees our friends get into the kids car, and boom, it’s all over.”

“Where is he now?”

“Getting pieces of his windshield taken out of his face. He’s in pretty bad shape.” Mario said “As a matter of fact, a lot of civilians are in pretty bad shape too. Whoever did this didn’t make things easy for us.”

“Yeah.” Tony said, looking down, and lost in thought. “Well, one thing at a time.”

“I’m not a cowboy; I’m not gonna go do anything stupid.” Mario said, then after a pause “Tony, I have to ask you, is there any chance this was ordered?” meaning was it sanctioned by the head of the family.

“None. I spoke with the old man five minutes ago, this is trouble. He’s not happy, and shit rolls….”

“..downhill, yeah I know.” Mario interrupted.

“OK. We don’t know. That’s your first order of business, go do your homework.” Tony said, patting Mario on the shoulder.

When he got back to the social club, Mario found Eddie Ferrara waiting for him.

“How you holding up?” Eddie asked.

“OK. You?”

“Like everyone else, I’m pretty fuckin’ pissed.”

Mario smiled at that, a sad smile but a smile none the less.

“What?” Eddie asked.

“This isn’t my boat, and this ain’t the middle of the night.” Mario said, referring to a situation they’d both been in that had similarities to the one they found themselves in presently. "This is different. This is business." Mario didn't say it in a 'preachy' way, but he did examine Eddie's face carefully to be certain Eddie understood.

"I'm not gonna make your life difficult Mario, you can believe that. In fact, I came here to give you some information."

"What's that?"

Eddie told Mario the details of the fight between Chick and Junior.

"I know it would have gotten back around what happened, but it probably hasn't yet, it was just last night." Eddie said.

Mario was silent for a minute, then he said "What do you think kid?"

Now it was Eddie's turn to contemplate, after a half minute he said "I just don't know. It's possible. Far as I know, Chick's not exactly an arch-fuckin'-criminal. Chip on his shoulder yeah, but that doesn't make him the Unabomber."

"That cocksucker never got over the fact that the old man's daughter didn't turn out to be the golden ticket."

"Well, he was definitely looking for trouble with Junior. It wasn't an accident…he came looking." Eddie said.

Mario motioned for him to proceed; this might be another piece of the puzzle.

"He came in, and sat a couple of stools away, and didn't say hello. Maybe he recognized us, maybe not. But then, a space opens up and he moves over next to us, that's when I noticed him, when he was moving." Eddie said in a reasonable tone "He moves over, he waits for us to recognize him, he insults Junior's girl and he just won't back off, it was too coincidental." he said, then after a pause "Yeah. He came looking to break balls."

Mario's eyes were darting this way and that, something was at the edge of his perception, and he wasn't quite able to put it together yet. "Well, there's more going on here kid, so don't do anything."

"Yeah."

They hugged and Eddie strode out of the club, Mario had about twenty phone messages, they were going to have to wait.

It had been almost forty eight hours since the explosion, and the cops were systematically going through every known wiseguy, looking for that thread that would unravel what had happened and who was responsible. There was no shortage of theories, from cops working the case, as well as informants. They didn't have, but what they most wanted, was reliable evidence. Mario had been approached, and pleaded ignorance. They didn't believe him of course, but that's the way the game was played. He was about to leave the club and head home, when one of his crew approached him and whispered in his ear. He immediately arranged a meeting with Tony Bianco, this time driving directly to the meeting.

"You heard?" Mario asked.

"What?" Tony asked.

"The son-in-law."

"Yeah?"

"They just found him in the trunk of his car." Mario said.

Tony didn't say anything. he stared at Mario for a few seconds then sat down and reclined in his chair. Mario sat down across from him, and watched Tony do his thing, hoping that he would arrive at the same conclusion he himself had an hour before. After a while, Tony leaned forward, stroking his face, still deep in thought but clearly coming to some sort of realization. His hand was covering the lower half of his face when it stopped in mid-stroke, his eyes darted up to fix on Mario's.

"OK. I need to speak to the old man first." Tony said. The look shared between the two communicated all that was needed.

"OK."

"Sit tight a little longer. Capisci?"

"Always."

Mario drove slowly, eyes scanning the row of parked cars in the crowded Westchester Square area of the Bronx. There! He spotted Eddie Ferrara's car parked in front of Annette's Coffee Shop.

"Filling out an application?"

"They made me an offer I can't refuse." Eddie said smiling.

He swallowed a bite of sandwich and wiped his mouth and hands with a paper napkin as he stood and hugged Mario, then the two sat back down at the counter.

"The guy from the bar, they found him in his trunk." Mario said casually.

Eddie didn't react immediately; he looked at his plate, his head nodding slightly in contemplation, then without raising his head he said "It's news to me."

"If I thought it was you, I wouldn't be here…and neither would you. There's something you want to do." he said deadpan.

"Yeah, what's that?"

Mario explained for the next five minutes. They stood and embraced and each went their separate way.

# Chapter 24
# *Loaves and Fishes*

*Brooklyn, New York City*

The place was noisy, and the smell of fresh baked bread permeated every room, large and small, every closet, hallway and storage space. It could lose its appeal if you worked here, but for some it never did. From three in the morning until three in the afternoon, thousands of loaves of bread made from about twenty different recipes that all traced their roots to the Mediterranean and reached back into antiquity. Green Olive Asiago, Herbed Garlic, and of course arguably the best classic Italian bread made in New York City, and considering that it was this particular city, that was saying something indeed! A small army of people clad in hair nets, white baker's aprons and splashed with flour, went about their baking with quiet determination. The noise was mainly from industrial sized mixers, shapers and conveyers that assisted the bakers in their daily tasks, six and a half days a week, 360 days of the year. In this particular bakery, about half of the work was still done manually, and a popular stop on a tour of the bakery was the ovens. A group of perspiration slicked men in clean white T-shirts, hats and pants stood in front of an enormous wall of ovens, loading perfect doughy logs and rounds, and unloading golden brown bread of such enticing beauty, that you could almost taste it with your eyes. Their perfectly coordinated movements, as they reached around, behind, across and over one another to maintain the flow of bread into and out of the ovens was impressive.

To the rear of the facility, in a large room piled from floor to ceiling with hundred pound sacks of ingredients, sat Tony Bianco and Mario Ruzzi. They made small talk, mostly about the Giants and Jets. Out on the factory floor, Moretti came walking through the maze of machines and people. When he came to the ovens, he yelled to one of the men and pointed to a golden brown round of fennel seed bread. The baker didn't put it together immediately, shrugging his shoulders and wondering who this mountain of a man was and where he had come from. When it registered that the baker didn't understand, Moretti put an annoyed condescending smirk on his face and gestured more aggressively. The light went on over the bakers head, and he tossed the loaf over to the huge man in the expensive suit.

His coworker turned his back to Moretti and said in broken English "He looks like a gangster."

The baker shot back in the same accent "He looks like a gangster, who ate another gangster."

Moretti tore into the loaf and broke off a fist-sized piece, the steam rose from the inside of the loaf, carrying the delicious smell with it. Moretti ignored the pain from the heat of the freshly baked loaf, and shoved the large piece into his mouth as he entered the stock room. He joined Tony and Mario at the circular wooden table, tossing the loaf into the middle. Neither of the two reached for a piece.

"Your message said it was important." Moretti said.

"Yeah." said Tony.

"By the way, I've got my guys on the street trying to find out about what happened to our friend and his son." Moretti interjected.

"Good. Good." Tony said "We know anything yet?"

"Not much, it may be bullshit, I'm still checking some things."

"What's bullshit? What are you hearing?"

"I heard that our friend's son got into it with somebody the other night. It may be bullshit, so take that with a grain, ya know?"

"Who was the other guy?" Tony asked.

"You're not gonna' like it." Moretti warned.

"Yeah, don't ruin my mood." Tony said sarcastically.

"Chick Fusco" the Fish said "from what I heard, they ran into each other at Steel Pier over by the track; the son got in his face and Chick didn't back down. Way it worked out, Chick got his ass handed to him. The son had a friend with him though, I don't know, maybe the two of them?" Moretti shrugged and stuck another wad of bread into his mouth. “In any case, I’m checking it out.”

“Chick?” Tony’s face changed from its habitually neutral expression to something approaching a scowl “This rat’s nest I don’t need…Jesus H. Christ…I need this like I need a fuckin’ hole in the head.” he said shaking his head slightly. “You’re sure it was Chick though?”

“The thing at Steel Pier? No question.”

“Seems a little thin, ya know, I mean Chick…” Mario spoke for the first time, letting the implication hang in the air.

“Yeah. We have to know, for sure, so, I’m checking.” Moretti said with a serious expression “This thing would give us less agita if it’s not the son-in-law, but whatever it is, it is. Maybe somebody should talk to him.”

“Somebody whacked him out.” Tony said.

“What? When?” Moretti said in surprise, playing his part perfectly his eyes immediately turned to Mario.

“Don’t look at me, nobody on my side did a fuckin’ thing.” Mario said to both Tony and Moretti.

“How do you know?” Moretti said “Sounds like you got a fuckin’ loose cannon in your crew.”

Mario began to protest but Moretti cut him off “I know it didn’t come from my crew, besides they have no reason to whack Chick.”

“Bottom line, Chick Fusco, I don’t know, but he just doesn’t seem like he’d do something that risky.” Mario said “The guy’s not that ambitious, never was.”

“When did this happen?” Moretti said.

“Yesterday.” Tony said.

Moretti made a show of being deep in thought, then said finally “I ran into him and we had drinks, just bullshit, but he seemed a little antsy ya know, like he had something on his mind.” Moretti said.

“Like what?” Tony said.

“Well you know…he thinks the fuckin’ world owes him because he married the daughter, but he was just on a jag about who was getting what, and why the old man didn’t appreciate what he could do for him and he should have a bigger part.”

“That’s thin, that all he said?” Tony asked.

"He was just bitching, but he made a comment about the son of our friend, probably didn't mean anything, just that he's gonna be handed his living by his father. He was jealous I guess… that's the way it seemed to me anyway."

"So what'd you tell him?" Mario said.

"What do you mean? I let him talk, he may not be fly shit in the scheme of things, but he's the son-in-law. I'm not fuckin' stupid." Moretti said, showing a little bit of indignation.

"It was only what…a day before that you had the thing with the guy though, the sit down, and it didn't get resolved right?" Mario said.

Moretti gave Mario 'the stare', and of course, it didn't work on Mario, who stared back. "You're gonna hang some part of this on me?" he said in a loud voice "Hey Colombo, I hate to disappoint you, but you don't know what the fuck you're talking about."

"You sure you didn't give Chick a little encouragement because of your beef with our friend?" Mario said, looking from Moretti to Tony.

Moretti, followed Mario's glance to Tony, who didn't protest or agree. It always frustrated Moretti that he failed so completely to manipulate Tony.

"What the fuck are you talking about? I got nothing to gain by killing Chick, and whoever did that piece of work on our friend and his son was a fucking moron. It had to be a fuckin' rank amateur; it couldn't have been done in a way that attracted more attention!"

Mario just shrugged and looked to Tony who had not moved a muscle.

Moretti continued "Our friend and his son are gone and I'm doing what I can to find out who. The son-in-law winds up in his trunk, I'll see what I can find out." the Fish tore off another piece of bread and stuff it into his mouth "I've had enough of this bullshit dragging me into it. You think I'm involved, show some proof, if you ain't got any, shut the fuck up!" Moretti screamed the last few words with a mouth full of bread.

Mario flinched, his body language subtly communicated that he was surrendering the confrontation to Moretti. Mario hoped that it wasn't too subtle for him to notice.

Tony finally broke his silence “OK. Opinion-time is over. Either of you have anything else I need to know?”

Neither said anything.

Turning to Moretti “Anything you get, I wanna know about it yesterday. Capisci?”

Moretti nodded.

Then to Mario “You go get control of things over there, and I’ll speak to the old man.”

Mario nodded.

The Fish left first, and Mario and Tony stalled a bit so they could have a chance to speak before leaving.

“You catch it? He doesn’t know Chick’s gone, and then he knows he was in the trunk.” Mario said.

“What am I, fucking stunad?” Tony said, mildly insulted.

“So?” Mario asked.

For a few seconds Tony stared deep in thought at the empty doorway; then he exhaled heavily and nodded.

# Chapter 25
## *Two Course Meal*

Double parking was a necessity here. The Brooklyn neighborhood hadn't changed much in appearance in the last fifty years. The brick storefronts, aged and densely packed, were set just a short distance from the curb. The sidewalks, once flat and even, now tilted this way and that from overgrown roots of trees and shifting soil. Some of the families that lived here had done so for two or three generations, and the majority of the businesses were locally owned. The homogenizing of American retail business by the nationwide chains had not yet touched these streets.

A burgundy Lincoln Continental moved slowly down the street, slowing further still as it approached the middle of the block; it double parked in front of Aldo's Pizza. The owner looked up from the pizza dough he was shaping, and saw Moretti waddling his way through the narrow glass doorway of his establishment. The face of the man, normally pleasant when his fingers were in the dough, instantly took on a guarded and completely disingenuous smile.

The proprietor 'Aldo' whose real name was Eliyahu Beretski, was a middle aged Polish Jew who had come to America at the age of five, prior to America's entry into the second World War. His parents didn't have the resources to travel as a family to America, and sensing what was coming, they sent their only child on ahead. Eli's uncle, his father's brother, agreed to take the child in, until his mother and father could find a way to follow. It was the last Eli saw of his parents, and in later years he'd learned that they had died in Chelmno, a Nazi concentration camp just forty miles from their home in Lodz.

Eli's uncle was manifestly a man of limited talents and ambitions; however he was a moral, hardworking and traditional family man, possessed of a gentle, soft spoken disposition. He raised his nephew as his own son, and instilled in him the qualities of reliability and hard work that were so well represented by immigrants of that era.

More than two decades ago, Eli, with wife Rita and new born daughter Regina, had taken his modest savings and became a partner in Aldo's Pizza with the original owner, the real 'Aldo'. Aldo Ferrara, also a hardworking immigrant from Naples, was also a family man. He lived in the Bronx with his wife Margaret and three children, a daughter Carmella, and two sons Peter and Eddie. Aldo and Eli had become good friends and the business partnership between the two was a happy and prosperous one.

Seventeen years ago, his partner Aldo died of a heart attack, and his widow Margaret had asked Eli if he'd like to purchase her interest in the business. Eli agreed and paid her a sum quite in excess of the value, doing his best to help her financially. Eli kept the name Aldo's Pizza and in the seventeen years since the original owners death, he'd become known to the new generation of neighborhood kids as 'Aldo'; although the older generation still knew him as 'Eli'.

The Fish's crew collected protection money from the small businesses in this area and Aldo's Pizza was not exempt from their outstretched palms. It had started suddenly; on several occasions a gang of unruly kids in their late teens and early twenties came in and trashed the place, terrorizing customers and destroying property. The police were not able to find the culprits, not surprising since they were part of the corruption themselves. Eventually a man showed up and said he'd heard of Eli's troubles and wanted to help; for a weekly fee he would ensure the safety and security of Eli's business from these criminals. Eli was in a position that offered him little choice, and he'd been paying each week for several years now. Aldo's Pizza made great food; pizza, calzone and stromboli, legendary cannoli, cheese cake and ricotta pie that his wife baked on the premises each morning. Eli's daughter Regina worked part time at Aldo's as well, tending the register and doing some of the cooking and prep work. Regina, now 21, was a sensual beauty; her large brown eyes were framed in long thick eyelashes and she had a voluptuousness common to women of Mediterranean descent, with a full chest, narrow waist and shapely hips. She usually wore her long slightly curly brown hair up in a bun, allowing her to cook without distraction.

Word had eventually gotten back to Moretti, from his man who collected from Aldo's, about the uncommonly delectable food, along with a comment or two about the uncommonly delectable owner's daughter as well. The Fish, who lived a considerable portion of his life upon the few square inches of the surface of his tongue, made it a point to visit the establishment when he had business in its vicinity.

"Ohhhh.... it's the kid from Israel." boomed Moretti's gravelly voice "What's good today." he fairly shouted to compete with Verdi's Rigoletto, more specifically this recording was Caruso's powerful tenor, coaxed by Toscanini not twenty miles from this very spot. It was as close to a friendly greeting as the Fish was capable of.

"Mr. Moretti! Good day to you sir."

Moretti plodded his way along the considerable length of the narrow dining room, finding his way to a table at the very back.

Aldo's was a pizzeria primarily, so patrons paid for and picked up their own orders at the counter near the register, in front of the massive pizza ovens. Moretti never paid for his meals since Eli had quickly found out from his neighbors who this man was and what he represented, further he found out what people thought he was capable of. Eli felt more caution than fear when Moretti was around, drawing some small degree of consolation and security from the fact that Moretti loved his food.

"What can I get you today?" Eli said as he placed a glass of Chianti in front of Moretti.

"What's that I smell?"

Eli almost smiled, he had to respect the mammoth Mafiosi's senses when it came to food, in spite of his obvious overindulgence, he did have a very discriminating pallet.

"Ahhh, you are my most appreciative guest!" he didn't say 'customer' since the Fish had never paid for a meal "My daughter's special chicken cutlet."

"Gina's chicken?" Moretti's eyes lit up, he wore the same expression when he looked at Regina as he did when eating a particularly succulent piece of veal. Moretti had tried to lay his best smiley bullshit on Gina with no regard to her father's disapproving looks, and his failure to charm her into his bed had not dampened his appetite for her. There had been times where he had let his hands brush against her shapely rear end. "Tell me about it." Moretti commanded.

"Tender chicken fillet, pounded thin, coated in seasoned flour and our homemade herbed breadcrumbs, skillet browned and then baked with a topping of basil ricotta and mozzarella, served with a spicy marinara and with a side of ziti."

"I'll have it." Moretti said with anticipation on his large round face, and added in his typical arrogant tone "And gimme some bread over here."

"Right away." Eli rushed off to get his order.

Regina emerged from the kitchen, bread basket in hand "Here you go Mr. Moretti."

"'Mike' Gina, you know my name, call me 'Mike'." he said grinning ear to ear.

"Enjoy your lunch." she said, smiling back and politely chuckling. She turned to return to the kitchen, but he was faster.

"This chicken Gina, is it as delicious as it sounds?" as he asked, his eyes moved from her face, down her body.

She ignored his gaze "Well you'll have to be the judge, won't you?"

He gently placed his hand on her lower back, just at the waist, and looked earnestly into her eyes "You should let me return the favor, and take you out sometime. I could show you a real night on the town, dinner, a show… whatdya say sweetheart?"

She smiled "You're a very generous man Mr. Moretti…"

"'Mike', Gina… 'Mike'." the Fish interjected.

"…Mike. I appreciate your kindness, but I don't have much free time. Maybe some other time."

"Well, if you're busy, you're busy." he said magnanimously, as he slid his hand down to her perfect rump and gave it a soft pat.

"Your food will be right out." she said smiling, as she seized the opportunity to extract herself and return to the kitchen.

In the mean time, two tables had become occupied, one with teenagers and another with three uniformed postal workers. Each group talked amongst themselves, each raising their voice to compete with the opera.

"She's somethin'…. you're daughter. Really something." Moretti said to Eli, who was behind the counter shaping a pizza crust, doing his best to hide his emotions. He kept his head down and worked the dough. "She's somethin' I said." Moretti repeated louder, thinking Eli hadn't heard him over Caruso.

"She's my jewel." Eli simply replied without looking up.

"That she is Eli, a jewel." he said, looking at the kitchen doors through which Regina had just disappeared.

Eli followed his daughter into the kitchen briefly and returned with a small chilled white plate that had a scoop of cold and creamy ricotta cheese, topped with a drizzle of warm sweet honey and a few flecks of lemon zest.

"A little something sweet while you wait." Eli said smiling.

"I don't mind telling you, for a Heeb, you make better Italian food than a lot of my paesano."

"We do our very best." Eli said, he didn't mind the derogatory reference to his Jewish ethnicity, but only because of who it came from. Moretti was a criminal, but more to the point, a criminal who lacked any sense of tact or manners. It would be like taking offense at a frog for hopping.

Nicky Trosa entered the eatery and came toward Moretti's table, his eyes scanning the patrons, some waiting on their food, others enjoying their lunch. He turned to Eli and leaning in, said something into his ear.

Eli came to Moretti's table with Nicky in tow "Mr. Moretti, if you'll follow me, I have a table for you that will provide a little more privacy. Yes?"

Moretti looked at Nicky, who nodded ever so slightly. "Aspetta, aspetta." he said in irritation as he stood and collected himself.

He followed Eli and Nicky down a narrow staircase into the basement. Cases of canned tomato products: crushed, peeled, pureed and paste, along with a plethora of dry goods set atop metal shelves that lined the walls. Eli made a sharp right and opened a door into a small private dining room that Eli used to have dinner with his family. The décor was simple and homey. Nicky stepped to the side and let his capo enter first, following him in and sitting after the Fish had settled into his chair, leaning forward onto the flower-print vinyl tablecloth. Eli appeared just half a minute later with a large circular serving tray, setting Moretti's wine glass, bread basket and half eaten ricotta in front of him.

"Something for you sir?" Eli asked Nicky.

"Not hungry. Thanks." Nicky said quickly.

"Please let me know if you change your mind." he said smiling, then turned to Moretti and said "Your food will be right out." closing the door behind him as he left.

"What?" he said, shooting an annoyed glance at Nicky as he separated a slice of bread from the loaf in front of him.

Moretti flicked his fingers and sent the bread basket sliding toward Nicky, who reached in and grabbed a piece, but not eat it.

"I got sent for." Nicky said.

That rated a reaction; Moretti stopped chewing and said with a mouth full of bread "Who? Who sent for you?"

"Tony B." he said, meaning Tony Bianco.

"When?"

"Just now, I just came back from Manhattan."

"What the fuck! You get sent for and I don't know about it?" the Fish spoke in a tone uncharacteristically quiet for him. Nicky had seen this look, predictably, Moretti's first reaction to unpleasantness was usually anger.

Nicky placed his wrists together as if he were in handcuffs "Hey, what am I gonna do? I got sent for, I go."

"You tell me first, that's what you do."

"I had no choice, that fuckin' Squib and the other guy, the big guy from the docks…" Nicky furrowed his thick brows, searching for the name "…what the fuck… Lil' Johnny. Anyway, they come to the club and say they got orders, I have to come in."

Moretti resumed his chewing, staring holes into Nicky's eyes. The next question was coming, they both knew what it would be, but Moretti waited a minute, letting Trosa stew.

"What did he want to know?"

Just then the door opened, and Eli came in balancing a round service tray. He set Moretti's meal in front of him and left.

Moretti ignored his food for the moment, and Nicky thought to himself There's a first! He must really be worried.

"He asked me about the recent car accident, and about the other guy they found."

"What did you say?" his eyes didn't leave Trosa's, while he cut a piece of chicken.

"I told him the truth…" Nicky said as he watched his boss's neck bulge as if he was going to gag on his food, quickly adding "…that you had us looking for the mutts responsible, but I told him that it looked to me like the son-in-law did something stupid and that fuckin' Mario decided to take revenge."

The flush that had begun in the Moretti's big round face, subsided just as quickly after hearing Nicky's 'truth'. Nicky Trosa was a soldier in Moretti's crew, and he functioned essentially as Moretti's number two man. However, he had not been part of the killing of late, that had been left entirely to Pat Vinci and Joe Cuomo. Since it was likely Nicky would take over for him if he was whacked for doing what he was doing, he'd be a bad risk to be in on it. Still, Nicky was perceptive and shrewd; a good business man. Moretti had little doubt that Nicky had suspected what was going on, perhaps had figured it out entirely.

"What did he say?"

"He asked me if I was sure." Nicky said "I said no I'm not sure, I didn't see Mario pull the trigger, it's just what makes sense."

The Fish noted how carefully Nicky had phrased that, separating his opinion from fact which added credibility, yet directing it completely toward Mario; Tony's question was really aimed at whether Moretti was involved.

"How'd he take that?" Moretti asked. He was relaxing and paying more attention to his meal, spearing a big piece of chicken and stuffing it into his mouth.

"Honestly, I can't say, he just….." Nicky searched for the right words.

"Yeah, I know. It's easier to read brail with your dick than to figure out what he's thinking." Moretti said, completing the thought for him “Then what?” Moretti was looking a little pale all of a sudden, as if he’d thought of some troubling detail.

“Then nothing. That was it.”

“So…” The Fish stopped in mid-sentence and rubbed his abdomen just above his massive stomach “Fuckin’ agita…all this aggrevation.” He face had definitely drained of color.

“You OK?”

“My stomach, I think this fuckin’ Jew gave me a bad piece of chicken." His mouth was watering and he pushed himself back from the table and spit on the floor. "I think I’m gonna throw up.”

Nicky rose immediately and helped his capo out of his seat, and said “Let's get you some air.” and lead him out of the room.

Nicky looked around and saw the half flight of steps up to the alleyway, he guided Moretti, now sweating and looking more uncomfortable, to the stairs and out into the alleyway to get some fresh air.

As soon as he was in the alley, Moretti suddenly stopped dead in his tracks, he felt a pain unlike any he'd ever experienced. It was as if an iron claw was inside his abdomen and was squeezing and tearing at his insides. The intensity of the pain completely paralyzed his legs.

“I gotta get to the bathroom, I’m gonna shit!” he said with urgency and a tortured expression, looking as though if he took too many more steps he might shit himself.

The Fish leaned against the back of a white delivery truck that was parked there. Suddenly the back door of the truck noisily rolled up and Eddie Ferrara extended a hand down to Nicky, who grabbed it and hoisted himself into the empty cargo compartment. Both men reached down and grabbed Moretti under the arms and strained to pull his huge frame backward into the truck. The Fish was in no condition to do anything about it; he lay on his back like a beached whale, trying desperately to hold his bowels against the effects of the 'cocktail' that Nicky had provided to Eli, who had incorporated it into the ricotta cheese mixture atop the chicken. The cocktail was made for Nicky by an equine veterinarian on Nicky's payroll at Yonkers Raceway, and per Nicky's instructions, it was far stronger than the minimum potency needed to tie the Fish's digestive tract into a knot before killing him. The pain was so excruciating that it completely paralyzed him.

Nicky quickly relieved Moretti of the contents of his pockets (car keys, wallet, etc.) and of course his gun. The two men hopped down from the truck and Eddie went around to the truck's cab and opened the passenger side door. Three huge dogs sprang out of the cab, wild but muzzled, nearly pulling Eddie onto the pavement. His muscles strained as he wrestled the monsters to the rear of the truck, and with Nicky's help, barely managed to hold them at bay. He had some little cubes of raw steak in his jacket pocket, which he held in front of the muzzled pack and then tossed into the compartment. The dogs tried to tear away and jump into the truck after the meat; they were truly ravenous. Moretti was in a fetal position, holding his lower abdomen and moaning in pain, and Eddie and Nicky could both smell that The Fish's attempts to hold his bowels had failed. Eddie removed the muzzle from each while Nicky held the leashes secure; they were all salivating and nipping at the air toward where they'd seen the few little cubes of steak go. Eddie's attempts to remove the muzzles quickly were proving difficult since the huge dogs were enormously strong and at a fevered pitch. Their ribs showed clearly through their sides; they were literally starving. A puddle of dog saliva had formed at Nicky's feet, and the dogs were so frantic that his grip on the leashes was fading quickly.

"Hurry up, I'm losing them!" Nicky warned.

One of the dogs snapped to the side and grazed Eddie's thumb, thankfully not drawing blood.

"Ahh. Fuck!" he grimaced "Come on, come on…"

Eddie finally removed the last muzzle as The Fish started to vomit on himself, his huge belly violently convulsing. Nicky let loose the leashes and the three behemoths launched into the truck. Eddie slammed the door of the compartment shut behind them.

"Now let that fat fuck be someone else's meal." Eddie said with genuine hatred in his voice, as The Fish's muted screams for help echoed from within the truck.

In his mind's eye, he could see his good friend Junior's smiling face, and Victor's as well. Where their deaths had been undeserved, unexpected, and quick, the Fish's would be quite the opposite. The dogs, in no particular hurry, would rip him apart and consumed him piece by piece. Well, to be realistic, Eddie thought, most of him; even they could only eat so much. As unbearably painful as the physical assault was, between the poison and the razor sharp teeth of the dogs, the horror of realizing that he was being eaten alive in the darkness and was helpless to stop it made it that much more horrific.

Nicky went back into Aldo's, while Eddie, rubbing his nearly chewed thumb, got into the truck and drove off. As the truck reached the end of the alley and merged into traffic, already Moretti's left ear and nose had been chewed off of his bulbous head and eaten by two of the dogs and they were now lapping and biting at the blood and torn skin. As he choked on the blood flowing into his sinuses from the mangled soft tissues of his face, the third behemoth, the one that had nicked Eddie's thumb just a minute ago, had opened his mouth widely and sank his teeth into Moretti's soft fleshy inner thigh just below his crotch, two of the dog's upper teeth piercing and crushing the Fish's right testicle. It pulled back with all of its considerable strength, jerking and tugging its head from side to side, ripping flesh from bone.

A minute later, Nicky emerged from the front of the building and drove off in Moretti's Lincoln. Two hours later the car was a cube of crushed metal that would be unrecognizable to even its late owner.

In the wake of the mysterious disappearance of Michael 'The Fish' Moretti, Nicky Trosa was 'bumped up' to capo, which came as a surprise to no one. Mario Ruzzi was similarly bumped up to capo of what had been Victor Forza's crew. Both crews, as well as Tony Bianco and the boss of the family himself, anticipated a more stable situation with the demise of the Fish. Victor's shoes would be hard to fill, but Mario was by far the most capable man in that regard; in fact, Victor had mentioned that very fact to Tony Bianco and had suggested and positioned

Mario as his successor, if and when the time came, and not his son as some had assumed.

A few years later Mario's life ended as he slept in his bed next to his wife, suffering a fatal heart attack. He had as peaceful an end as anyone in 'the life' could hope for. Three days later at his funeral, Angelo Cento learned that he was to succeed Mario Ruzzi as capo. Angelo shared many characteristics with his late captain; he was intelligent, shrewd and careful, with a tendency to maintain a very low profile, continuing in the style and tradition of late Victor Forza.

# Chapter 26
# *Evaluations*

*The Bronx, New York City*

***Present Day…***

Early morning sunlight flooded the room with the promise of a new day. Eddie sighed with resignation as he closed his eyes, stifled a smile and shook his head slightly as if to say 'Here we go again.' Antonia was staring off into space, her head resting on his shoulder and her fingers playing with his chest hair. She had a serene smile on her face, lost as she was in pleasant thoughts. Upon hearing his sigh, she looked up at Eddie and arched her eyebrows inquisitively. He marveled at the sun glinting off her long eye lashes and the exquisite almond shape of her eyes for the ten thousandth time, and as always it came to him as if it were a new discovery.

"I know that look." he said.

"Hmmm?"

He smiled and chucked to himself, shaking his head again.

"Have you considered the fact that I know you better than any living soul?" he said.

"Have you considered the fact that I know you better than any living soul as well?"

A pause, a furrowed brow and a slight frown.

"Now that's a scary thought." he said looking mildly troubled "I know some people who would pay for that information."

"They could pull my fingernails out, I'd never tell."

"And what lovely fingernails they are." he said as he picked up her hand and inspected her fingertips and then the entire delicate hand.

He pressed her palm to his lips firmly and kissed.

"I love you, but I'm not having this discussion right now."

"What discussion?" she said, trying her best to look credibly innocent.

"Fine."

"Something on your mind?" she said, maintaining her innocence.

"Jesus! You have no scruples. None."

"Are you feeling alright?" she said "Because I don't know what you're getting at."

Sixty seconds of silence. Fingers gently tousling chest hair. Then the hand doing the tousling comes to rest and her face looking angelic, bathed as it is in the morning sun, and turns squarely to his with a broad smile of admission.

"You'd fold under cross-examination." he said laughing.

She joined in, giggling.

"I love you." he said, staring lazily at the ceiling.

"This I've always known." she said.

"Isn't that enough?"

"Is it enough for you?" she asked.

He paused, thinking carefully, searching his feelings and looking for an answer that wasn't found with intellect, but with wisdom. Was it enough for him? It was a yes or no question. He'd avoided determining the answer to that question for many years, principally because either answer led to a difficult test of commitment. The subject of marriage and children had come up occasionally between them once they were both aware that each had found their soul mate in the other. Eddie's reservations were completely based upon complications that could, and if he was being honest with himself in all likelihood would, arise due to his occupation.

He loved Antonia beyond question and measure, and to some degree she would be put in jeopardy if they were to 'tie the knot'. If a situation arose where someone wanted to 'get to him', a major vulnerability he didn't currently have was a wife or children who could be used as leverage, or to exact vengeance. If a situation arose where he had to run, had to do extended prison time, had to fight it out with a rival, it was he and he alone who would suffer any consequences of his failures. The possibility of others having to suffer, others whose lives he valued more than he valued his own, was simply not tenable to him. He couldn't willingly allow such a situation to develop.

The alternative was of course, to leave 'the life'. If he were to go 'legit' then the equation would change and there was the possibility of a married life that he felt Antonia deserved. There was danger here as well. He was entrusted with information about the organization and nature of the family's business to a degree normally reserved for 'made' men; and made men…members…never leave the family, at least not with a beating heart. While the knowledge and trust he engendered made him more capable and powerful within the life, it worked against his being able to walk away from it, even though he wasn't a member. It was a 'Catch 22'. He could easily envision a sit-down between Angelo and the other capos, where someone within about ten seconds would say "Why take a chance?", and others would nod. Would Angelo nod? Probably not. In the end he felt that Angelo trusted him. He smirked in spite of himself, and reflected that it would be the height of foolishness to attach much confidence to that assessment. You never knew about people in the life, you just had to believe that anything was possible. If you didn't, sooner or later you'd get a real 'come to Jesus' experience…literally. Whatever Angelo's leanings, once there was agreement among the majority of the captains, the pressure to go along to avoid a conflict would be intense.

The thought came back to him; it boiled down to a question of commitment. 'The life' excluding marriage and children under the conditions that he'd abide, or going 'into the wind', dropping off the face of the earth and all of the risk and work that it entailed. His destiny with Antonia versus the determination and resources of the family. These thoughts begged the question, why was he involved in the life at all? Much as he saw himself somewhat as a master of his own destiny, his insights compelled him to admit it was circumstance and environment that lead him here. If he was to extricate himself from the life, he'd have to construct circumstances that would ensure his survival. That, he thought, is one hell of a formidable problem. To his surprise, and for the first time, he found himself considering the latter alternative, and what would be required to achieve it successfully.

Eddie was the kind of thinker who perceived things in a 'cause and effect' way, he didn't see isolated events, which is to say, he didn't see any event in isolation. He tended to think along 'timelines' and questioned the contexts of his perceptions. Consequently, when he planned, his perceptions came to him as sequences of events, cascading in time as water along a riverbed. Nothing was considered on its own, every detail was perceived as one part of a larger network of events. He'd once read a book on the life of the eminent physicist and native New Yorker Richard Feynman, which had a black and white photo of the great scientist on the back cover, standing at a blackboard that was covered by equations. When he reflected on the difficulty of successfully leaving the life, and the network of circumstances that would be necessary for it to be successful, he smiled for a moment picturing that same photo of Feynman with a caption that read "calculating the solution set to Eddie Ferrara's Survival Matrix".

"Giving me the silent treatment?" she asked.

Tearing himself away from his introspection, he finally replied "I have to think about it." He glanced down at her "OK?"

"OK" she said, smiling. She knew from the contemplative way he had considered her question, he was reconsidering his options. Antonia was wise enough to connect the recent incident at Lincoln Center with his willingness to re-evaluate his life; it was a common result of facing the possible loss of something or someone you love, and in her experience it was almost always a good thing.

# Chapter 27
# *Western Influence*

*San Francisco International Airport*

Joey Ross, known as 'Joey Bags' by his associates in New York, stood by the Preferred Members Club electronic bulletin board while his partner, Sammy 'DMV' Cotti, entered the little rental car satellite building. Emerging a few minutes later, ‘Mr. Jacobsen’ - Sammy rarely paid for anything under his real name - headed for parking spot K39 where a brown Chevy Tahoe sat idling with it’s cargo door open. His associate joined him at the parking spot and loaded their suitcases into the back of the vehicle. Pulling out of the spot with a screech, they exited the rental car area and then the airport itself, merging onto 101 heading south toward San Jose. Joey Bags pressed the volume dial to turn the radio on; it had been last tuned to a classical radio station and the driving saga of Holst’s Mars, Bringer of War eclipsed the road noise. Joey Bags gave his partner an evil grin as if to say ‘I love it when a plan comes together’. As DMV drove, his eyes continually scanned the road and his mirrors, not for traffic, but instead for cops, while Joey Bags unfolded a map and began to orient himself.

Joey Bags had gotten his nickname when he was in his late teens; he had hijacked a truckload of luggage and over the course of the following year was constantly peddling the bags to everyone. Joey’s partner, Sammy ‘DMV’ Cotti, had a sister who worked at the New York State Department of Motor Vehicles. Sammy would occasionally offer to help someone out with a driver’s license or a vehicle registration, for a price of course, which he would then split with his sister.

“About a half hour, maybe forty minutes depending on traffic.” Joey Bags estimated.

DMV barely nodded.

“You’re a cheery fuck. What’s up your ass?”

"Nothing." he said, rubbing his eyes "Long flight. I hate flying."

"Yeah, well six hours on a plane will do that to ya." the Joey said, folding the map into a square that showed the limits of their excursion today. "We'll sleep on the way back tonight."

The two had caught the earliest flight from New York's La Guardia Airport to San Francisco, and nearly six hours squeezed into coach seats had been only bearable for the two who were built like NFL lineman.

"I can't get to sleep on a plane. I hate flying." DMV said "What was that, the first flight out? Fuckin' early."

"Brutal." Joey grunted in agreement, he hadn't slept on the long direct flight either, and was just coming out of the flight induced coma himself "Hey, at least there was no traffic over the bridge this morning."

DMV nodded, even though that was not entirely true, there was always traffic, but for New York City it had been comparatively light on the way to the airport that early in the morning. The men were in the commuter lane when they saw traffic slowing ahead.

A quick look at the map "We're coming up to 85, head south."

"Th'fuck is this?" DMV mumbled, coming to a stop in a sudden sea of bumper to bumper traffic.

Twenty minutes later they had moved barely a mile, and could see the sign for the 85 interchange in the distance.

"There's no fuckin' bridge or anything, it must be a real pile-up..." he shrugged peering out the windshield intently "…or something bad to cause this kind of delay." Joey Bags offered.

"How we doing on time?"

"Depends on how far this shit goes on for. How far ya think it goes?"

The driver just shook his head. They could see only traffic backed up to the crest of the next hill.

*San Jose, California*

It was getting close to lunch time at ExchangeVault, and Vincent's stomach had been groaning for an hour now. He picked up his phone and dialed three digits.

"Great Wall?"

"OK."

"I'm starving. Eleven?"

"Eleven thirty."

"Come on man, my stomach is starting to eat itself."

"I'm not that hungry dude, eleven is like... practically breakfast."

"You will be ready to eat at eleven." His voice taking on a Obe Wan Kenobi softness.

"Your Jedi mind-tricks will not work on me homey..." Chuck shot back.

"Pleeeease." Vincent interrupted, the Jedi in his voice giving way to Lucy Ricardo.

"Yeah OK." Chuck said and hung up.

Vincent dialed Scott's extension and the two short rings indicated it was a call from inside the building.

"Who's your daddy?" Scott answered.

"Chinese." Vincent said.

"Great Wall huh?" Scott guessed. "Thanks but lunch is for wimps pal."

"It's sad that you think of yourself as a Gordon Gekko type."

"Let me tell you something 'Dear Leader', Michael Douglas has nothing on me. Nothing!"

"Except."

"What? You're not gonna throw that Catherine Zeta Jones thing in my face again. You're stuck in a loop my friend."

"Hey, she wants nothing to do with you. Sadly that's a fact that everyone but you seems to know..."

"She's just being coy." Scott interrupted "This is old news. She's just..."

Now it was Vincent's turn to cut Scott off "Married? Dude, face it, she married him."

"You have no sense of romance!… Of drama!… She and I are just taking part in the timeless art of seduction my friend. The primal dance of courtship. Look it up." Scott said sarcastically.

"I did, it's a pay site, I can't get past the welcome screen."

"So what were we talking about?"

Vincent laughed at the absurdity of the spontaneous conversation "Christ I forgot. Oh yeah. Great Wall."

"I can't, I'm swamped." Scott said, but added "What time were ya thinking?"

Vincent looked at the clock on his computer "Now actually."

There was silence for a few seconds "Vincent, it's eleven o'clock." Scott said deadpan.

"Remember that scene where Gordon Gekko meets Bud in the fancy restaurant for lunch and gives him that big check..."

"It's not gonna work." Scott interrupted, chuckling and giving Vincent props for persistence. "Really man, thanks, but I can't make it today, I have a lot on my list."

"It's all good." Vincent said "Want me to bring you back something?" Vincent wouldn't offer this to anyone, other than Scott. He had huge respect for his unassuming, quick witted and talented colleague.

"That's a dog with different fleas pal." Scott mimicked Gekko the Great "Thanks though. And I won't tell anyone you just made that offer. I wouldn't want to ruin your image." Scott said smiling.

"What offer?"

"Exactly."

*Mountain View, California*

"Cock. Sucker." Joey Bags said slowly and in utter disbelief as they passed the source of the traffic jam.

A California Highway Patrol car, roof lights flashing, was parked on the shoulder behind a brown Mazda Miata that was in the process of being attached to a tow truck. In the rear of the patrol car, behind the wire mesh, sat a young man with a bored expression on his face. As the cars in each of the three lanes reached the point of the 'spectacle', they accelerated to normal freeway speed. Joey Bags and DMV approached the scene and their attention was almost completely focused on the slow moving cars around them; instead of the police car that everyone else was paying attention to.

"You've got to be fuckin' kidding me right?" the Joey said in irritation.

"Jesus Christ these people are living on the moon." DMV said in disgust "Back in NYC you couldn't get people to slow down like this if the Pope was lying dead in the middle of the road!"

After they'd accelerated back to a more normal cruising speed, DMV said "It's fuckin' oobatz!" and shaking his head asked Joey Bags "How we doing on time?"

"Late."

He hit the accelerator as he stared at the cop car just disappearing in the rear view mirror and muttered "Un-fuckin' believable."

*San Jose, California*

Twenty minutes later the brown Tahoe pulled into the ExchangeVault parking lot, and proceeded to the employee parking lot at the rear of the building. A minute later DMV saw their target first.

"Grey Prius, UCLA sticker."

They were about to park, when the rear door of the building opened and two young men emerged. One looked as though he could be the man they came to see. Joey and DMV watched the two young men cross the parking lot to the Grey Prius with the blue UCLA sticker.

"Well, he's got company." Joey said.

"We wait?" the driver asked.

Joey glanced at his watch "It's lunchtime, they'll be back. Take off and let's go find some place kill a few hours. We'll grab him later when he's alone."

They struck out from the ExchangeVault parking lot in search of a place to eat lunch and have a drink or two. At five in the evening they passed through the parking lot again, and saw that the Prius was in the same spot. The passenger unfolded his map and studied it for a few minutes.

"Let's go see how it looks where he lives."

"Where to?"

"Get back on 101 and head south, look for Bernal Road."

Twelve minutes later they were driving through the townhouse complex where Vincent lived, perhaps ten or so years old and well maintained, it was the epitome of 'urban isolated'. There were no children to be seen, no neighbors in conversation, the very flower of the industrial revolution. Each townhouse had a two car garage, and shared a common driveway with its neighbor.

"I don't like it." Joey said, in spite of the fact that he could not see a single soul. "Too many windows and doors."

"Plenty of chances to be seen too if we have to get out of here in a hurry." DMV agreed.

"Take a drive around the block, let's see the approach." meaning that perhaps there was more camouflage heading into the development.

The complex had only one entrance that was easily accessible, and they drove a circuitous path out from it, in the direction of the highway. Two blocks away the driver pulled over at a four-way stop sign intersection and parked. The two sat in silence for a minute, studying the surroundings. This particular intersection was two blocks from the closest major street, Bernal Road itself, and was unique in that it had no houses facing the street directly. It was about as good a spot as they were going to find.

"Bump him?" DMV suggested, meaning they would roll to a slow stop behind their target's car, and hit him from behind, hard enough to do some damage.

Joey Bags surveyed the surroundings and knew that his target would pass this intersection on his way home, and that many others would as well. They had to expect that there would be a line of cars behind the target.

“Yeah." he pointed to a stretch of painted curb in front of a fire hydrant and under a tree, about fifty feet away. "Then lead him over there right away.”

“We going to be able to catch a flight home tonight?”

“I was just thinking the same thing.” Joey said with a frown.

Normally someone would have checked the flight information for the latest flight out, but they both knew from experience that they needed to focus on doing what they came here to do, and to get it done without fucking it up. They also did not call to make a hotel reservation in case they missed the last flight out, since it might serve as one more data point if anything went wrong. Even though the arrangement would be made under a false name, still it would be the same false name that the car had been rented under. In this line of work, you learned almost immediately and usually from the misfortunes of others, to leave no tracks and cover any you’re forced to leave.

Just before eight that evening, DMV's brain was ready to shut down. He’d been watching for a grey Prius and he felt as though he’d seen one every five fucking minutes, but one with a blue UCLA sticker in the rear window, that he'd not seen yet. It was like watching a stream of water for three hours, looking for a single drop of ink to appear, and since that drop could appear and be gone in a moment, he had to watch constantly.

“What time is it?” DMV asked.

“Who am I, Big Ben?” Joey replied from his reclined position “See those glowing numbers on the dash...”

DMV glanced at the clock on the dashboard, he had not asked the time to know the time, he’d done so simply to lament the boredom he felt.

“Who is this guy, the fuckin’ Donald Trump of computers? Who works this late? He’s a kid, he should be out getting laid for Chrissakes.”

The fact that the ‘kid’ was only five years younger than Sammy himself didn’t occur to him. The picture they had of 'the kid' made him look five years younger still.

“He’s a computer nerd, he can’t get laid.” Joey said from under his arms, which were crossed over his face.

“Naaa. It’s different out here, they’re all computer nerds out here.” DMV said as he saw in his rear view mirror, yet another grey Prius coming into view behind him.

"So? Who they gonna' fuck if there all computer nerds?"

“Computer nerd women.” DMV said as if it were obvious.

As the Prius passed him, he saw the blue sticker in the rear window.

“Hallah-fuckin’-lujah!” DMV exclaimed.

The engine had been running, and DMV wrenched the big Tahoe out into the stream of traffic, cutting off the driver following the Prius. Joey bolted upright and rubbed his face; he grabbed an empty Starbuck’s cup on the dash in front of him and tossed it out the window. A block later, the Prius slowed to a California-style ‘rolling stop’ at the stop sign, and was promptly rear-ended by the Tahoe. Vincent Ko got out of his car, but then saw the driver of the Tahoe point at an empty stretch of curb to their right and out of the flow of traffic. The Tahoe had pulled slowly around him and to the spot he'd indicated.

As Vincent pulled up behind the Tahoe, he saw the driver inspecting its front bumper, clearly embarrassed and annoyed. Vincent got out and surveyed the damage to his own car’s rear bumper, there were cracks in thin parts of the bumper cowling; nothing major but repair prices being what they were, insurance would have to be involved.

Vincent had expected the driver to say something, and when he didn’t Vincent asked “Are you OK? No one hurt?” his words sounding a little ludicrous to his ears, since it was he who was rear-ended.

The driver looked at him oddly. There was no hostility in his demeanor, it was just odd that he was staring at him and saying nothing. Just then, Vincent was startled by a hand closing around his upper arm, and it hurt. He turned to see the primate applying the grip on his arm, and found himself staring into the broad chest of a hulk. His glance followed the line of buttons on the man’s shirt, up to his impossibly wide neck, coming to rest on a clean shaven square jawed face.

“Fuck!” Vincent said under his breath at the pain in his arm.

“No thinks.” the huge man said, sporting an evil smirk “Get in the car Vincent.”

“Do I know you?” Vincent asked reflexively at hearing his name from this stranger “Let go of my arm.”

The strange looked directly into his eyes, Vincent sensed no emotion there, just a blank gaze “I’m not a patient man Vincent” the man said, accentuating his name “and arguing with me is never smart.”

Unbelievably, the grip grew even tighter. Vincent didn’t know what to do, however the issue was solved for him when the grip forced him back into his car. The huge man folded his large frame into the passenger seat of the Prius.

“OK. Buckle up for safety!” the man said grinning, and when it was clear that this behemoth meant it, Vincent fastened his seatbelt. “Now, some ground rules so we understand each other. You’ll drive safely, don’t pass a stop sign, don’t speed, don’t break any traffic laws. Also, and you'll wanna sit up and take a sip of coffee for this one; if you pull anything and we get stopped by a cop, you'll leave me no choice. After I kill him, I’ll have to kill you.” He was still smiling “Makes sense, doesn’t it?” the man said, as if he was helping Vincent with his math homework “See what I’m saying? It’s not rocket science.”

Vincent just stared back at him blankly, suddenly distracted by almost irresistible urge to urinate; he was trying desperately not to piss himself.

“Vincent? You with me? This is important stuff here, you don’t want to miss this.”

Vincent nodded slowly.

“Good. Now finally, and I’m sure this one’s gonna be your favorite. If you do exactly as I say, when I say…” he paused “…nothing happens. We have our little talk, and that’s that.” He spread his hands, palms up. “Isn’t that great? Sounds reasonable, right? I mean if I wanted to kill you, you'd be in the trunk instead of behind the wheel. See what I'm sayin'?”

Another nod.

“Good Vincent. You're a good listener, I like that. So it’s up to you, remember that. If you try to be cute with me, it’s all over…it’ll all be over and there’s nothing I can do about that. That’s just the way it is.” he said with a resigned expression whose sincerity caused a chill to run down Vincent's spine. "If you do what I tell you, we have our talk and nothing happens." As he was making this final point, the smile had disappeared and had been replaced again by the 'dead-eyes' stare.

Vincent stared back at him, fear in his eyes.

The man faced forward "Drive. Follow him." indicating the brown Tahoe.

"I have to take a piss." Vincent said as he started the car and shifted into gear.

"Hold it."

# Chapter 28
# *Contact*

*The Lower Westside of Manhattan, New York City*

Scott unpacked his suitcase and grumbled at the creases, it was so late when he'd entered his hotel room that he'd dropped his suitcase, shed his clothes, set the alarm clock and passed out. He felt like he could use another four hours of sleep, in fact his body, still on California time, thought it was four in the morning. He hung his slacks and shirts in the bathroom and let the steam from the shower build up as he shaved and brushed his teeth. Twenty minutes later, with his stuffed computer bag slung over his shoulder, he left his room grabbing the free copy of USA Today placed in front of his door. As he made his way silently toward the elevators, his mind settled on the thought that his comfortable bed was now about sixty feet behind him and the distance was growing rapidly. With a scowl he hit the elevator button.

*San Jose, California*

"We're going to Santa Cruz on Saturday, you're coming I assume?" Chuck said.

"No thanks." Vincent said, not looking up from his computer monitor.

Vincent had been quiet for the last couple of days, unusually so even for him. Chuck didn't know what it was, but it was definitely something. Occasionally he and Vincent accompanied some of the crew from product testing on mountain bike excursions in the hilly terrain of Santa Cruz. This was usually followed by either pizza at Figaro's or an all-out raid on Sushi Boat #2. This time, Chuck had actually sparked the idea with the product test people, with an eye on ending Vincent's self imposed quarantine.

"Dude. Biking, food…the beer and sake will flow."

"I gotta' pass this time. I have some stuff to do."

"Paaassss…" Chuck said accentuating the word with disdain "Paaassss? What the fuck is THAT.. Paaasss… what the fuck IS that!" he said, doing a fair impression of Vincent's critique the week before. Seeing no reaction, he asked "C'mon man, what's wrong?"

"Nothing's wrong. I'm busy, I have stuff to do." he said, still not looking away from his monitor.

"Bro, you've been keeping to yourself the last couple of days, more than usual." Chuck paused "Something's up, what is it?"

"Nothing's up." Vincent said flatly, eyes locked on the screen "Chuck." he said, finally meeting his friend's gaze.

After a few seconds of silence "Mmmm?"

"Let it go, I'm busy OK, stop bugging me."

"Yeah yeah, I'll drop it." Chuck said, and as he started to leave, turned back and added "For now."

A minute after Chuck had made his retreat; Vincent got up and headed to Diane West's office. He slowed down as he approached her doorway, commanding himself to project a nonchalant demeanor.

"Hey Diane."

"A Vincent Ko sighting!" she said, pointing at him.

He gave a token chuckle "How ya doing?"

"Oh just fine, and you?"

"I'm good, thanks. Hey Scott's away at that boondoggle right?"

The 'boondoggle' in this case was a conference, a trade show really, in New York City at the Javits convention center in Manhattan. People from all over the map converged on NYC once a year, mostly to bore the shit out of each other with ideas and news regarding computer security protocols that specifically related to the financial industry. Scott had been invited to give a fifteen minute overview presentation on ExchangeVault. Although not a software security specialist in the purest sense, he did know a good deal about it, and had spent several years writing code as well. To this audience, he'd have more than enough competence to give a very credible fifteen minutes. Clearly, the time spent at the conference would involve no glamour or glory, however it was an unwritten rule in high tech that anyone traveling to any industry-event, like a trade show or conference, was to be criticized for wasting time and money, as if they were meeting movie stars and dining on wine and caviar, rather than watching soft-core porn on the hotel room pay-per-vision and eating dried-out hotel chicken washed down with something from the mini-bar.

"Yupper. He's flying back Sunday, so I'd imagine you'll see him in here on Monday." Strictly speaking, Diane's responsibilities did not include Scott's travel plans, however she was tasked to keep tabs at all times on ten people in the company, and Scott was one of them. Closer to the point though, she and Scott had a rapport and she would know when and where he was traveling even if he weren't on the 'ten most wanted'.

"OK. Thanks." he said, ducking out as quickly as he'd appeared.

*The Lower West Side of Manhattan, New York City*

At the end of the first day of the conference, Scott felt wiped. His brain-fry was coming along nicely, he judged that by nine that night, assuming he went to the evening session, that he'd lose his ability to safely operate a ball point pen. In his opinion, when he was this spent, he was a danger to himself and others. He'd taken a late flight to New York the previous night and didn't get into his hotel room and asleep until after two in the morning. He had to rise a few hours later to work on his presentation. Even though it was against his nature to 'wing it', when it came to presentations that were not specifically related to his immediate work, that is, presentations at tradeshows and the like, he never seemed to prioritize having it done and in final form before he got on the plane.

He opened the curtains and looked out on the city from twenty floors above, wishing that he wasn't going back to the evening session. A slight smirk formed on his lips.

“Fuck it.”

He decided on impulse that he would skip the boring, and strike out in search of food…Italian food. Suddenly feeling somewhat refreshed, he got cleaned up and headed out of his room and toward the elevator with a just a bit of a spring in his step.

Nothing appealed to him for several long city blocks as he walked in the direction of Broadway, toward Herald Square. He came upon several fine eateries with white table cloths and a wine glasses, silverware and fancy folded napkins neatly arranged on each table. He smiled as he thought to himself 'Back in the Bay Area they roll up the streets at ten, here…its like they’re just getting started at midnight.'

His appetite was working on him and when he could resist no longer, he wandered into Pagliacci e Amanti. He was seated immediately and took a cleansing breath before opening the king-sized bound menu, savoring the enticing smells and unfamiliar surroundings. A waiter came to the table and took his drink order, a lower priced bottle of crisp Pinot Grigio, and cleared the extra place setting before leaving. The menu was divided into five sections: L’antipasto, Il Primo, Il Secondo, Il Contorndo and Il Dolce. Under each heading were four selections, the description of each given in both Italian and English. After carefully perusing the menu, Scott settled on a bowl of stracciatella, followed by pansotti with walnut cream sauce. He'd worry about desert later. The waiter arrived with the wine and went through the tasting ritual. Scott sipped the wine and was immediately impressed; although he was no sommelier, great was great, and this tasted surprisingly great for a thirty five dollar bottle of white wine. He took another long sip and as he was surrendering to the crisp, delicately balanced flavor, he glanced at the wine bucket beside his table; this was not the bottle he ordered.

“Surprised?” a voice came from behind him.

Scott looked up and behind him, not knowing quite what to say. The voice continued, as the speaker walked around to the other side of the table to face Scott.

"No offense but the bottle you ordered…well…it just doesn't cut it." the man said matter-of-factly "You only go around once in this life, you should really treat yourself better."

"It's very generous of you. Thanks." Scott said, with a flat tone that implied 'Sorry, but I'm not gay.'

For a moment Scott thought it logical that this could be the restaurant manager, however this glimmer of a notion didn't survive long, the man seemed more like a…well, he didn't know what, but definitely not a representative of the food and beverage service industry. He was perhaps six feet tall and broad shouldered, made to look broader still by what had to be a very expensive blue suit. The powder blue shirt had thick French cuffs which drew attention to expensive looking gold and onyx cufflinks. Some people you meet seem to…project, Scott reflected, and this guy had it in spades.

"Mind if I sit down for a moment." It wasn't a question as the man seated himself; almost simultaneously a wine glass appeared in front of him. The waiter reached for the bottle but the man politely waved the waiter away.

"May I?" he said motioning toward the wine bucket.

Scott nodded, still confused.

The man poured a half glass and took a thoughtful sip, savored it for a moment then carefully placed his glass down.

"Not bad. I don't drink white wine often, I'm more for reds, but there are a few whites that really have something to say."

At this point, Scott was clueless. Further, he was aware of being clueless. The only suspicions he had so far were negative, he didn't think the guy was making a pass at him, he also didn't feel like the guy was a con man of some sort. He didn't, at least yet, seem crazy in any way, and he sure as heck wasn't a wine salesman. The man's charisma tended to make Scott feel all the more off balance.

"Here for the convention."

"Yeah. You?" Even as he asked the question, Scott realized that the man was making a statement, not asking a question.

"No. No, gratefully I didn't have to endure that many hours on a plane." he said, smiling and shaking his head.

Scott chuckled and nodded in agreement.

"Flying westward is easier, at least the clock is with you. Coming east though, by the time you grab your bag and clear the airport traffic, it feels like you have five minutes to sleep before you have to be up again."

"That's true enough. I'd hate to have to do these back to back like some guys in the industry. I have buddies who for all practical purposes live in airports." Scott said.

The man took a sip of his wine "It's the nature of the beast, isn't it?"

"True dat." Scott grinned and shook his head.

"There are a lot of things about the business that, despite the changes in technologies and the market, stay the same though. Don't you think?" the man said, waxing philosophic.

"Yeah I'd have to agree." Scott said, sipping at his wine and becoming engrossed in the conversation. As a matter of fact, the strangeness of the introduction was quickly fading from his attention. "Some things prove their value and survive, that's for sure. The quality of the people you hire, for instance. People to run the business, people to do the creating, people to coordinate it all and keep it running on a schedule, having good people in all these areas makes the difference, ya know?."

"That's a wise observation." the man said "Also, there are some realities that just 'are', and if you ignore them, you'll fail nine times out of ten. Launching at a particular time of year, price points, service and support. You've got to compete. You've got to pony up, or you'll eventually fail. No?"

"Agreed, and more to your point, they're necessities." Scott said. "In fact, it's ridiculous how often we forget lessons already learned, lessons that cost us money." Scott raised his eyebrows "The issues there are never sexy." Scott chucked and took a sip of wine "The no-brainer aspects. It's funny; manufacturing stuff, customer service stuff, these are the folks that create loyalty, not the flashing lights and sexy paint job that get you the first sale."

"Yeah…call em the 'Facts of Life', the wisdom you get from experience, right? What works, what doesn't…"

Scott nodded as the waiter magically appeared at just the right moment to refill both their glasses.

"So. You a VC?" Scott asked, his best guess at this point was that this man worked for a venture capital investment firm.

“Not really, no.”

“Well you talk like one. No insult intended.” They both laughed at that double entendre.

“None taken.” he chuckled again “Still Scott, we do have a common interest.”

“That so?” Scott asked, still smiling, the amusement of his earlier comment hadn’t quite faded.

“Yeah. All in all it’s fortuitous that you didn’t attend the night program.”

“I really should have, but the guilt is fading.” Scott said, gesturing toward his wine glass. Something in the back of his brain was trying to assert itself, unsuccessfully so far, more from fatigue than the wine.

“Yeah, I know how you feel, it’s not torture is it?” he said with a broad smile.

Scott opened his mouth, then closed it and furrowed his brow as the notion finally registered “So… what… you a recruiter? A partner? An investor? What? I mean you know my name though I’m sure we’ve never met.”

“You may think who I am is important, but for the moment…it really isn’t. What is important is what I have to tell you. Information. Understand?” his voice retained its friendly tone.

“No.”

Eddie laughed “Good. You didn’t get to where you are by bullshitting your way through things.”

“Who are you?” Scott said, with a little more intensity than he wanted to show.

“My name is Eddie, and I’m here to do you a favor believe it or not. Listen to me carefully Scott. Then if you think I’m full of shit, feel free to get up and walk away. It’s no skin off my nose.”

His eyes were boring into Scott’s now, his casual demeanor replaced by a total earnestness. “But if we continue our conversation, you’ll have to pay a little more attention. My time is valuable, as is yours, agreed?” He sat back, clearly prepared to wait for Scott to think it through and make a decision.

Scott nodded.

There was nothing threatening about the guy, yet it was clear that what he had to say was important, to him at least. What did he have to lose by listening? He considered it for a moment…nothing.

"OK. What is it I need to know?"

Over the next ten minutes Eddie explained what was going to happen, and as he did so Scott's face betrayed the expected array of emotions.

After half a minute of silence Scott said "I believe you." but his expression said 'But, you're crazy if you think I'm not going to the FBI.'

Eddie's face was suddenly sympathetic, and the expression confused Scott.

"Look. You have to know that I'd guess…anyone with half brain, would guess your next move."

Scott didn't know what to say to that.

Eddie hadn't told Scott the truth, not the entire truth. He hadn't told him that in fact, he himself was tasked by his capo to oversee the theft originally, and that only when Richie Scala got involved did the wheels come off the wagon. Eddie had cultivated many sources of information, many sources, and one of them had let him know that two of Richie's guys had booked tickets to California; knowing Richie's way of handling people, there was little doubt as to why. What the hell, the reality was that now Richie was in the picture and if they didn't do something then somebody, some working stiff, was probably going to go missing. Considering the amount of money involved, Eddie was fairly confident that Richie would erase any possibility of a trail leading to him. If Richie had cooked this up on his own it wouldn't be Eddie's problem. Instead, Richie muscled in on Mikey Zirella, started salivating at the sight of the amount from this internet thing, found out what he had to, and then whacked him, fearing that Zirella would eventually go to Angelo about the situation. Riche was correct about that, Eddie had no doubt that Zirella would have gone to Angelo after his initial fear of Richie had faded even slightly. In all, the story he was telling Scott was a judicious mixture of fact and omission, principally based on his desire to avoid confusing Scott, who saw this as a moral situation. There were others who saw it simply as business.

"Hey, knock yourself out. Make the call, get the FBI, the cops, whoever you want to call… it's your neck, not mine. I'm not behind it, you don't want to believe that, go ahead and make your calls."

"What's to stop me?"

"Well, this situation, it's like kicking over a nest of hornets. You can take the initiative and kick it over before anyone stops you. But when you do, you're gonna get stung. Of that there is no doubt. Zero."

"Is that a threat?"

Eddie's serious expression gave way to a sympathetic one "Are you still listening to me Scott? These people do what they do, and they know their business. You can go make your phone calls and do whatever your rationale tells you to do, and you know what'll happen in the end?"

"Tell me."

"They'll get what they want, and you'll disappear."

"So you are threatening me."

"For a smart guy, you're not much of a listener. I'm not the bad guy here."

"Well let me ask you something. Why are you here then, what's in it for you?" Scott said smiling a mirthless smile.

"The bad guy, in this case…?"

Scott nodded.

"Not on my Christmas list."

"Really." Scott said, in a sarcastic tone.

Eddie just stared at him.

"So, what then? You win if he loses?"

"Ya know when you do listen, you catch on fast."

"How do I know all of this isn't a crock?"

"I guess you can't know that. Not yet anyway."

"Not yet?"

"When you're lying in the back of a van with hands and feet bound … I think at that point you'll be a believer. Unfortunately at that point, there is nothing you can say that will save you." Eddie said casually "If you need that to convince you, my conscience is clear."

"So you're doing this out of the good of your heart…"

"Not really." Eddie cut him off with a wave of his hand "Our interests, yours and mine, are…'aligned' temporarily. Beyond that, if it saves your life or the life of one of your guys…" Eddie shrugged "…so much the better."

"I can't just let this happen." Scott said after a pause.

"Let me ask you something. Why else would I have told you all this? Why let you in on what's going down? If I was behind it, and it was just about the money, I wouldn't be here. Take a minute and process that." Eddie said, and sat back, taking a sip of his wine.

Scott's eyes were fixed on the table, his eyes darted this way and that, as he carefully sifted through what he'd been told. After a full minute, he looked up at Eddie, another half minute of silence passing while he studied his face for any sign of deception.

"How can I let it happen, it'll ruin us. I've invested two years of my life into this."

"Allow me to advise you Scott, it may be hard for you to trust me, but believe me, I'm as accomplished in this area as you are in yours. There are some 'Facts of Life' that you learn from experience in this thing, and if you make the wrong kind of mistake, the cost is…well… absolute."

"Yeah, so?"

"There's nothing you can do to prevent this, in fact, if you could, and you did, as I said before, you'd ultimately lose anyway." Eddie leaned forward "Hey, there are worse things in life. It's just money."

"It's not just money, we'd be ruined."

"Possibly. Worst case. Maybe not though, it depends on how it's reported to some extent, when and how it comes out. We can get to that later." Eddie said "This is simple, this guy and I, we're like two huge semi's speeding down the highway, and you're just a guy…a guy in a friggin Beetle up ahead. You either get very, very lucky and thread the needle, or badda-bing, you're road kill. Collateral damage. Believe what you want, I'm telling you the best way to handle this because it helps me too. Ultimately, I know you're gonna walk out of here and you're gonna do what you gonna do." Eddie shrugged.

"If, as you say, he's going to come after us after the money changes hands, what's to stop him? I mean, when he finds out he doesn't have the money, not really, wouldn't that just piss him off more? If there was any doubt about what he was going to do, there'd be none when he found out. Right?"

"Well, let's just say that in this case, you can't get out by going right or left, or backward for that matter. The only way to get out of this is to go through." Eddie said, explaining further for a few minutes more. "If this guy and I didn't have a problem, you and I wouldn't be having this conversation, and you'd be in sorry shape. It may not be fair, but it's reality. This is not about the money for you and yours, it's about survival."

"I have to think about it."

"Yeah, I know." Eddie got up to leave.

"How do I get in touch with you?" Scott asked, clearly unprepared for Eddie's abrupt departure.

"Don't worry, I'll get in touch with you." Eddie said "Think it through Scott Munson. Use that big brain of yours, and think it all the way though. That my friend, is the key to survival; you don't wanna be ROM on this one." Eddie said, using tech jargon for Read-Only Memory, that is, a memory chip that doesn't take in information, but instead only puts out information it already has, intimating to Scott that he should try to consider his situation with an open mind. Eddie smiled a friendly smile, and left.

As if on cue, the waiter brought Scott's soup and a new bottle of wine, his guest must have arranged it with the waiter.

After he had opened the bottle and refilled Scott's glass, the waiter said "Sir, the check has been taken care of."

"Who was that guy?"

The waiter completely ignored his question and as he took his leave said "Bon Apetito."

Scott stared into his untouched soup for a few minutes, stunned at the evening's turn of events. Slowly, he picked up spoon and dipped it into the hot broth and egg mixture, as confused as he was, he did feel certain about one thing; his life had just gotten more complicated.

Connected.

# Chapter 29
# *Stratagem*

*The Bronx, New York City*

"You have a nice day Mrs. Ayala, and say hello to Mr. Ayala for me."

"OK. I tell him 'hello' for you." the old woman answered, the creases in her worn face were concentrated at the corners of her mouth and the bottoms of her cheeks, from the years of smiling at her neighbors.

"Jackie, for goodness sake, when are you gonna settle down and get married, huh?"

Jackie's back was to her, but he smiled anyway. He found her periodic appeals amusing.

"Good looking boy like you. You can't meet a nice girl? It's a sin." she said in a lighthearted way. "I have nieces that have no husband yet, beautiful girls."

"Mrs. Ayala, if they're your nieces, I'm sure they are as beautiful as you are, and have a crowd of men around them…"

"Please…" she waved her hand, interrupting him "…you should see the bums they bring home. Bums! Some of them don't even have a job. Some have the long hair…the beard. Please." she shook her head in disapproval "They need to meet someone like you. Nice boy, clean, hardworking; someone has respect for the mother and father." she said in her strange accent, a melding of Spanish and Italian that never quite made peace with each other.

"Mrs. Ayala, you're very kind and I don't deserve your compliments." Jackie said in his thick Bronx accent "You stay well and I'll see you tomorrow. And please say hello to Mr. Ayala for me."

"I tell him. God bless you Jackie, I gonna light a candle for you find a wife."

Angelo Cento sat reading his New York Times, a little cup of espresso in front of him and the sweet smell of the Anisette he'd added to it caressed his nostrils. Though he was reading, he'd heard every word exchanged at the register. Angelo wasn't the guy you wanted present when you didn't show respect to the elderly, in fact, on a few occasions he had 'reached out and touched someone' who'd been blatantly rude to old people from the neighborhood, many of whom had lived there for decades. It was a typical irony, characteristic of many older generation made men; if you didn't pay your debt you might wind up in a dumpster, yet if you mugged an old woman or put your hands on someone's daughter from the neighborhood you might wind up in that same dumpster, minus your cock.

The door opened and in doing so struck the tiny bell attached to the top of its frame and in walked Eddie. The smells of fresh baked bread and chocolate hit Eddie the moment the door closed behind him, he glanced at the incredible array of pastries, breads and cakes, and felt a tremor in his empty stomach. Fortino's Bakery. If some diet guru ever went crazy from self-denial and wound up with his picture in the paper, surrounded by all the food that you 'weren't supposed to eat' smeared on his face and all down the front of his shirt… this was the place where it would go down. Eddie smiled to himself and thought 'I'd love to see Richard Simmons locked up in here overnight.'

"Jackie. Come va?"

"Buono." Jackie smiled "Hey Eddie. How's the cannoli?"

Eddie laughed, made a quick gesture as if he were sipping coffee from a cup, and flicked his head toward Angelo. Jackie nodded back.

"Good morning Ang."

Angelo looked up and smiled at Eddie, simultaneously pushing out the empty chair opposite him with his leg from under the table.

"These Yankees" he said, glancing down at his paper "These fuckin' Yankees. I'd like to have a talk with this guy. It makes no sense."

"The trade?"

"Yeah." he shook his head "This guy couldn't find his ass with both hands."

"Well, what're ya gonna do." Eddie shrugged.

"Yeah." Angelo said in resignation. He folded the paper and picked up his coffee "So how's business."

"Well, the guy, our friend who's not much of a friend."

Angelo nodded.

"I think we were right about that thing, I think the guy decided to take what he wanted."

"We have proof of this?"

"No. It's circumstantial."

"You?"

"I'm convinced."

While it would not be hard to prove that Richie Scala was extorting money from the late Mikey Zirella's sex establishments, it didn't prove conclusively that he was the one responsible for killing him. Added to that, Mikey was not a made guy, or even a half-assed wiseguy. He was connected, for protection, but not a guy who did other business for the family. Considering the delicacy of the Internet theft planned, having Seiden come in for questioning could wind up killing the goose that laid the golden egg. There was too much money at stake to risk that. So the net effect was that the situation was looking more and more like it called for a non-sanctioned solution. Something creative, something like the one Eddie had suggested to Angelo recently.

After a long pause, Angelo said "How's that other thing coming?"

"Plans for our friend, or the thing itself?"

"The thing."

"The asshole sent a couple guys to the west coast to have a talk with somebody."

"What?"

Eddie just stared back at him.

"That fucking jadrool. To arrange something?" Angelo was asking if the people dispatched to California were arranging some kind of cooperation with the family out there.

Eddie shook his head "No way. Not the right guys. Low level guys, two fuckin' lackeys."

"This guy is fucking up three ways to Sunday." Angelo looked disgusted "What about you?"

"Well, I had a talk with a guy from the tech company, he was out here at a conference at Javitz."

Angelo's response displayed the trust he had for Eddie, instead of assuming that Eddie had made matters worse by threatening yet another person who wasn't supposed to know anything about it, until it was too late, he opted for an explanation first.

"How'd that go?" Angelo asked.

"To be honest, I'm not sure yet, but I do think we have a good chance to get this done without that crazy bastard making too many waves." Eddie said meaning Richie Scala.

"This thing has to be handled the right way." Angelo said.

"Somebody decided the rules don't apply to him and badda-beep badda-bop badda-boop… I'm the one who's gotta walk on eggshells."

"Yeah yeah…that's why you got the job, so let's move on. What about your plans, you look into that thing?" Angelo said, meaning the possibility of taking Richie out of the picture in a way that didn't point to them.

Eddie took a breath as Jackie placed a cup of cappuccino in front of him. After Jackie had returned to his counter and resumed his work, Eddie looked at Angelo said slowly "It depends."

"Everything depends." Angelo shot back.

"It depends on Nicky…" he stopped himself, and started over "It depends on how well we can predict how he'll react."

"If you're thinking that it's as simple as letting him know what Richie did, you're gonna disappoint me." Angelo said, a cold stone-like face instantly appeared. It was like the temperature in the room instantly dropped ten degrees.

Eddie chucked "Take it easy, take it easy. What am I, fuckin' oobatz?" he said smiling "I'm talking about his knowing what his guy did, yeah, but also how he'll react to having his problem solved for him. Will he look the other way? Will he let it go or is he gonna look to send a message."

Angelo sat back, contemplating for a moment "Well now that depends."

Connected.

"Exactly." Eddie smiled.

Over the next ten minutes, Eddie described what he had in mind. When he was done, he sat back and waited for a reaction, but Angelo, true to form, sipped his coffee and with an expression on his face as though someone had just told him that oranges were on sale today at the local supermarket.

# Chapter 30
# *Changeling*

"I'll tell you what you do…nothing!"

"All due respect, that cocksucker is in my way."

"Everybody's in your way. Get off your high horse."

"It's not like he's a friend, not a friend of ours."

"Why the fuck are you wasting my time telling me things I already know."

"Because that fuckin' strunz is in my way."

Nicky Trosa gave no response; silence, used judiciously and skillfully, was a potent weapon. He absentmindedly turned the page of the worn Sports Illustrated Swimsuit Edition that someone had left on the table.

"You expect me to cover my nut every week, but you keep my hands tied." Richie said.

"You not gonna make your numbers? Is that what you're saying?" Nicky's eyes showed his impatience with this conversation was growing by the minute.

"What is this punk to you anyway? He's a fuckin' punk…"

"What is he to me? IT'S NONE OF YOUR FUCKIN' BUSINESS WHAT HE IS OR ISN'T TO ME!!" Nicky took a breath and continued "You better watch your step 'cause you're skatin' on thin ice." Nicky was smiling a strange smile, but his eyes possessed a deadly earnestness.

"A'righ a'right, calm down." Richie said, his hands held in front of him in mock surrender.

"Now you're gonna tell me what to do?" Nicky's eyes were like two red hot embers, and the smile was still there.

"That's not what I meant. I'm sorry. I stepped outta line." Richie said, but saw that Nicky's face remained frozen "I was outta line." he repeated in a softer voice, his tail tucked between his legs.

For a minute longer, Nicky remained frozen like a statue, then gradually he started to breath again. Richie decided that changing the subject to make a strategic retreat was the best option to calm things down.

"Zatz?" Richie asked.

Nicky shook his head.

"Fuck."

"Yeah." Nicky agreed.

"No chance?"

Nicky shrugged, then shook his head again.

Matthew Barra, aka 'Zatz' had gotten careless, and was caught in a large heroin deal. The least of his transgressions was that it was clear that he was not planning on paying his tribute, which in many cases carried a death sentence. But that was the least of his offenses; the greatest of his sins was that rather than face the hospitality of thirty years in the penal system, he was going to cooperate with federal prosecutors and give them information about the operations of the organization, testify against family members and enter the federal witness protection program. In short, break his oath of omerta. Although this wasn't an everyday occurrence, it had happened enough that further discussion wasn't necessary, at least not between a capo and his soldier. Of course there was always the chance that some fuck-up could afford them the opportunity to help Zatz meet with his creator before he sang his song in court, but the odds were against them.

"We're done here." Nicky stood and fished his car keys from his pocket.

With many of the other 'members', an embrace and a kiss would have followed Nicky's standing, but it had only been the case with Richie Scala on the day he was 'made', and perhaps once or twice immediately after. He was generally not liked by his associates, as members go, but his track record of earning illustrated more than anything that the family was a business first and foremost.

"Pope… c'mon take a ride down the street." Nicky called to Ronnie Simonetti.

Nicky headed out of the club and a minute later was driving no where in particular. He turned to his soldier.

"I want you to do something for me, and I don't want anybody to know about it. No one, capisci?"

"Yeah."

"Richie's got something under his fingernails. Find out what it is."

"What's the story?"

"He's busting my balls about the kid, ya' know Angelo's guy, but when it comes to an explanation he's bullshitting around. I want to know what's going on."

"Yeah, OK. Any thoughts?" the Pope asked, hoping that Nicky had a suspicion; Nicky was, after all, a pretty sharp fuckin' cookie and had more of a sense for this kind of thing than anyone else the Pope knew.

"You're the guy with the big brain." Nicky said with a smirk.

Ronnie 'The Pope' Simonetti got his nickname from his one truly distinctive physical feature… his forehead. He had a very high forehead, and unfortunately for him, a receding hairline that augmented it further still. Even as a teenager it's appearance bordered on the absurd. At some point, someone made the observation that it made him look like the pope, referring to the large crested ceremonial head piece, the mitre that the pope wore on special occasions. As with most unflattering nicknames, Ronnie's protestations had simply served to ensure that it stuck.

When Ronnie had no reply, Nicky continued.

"È un maiale ingordo. He's eye's have always been too big for his balls. Maybe he's got something he's keeping to himself." Nicky shrugged.

"Ya think?" Ronnie said absentmindedly.

"Yeah I think. But I don't know." Nicky said in an irritated voice.

"I'll take care of it."

As Nicky was dropping the Pope off, down the block from the club, he reminded him as he was getting out of the car "Under the radar."

"I heard you the first time, I'll handle it." the Pope said, closed the car door and made his way back toward the club.

If this was a chance to get rid of that fuckin' Richie, if he was doing something as moronic as holding out on Nicky Trosa, then he'd make it his personal goal in life to find out. The fact that Richie was looking for permission to whack Eddie Ferrara, who was good people, was just gravy on the pasta.

The Pope walked back into the club and casually ambled by Richie, who was bullshitting with Al Cusimano, and as he passed the table he firmly smacked the side of his cell phone into his hand.

"Fuck this thing." He stared at the display, which of course looked normal "Come on you cunt." he said with a little irritation. No need to overact here. "Hey Richie, gimme your cell for a second I gotta call my goumada."

Richie handed his phone over and the Pope dialed a number from memory; wiseguys on the outside of prison bars don't write things down, and don't store numbers in their cell phones.

"Hey, it's me."

'What's up?' the voice on the other end said.

"Hey I'm gonna be late."

'That's nice. What are you talking about?'

"Yeah, I gotta get another cell, a friend lent me his that's why the different number."

'OK, I have the number. Trap and Record, or just Trap?'

"Yeah both are good."

'This number you're calling from now, right?'

"Exactly, exactly honey."

'Understood. Sweetheart.'

"OK I'll call you when I'm done. Alright? Don't be upset."

'Jesus it looks like rain outside. Fucking drive home is gonna' take twice as long.' the voice on the other end said, as he pressed his head against his office window. The essential information having been exchanged, he waited for the Pope to finish his bullshit routine for whomever the dumb fuck was who had willingly handed his cell phone over.

"OK." He felt like saying 'I love you.' which would have been more realistic, but he would only go so far with a guy on the other end of the line, acting or no. Richie and Al were still knee-deep in bullshit, and the Pope took the opportunity to really dial his goumada's number, when it rang the second time he hung up. He didn't think Richie would be paranoid or let's face it, smart enough, to check the number he'd dialed but if he did he didn't think he'd go deeper than the last number, which of course now really was his goumada's.

This would cost him a few beans, but he'd have the list with all the numbers Richie dialed and received, how long the calls went, and the most expensive part, recordings of the conversations he had.

"Mark my words, she's gonna fill my fuckin' ear about it later." the Pope said as he handed Richie back his cell phone.

"So?" Richie looked at him as if he were insane "Give her a smack in the mouth."

"Naaa. I like this girl. She's a nice girl." Besides the Pope thought, 'I don't feel the need to hit women like some needle-dicks I know.'

"Grow a pair…" Riche said "…I'm telling ya', they need it once in a while. What's right is right, besides, once in a while it turn's em on."

"Yeah, you're probably right at that." the Pope said, patting Richie on his shoulder as he walked towards the tiny bathroom at the rear of the club.

"Fuckin-A I'm right."

Jacob Seiden stood on the steps of the New York Public Library, squinting as he scanned the torrent of faces climbing the steps. Like many in the software industry, he had an analytical nature. As he stood and surveyed the torrent of people moving here and there, he thought about chaos theory and the nature of randomness; a young Asian woman, who couldn't weigh more than eighty five pounds, was followed by a mountain of a man who couldn't weigh less than two hundred and seventy. The man was nearly twice the height of the young woman, and to his surprise the hulk walked right up to him.

"Mr. Seiden." It wasn't a question.

Jacob just looked up, opened his mouth and closed it again.

"I'm a friend of Eddie's. Come with me please." Philly said, and turned without saying more, heading back down the stairs.

Five minutes later they were in Philly's car, heading uptown.

"Where are we going?"

Silence. The man looked like he barely fit behind the wheel of the Escalade, not a small vehicle to begin with. Jacob resigned himself to the fact that he was going to go where ever this walking Sherman tank was taking him, and worrying about it was 'inefficient'.

Ten minutes later Philly double parked in front of Milano Wine Merchants. As he led Jacob into the storefront he tossed the keys to a kid who couldn't have been more than fourteen, leaning against the front of the building. The young man hopped in and backed the car, at reckless speed, into a tiny driveway that looked barely wide enough to accommodate the large SUV.

"Jacob." said Eddie, extending his hand.

"Eddie." Jacob said, accepting the handshake, but wearing a worried expression.

"So he reached out to you, did he?"

"Yes. I left the office late, and he was waiting a block away." Jacob said, the words rushing out, he was clearly afraid "He knew about the project; he said that it was still to go forward and asked if there were any problems."

"What did you say?"

"What did I say? I said there are no problems! I may not be psychic but I know what I sensed his reaction would be if I said there were any problems. Did I misinterpret?"

Eddie paused, smiling, "No, I'd say your senses are working perfectly."

"I fail to see the humor." Jacob said, somewhat light-heartedly.

"Same guy then…that you saw with Mr. Zirella that day, the one in the car?"

"Yes yes, the same man."

Eddie lowered his head in thought.

"Mr. Zirella, I never got the impression he was a… what'll I call it? Leg-breaker?" Jacob said softly "But this man, I feel like I should take a vacation, get out of town for a while. Perhaps a long while."

Eddie shook his head.

"My brother lives in Israel, I could go stay with him."

In a very casual tone Eddie said "Naaa. I'd advise against that. He find you and kill you."

Jacob looked at him, speechless.

"Believe me Jacob, people always think they can hide." Eddie said, then added "Which makes it twice as disturbing when they turn a corner and get popped, just like that. Believe me. You could hide in an ice-hut on the Siberian tundra and you'd be found."

Jacob's look of surprise turned into one of despair.

Eddie smiled at him "Fuhgetaboutit. You're in good shape."

"How, may I ask, do you come to that conclusion?" Jacob asked sarcastically.

"Because you're going to give him what he wants."

"I am?"

"Sure. Well almost." Eddie said, smiling.

"You'll have to explain that. But first, suppose he decides to get rid of me after the fact?"

"Won't be any 'after-the-fact'." Eddie said enigmatically.

"Meaning?"

"A little bit of situational Aikido."

Jacob just looked at him quizzically.

"Let's let him do the heavy-lifting. We don't need to exert any energy here if we know what we're doing. He'll provide the momentum, and all we have to do is pivot. Capisci?"

"In the abstract I suppose."

"Here is the information you need, make sure that the module incorporates these numbers." Eddie said, sliding a flash stick across the table, and then leaning in "And for all of our sakes, check the numbers a few times after you enter them. One wrong digit could ruin our day."

"Yes. I'll be very careful."

"The file is encrypted, the password is 'Halakha'."

Jacob smiled at the reference. "Seriously?"

Connected.

Eddie returned the smile. “Jacob, I’m always serious.”

# Chapter 31
# Commission

*San Jose, California*

The sun was setting behind The Tech Museum of Innovation in downtown San Jose, and people were hurrying, or at least what passed for hurrying on the west coast, to and fro. The Christmas in the Park display, which occupied the entire grassy island in front of the Fairmont Hotel, looked completely unremarkable in the daylight. In just an hour or so, as dark descended, it would be transformed by a million colorful lights into the traditional spectacle for children and adults alike, an army of father's with toddlers perched on their shoulders.

Just to the south of the display area, at the corner of Market and San Carlos was a well known local Italian restaurant, and if you sat at the counter you could watch the cooks do their thing; the separate kitchen that was hidden from view contained dish washers, storage, a tiny office and little else. Out in front though, hungry patrons dipped pieces of sourdough bread into extra virgin olive oil and balsamic vinegar, while watching huge sauce pans with pounds of fresh mushrooms being doused with a half bottle of wine, salt and sticks of butter. Large perfectly cooked slabs of meat: ribs, chops, steaks and fillets being removed from the large inferno of an oven. Waiters in bow ties moved in and out of the line, retrieving their dishes and in some cases plating them with sides, as they exchanged quips with the line cooks. Organized chaos. The noise level inside the cavernous interior of the establishment was decidedly quieter than being on the runway at the nearby Mineta airport. To offset the cacophony of chatter and the background music courtesy of Dean Martin, Frank Sinatra, Tony Bennett and others, was a symphony of smells. The same open architecture that allowed the sound to travel, similarly allowed the odors from the sauté pans to waft throughout the space; one seemed to perfectly balance the other.

At the last two counter seats, the ones nearest the front window, and nearest the broiler, sat two obvious 'techie types', quietly slurping soup from coffee mugs. They perspired a little, perhaps from the red pepper flakes that gave the soup its kick, but more from the bath of infrared being radiated from the broiler eight feet away.

"Shhhhhh." Scott said.

Vincent said nothing.

"Shhhhhhhhhhhh." he persisted.

"Yeah." Vincent said, knowing Scott would keep it up until the end of time unless he got a reaction.

"Well, we come down here for dinner, what… a few times a year? I figure you're either in a festive mood, or you have some news to tell me…" Scott stopped and looked at his friend seriously "Vincent! You're gay!"

"Cut it out."

"Don't let them judge you Vincent." Scott said earnestly "You go girl!"

Vincent didn't even smile. Scott knew he'd hit a double at least, and not even a smirk. Something was wrong.

"OK then. Let's have it."

"Have what?"

When Scott said nothing, Vincent looked up at him and saw the face Scott reserved for 'Don't waste my fucking time.' situations. It was a rare occasion when that face was seen, but, he supposed, this definitely qualified as one of them.

"Something happened." Vincent mumbled.

"Yeah…?"

"I'm not supposed to tell anyone. I don't know what to do."

"Something at work? Personal? What?" Scott said, keeping his voice neutral.

"Yeah."

"Yeah which?"

"Yeah both."

Over the next fifteen minutes Vincent relived for Scott, what had happened: the hulk, the drive, the 'talk'. Although he was embarrassed and felt emasculated by his abduction, he never the less left no detail or emotion out of his narrative. Predictably, the emotion woven throughout the experience, and the one most present in Vincent's eyes now, was fear. Then again, no one had ever accused the hulking man who'd paid the visit to Vincent, of not knowing how to do his job.

Scott felt numb. Although he knew that his experience in the restaurant in New York had been something he'd have to deal with, over the weekend he'd put it out of his mind. His return to work and its familiar surroundings also reinforced the sense of normalcy. Now, unexpectedly, there was a grim reminder of the reality and the gravity of the situation he found himself and Vincent in.

Misconstruing Scott's silence, Vincent said "I'm not making this up. You know I'm telling you the truth? I mean, you believe me right?"

"Unfortunately, I know it's true." Scott said.

"They threatened you too?"

"Not exactly." Scott said.

"What happened, what'd they do to you?"

"Bought me a very expensive dinner." Scott said.

Vincent just stared, not sure if Scott was serious.

Scott turned to face him fully, raised his eyebrows and said "The wine was even better than the food, I'd even say exceptional."

"Dude." Vincent opened his mouth, then just sighed in frustration "Did we switch subjects here? What the fuck are you talking about?"

"A guy paid me a surprise visit too, while I was in New York at the conference."

"He bought you dinner?"

"Yeah."

"What did he say?

"He predicted that what happened to you would happen to one of us."

"So he did threaten you." Vincent said with a note of satisfaction.

"Not really, he said that he and his friends were not behind what was going down, and that there was a way to protect ourselves."

"How's that?"

“Well, as it happens, the guy I met is no friend of the guy who is behind it, and he’d like nothing better than to settle an old score I guess. He said… something like ‘our interests are aligned’ in this. Something like that."

“So we don’t have to go through with it, he’s going to help us.”

“No and yes.”

Now it was Vincent’s turn to arch his eyebrows.

“We have to go through with it, and he’s going to help us.” Scott said.

“So either way we’re stuck. Why are you talking about this guy like he’s helping us? We have to help him steal the money; he’s the same as the other guy. What the hell’s the difference?”

“The difference is if we go with him, no one gets hurt and I guess this other guy is out of the picture somehow, or at least no longer a threat to us. He didn’t elaborate and I didn’t ask.”

“He told you he’d chop you up in little pieces if you didn’t play ball, right?”

“Not exactly, no.”

“What did he say?”

“Basically, he said do whatever I thought was best.”

“Now you’re shitting me.”

Scott chucked morosely “I shit you not. He didn’t say not to go to the cops, only that it would result in one of us disappearing, that this bad guy had friends everywhere. He said I didn’t have to believe him, that I could just either go to the cops or cooperate with the bad guy, or do whatever. Basically he was saying that the theft was going to happen, nothing was likely to stop that now, that it was only money and that it was fortunate for me, for us I guess, that this guy was not his best friend, because it’s unlikely that he would leave a ‘loose end’ that has the ability to testify in court.”

“Let me guess, I’m the ‘loose-end’?”

Scott nodded.

“Are we being naïve here, I mean maybe they’re together, and working us from both ends? Good cop, bad cop.”

“You watch too much TV.”

“So you believe him?”

"I can't be sure." Scott shook his head "But there was something about the guy…my sense, and it hasn't changed over the weekend, I think he's being truthful. I know that sounds absurd but…I don't know…I just get that feeling."

Neither of them said anything for a minute, as their soup mugs were taken away and two huge plates of steaming spinach gnocchi took their place.

"What exactly does this guy want us to do?" Vincent asked.

"The account numbers those guys gave you?"

"Yeah."

"Just a little modification."

The pasta, enticing and perfectly prepared, remained untouched. Vincent was looking at his shoes, deep in thought. He looked up to his friend.

"What do you think we should do?"

Scott exhaled heavily and said in a soft voice, as if he was saying a prayer "Go with my guy."

"He have a name?"

"Eddie."

"Gave you his number?"

"Nope."

"Well then how are you going to get in touch with him?"

"I don't know. He said he'd be in touch with me." Scott said shaking his head "Fuck it. We're in some kind of shit Vincent, let's just take a few minutes and enjoy the food…a little mental holiday bro."

Vincent tossed some fresh grated cheese onto his dinner, speared a piece of gnocchi with his fork and stuffed it into his mouth. With his free hand, he reached for the wine list.

"Fuck it."

"Word." Scott agreed.

# Chapter 32
# *Disclosure*

*The Bronx, New York City*

Eddie, Philly, Vin and Tony D. emerged from the darker interiors of the social club and out into the street. All four of them reached for their sunglasses as they squinted into the winter sun. The air was clear and crisp, and they looked like that scene from the beginning of Tarantino's Reservoir Dogs as they walked down the block to Vin's car. All that the other three knew about the meeting Eddie had a few minutes ago with Angelo Cento was that it was short and that Angelo didn't look happy, hard as it was to tell when Angelo was happy. No one asked Eddie for detail, but each of them assumed he'd give it to them at the right time.

"Where to?" Vin asked.

"The Shore Inn." Eddie replied.

"Pete?"

"Yeah."

Vin merged onto the Cross Bronx Expressway.

"Let's have a drink when we're there, I need to run something by you guys."

"You buyin'?" Vin asked, trying unsuccessfully to hide a grin.

"Vin I know you have money in your pocket. Know how I know?"

"That bulge is my cazzo, stop looking at it you're creepin' me out."

"Oh, I thought it was a roll of dimes."

Philly cackled at that.

"Anyway, I can tell that you have to have money in your pocket, because you sure ain't wearing it anymore." Eddie said, picking at Vin's vanity.

"Yeah yeah, you're not gonna bait me Eddie, so save it."

"I mean you used to dress so nice, we looked like a pack of dogs compared to you. I never said anything because, ya know, I got my pride." Eddie said "Tony, am I right or am I right?" he called over his shoulder to Tony in the back seat.

"I thought we agreed not to talk about it in front of him?" Tony said in a reasonable tone.

"Not talk about what?" Vin said hotly "Fuck you! You dress like shit Tony, and you know it." Vin took the bait faster than even Eddie thought possible.

"What are you fucking deaf Vinny? That's what Eddie's saying. You don't listen, that's your problem."

"See these fucking shoes asshole…" Vin said.

"Oh god, not with the fucking shoes again!" Philly pleaded "How many times I have to hear about your fucking footwear? Like that day you had to climb that crane? Jesus it's worse than doing a job with Donatella Versace with your fuckin' shoes. It's a little gay Vin, this thing you got for footwear."

Vin exploded "Gay! I'll put a bullet through your fucking head you…" Vin stuttered in anger "…you're like a fucking dump truck with lips."

Philly tried to interrupt, but Vin wouldn't have it "And you should be the last one to open your yap about the way I dress, you wouldn't know a decent suit if it bit you in that big fucking ass of yours!"

"You're taking this way too personal Vin, Jesus H. Christ, we're just trying to let you know something, and you have to make it a big fuckin' opera…switch to fuckin' decaf already!" Eddie pleaded. After a few seconds of silence he added "Again, you bring up the shoes…and those shoes don't match what you're wearing at all...."

"I tell you motherfuckers what…" Vin said, his voice low but white hot with anger "we get to Pete's I'll buy the drinks, if you do one god damn thing for me."

In the back seat, Tony D. looked at Philly, as if to say, 'That was easy.'

"What's that?" Philly asked innocently.

"SHUT THE FUCK UP!"

All three of them responded, talking on top of each other in low tones that it was no problem, he should have just said so if it was bothering him, and so forth.

In the back seat Tony D. smiled to himself, his friend Eddie was a fucking genius. It was really fun to watch.

They arrived at the Shore Inn, went inside and took seats at the bar. Eddie went back into the kitchen to see Pete. Vin, Phil and Tony made small talk and after ten minutes Eddie emerged from the back room and motioned for the other three to sit with him at a table in the corner of the room.

“The prick sent two people to California to fuck with Angelo’s business. The civilian he sent them after..." Eddie shook his head "...stupid. As usual.”

“What are you talking about?” asked Vin.

“Zirella. It was Richie the prick. The clubs weren’t his only interest. In fact, they weren’t even his main interest, they were gravy.” he looked at Philly “Remember the guy you picked up for me at the Library?”

Philly nodded.

“He’s the key, and he’s the one Richie really wants.”

“How’s that?” from Tony D.

“There’s an internet company, they’re kind of a glorified escrow company. They specialize in online transactions; very large transactions.” Eddie said, taking a moment to look at each of them.

Tony D. shrugged, as if to say ‘What’s the angle?’

“Zirella had a contact in the company that was contracted to do the software security for them.”

They looked at each other, but no one said anything.

Eddie continued “See, if the company that does the security of the software is in your pocket, then you can basically put some hooks in there to route the money to a specific account, then essentially erase the trail. The money disappears and no one knows where. It’s like having the security guard at Fort Knox in your pocket.”

“But it’s not real money, it’s just internet money.” Tony said.

"Tony, it's the same thing, there's no difference." Eddie said with a little condescension.

"Yeah? Since when?"

"Since the Internet."

Tony said nothing for a few seconds, and then whispered "Holy shit."

"My thoughts exactly." Eddie agreed.

"How do you erase the trail though, don't they keep records of all that. fucking ehhh 'backups' or whatever they call them."

"That's the real genius of this thing, it's not so much the grab itself, that's the easier part of it, it's the way the trail is erased, in fact it's the way it's created to begin with. Anyway, no disrespect but it gets technical."

"How much are we talking about?" from Philly.

Eddie made a gesture indicating that the information doesn't leave the table, and said "Four."

"Four?" Tony asked with a furrowed brow "So what. Four large?"

Eddie slowly shook his head 'no'.

"Fuck me." Tony said in a low and calm voice, but his face gave evidence of his surprise "Four?"

Eddie just stared at him.

"Four." Tony repeated.

"Yeah."

"Get the fuck outta here."

Eddie just stared at him some more.

After a long pause, Tony spoke, and when he did the question he asked was exactly the one they were thinking at that moment "Why are you telling us this?"

"If anyone knew I was telling you…click, bang and I'm gone." he said looking with guileless eyes at Tony "But."

"There's always a 'but'." Tony said to Philly.

"There are extenuating circumstances."

"What circumstances?"

Eddie paused "Let's get another round and I'll tell you."

As if on cue, all three looked at Vin.

As he rose reluctantly to order another round, Vin smiled and said "Fuck you all."

A minute later Pete came out from behind the bar and put the drinks down on the table, announcing somewhat formally "Gentlemen, these are with Vin." absolutely straight-faced.

The three of them cackled a bit, then toasted each other "Salute", and took long pulls on their drinks.

"So. Circumstances." Eddie continued "I've decided to ask Antonia to marry me."

The three smiled and there was a subdued outpouring of congratulations.

"Thanks." he looked at each of them "But I've got to tell you something, and again, I'm telling you something that could mean my head, and probably Antonia's too."

Smiles disappeared, replaced by concerned stares. He waited but no one moved a muscle, hanging as they were on his every word.

"I won't marry her and be in the life. I have my way of looking at this thing, and risking my own skin…that's one thing."

They sat in silence for a full minute, each considering the changes that Eddie's news implied, and when the silence was broken, it was Tony who asked the question on everyone's mind "So what are you planning to do?"

"I'm going to take my share of the money from the internet thing, and give Angelo what's his." Eddie said, then after a moment "Then I'm gonna' take care of that pain in the ass Richie and my problem at the same time."

Tony D. said "Eddie, whatever I can do to help you, you know I'm gonna do it."

Philly and Vin expressed their support as well.

"What about Angelo?" Philly asked.

"Yeah, that's a little tricky. I don't want to put him in a position where he has to make a call, at least not publicly."

"Well then what's the plan?" Tony D. asked.

"Let's deal with first things first. First thing we have to do is pay off those two that Mr. Sunshine sent out west. If Bags and DMV aren't out of the way they might get vindictive and go tell some stories. Also though, none of us need Batman and Robin doing a number on one of these guys out in California, that's a fuckin' federal case waiting to happen." Eddie said.

"You know it was them?"

Eddie nodded.

"Well, I'm up for a ride to the country with the Dynamic Duo." Vin said.

"Not this time." Eddie shook his head.

"Oh?" Tony asked.

"Nope." Eddie smiled; the explanation took only a few minutes.

The four got back in the car and as Vin pulled away he applied a little too much gas; the sound of loose gravel hitting the custom painted and hand waxed quarter panels prompted a scowl.

Connected.

# Chapter 33
# *Cartography*

Joey Bags sat in a black vinyl bucket seat that was set on the concrete floor of the long defunct Jacobi Bros. Tool & Die building. The seat was from a '67 Chevy Camaro and had probably been in the building for at least two decades. The inside of the structure was cavernous; the ceiling was three stories above the floor, with no intervening floors, and the length and breath of the building could almost accommodate a regulation indoor soccer field. Much of the space was filled however, with rusting machines of nondescript function, along with the litter of broken rusting tools, rusted scrap metal and cardboard boxes that were soaked, falling apart and brimming over with refuse. The place had a strong sour-musty smell that was impossible to ignore or become accustomed to.

Joey was thumbing through a Hustler magazine and beside him were a New York Daily News, a glossy brochure from Pyramid Porsche of the current model Boxster, and the current Motor Trend magazine purchased recently at the San Francisco International Airport. Next to the stack of reading material was an empty Starbuck's cup, the cryptic shorthand Sharpie'd onto the brown recycled cardboard sleeve identified it as the remains of a Venti Non-Fat Latte. About three feet to the left of the empty cup was a puddle of reddish foul smelling liquid, and directly above that puddle, suspended upside down from the ceiling by a long chain attached to his ankles, was the bound and gagged Crazy John Morozov. Joey Bags and DMV had both taken part in the beating of Crazy John, getting what they wanted in less than half an hour. DMV was out on an errand retrieving a package that belonged to Morozov, well… it didn't belong to Morozov any more. Joey Bags sat, read and waited for DMV's return; his considerable bulk looked absurd perched in the little bucket seat on the floor. Even though Crazy John had been told repeatedly that they only wanted the drugs, and lent credibility by threatening the consequences if he were to seek retribution when he was freed, they were going to kill him once DMV returned with the package.

Morozov was a bloody mess from the shoulders down, in this case 'down' was his shoulders to the top of his head; the puddle was a mixture of blood, urine and a still running steam of saliva that oozed from around the gag in his mouth as he had screamed in fear and pain. He had been moaning loudly for about five minutes when an irritated Joey exhaled heavily, struggled to his feet and from a nearby pile of refuse grabbed a dirty length of wooden two by four with two rusty nails protruding from it's end. He planted himself in front of the source of his irritation, raised the two by four above his head and struck downward, the end of the beam with the nails hitting Crazy John squarely on his testicles.

"SHUT THE FUCK UP ALREADY! You're giving me a headache."

Crazy John made a tortured unnatural sound as he tried to contain his whimpers of pain. Seemingly mollified having vented his frustration, Joey sat back down, picked up the Hustler, and resumed his 'reading'.

A few minutes later Joey Bags suddenly felt a sharp and painful impact at the back of his head. He had excellent reflexes in spite of his bulky physique; he sprang to his feet and spun around with lightning speed. However his brain had not caught up yet, so his hand had not moved toward the nine millimeter Smith' tucked into his belt at the small of his back. He was now in a position to see Tony D., Vin, and Eddie who was holding a pistol leveled at him and obviously the cause of the pain in his head.

Eddie smiled at him "You waited too long."

Joey didn't react, not a word nor as much as a twitch of a muscle. They both knew that Eddie was referring to Joey's delay in reaching for his weapon, and they both also knew Eddie was absolutely correct.

Suddenly, the suspended Mr. Morozov started to shake violently; he didn't make a sound but just shuddered steadily for about thirty seconds and then went quiet. Tony walked over to him and felt for a pulse on his neck. Feeling none, he wiped his blood stained fingers onto leg of the dead man's pants.

"Well, he's gone." Tony D. said evenly to Eddie "I guess they got a little carried away."

"Ah well, mistakes happen." Eddie sighed, and shot Joey Bags in the heart.

Joey collapsed like a pile of lead bricks; they left his weapon in his belt.

A minute later, DMV came walking into the building slightly bent over, and as he got closer, Eddie could see Philly behind him. Philly had DMV by his hand somehow, twisted as it was behind his back. He looked like he was in a lot of pain but coping with it for pride's sake. Philly was wearing a pair of leather work gloves, and in his free hand he held DMV's pistol. Once he was close enough to see Joey lying dead on the floor, the large expanding red stain on the chest of his shirt, DMV turned white with fear. To his relief, Philly released his fingers from the iron grip as Eddie spoke to him.

"Look in that corner tough-guy, and tell me what you see?"

DMV cautiously turned his head to look in the corner behind him, and as he did so, Eddie shot him in the stomach; DMV fell down screaming and clutching at the wound.

Eddie stepped over him and aimed at his head, firing again.

Philly shoved DMV's pistol back into its holster on the dead man's ankle, then with the gloves still on, reached into a deep pocket inside of his jacket and produced a very large syringe filled with a clear yellowish liquid.

"Drano?" Eddie asked.

"Liquid-PLUMR. It was on sale." Philly said reasonably as he stepped over to Morozov's corpse, struck downward with the needle through Morozov's pants and injected the liquid into his scrotum.

"Ouch! " Vin said.

"His car outside?" Eddie asked Philly, who nodded in return.

“Let’s hope this poor bastard wasn’t bullshitting them.” Eddie said and carefully retrieved DMV’s car keys from his pants pocket.

Out in the parking lot, they opened the trunk, and a minute later found a hidden compartment behind the spare tire that held eight quarter-kilo clear plastic packages of heroin. The four men walked two blocks north with the heroin in a Macy’s shopping bag carried by Philly. When they reached Vin’s car, they got in and Philly sat in the front passenger seat, shopping bag on his lap.

“Casa de Bastardo?” Vin asked.

Eddie nodded.

The car pulled over to the curb around the block from the apartment building that Richie Scala called home. From this vantage point, at the rear of the building, Richie’s window could be seen. It was dark inside, and looked as though no one was home. None of the four had ever been inside the apartment, and it was decided that if Richie had installed any security devices there was little they could do about it. It was a risk that had to be taken. The four of them all emerged from the car, walked over to a spot where the street light cast a dark shadow, and hopped the chest high wrought iron fence that separated the courtyard in the rear of the apartment building from the sidewalk beyond.

At the rear door Vin said “This is an old building, I don’t think we’ll find cameras, but let’s take it easy.”

“Agreed.” from Eddie.

Philly removed a very large screwdriver from his inside jacket pocket but Eddie held his hand up. He reached down and tried the door handle. It wasn’t locked. He turned his head slowly and smiled at Philly.

'Fuck you.' Philly smiled back.

Eddie slowly opened the door a crack, stuck his head in and peered around the corner and into the hallway. It was empty. He took the shopping bag from Philly and entered the hallway, followed by Vin and Tony D., who quietly shut the door behind them. Philly hopped back over the fence and walked at a leisurely pace around the block and sat down on a bench at a bus stop. He had a perfect view of the front entryway of the building. Inside, the other three found their way to the elevator and took it to the sixth floor. Vin and Eddie emerged from the elevator, the faint smells of paint and some sort of cleaning fluid were noticeable. The hallway was painted in two tone blue; dark blue on the lower half and light blue from eye level on up. The hallway itself was carpeted so their footsteps would be unnoticeable, but of course the doors all had peepholes. Tony D. stayed in the elevator as the doors closed, pulled a newspaper that was folded in his pocket, and would ride the elevator for the few minutes that Eddie and Vin were in the apartment.

"No sound, we move straight in." Eddie said to Vin.

Vin followed him down the hallway to the apartment door marked '6F'. Vin picked the lock on the door knob, and then the dead bolt. He took his time, trying not to leave scratches that could later identify the lock as having been picked. When the door swung open, Eddie stepped in, immediately followed by Vin who quietly closed the door. Eddie quickly found the bedroom went straight over to the dresser and removed the bottom two drawers. He produced a roll of silver duct tape from his jacket pocket and began taping the bags of heroin onto the bottom recessed surfaces of the drawers. Vin followed suit with the second drawer. They wiped their finger prints off of the tape and plastic bags with their sleeves, flipped the drawers over, arranged the contents and then slipped them back into place.

As soon as the drawers were replaced, Eddie and Vin headed for the front door; on the way Eddie stepped into the kitchen picked a drawer at random, and found it had several dish towels in it. He lifted up the rear-most pile and placed DMV's car keys underneath. He closed the drawer, and quietly exited the apartment.

Five minutes later they picked up Philly a block west of the building and faded anonymously into the nighttime traffic.

# Chapter 34
# *The Uncertainty Principle*

*San Jose, California*

Scott left work early. It was still light outside, and being winter, it was cold, by California standards anyway. It couldn't be more than fifty five degrees and as the sun set it would get colder still. Scott smiled to himself…California. This was beach chair weather where he grew up in Minnesota. Back home at this time of year, it was so cold that if you weren't careful things on your body might inadvertently snap right off. In spite of his early departure from work, he headed to his favorite wireless working office-away-from-office, The Coffee Terrorists, and looked for a free table near an electrical outlet. There was only one free, it was near the entrance. He considered the trade-off; be distracted by the stream of people walking from the door to the register but be able to operate his laptop in Performance Mode which ate power, or sit in the back of the shop where it was quiet and operate in slower battery operated Travel Mode. He opted for the peace and quiet of the back area and went out to the little patio area, which to his glee, was empty.

Foregoing his usual Grande Osama Bin Latte for a simple Venti Qadhafi Americano, he spread out his materials, fired up his laptop and set about reducing the size of his inbox. Twenty minutes into this mindless orgy of electronic communication, he was startled by a voice behind him.

"So?"

He flinched, surprised since he hadn't noticed anyone come into the patio area. Turning he saw Eddie sitting behind him, with a half consumed cappuccino, and his first thought was that if it was half empty, how long had Eddie been sitting there?

"So." Scott returned.

"What do you think?" Eddie gestured to the sky "Me? I say it's gonna rain. That guy on the news is full of shit."

“What do you want?” Scott asked, neutral, not challenging.

Eddie leaned forward “What do you want?”

“I want this to go away.”

“It’s going to, one way or the other.” Eddie said “It’s just a question of how.”

Scott just stared at him.

Eddie stood “Well, if you don’t believe me, you don’t believe me.” he said, buttoning his jacket “I’ll find a way to get the guy, it just would have been easier for both of us if it was with you.”

Scott still said nothing.

“You’re on your own.” Eddie said, as he patted Scott on the shoulder. He walked out of the shop at a leisurely pace, and was about to cross the street when he felt a tug at his elbow.

“How do I know?” Scott asked “How do I really know?”

“You can’t. This business, the circles that I travel in, it’s usually done this way...a way that you can’t really know. It’s like the inverse of your business.”

“But then how do you know you’re not going to get ripped off?”

“Simple. There are rules, you break em’ and get caught, you’re gone.” Eddie said, noticing a sour look creeping across Scott’s face “Listen, you’re a logical guy right? It’s the only way to make sure people like… like the people I deal with, it’s the only way to make sure that they don’t steal from each other, not too much anyway." Eddie chuckled "They steal, they die. In a way it’s the only thing that they truly understand.”

After a few moments pause, Scott said “OK, come back inside and let's go over it until I know it cold.”

The two returned to the table. It was a short conversation.

# Chapter 35
# *Handshake*

*www.exchangevault.com, Cyberspace*

ExchangeVault's services came online at precisely seven minutes after nine o'clock on a Monday morning. The first transaction was a large one. One designed by the sales and marketing people, one that could be referenced and exploited later to gain the trust of future prospective clients. It's easier to gain that trust when you can show the corporate logos of customers you've served and they happen to be well known companies. So this first 'showcase' transaction involved Mediex, a company that was one of the removable-storage-media industry's leaders, they made compact discs, DVD's, magnetic tape cartridges and the like. The other principal, the buyer in this case, was Parker Content Co., a start up company that had a new twist on delivering content to educational institutions, the military and other government agencies. All of the financial transactions and accounting would be handled online by ExchangeVault, including transfer of the four million dollars from the Parker Content's bank to the Mediex's, for the large shipment of security-enhanced optical discs along with the licensing fee and some development software. ExchangeVault also functioned as the software escrow company in this transaction, keeping a copy of the Mediex source code in case they ever went bankrupt.

At twenty one minutes after nine, the electronic handshake that represented the transfer of funds took place; it went smoothly.

*San Jose, California*

Connected.

At thirteen minutes after ten, Ray Phillips, the EFT service representative at Mediex's bank, called his contact at ExchangeVault, Suri Poria to ask when the funds would be wired.

"They were wired at nine twenty."

"We didn't receive it."

"I'm looking at the confirmation."

"You're looking at it?"

"Yeah, I have it in front of me. I'm looking at it."

The two exchanged relevant information that each had.

"Well can you go check again? Maybe your notification system had a hiccup."

"Never happened before, but anything's possible. Hold on."

Several minutes pass.

"Nope. I got it from the source. Nothing was received."

"OK. Let me check everything out on our end. I'll give you a call back."

"Sounds good."

ExchangeVault's product had redundant systems in place to keep very detailed traces of transactions. When the trace logs were called up… they didn't exist. All details of the four million dollar transaction were corrupted and unreadable. Suri went to the second level 'protected' backups, made in real time. Same story, corrupted data. He checked other sample transactions carried out earlier that morning by the engineers; no sign of corruption. Whatever happened, it had to have happened after the last sample transaction was run. A virus was the most probable explanation, but how had it penetrated the system? The levels of security were considerable.

Suri called his contact at Parker Content's bank, Lynn Jones, and told her there were some glitches that he was trying to work out. He was cautious, he'd like nothing more than to be able to keep this bug and it's fix 'in house' to save face. He'd get the engineers working on it, have a fix in place and move on down the road with no one the wiser. Maybe.

"I have an electronic confirmation from their bank, but the bank itself says they never received the funds."

"Our records show we did transfer the funds."

"Read me the confirmation information."

Lynn read the long string of numbers.

"That doesn't match what I have." Suri said.

"Are you looking at the database itself?"

"No, I'm looking at the electronic notification log."

"Can you take a look at the database itself, the source, so we know we're looking at the raw data?"

Suri could look at the database, in fact he just had, and it was a senseless mass of numbers and letters, a thoroughly corrupted mess. He wasn't prepared to let anyone outside the company know anything yet.

"The development folks are hogging it at the moment, but I will and I'll get back to you."

"Do I need to be worried Suri?"

"Naaa. It's a new system, I'll work it and call you back, no problem."

"OK. Call me."

Suri pushed back from his desk, and leaned back in his ergonomic chair. The facts as he knew them so far were: four million dollars was transferred from Parker's bank, the money was not received by Mediex's bank, the data files were corrupted on every trace he'd seen on this transaction alone, the confirmation number on the notification email didn't match the number from the bank that made the transfer. What a pain in the ass, and unexpected too, they hadn't seen anything like this happen in all the exhaustive testing. Four million dollars was missing, and the only records of exactly where it went were unreadable. He paused and ran the thought through his head again. Four million dollars was missing, and the only records of exactly where it went were unreadable.

"Holy shit." his hands unclasped from behind his head as he leaned forward, looking at the carpet between his shoes, running the problem through his head a third time. "*No fucking way.*" he whispered in disbelief.

*Lower Manhattan, New York City*

"Where the fuck is my money?"

Jacob Seiden, resisting the almost uncontrollable urge to run away and hide today, followed Eddie's advice and went to work in order to maintain the appearance that nothing was wrong. It took him fifteen minutes to work up the courage to execute the next part of the plan, going to lunch. There were several 'errands' outside the office building that he was to carry out, all with the aim of allowing Richie Scala to grab him. 'This is insane.' he thought, but carried out his part never the less. He didn't have long to wait, the first excursion, lunch, found Richie lying in wait.

"Where the fuck is my money?" he repeated. Richie didn't yell or attract attention, he didn't lay a finger on Jacob. His eyes said it all.

"They did the transaction today. I did exactly what I was supposed to do. You didn't receive it?"

Richie was speaking slowly, working hard to control his anger "Would I be here if I did?"

Jacob looked down, deep in thought; rather, he worked at looking like he was deep in thought.

"I don't know what happened." Jacob said, then before Richie's hand had moved, he added "But."

"But what?" anger more than inquiry.

"But, I think I know a way to find out." he said in a contemplative tone.

"Don't try to bullshit me, you don't have my money you're gonna fucking regret it. I'll cut you up and do things to the pieces."

Jacob felt a sudden urgent need to visit a bathroom, it came upon him suddenly, and he started sweating as he held his bowels. Richie was without a doubt the scariest man Jacob had ever seen.

"You're forgetting something." and before Richie could ask, Jacob continued, summoning up every last ounce of courage that he had left "I have invested a lot of effort into this project too, and I'm taking a lot of risk. I want to be paid what I was promised."

Richie's face was stone. Silence.

Then, after having considered the matter he said "You'll get paid, but if you don't find that money, you'll get what's coming to you."

"If I find out where it went, you will go and get it, and then you will pay me, yes?"

"Just find it! And I mean right fucking now!" then with a sarcastic smirk "I'll be in touch."

Jacob called to him "How will I find you?"

Richie turned and said with an evil grin "We're watching you, you won't have to look."

Arriving back at his office, Jacob took out the cell phone that Eddie had given him and called the number he'd been given.

"He bite?" Eddie asked, not even asking who it was.

"Yes."

"Good. Stay calm and don't do anything stupid."

"I won't."

"You remember what to do next, right?"

"Yes. Don't worry, I know what to do. Just keep me alive."

"Stick to the plan. It's a good plan." Eddie said, and hung up.

*The Bronx, New York City*

Nicky Trosa's Cadillac slowed to a crawl as he looked into the storefront window of Plaza Travel; he could see the Pope sitting inside. He pulled down a narrow alleyway, and parked in Plaza's 'Patrons Only' parking. He knocked on the rear door.

"Morning Nick." said Elaine with her usual big smile.

"Morning hun. Ronnie here?"

"Sure is. Come on in." she said as she stepped back and out of the way allowing Nicky to enter and exchanging a hug and a peck on the cheek.

Elaine Caforo was married to Nicky's cousin Frank, and Frank Caforo was Nicky's favorite and closest cousin. Elaine's five feet and six inches was decidedly curvy. She was big breasted, but usually wore a tasteful blouse that showed some cleavage but didn't 'feature' it. Her warm and genuine smile went perfectly with her voluptuous body. The fact that his cousin, who was as close as a brother, had found such a wonderful wife was a real source of satisfaction for Nicky.

Elaine led him to the main space in the travel office, where he saw the Pope talking on the phone. Plaza Travel was lucky if it broke even on its own merits at the end of each year, it was really a front for a few less legal concerns that Frank Caforo ran. The Pope hung up and stood to embrace Nicky then they both sat down at adjacent desks. Elaine knew the drill and wandered off to the back room while Nicky and Ronnie spoke.

"So?"

"Bad news." the Pope said, although his feelings were quite to the contrary.

Nicky stared and waited a moment, then said "The light's green."

"I've heard a few conversations…" the Pope said "…the first was on Saturday, at about six in the evening…"

"Bottom line." Nicky said "We can go over the detail later."

"He's in business for himself."

Nicky noticed how the Pope had said it. Not 'I think…' or 'It looks like…' but just a flat out conclusion. He considered the two obvious scenarios, either the Pope saw enough to convince him, or he had it in for Richie and was playing the situation. 'What the fuck…' he thought, '…who doesn't have it in for Richie.' He was starting to wonder if the time had come to consider whether Richie more trouble than he was worth, regardless of whether the Pope was being straight with him or not. The Pope was easy going as wiseguys went, and he picked him because he had good sources of information, was a little anal about detail, a plus in this kind of thing, and would not do anything too bold. He wouldn't out and out lie, even if he did put his own slant on the story.

"You heard about Mikey Zirella right?"

Nicky nodded.

"The way I see it, it was probably our friend who clipped him."

"That guy was with Angelo, he was under Angelo's protection." Nicky said, understandably irritated.

"Yeah, he was." the Pope said, his face darkened.

"What?" Nicky said.

“He’s got something going with some guy in Manhattan. There wasn’t much detail from the calls but it was connected to Zirella so again…he’s got his hand in Angelo’s pocket. I've been tailing Richie a little…”

Nicky reacted to that, he was about to say something, but the Pope was too fast.

“You can relax, he never caught on. I told you I’d handle it.”

That seemed to calm Nicky a bit, and he gestured for the Pope to continue.

“Anyway, I saw him put the arm on this guy, the guy from Manhattan, and he’s pissy because he’s got some scam that was supposed to go down with him, and something went wrong, and you know Richie….pay me or I’ll chop you up into little fuckin’ bits. I followed the guy on the way back, and he’s a computer guy. Engineer or some shit like that.”

“What does his company do?” Nicky asked, knowing that the Pope, true to his nature, couldn’t resist the urge to get the background, to satisfy his curiosity.

“Listen to this, the company he works for, they write computer programs and other companies use the programs they write in their programs. They're…ya know…a subcontractor…but instead of painting or concrete…it's computers.”

“OK…so what? What's the scam?”

"I don’t know, but these guys, I looked it up on the Internet, they do some work in the financial sector. All the online business, the money that changes hands on the internet…billions, processing credit cards and whatnot…capisci?”

While the Pope’s understanding of what Seventeen O Three did was neither elegant nor comprehensive, it was just as effective as if it had been. Money, Internet, Richie, Freelance…that’s what it boiled down to. If Richie did whack Mike Zirella, add another layer of bullshit he’d have to wade through with Angelo; and that’s if he could keep it contained to Angelo. He didn’t need the sometimes volatile underboss Frank Carbone getting involved; if Frank got involved it would most likely cost him money. Frank was famous for ‘taxing’ people for their mistakes, of course he wound up keeping a chunk of that tax, the greedy fuck, but it was his prerogative.

"You had Joey Bags and DMV take care of that landlord thing back in September with Richie. After that job I saw them hanging with Richie a lot." the Pope said. "I'm not the only one who would say this, but they were beginning to sound more like Richie…ya know…acting like everything belonged to them." the Pope shrugged "Like Richie was rubbing off on em or something.. I dunno."

Nicky stared at the Pope for a long moment, and asked "You're sure?" in a tone that clearly communicated 'Lie to me and I'll cut your fuckin' heart out and feed it to you.'

The Pope didn't hesitate "Yeah."

"Go take a ride for me. I wanna talk with those two. Don't say anything; just tell them I want to see them right now. I sent them down to talk to a guy who owes us some money. They should be down at the Jacobi building down by the bridge. Go get them and bring them here."

Nicky had no way of knowing that Joey 'Bags' Ross, was in no condition to come tell him anything, since he was lying dead at the Jacobi building, a hole the size of a half dollar drilled into his chest by Eddie Ferrara. Similarly, Sammy 'DMV' Cotti could offer nothing as well.

# Chapter 36
# *Compass Needle*

*Lower Manhattan, New York City*

Around the time that Nicky Trosa sent for Joey Bags and DMV, Richie Scala was holding Jacob Seiden by the hair on the back of his head, in an alleyway two blocks from the offices of Seventeen O Three.

He slapped Seiden across the face and tugged his head roughly from behind, causing Seiden's yarmulke to fall off and land at his feet.

“Listen to me you Jew prick, what the fuck took you so long?”

“This takes time…" he stammered "…what we’re looking for. What good would it do if I came out and had nothing?” Seiden said, his voice cracking with fear.

“Don’t get smug with me or I’ll crack your fuckin' skull.” Richie said menacingly.

“I’m telling you I have an interest in finding that money too. I’m doing that.”

“WHERE’S MY FUCKING MONEY?”

“Someone stole it.”

“What are you a fucking comedian? We stole it.” Richie shot back.

“Yes we did; then someone stole it from us.”

“What?” Richie let go of Seiden and took a step back, trying not to show his surprise while being caught completely by surprise.

“Tracing what happened is very difficult, in fact for anyone else but me it is impossible. That was my contribution, to be certain that the tracks would all be corrupted.”

In fact, the tracks had been essentially erased, so extensive had been the corruption. Jacob knew this of course, he’d written the algorithms, but he also knew that Riche Scala didn’t know that. It would be logical and believable to Richie that the guy who did it would be able to un-do it. Believable, but completely untrue.

"Corrupted?"

"Forgive me. Scrambled. The information in the computer systems that could lead to where the money actually went had to be scrambled into nonsense, made unreadable, the term we use is corrupted."

"So if that was done, how could you read it?"

"I wrote the part of the computer program that did the scrambling, so I alone know how to unscramble most of it."

"Most of it?"

"The way it works is that some pieces of the information are gone for good, completely randomized, but other pieces, a lot of them, well…I am able to get them back."

"I hope for your sake, you were able to tell me where my money is."

"I know where it went."

Richie stared at him, he was practically salivating, totally focused on getting the name, killing the offender, and taking his money back. After a few seconds of silence, it came to him that Seiden was not speaking.

"Don't get fucking cute."

"I want to know…I have to be sure, that I will get what is due to me."

"You'll get your end." Richie said.

"What's to stop you from simply killing me and keeping all of it?"

"There's something people like you don't seem to grasp about people like me…that's always a possibility. The best way to avoid that is not to piss me off and keep your commitments to me. You'll get your end."

Seiden knew in that moment that he'd receive a bullet as his payment; he had no doubt about it.

"The money was intercepted, someone else was working their own scheme and the cash was routed to a shell account, that is, an account whose purpose in this case is to shield the identity of the thief. Unfortunately for the owner of that account, I have certain skills in this area, and tracked the money to its final destination, AN Development Corporation. Even the authorities will never know where the money went."

“And?”

“AN Development is listed here, in Manhattan.”

*The Bronx, New York City*

Nicky Trosa stood as still as a statue, studying the bodies of Joey Bags, DMV and Crazy John Morozov, as the Pope took another turn through the building to satisfy himself that he and Nicky were alone. A minute later the Pope was satisfied.

“They both have their pieces.” Nicky said “Bags didn’t even reach for his.”

“Taken by surprise?”

“Surprised that it was a friend.” Nicky said “In this situation if anyone had come in, even if it was someone they knew but wasn’t a friend, Bags would have had his piece in his hand. No, this had to be someone they both trusted.”

Nicky thought for a moment, then continued “The guy pops Bags in the chest, right? DMV goes for his piece but not fast enough, and he takes one in the stomach. Stomach makes sense since who ever shot him is in a rush to drop him before he gets nailed himself…doesn't wanna miss; so not a head shot. Then he steps closer and finishes the job once DMV is on the ground.”

“All of that makes sense to me. The one thing that doesn’t is this guy hanging here.” the Pope said.

“They were supposed lean on this guy… just lean on him. He owed us money. He had something in the works to pay us what he owed.”

“Yeah, but the needle.” the Pope said “I don’t know what that shit is in the needle, but it smells awful. Jab a guy in the balls with that, you're not expecting him to live. Why do that if you need him alive?”

“Unless they got what they needed.” Nicky said.

"Got what? They were supposed to smack him around you said, what could they have gotten that you needed?"

"I said what they needed, not what I needed."

After a few seconds of silence, the Pope said "I'm sorry Nick I don't follow."

"They guy had some babanya he was gonna wholesale, to pay us."

The Pope furrowed his considerable brow "They take his powder; he has no way to pay."

"Well…" Nicky said contemplatively "…they were clipped by someone they knew. The guy is dead too." he put his hands on his hips and looked at the ground, walking through the situation carefully "I'll lay odds his junk is gone too, wherever it was." then looked at the Pope with arched eyebrows "A needle in the cazzo and he'd have given up his mother."

"It's weird, a needle to the balls." the Pope said "I've seen a lotta shit Nick, that's a new one on me."

Nicky's gaze locked onto the body, then he looked at the syringe lying on the floor where the Pope had dropped it after pulling it out of Morozov's scrotum. His eyes went back to the body, then back to the syringe, and then they narrowed. He heard about that being done before, but only once, a few years back. The Pope saw the look of recognition spread across Nicky's face.

"What?" he asked.

"C'mon, take a ride." Nicky said, turning toward the exit.

After they were in the car and pulling out into the street, the Pope turned and asked "Where to?"

"Know where Richie lives?"

The Pope nodded.

"Let's make a house call."

*Lower Manhattan, New York City*

"I told him. He believed me, and he was very angry." Jacob said.

Eddie chuckled "Yeah, that's good Jacob, you did good." he said in a tired tone.

"You look like you could use some sleep." Jacob offered, seeing the lines around Eddie's eyes.

"I could." Eddie said rubbing his eyes "I had a long flight and haven't gotten a chance to sleep yet."

“So what now?” Jacob asked.

“What were you going to do before? Originally I mean.”

“I made arrangements to go live with my brother in Israel for a while.”

“Let me see your cell phone." Eddie said, holding his hand out.

Clearly confused, Jacob removed it from his belt clip and handed it to Eddie.

"Anything critical stored in this that you don't have at home?" Eddie asked.

Jacob shook his head.

Eddie removed the battery, dropped the phone on the ground and with one powerful stomp, crushed it into pieces.

“I’m going to give you a number, this is very important Jacob, memorize it. Never write it down anywhere. Don’t write it down when you leave here.” Eddie said in a reasonable tone "Don't write it down. Ever."

Eddie gave Seiden the number, and watched him for a minute as he moved his lips, silently memorizing the sequence.

“Call that number in two weeks, I’ll get you your money, the way things are, you have to hang in there and trust me.”

“Two weeks.” It was a confirmation, not a question. Seiden figured that as things stood, if Eddie was out to screw him, there was really no way to stop him.

“How are you going to get to your brother’s without booking a flight in your name? Once you don’t show up at work, they’ll assume you were involved and the FBI will be looking for you.”

“Before Mr. Zirella died, he was able to get me some false identification. I insisted on getting that before I went any farther. I’ll travel under that identity then discard the documents. My brother can help me once I’m in Israel.”

Eddie reached into his jacket pocket and produced a cell phone, handing it to Seiden.

“Here…you can use this one for now…can’t be traced to anyone. Don’t be careless and use it unless it’s essential.” Eddie said “If anything comes up, call me from that phone…I’ll do the same if I need to get in touch with you. Jacob…” Eddie grabbed his arm gently “…don’t store the number I just gave you in this phone, and make sure you destroy it before you get on a plane to go anywhere. Clear?"

"No problems, it'll be as you say."

"Good, OK, so two weeks." Eddie said.

"Two weeks." Jacob agreed.

# Chapter 37
# *Race with the Devil*

*Mid-town Manhattan, New York City*

More than anything else, Richie Scala was vengeful. His unforgiving nature exceeded even his avarice. If he saw something he wanted, he was relentless in pursuit and remorseless in action. If however, he felt the he'd been wronged, then the spite and cruelty he was capable of was truly disturbing. He was someone who had to have his revenge.

After some digging into AN Development and the mutts who had stolen his money, the results shouldn't have been surprising. As a matter of fact, he felt annoyed for not having suspected the person from the moment he'd heard the bad news. AN Development was a company that had financed a few restaurants in Manhattan. Nothing major as far as Richie could determine, just relatively inexpensive joints that were all bankrolled by the same corporation. The 'AN' in AN Development stood for Armando Navas.

Exercising caution, Richie had one of his muscle-bound collectors pay a visit to Armando, and learned that a boyhood friend had offered Navas a way to make some quick money. If he agreed to receive payment of a large sum of money that would be wired into his business account, then his friend would pay Navas ten thousand dollars. The money would be wired out of his account later the same day to a bank in the Caiman Islands, but for helping him with the transaction he would be paid the ten thousand in cash in two days time. Richie's emissary 'leaned' on Armando and was convinced he was telling him the truth; Armando told him that the boyhood friend behind the deal was a guy named Eddie Ferrara.

*The Bronx, New York City*

It was New Years Eve. Nicky Trosa and the Pope parked outside of the social club and entered with a garment bag slung over the Pope's shoulder. Taped inside the garment bag were eight quarter-kilo plastic bags of heroin and a set of car keys. The two men walked to the back of the club, and into Nicky's tiny office area. When the door closed Nicky wasted no time.

"Send for him."

The Pope gravely nodded to Nicky and left the room, closing the door behind him. As he walked to the front door, he had a hard time keeping the smile off his face. Nicky called Al Cusimano into the office.

"What's up Nick?"

"Stick around, I might have a job for you."

Al was smart enough not to ask and left Nicky to whatever was troubling him.

Nicky sighed heavily and flipped open his cell phone and dialed a number, it rang six times before he got an answer.

"Yeah?"

"Happy New Year." Nicky said.

"Happy New Year to you too. You loaded yet?" the voice on the other end said with cheer.

"I plan to be, but no, not yet." Nicky said, his tone carried the message clearly I wish I was carefree and drunk, but something is giving me heartburn. "I was heading over by the golf course to pay my respects."

"Oh yeah? Hey maybe I'll take a ride over there. It's been too long."

"Half an hour?" Nicky asked.

"See you there." the voice said, and hung up.

Half an hour later, Nicky was standing at the edge of a small waterway in front of Calco Salvage, Inc., looking across the water at the rolling greens of Pelham Split Rock Golf Course. The junkyard was closed for the holiday and the area, which normally saw only light traffic, was completely deserted. He heard footsteps behind him.

"Been a while...since you and I were here." Nicky said without turning.

"True. That was a…productive day." said Eddie Ferrara with a slight chuckle.

The 'productive day' Eddie referred to, occurred many years ago when he and Nicky had rendezvoused at this junk yard. They'd watched carefully as the late Michael 'The Fish' Moretti, the truck he had died in, and his car, were burned and crushed.

"Yeah." Nicky smiled "That alone would have cleared the way for you." meaning that his part in the killing of the Fish would have clinchedEddie's being 'made' into a full fledged wiseguy.

"Yeah, it would have." was all that Eddie said.

"That when you turned it down?"

"It wasn't easy. Do it the wrong way..." Eddie left the thought hanging, meaning everyone in 'the life' wanted to be 'made', and there was a distinct possibility that if you refused such an honor it would cause suspicion and lead to your prompt demise.

"Why refuse? You'd have been a capo by now." Nicky asked.

"What can I say Nick, I just have my own way of looking at things. The way it was, the way it is, I don't wanna make that commitment…" Eddie said in a serious but reasonable tone "…once you do, it's…ya know…there's no going back."

Nicky smiled "Hey, you're no fucking jadrool, the things you're trusted with now, you're in that box already kid."

"Maybe so…" Eddie paused a few seconds "…but not on the record."

"For whatever difference you think that makes." Nicky said in a neutral tone.

"It could make a difference." Eddie said in a way that communicated that he didn't wish to elaborate "So, this agita, what is it and how can I help?"

Nicky took a deep breath and turned to face Eddie "Richie."

Nicky and Eddie spoke for twenty minutes, Eddie was in Angelo's crew, so technically having this conversation carried with it some risk for both men. Nicky pursued information that would fill out the picture of what Richie was up to and exactly what he had done; also if Nicky had Eddie as an ally to keep the information contained and act as emissary to Angelo, perhaps they could keep Frank Carbone out of the picture and out of their pockets.

Eddie's interests lie in solidifying the chances of his plan succeeding, and by doing so he would undoubtedly help both Nicky and Angelo. Eddie wanted Richie to get what he deserved, wanted to get Angelo his money, and he wanted to get out of 'the life' and marry Antonia. If this chance to talk to Nicky was handled the right way, it could help him accomplish each of those goals.

As they were concluding their conversation, both men were now unconsciously shifting their weight from one foot to the other in an attempt to keep them warm against the frigid air coming off the water.

"You believed her, this whore?" Nicky asked.

"Yeah. She was scared. She wasn't lying." Eddie said "She has no reason to in any case."

"I may have to send for her…" Nicky said.

"…yeah, I know…Richie's a member." Eddie completed Nicky's sentence for him.

"Don't get cute." Nicky said good naturedly "I've already sent for Richie."

This caught Eddie by surprise, although he didn't show it. He'd counted on the holiday to give him at least another day to take care of things. If Richie had been sent for, and in light of the things Richie had been doing, he'd easily put it together and make a stop at the bordello to kill Honey, since she was a witness to his meeting with Mike Zirella. Eddie didn't want to have to use Jacob Seiden in any way as a witness for Nicky's purposes or for anyone else's; the amount of money was too large to risk anyone talking about it down the road, witness protection program or otherwise. He felt that Honey had to be saved from that marauding strunz; besides she did provide the link that put him wise to Richie's involvement so why let either Richie kill her, or depending on how things played out, Nicky might not want to risk leaving her alive.

"Well, it's not my place to stick my nose into your business. No offense but if I was in your shoes, I wouldn't want anything to go down and attract Frank's attention until I was ready for it." Eddie said.

"Well, you're right…that's not your business. That's my business." Nicky said in a neutral tone.

"Who knows, maybe things will work themselves out." Eddie said enigmatically.

Nicky looked at Eddie for a long moment, evaluating his best course of action to put this whole issue to bed. He decided that Eddie had done well for himself, in fact extremely well considering he'd done it without being a made guy.

"Yeah…maybe." Nicky finally said, giving Eddie the most fleeting of nods.

They both turned and headed back toward their cars.

"Happy New Year kid."

"Same to you Nick." Eddie said with an earnest look.

*Mid-town Manhattan, New York City*

Armando Navas sat behind his desk. A casual observer would have trouble seeing a desk at all. His office was not what one would call 'neat and organized'; the two file cabinets were full but contained not a single 'file'. Instead there were free sample cases, plastic letters, some binders and catalogs; a small tool kit… an entire bottom drawer of one of them was filled with a broken exhaust fan motor. His desk was piled high with bills, magazines, newspapers, correspondence; it was shaped like a pile too, round on top and squat like a pyramid. There were boxes of stuff everywhere, on the floor on the shelves… if you wanted to sit you were on your own, you had to clear a space.

At the center of this storm of disorganized debris, was its pilot, Armando. He'd come a long way from selling knock-off New York Yankees T-Shirts for his uncle back in his boyhood days in the Bronx. The 'mess' for lack of a better word, was decidedly not a manifestation of how his mind worked; he was focused and thoroughly a pragmatist. His days hustling for business on the streets, fencing stolen goods and so forth, were well behind him. However, those days instilled in him a lasting quality of decisiveness; experience had taught him that making ten decisions and getting a few wrong produced better results than making no decisions.

Armando was going over the expenses from a midtown pizza place he was part owner of, when the phone rang.

"Hello."

"Armando, it's me." Eddie said.

"Eddie...you know some fuckin' guy came asking about you..."

"What guy?" Eddie interjected.

"He didn't exactly leave a card. Some gorilla, asking me about the money."

"You tell him?"

"Not right away, but yeah I did."

"You OK? No offense Armando, but did he lean on you?"

There was a long pause, then Armando said "Yeah well what could I do, I'm not Rambo."

"You alright?" Eddie asked.

"Yeah, he smacked me around a little bit man, it was humiliating but I'm in one piece."

"I'm sorry, it's my fault and my bad timing." Eddie said apologetically "What did he look like?"

"Look like?...BIG! He was fuckin' BIG Eddie." Armando said deadpan.

"Hair, eyes, tattoos, facial hair."

"Brown hair and eyes, clean shaven, didn't notice any tattoos. I dunno."

Oh shit, if it was Richie Eddie thought Armando is lucky he's still breathing. "How tall?"

"Six two, maybe taller." Armando said.

"How old?"

"Who are you.. Joe Friday? I dunno how old."

"It's important Armando, how old would you say?"

"Maybe thirty...early thirties at most."

Eddie exhaled It wasn't Richie himself, he sent someone else.

"I'm sorry Armando, I'll compensate you."

"No, you don't have to do anything, it's over, but just...ya know...don't put me in that position man."

"Armando…listen to me, I have to put you in that position again."

"What? Are you listening to me?"

“I need you to bring someone to me…a girl.”

“Call a pimp.” Armando chuckled.

“This is important, I know what I’m asking...but this could be some shit.” Eddie said, his tone neutralizing any possibility of humor.

“Some shit huh? Sounds dangerous.” Armando said.

“It might be. I don’t think so, but…you need to find her and get her away from where she is…you’ll have to persuade her and I don’t know how she’ll react.”

“Just out of curiosity, why me?”

"I can't put some of my guys in a position to have to lie about being involved, lying about it could cause a big fuckin’ problem. No one knows who you are…no roads will lead to you."

“It’s that important?”

“It’s that important.”

“Where do I find her?”

“She’s a hooker, you’ll find her at the Hi-Class bordello over by Morris Avenue. She goes by the name ‘Honey’. Blonde, skinny, about twenty five maybe, but dressed up to look teen.”

“So I’m not your pimp, but I’m going to a whorehouse to get you a whore? You’ve got to be fuckin’ kidding me.”

“We know each other a long time, you hear me laughing?” Eddie said in an intensely earnest voice.

Armando interrupted him “I’ve been a knock around guy, you know that, but I’ve never even been to a whorehouse. What the hell do I say? How do I do it?”

“Just knock on the door, don’t say anything, they’ll let you in. You go up to the guy in the waiting room and tell him you want a date with Honey.”

“Then?”

“Then you go into the room with her; instead of fucking her you tell her what I told you. You’ll have to get her out of there without anyone noticing and bring her to me.”

“Yeah, well suppose she won’t come with me?”

“Be persuasive, it’s her neck if she won’t come, not yours. But get her to come and do it fast. Don't hang around…the clock's ticking.”

“Where are you?”

“No time to explain…grab her and we'll meet at your uncle's diner by the bridge?"

"Three Stars? OK."

“Right now. Seriously, drop whatever it is you’re doing, and get her right now.”

Eddie said it with more stress in his voice than Armando could remember ever having heard; it alarmed him since Eddie was always easy going and in control, and it made you feel more confident being around him. He didn’t sound that confident now so the situation must be dire.

“I’m on my way. Do I need to bring protection?” He didn’t mean a condom, he meant a gun, but smirked as he realized the double-entendre.

“Don’t bring it unless you're ready to use it.”

“OK, I’ll see you in an hour.”

*The Bronx, New York City*

Richie stormed into Hi-Class, pushing past a very large guy guarding the door, snaked his way through the narrow dimly lit halls and exploded into Gio’s office.

“Where’s that little blonde bitch!”

“What…who?” Gio asked, shocked. The last person he’d expected to come charging into his office, aside from Mike Zirella of course, was Richie Scala. So deep was his fear of Richie, that his mind instantly raced, searching for reasons that Richie might be here in his office and looking fierce. In a way it was like having Hannibal Lecter as your proctologist… one way or another, something bad was going to happen.

“Don’t give me ‘who’ you fucking snake. I’ll grind you into this shitty carpet for the bug you are.” Richie said, red faced. He was waving something in his hand at Gio as he spoke. He sensed Gio’s fear, which only served to feed Richie’s fire. “WHERE THE FUCK IS SHE?”

"Who, Honey? The girl you were with last time?" Gio stammered.

"Yeah, that's her, Honey. Where is she?"

"What happened, did she do something? Richie for Chrissakes, tell me what's wrong!"

"That little cunt lied to me; she told that fucking bastard that it was me, didn't she? Now he took what's mine, and she's gonna learn what happens to people who talk too much. First I'm gonna cut off her tits, then I'm gonna cut out her tongue." he paused and smiled…it wasn't a happy smile "Then… then I'm going to hurt her for a few hours."

"What happened?" Gio stammered, he was more afraid for his life then he'd ever been. His eyes locked onto the object in Richie's hand, a roll of tape of some kind. In an absurd moment, Gio wondered to himself 'He's going to hit me with a roll of tape?'

"I don't have to tell you anything!" he said, and slowly circled around the desk, setting the roll down on the edge of the desk.

Gio was on the verge of panic, he stood up and turned to face Richie, the space was so small that he had to bend backward, nearly falling over backwards onto his desk as Richie leaned into him. His hands shot backward to stop himself from falling backward, his left hand supporting his weight, flat on the desktop, but the right landed on something unstable. His desk phone. Richie launched a right hook at Gio, catching him with a glancing blow as Gio turned his head to look down at the phone under his hand. Gio, shaking with fear, was startled by the punch, even as it grazed him, pulling at the soft skin beside his left eye and tearing it.

By some unconscious reflex Gio wrapped his fingers the phone's receiver and swung it like a club, hitting Richie on the left side of his head. The receiver was made of only light plastic, so the only thing Gio accomplished was to make matters worse.

Richie took a step back and looked at him calmly. In the moment Gio didn't know what to think, it seemed unbelievable that Richie would stop his attack for something as inconsequential as a light piece of plastic bouncing off his rock-hard skull. He was correct. Richie closed the small remaining distance to Gio, and in a slow and deliberate motion, reached out and grabbed him by the neck. Gio was wide eyed, he couldn't come to terms with the intensity of the grip that had him, Richie's hand was like a vice, it felt inhuman. He reached up with both hands and grabbed onto Richie's forearm, trying with every ounce of his strength to shake it loose, but it didn't budge in the slightest. Richie stood there, calm and unaffected for a few seconds, holding Gio by his neck and completely in control. His eyes never left Gio's as he slowly reached out and removed the gold metal pen from Gio's shirt pocket. He brought it up in one smooth deliberate movement and forced the pen slowly through the center of Gio's throat. Richie maintained the strong grip on his victim for several minutes, watching from a few inches away as the life drained out of his eyes.

Richie released his grip, dropping Gio to the floor and left the tiny office, grabbing the roll of tape from the desk and closing the door behind him. He looked down the hallway to the left. There was a metal door painted the same dark red color as the hallway, it had a latch that ran horizontal about waist high, white with large red block letters on it that read "Fire Exit. Alarm Will Sound." Richie went right, and began a slow methodical search of the establishment. As he rounded the first corner he looked back at the closed office door, the fingertips of his right hand unconsciously feeling the contours of the knife in the pocket of his pants.

'It's time to silence that little whore, she won't be telling anyone anything anymore…not Eddie, and not Nicky. All this aggravation from that fucking Eddie. He isn't even a member that fucking pucchiacha…it was going to be very satisfying doing the work on him.'

# Chapter 38
# *Last Door on the Right*

Armando made it to Hi-Class in record time; he was able to get past the front door-man, and as instructed, asked the guy in the room with the grungy sofas for Honey. The guy sat on a tall stool in front of a doorway that had no door, only hinges painted the same dark red color of the walls and ceiling. The door would have been redundant anyway, the guy was big, and he could have easily filled the space himself; at the moment he was engrossed in a conversation on his cell phone, and he simply leaned back on his stool and yelled through the empty doorframe for Honey and went back to his phone conversation. When no one emerged, he yelled again. Again, no one appeared. Considering the body language, Armando thought, it had to be the guy's wife or girlfriend; who else could put a guy this big on the defensive?

Armando, sensing a chance to get by this guy quickly due to his phone distraction, gestured as if to say Should I just go on in? The cell phone won his attention and he turned to Armando, looking irritated, and said "End of the hall, last room on the right." and waved him through.

Armando crept down the dingy hallway to the last room, and stood in front of the last door on the right. It was closed and he stepped up close to it, his nose was almost touching the door, as he listened for any sound inside. At first he heard nothing. Then he heard a grunt, and some movement. Then a whimper, it definitely came from a woman. Armando was a little nervous having never been in a bordello. Apparently, the woman he came to get was 'doing business'. Figuring he'd just wait for the 'transaction' to be over, he turned to head back into the waiting area, when he heard the woman's pleading muffled voice. It didn't sound normal, it sounded like there was something in her mouth and it was definitely a sound of distress. Armando shrugged, figuring she was doing something 'special' for a client perhaps, but as he turned again to leave that notion vanished completely. The woman's voice screamed in pain, but was muted as though her mouth was covered and all of the sound was escaping from her nose. In a flash Armando decided that the girl he was here to save for his friend Eddie, needed saving right now. He scorned himself for having not brought his pistol, and looked around for something to use as a weapon; the only item in the hallway was a fire extinguisher mounted on the wall to his left. He moved quickly to it, lifting it from its mount and moved back to the door. Now he could hear muted crying, and a grunt again from a male sounding voice.

Armando gripped the doorknob and slowly turned it, and opening the door quietly, hoping to be able to get positioned without the bad guy knowing. As the door opened, he felt a silent gratitude that the hinges didn't squeak, and there in front stood a very stocky man of average height standing over a helpless young girl. It had to be Honey. She was completely naked and bound with duct tape to a fabric covered folding chair. Her hands were bound together and stretched tight up over her head, a thick band of tape pulled them back and fastened them to another band of tape around her torso and the back of the chair, just below her breasts. Her ankles were taped to the rear legs of the chair and her mouth was completely covered with tape as well. Tears were streaming down her cheeks, which were flushed red with torment.

The man wore expensive looking pants and shoes but had taken off his shirt and jacket and thrown them on the bed. All he was wearing on his upper body was a tank top undershirt. His right side was almost facing Armando, and there was a large tattoo of a dragon that ran from his elbow, down his forearm and ending in a fierce dragon's mouth just above his knuckles. That dragon mouth was holding a large stiletto knife and as he shifted to his left a bit, Armando could see a bleeding wound in the bottom of Honey's left breast. Clearly this was the source of the muffled cry of anguish he heard a moment before. In two or three seconds he'd taken all of this in and his brain was beginning to catch up to the events. Just as he was beginning to feel rage at what his eyes were seeing, the man brought the knife to Honey's other breast. While staring into her terror filled eyes, he began to slowly force the knife upward into the underside of her right breast, duplicating what he done to the left one.

Something inside of Armando snapped.

Being in the room for four seconds was enough for all of his brain to fully comprehend. He raised the fire extinguisher over his head and grunted as he brought it down with all of his rage, aiming for Richie's head. Richie flinched as he heard the grunt behind him, and that saved his skull from being crushed. The heavy metal cylinder missed his head and his upper back took the full force of the blow. He went down, the wind had left his lungs and the pain he felt was paralyzing. He lay on the floor, face in the smelly carpet, dazed. Armando, raised the fire extinguisher up again, and this time threw it down as hard as he could at the center of Richie's back. Armando watched for a few seconds and saw no movement from the man.

Armando picked up the stiletto knife that Richie had been using and quickly slashed away all of the tape, leaving the piece over her mouth for last; as he grabbed the corner of it, he gestured for her not to make a sound.

"Your coming with me." he said, as he uncovered her mouth.

"Who are you?" Honey asked, tears still falling with the pain she felt in her breasts, and still not believing that she wasn't going to die in that room.

"I was sent for you."

"By who?" She asked.

"C'mon, we're getting out of here."

Her clothes were ripped apart and useless, so Armando took off his winter coat, a large dark green nylon parka with fur around the hood, and wrapped it around Honey. Once on her spare frame it looked absurdly big, and came down to her knees. He led her to the door, and opened it. As he watched her step through the door, a flying metal cylinder barely missed him, grazing his cheek as it sailed by. However, it did not miss Honey, striking her head with a gruesome clang. She immediately went down, knocked unconscious. Shocked, Armando turned and saw Richie bent over in pain, with a grin on his face. Armando picked up the fire extinguisher as Richie went for his knife which Armando had left by the chair after freeing Honey. In this race, Armando was faster, and hit Richie solidly on the side of his head with the extinguisher. Richie went down again. This time he was out cold.

Honey lay unconscious in the doorway and apparently no one outside the room knew what was going on. He looked at her helpless body and then glanced down at Richie, and for a moment considered killing him. His gaze locked on the dark green dragon tattoo; there was something familiar about it but he couldn't quite put it together.

In a moment, he shook his head to clear it and decided that the smart thing to do was get out of there, and quickly. He rushed over, picked up Honey, and carried her out of the room. He tip toed down the hallway and rounded the corner to his right. Looking past the open doorway that was guarded by the big guy, still on his cell phone, Armando could see a fire exit at the far end. He waited until the guy had leaned forward and had his back completely them, and quietly carried Honey past. As he approached the fire exit he saw a closed door to his left and prayed that it wouldn't open for just a few seconds more, unaware that Richie made certain of that. He reached the exit door, took a deep breath, and eased the horizontal latch delicately so as to avoid any noise. As the door slowly opened, blinding sunlight assaulted his eyes. Armando eased out of the door to find a flight of metal stairs leading down to an enclosed concrete area behind the building. When he got to the bottom of the stairs, he exhaled, thankful that no alarm had sounded. He looked around the brick walls of the buildings around him, seemingly trapped, then looked up to the top of the stairs and felt relief that the big guy inside hadn't followed. Armando took another look around the courtyard and noticed a gap in the far corner, moving closer he could see it was a very narrow passageway between two adjacent buildings that was just wide enough for him to fit through, if he carried Honey over his shoulder.

He emerged from the passage onto the sidewalk the next block over from Hi-Class. Taking Honey off of his shoulder and carrying her in his arms again, he turned right and headed for his car, just becoming aware of the frigid weather. The street was fairly empty at the moment, by New York City standards, and he ignored the looks from the few passersby as he carried the unconscious Honey to his car. Upon reaching it, he lay Honey across the back seat; she was still completely unconscious and the front of the green parka had two small red stains where the blood from her breast wounds was beginning to soak through the fabric. He jumped into the car, turned on the heater full blast and pulled out quickly into light traffic.

As Armando bobbed and weaved his way through traffic, he dug his cell phone out of his pocket and dialed Eddie relaying everything that happened, including remembering the tattoo. He'd have to get Honey to a hospital and they'd be sure to ask questions; Eddie had it covered.

Connected.

# Chapter 39
# *A Death By The Shore*

Eddie, after receiving an excited call from Armando, immediately dialed another number.

"Jacob."

"Eddie. I didn't expect to hear from you."

"I know. I need you to make a call." Eddie said.

"A call… to whom?"

"Your friend Richie."

"You're joking!"

Eddie laughed "I'm not. You're going to tell him about our meeting tomorrow."

"We have a meeting tomorrow?" Jacob asked in confusion.

"Well, not really, but Richie should think we are…" Eddie explained just enough for Jacob to be able to navigate his way though a conversation with Richie. He gave him Richie's cell number and reassured Jacob that things would all work out.

Eddie placed one more call, to Pete Oh'Alin at the Shore Inn.

In the late afternoon on New Year's Day, Richie's Cadillac skidded to a stop on the loose pebble of the parking lot in front of the Shore Inn. His head was aching and his back felt like he'd been hit by a truck. Bounding out of his car, he found the front door locked and headed for the kitchen door at the rear of the building. He pounded on it with a meaty fist; hitting something, hitting anything, felt good right now. The door opened under his assault, and an unruffled Pete Oh'Alin emerged, a white kitchen apron tucked into the waistband of his pants and a dish towel draped over his right shoulder; a cigarette dangling from his the corner of his mouth.

"We ain't open yet."

Richie pushed his way in, shoving Pete back a few steps, and proceeded to quickly search the kitchen, hallway and main barroom. Clearly unsatisfied with the result of his search, Richie planted himself menacingly in front of the proprietor and demanded to know where Eddie Ferrara was.

"He's not here. Who the fuck are you?"

"I'm the guy who's gonna ruin your fucking day if you don't wise up." Richie said in a low threatening voice. "Now I know he's supposed to be here, you wanna play fucking games with me?" he said, giving Pete the 'dead eyes' stare.

Pete was clearly not intimidated, his expression didn't change a wit as he turned to the big stainless steel kitchen sink full of sudsy pots and pans, and turned off the faucet. He casually turned back to Richie.

"You got business with Eddie?"

"I'm asking the questions." poking Pete in the chest with a stubby finger.

"Well, he'll be here." Pete said in his best 'same shit different day' tone, "Wanna wait in the office?"

Richie stepped back with one foot, gesturing for Pete to lead the way. A doorway in the dimly lit hallway opened to a darkened flight of sturdy but worn wooden steps. Upon reaching the bottom, Pete headed to the right, winding his way through cases of beer, liquor, canned and paper goods stacked from floor to ceiling. They reached a clearing in the forest of boxes, and against the far wall was a battered old grey metal desk, upon which set a morass of loose paperwork. The ceiling was uncovered, comprised of the simple beam and floor-board wooden structure of the floor above. Hanging from the beams overhead, were two long florescent lighting fixtures that bathed the cramped 'office' area in a blue-white pallor that seemed appropriate to the musty smell that hung in the air.

"Make yourself comfortable." Pete said in a sarcastic tone that could not be missed "I'll tell him you're here when he shows up."

Richie didn't move, his considerable size blocking Pete's egress "Sit down and relax."

Richie decided that this bar owner would be joining Eddie on his trip to the other side today, he didn't like the guy's attitude. He didn't like anyone who didn't fear him. Pete sat down in his creaky office chair behind his desk, its arms had been wrapped in black electrical tape and the repair had to have been made when Nixon was president because the tape itself was nearly worn through.

Pete looked up at Richie "If you wanna stand, it's no skin…" and leaned back in his chair, lacing his fingers behind his head.

Richie just stood in front of him, looking at him, and gradually started to take in the surroundings, glancing at the cases of supplies and roughly estimating how much he would make from the sale after the man seated in front of him was dead.

After a couple of minutes, Richie said "Call him." picking up a what looked like a small personal ledger or phone book with a worn black leather cover and handing it to Pete.

"It's not a phone book." Pete said, dropping the book back on the desk "It's the tab."

Richie just stared at him.

"When you own a saloon you have a lot of debts to keep track of. I'm careful, the details are the business, I write it down so I'm sure nothing goes unpaid." Pete said "The devil…right?"

"Huh?"

"The devil. The devil is in the details." Pete said.

Richie grunted.

"That's what works for me anyway." Pete said amiably "I keep track of everything. Sooner or later somebody will show up again who has a tab that they owe, and because I keep track I can cross it off the list. Then you're even." he said as he lit another cigarette and shrugged "Well anyway, that's what works for me. Everybody has their own way of doing things."

Although Riche's face could have been made of stone for all the emotion it showed, inside he was quite amused. He was going to scratch Eddie off his list, and this poor fuck was about to have some bad luck himself. First things first though, and he needed Eddie within reach to be that first thing.

"What's that?" said Richie, motioning with his chin toward a metal door with chromed hinges and handle, built into the wall between two stacks of crates. The door was obstructed by the crates and covered with pictures, newspaper clippings, delivery schedules and other printed matter, making it difficult to recognize as a door.

"Cold storage." Pete said.

"Show me."

"There' nothing to see in there, it's just meat and stuff."

"Let's go, show me." Richie said, beckoning Pete with a gesture that said the issue was not up for debate.

Pete got up and squeezed by Riche's big frame, flipped the latch/lock mechanism and pulled the door halfway open "See, it's just meat."

Richie, mentally bumping up his estimated profit, smiled and said "All the way." indicating for Pete that he wanted to see more.

Pete opened the door the rest of the way, and stepped aside. Richie slid past him and stuck his head into the box, squinting as he tried to make out what the contents were.

"There's a light switch on your left side."

As Richie stepped over the metal threshold, the cold air registered on his face. His hand slid up the surface of the wall on his left and finding the switch, flipped it on. The small caliber bullet was sent into a tumbling motion upon penetrating the bone that comprised the rear of Richie's skull, and its end over end rotation as it moved through the soft tissues of his brain, drilled a much larger hole than the diameter of the slug itself. After traversing the skull cavity, the bullet reached the inside surface of his forehead an inch below his hair line; however, it had lost enough velocity to prevent an exit hole. Instead, the slug dimpled the surface of the bone and ricocheted, careening around inside his skull; the 'tunnels' of vaporized brain pulp and blood tracing the bullet's path.

Richie Scala's last conscious notion was of course, fleeting. In the flash of time before his brain shut down, he associated the physical shock he felt in his skull with flipping the light switch, and for an impossibly brief instant, thought that he had been electrocuted.

Pete leaned over the body, took careful aim and fired another round into the back of Richie's head. He gazed down at the corpse for a few seconds, his ears still ringing from the shots which sounded incredibly loud in the tiny space. He backed out of the cold box, turned the light off and shut the door.

"What goes around..." Pete said in an indifferent tone that gave no outward sign of the intense mix of emotions he was feeling. He leaned against the door with one arm, while the revolver hung from the other, swinging slightly back and forth as a pendulum in a clock. He took a deep breath and slowly allowed his legs to give way, his weight pressing against his shoulder, which slid down the front surface of the closed door to the cold storage box. In the considerable collage of paper scraps taped to the outside surface of the door, his eyes found and focused on an aged newspaper clipping whose ink had deteriorated almost to illegibility. The article had a picture inset of a smiling and attractive young couple, the head line read "Couple Murdered In Apparent Case of Road Rage". The article began "Authorities are seeking any information relating to the brutal murder of a Bronx couple who were driving home after attending a family wedding...." Under the picture, the caption read "Murder victims Carolyn Oh'Alin-Fontana and Dominick Fontana, husband and wife. Their brutalized bodies found on the service road along I-95."

Pete felt grief rush into him as he recalled how precious and full of life his niece had been. He was certain that her death was the reason his brother and sister-in-law both died at a relatively early age; they had never recovered from the ugly and tragic death of their daughter. Whether his brother would approve of his actions he did not know and never would. What he did know, what he felt sure of, was that what he'd done was necessary. He stood slowly, made his way to the phone on his desk and made a call. After the call was made, he sat in his creaky desk chair and thought back to the time before the animal lying dead in the cold storage box had come crashing into the lives of his family.

Ten minutes later he was jarred from his introspection by a loud banging on the metal storm doors that lead from the rear parking lot down a short stone staircase into the basement. Pete made his way through the labyrinth of boxes and up the short flight of pocked and stained concrete steps. The metal storm doors lay at a forty five degree angle and were quite heavy, Pete slid the thick metal latch and pushed hard upward, and almost fell over. The door's bulk seemed to fly open of its own accord, until he could see that Eddie was pulling it open from the other side.

"How ya doin'?" Eddie said, looking as calm as if he was ordering a bowl of soup.

Pete didn't say anything; he turned and led Eddie to the body. Eddie squatted down and looked carefully at the body, then after a few seconds of silence said "Couple of guys will be over here in twenty minutes to clean up. OK?"

Pete nodded.

"Anything I can get you Pete? Anything you need?" Eddie said as he took the pistol from Pete's hand.

"You've done enough Eddie. I won't forget it." Pete said solemnly.

"Call me if you need anything. I mean it Pete, I'm the first call you make. OK?" Eddie said, putting his hand on Pete's shoulder.

"I'm good Eddie." Pete saw that Eddie was skeptical "I'm fine, I'm OK!"

"Alright. You know how to find me."

He was about to turn and head back to his car, but he noticed an unspoken question on Pete's face. He knew that Pete wouldn't ask him, but he also knew that closure was what he could give his friend, closure that the man he'd just shot was without a doubt the man who'd killed his brothers only child. Pete took it on faith that Richie had been that man, but if there was any doubt it would cause Pete some pain. This was not business, this was personal so he decided to volunteer the links between Richie and his niece.

Eddie saw the questioning look and said "When I started out, I had a friend who I did business with down by Yankee Stadium. Sometime after Mario Ruzzi's son died… remember little Carmine Ruzzi?"

“Yeah I remember him, Buddy ya mean. Yeah.” he said solemnly.

“Yeah, Buddy.” Eddie paused, a somber expression suddenly appeared on his face “Well around that time, this friend of mine decided to go straight; he had an uncle that owned a diner near the bridge, and he went to work for him managing it.”

Pete waited, as still as a statue.

“Your niece and nephew stopped at that diner on the way home from the wedding that night.”

“I never heard that before.” Pete said.

“No one knew. No one connected it until my friend saw the guy. It was a lucky coincidence. It was coming to a head with this fuck anyway, but when I found out it was him...that he’d killed your niece…” Eddie paused between each dot, long enough to be sure Pete drew a line “Yesterday my friend recognized the guy; he was the manager in the diner that night. Christ he broke up a fight between your son in law and the guy; the tattoo is what made him remember. No question. He told me about that night, he remembered everything about him once he saw that tattoo. They all left at essentially the same time…the diner’s two minutes from where they were killed…it was him Pete.”

Pete looked a little less upset. “This thing stirred up some shit from the past that I’d be happy to forget now. Thanks again Eddie, I appreciate you remembering my family.”

“Pete, you gotta know, this guy was gonna go no matter what. Don’t have second thoughts tomorrow. OK? The line of guys who wanted this guy dead is longer than my dick, you just had the best reason…and for this fuckin’ guy, that’s saying a lot.”

“Does he have friends?” Pete asked, meaning was the guy he had just killed a ‘made man’; Pete asked this with more poise than most men in his position would have.

“Yeah, but fuhgetaboutit. Not a problem.”

Pete stared at Eddie, and after realizing that there wasn’t more explanation coming, said “Well it’s usually a pretty big fucking problem.”

“It was taken care of before you ever heard about him.” Eddie said reassuringly. “Don’t go looking over your shoulder.” Eddie didn't have to tell him to keep quiet; Pete grew up in the environment and understood how things worked.

They walked up to the parking lot through the storm doors, and as they shook hands, Eddie said “Twenty minutes.”

He opened his trunk and threw in the weapon he’d taken from Pete, got into his car and drove out of the parking lot slowly, watching Pete in his rear view mirror as he disappeared back into the basement, closing the big metal doors behind him.

Connected.

# Chapter 40
## *Phoenix*

Honey felt a far off sensation; it felt like a huge pair of pliers was squeezing her skull. Every few seconds a dull throbbing started at the back of her head and then spread out like the wave from a stone dropped into peaceful lake. As she gradually awakened, the intensity of the pain followed suit. Her eyes felt like they were glued shut and she made a weak effort to open them, but they didn't budge. She slowly took a few shallow breaths and as the fog started to clear she tried again, forcing her eyes to open slightly. She took in….a big blur. She wasn't able to focus and the anesthetic in her system ensured that she was in no particular rush to do so; instead she felt content to continue 'floating' for a while. As she closed her eyes, she became more aware of her breathing.

Several minutes later she opened her eyes again, squinting and seeing a more detailed blur…even though she couldn't see clearly, she felt certain there was nothing familiar about this place. Some time later, how long she could not tell, she opened her eyes again and found that she was in a hospital room. The room was empty and as silent as a tomb; the air a bit too cool for comfort. When she tried to move her head slightly a burning pain shot up the back of her skull, terminating at the very top. She scanned the room as much as she could without moving her head; she could see an IV tube sticking out from underneath a patch of white medical tape on the inside of her forearm. Her head was now somewhat clearer, but she still wasn't conscious enough to ask herself why she was in a hospital bed.

Then, quite suddenly, a fragment of the why flashed in her mind; a burly hand sporting a dragon approaching her face too quickly for her to move out of it's path, a frightening gravelly voice shouting in anger, being bound and gagged and tortured, an impact on her skull as if it were an empty shell with no feeling at all, and finally…nothing. In the space of perhaps sixty seconds, she'd gone from 'floating' carefree to trembling with fear, and she was recalling more about her situation as the seconds ticked by. He would find her, he was immensely powerful and his anger was equally powerful. He would find her and he would finish what he'd started, and of that she had no doubt. None at all. A deep depression formed in the pit of her stomach, a feeling she'd lived with for the last eight years.

In truth, she was a girl who'd never caught a break. Honey was born in the Midwest to a mother who lived for her next high and a father who'd left before she'd even been born. She was made a ward of the state and spent the next fifteen years in institutions and foster homes where she was molested, abused and perhaps most injuriously of all, ignored. At fifteen, she saw no advantage in staying put, and never knowing stability or love, ran away, eventually arriving at Grand Central Station in New York City without so much as a suitcase. There she fell prey to a scavenger whose trade was exploitation of the weak and helpless. Her antagonist did his best to addict her to heroin in order to control her, but in a rare reversal of fortunes she somehow rejected the drugs during the following year, and stopped using altogether. Her situation and the psychological scars she carried made her 'pliant' enough for her pimp never the less.

Honey had as much of a capacity for love and self-respect as anyone, but between the orphanages, foster homes and now the bordello, she'd never been in an environment that encouraged or even afforded it; she'd never had a chance in her life for it to develop. In fact, for someone who'd been through what she had, it was ironic that she was neither cynical nor manipulative; she was primarily…a victim.

Nibbling at the very edges of the silence of her room, she began to hear faint noises; talking…a door…it was hard to discern. As the sounds grew louder a panic started to grow inside of her, but it soon turned to a resignation that he'd come back…to finish what he'd started. A feeling of misery washed over her. Her stomach began to ache and her eyes welled up with tears of hopelessness, 'I'm tired.' she thought 'I'm tired of living.'

Suddenly the door burst open and she braced herself for the hammer that was about to fall.

“Well well well… how ya doin’ Hun?” Eddie asked boisterously.

He looked larger than life to her, healthy and strong. More to the point, he wasn’t the killer she’d expected. She didn’t react, she didn’t know how to in this moment.

“Jeeze you look awful.” Eddie said, his tone somewhere between seriousness and humor “Believe me, I’ve seen worse. They treating you OK?” he asked with a huge smile.

No response, a look of complete confusion registered on her face. Eddie recognized it and decided to take the direct approach. He reached out and gently took both of her hands, held them together in his. She noticed his were warm…large and warm.

“Look at me.” Eddie said.

He leaned over the bed, bringing his face close to hers. She looked into his eyes. He was very wide, she noticed, his shoulders filled her field of view at this distance. His eyes were clear and unflinching, his stare intense, almost mesmerizing, and he was just inches from her face.

“You’re safe now. He’s gone, for good. Understand?” he said in a gentle but firm voice.

She began to look away, not ready to give up her fear.

“Look at me Hun…” he said again, coming even closer to her face, squeezing her hands just a bit more. “…he’s gone, for good. I mean gone. OK? Do what I tell you and you have nothing to fear. Believe me.”

It wasn’t a question…he was not asking to be believed. He was telling her. She found his words irresistible; he didn’t flinch and there was no hesitation or doubt in his stare or his voice. What was it she was feeling about this man, his grip was strong and...'protective' she decided, 'Protective but not domineering'. Perhaps she should trust him; she’d arrived at a point where she needed to trust someone.

In spite of the pain, she nodded slowly.

“Good” he let go of her hands, and touched her cheek gently “Good.”

Tears were still falling gently down her cheeks, but now they were tears of relief.

"Remember this guy?" Eddie said with a wide grin, and stepped aside.

"How you feelin…" Armando said, and for some reason she could not fathom, his round jovial face had an immediate calming effect on her. "…or are you feeling anything yet?" he asked with a good natured and sympathetic smile.

She smiled at him, not a painted on smile but a genuine and quite angelic one.

"I can't explain everything to you right now." Eddie said. "You're going to heal up here, and when they say you're well enough to leave, you'll go with Armando. You'll be working for him now."

A troubled expression immediately flashed across her face.

Eddie noticed it and touched her cheek "You've had a rough trip kid." he shook his head in sympathy "A rough ride." he stared at her for a moment, then smiled "Relax. You don't earn a living on your back anymore. We understand each other?" he said, suddenly serious.

It was a little frightening, he was smiling but his eyes said something else entirely.

"Armando is a good friend of mine. I've know him for a lot of years and I trust him." Eddie said "He's completely legit. He's going to take you in with him, as a favor to me. That means if you screw up, it's on my head." he said "This is your chance to make things right for yourself…or yours to throw away, if that's what you want to do." his look was chilling. "You've been made to suffer enough in your life kid, but you made it through. You lasted long enough to catch a break. This is it."

Eddie was silent for a few seconds as he turned to study the setting sun through the window; after a contemplative pause he said in a gentle voice barely above a whisper "It's not your fault kid…it never was."

She looked solemnly from Eddie to Armando and back again, struggling to hold back the tide of emotions she felt suddenly welling up inside of her. She nodded, though she wasn't sure he'd seen it.

Armando, wanting to lighten the mood, spoke up "I'm opening a new restaurant, it's been my dream and now it's finally going to happen." he continued with a frustrated smile "I'm buried. If you can step up there's a real opportunity. It's a tough business; we'll either sink or swim...but I'd rather swim." he chuckled.

As she listened to his words his enthusiasm was contagious...but there was more.

"Who does the cooking, you or your wife?" she asked in a quiet voice.

"I have a really good chef I'm working with on the menu and wine selection, he's the best." then added as an afterthought "I'm not married."

She found herself very interested in that last bit of information. There was an odd feeling she had about this man, she'd never felt this way before and it was disorienting, inexplicable and pleasant all at the same time. Her eyes began to tear up again.

Armando stepped close to console her "It's OK. It's going to be OK now." and then he reached out and gently took her hands in his and asked "What's your name?"

The tears that began as a trickle became a river. Her shoulders shuddered and trembled as she felt an emotional release unlike any she had experienced before. Her face was contorted in pain and her mouth was gaping wide open, but she didn't make a single sound. Armando thought it an apt metaphor for the pain this girl must have silently endured and it deepened his empathy for her beyond measure. In a moment of self-discovery he realized that regardless of her past, there was something about her that touched him. He could not get his arms around it, but it prompted a sort of wonder. In that moment, with her wet anguished face pressed to his shirt, he knew that he'd do whatever was necessary to protect her, to take care of her. While it was a completely unexpected and improbable development ...but there it was.

When her sobs had slowed, she gathered herself up emotionally and looked up into his eyes.

She hesitated, and then took the first step into the rest of her life, whispering "My name is Mary Elizabeth." as if she was telling a secret that she'd had to hide for a very long time "Mary Elizabeth Wynn".

Eddie had already slipped out and was getting into his car. He squinted through the salt-streaked windshield at a blazing red sun that was setting behind the west wing of the hospital, and smiled.

# Chapter 41
# *Beginnings*

Eddie went to the social club looking for Angelo. Not seeing him, he took a seat and fished a paperback out of his pocket, reclined in the creaky wooden chair and waited.

"Crimes and…?" a Voice said from behind him.

He turned to see Jimmy Knievel squinting to read the title of the book from tiny printing in the margin at the top of each page.

"Crimes Against Logic." Eddie corrected him.

Jimmy gave him a blank look and a shrug.

"Fuhgetaboutit." Eddie said with a wave of his hand. "The old man around?"

"Yeah. We had a sit down with our friend about the Prick." Jimmy said, meaning that Angelo and Nicky Trosa had a discussion regarding Richie Scala.

Eddie nodded, he knew not to ask about it; it wasn't Jimmy's place to say, it was Angelo's to reveal if he chose to.

"I need to see him." Eddie said.

"Yeah, sit tight a minute." Jimmy said patting Eddie on the shoulder.

A few minutes later, Eddie heard Angelo Cento's voice behind him and turned in time to see him gesture to Pin for an espresso. He sat at his usual table and motioned Eddie over.

"How're things?" Angelo started.

"That depends." Eddie said, grinning. He sat down and placed his hands flat on the table top.

"Smartass." Angelo said in a good natured way.

"Can I ask about how it went with Nicky?"

"Yeah. You can ask. Tell me what you have to tell me." Angelo said.

Eddie slid his right hand forward between Angelo's hands and then pulled it back, leaving a tiny folded piece of paper. It looked like a magic trick. Angelo glanced at it and put it in his pocket.

"It's all there?" Angelo asked.

"Minus my end, what was owed to our guy on the inside, and a little bit for a friend of mine who helped us out…yeah it's all there."

"Loose ends?"

"Nothing I can't handle." Eddie said "Which leads us to…" he let it hang in the air.

"Yeah." Angelo said, waiting until Pin had placed the espresso in front of him and retreated "The guy, the problem, he's been sent for. It looks like he was holding out."

Eddie noticed how carefully Angelo said that, not 'He was holding out.' but instead 'It looks like he was holding out.' It was Angelo's way of reminding Eddie that the nature of the problem had always been political.

"Not surprising." Eddie observed.

"Nicky was worried that he was stepping on our toes." Angelo said.

"Really?" Eddie asked rhetorically.

"Did you just hear me say so?" Angelo asked; his tone demonstrating that there was nothing casual about any of this.

"So he's been sent for."

"Nicky's smart." Angelo said reassuringly.

Angelo meant that Nicky Trosa almost certainly knew more than he'd admit to knowing; how much he knew…well that's the way the game was played. Since Nicky called for the sit-down with Angelo, in essence confirming that Richie had gone over the line, it meant that whatever Nicky did know didn't cause him any great angst toward anyone but Richie.

Angelo read the expression on Eddie's face, aside from Antonia he was probably the only one that could "It's not all said and done. They're not gonna find him?"

"I doubt it." Eddie confirmed.

"Well, Nicky's had enough aggravation over the years, he might get irritated, but I don't think he'll want somebody's head. It was his guy freelancing, not mine. If you're gonna do that you take your chances."

Angelo took a sip of his espresso.

Eddie was at a decision point, he'd thought about it from every angle, and now that it was here, he still felt some trepidation about having overlooked or misjudged some aspect of his situation. True to himself though, he took a breath and pushed forward.

"Maybe a gesture, to save face?" Eddie shrugged.

"Save face huh?" Angelo asked contemplatively.

"Well, God forbid they don't find him, he was a member."

"Yeah." Angelo agreed.

A few seconds of silence passed, then Angelo continued.

"Like I said, I don't think he'll call for anybody's head. He'd have to open that can of worms again. He won't want that."

In the next moment Eddie would find out how well he'd gambled. Angelo spoke again.

"But short of that, he might want some gesture." *If you ask me to leave the life, I'm not going to kill you.*

Eddie nodded "Yeah, I was thinking that too." *I want to leave.*

"How's your crew, everything in line?" *Who do you think is the right guy to take over?*

"Good. Solid. Tony Donato has been stepping up, he's a good man." *Tony D. is who you want.*

"Yeah, he's a sharp kid." *I agree.*

Just then, Pin set down two shot glasses of Johnny Walker Blue Label on the table, and left.

Angelo picked up a shot glass and handed it to Eddie; picking up the other he raised his glass "No one could have done it better kid. Salute."

Both men threw back their drinks and set down their glasses.

Angelo said "OK, it's time for you to leave. I got some things to take care of." he spoke with an expression on his face that Eddie found curious.

Eddie felt confused; the scalp on the back of his head was tingling. He was missing something. They both rose and uncharacteristically Angelo gave him an embrace and kissed him on both cheeks. In spite of this, Eddie didn't sense danger, it was more like a feeling that something was staring him in the face and he just wasn't seeing it.

He turned to leave and heard Angelo ask "How's that girl of yours?"

He turned back to face Angelo "She's fine."

"That's a solid girl you've got, a good girl. You really ought to marry her before she finds out what a strunz you are." Angelo said, half smiling.

Eddie smiled and before he could reply he heard the door open and turned to see Tony D. coming in out of the cold. Angelo gestured to Tony that he'd be a minute. Eddie turned back to Angelo, that curious half smile still on his face.

"Go on, get out of here…I gotta take care of some things." *Goodbye Eddie Ferrara.*

As Eddie passed Tony, he said "I'll give you a call tonight."

Tony nodded, glancing at Angelo with a worried expression on his face.

'He hasn't figured it out yet.' Eddie thought 'He'd better get his brain in gear if he's going to handle things.'

"Smile, things are good." he said to Tony.

"Yeah?"

"Yeah." Eddie chuckled "You worry too much."

"Fuhgetaboutit." Tony said, hugging Eddie and then heading over to Angelo who was ready for him.

As he opened the door to leave, a burst of frigid air hit him squarely on the face; he turned and took a last look inside the club. His eyes fixed on Angelo and Tony D. sitting at the table, and he smiled and thought to himself 'That Angelo…he saw it coming…he was already there. He's a cagey bastard.' He pushed himself out against the wind, and for the last time, left the club.

*San Jose, California*

Scott, Diane, Vincent and Chuck were sitting in ExchangeVault's employee break room. It was nearly eight o'clock, the sun had set and the four were spread out, feet up on adjacent chairs and wanting to see the article in the San Jose

Mercury News about the recent arrest at their company. Scott had the only copy and said he would read it aloud, but out of habit started to read the first paragraph to himself.

Vincent scrunched his face up, as if he was totally mentally focused, and placed the tips of his fingers at his temples as he leaned toward Scott.

Scott noticed strange pose and inquired "Hmm?"

"I'm trying to develop psychic power." Vincent said, continuing his 'mind-reading' pose.

"What?" Scott asked, confused.

"How are we supposed to know what the hell your reading!" he said irritated.

"Excitable. Asians. Don'ya think?" Scott said to Diane.

"We're waiting." she returned, straight faced.

"On Friday police arrested Barton Peale at his office in the newly founded valley company ExchangeVault. Mr. Peale, Senior Vice President of Sales, was charged in connection with theft at the company a week ago. The nature and amount of the theft has not been released to the public, but sources indicate it was substantial. Mr. Peale allegedly conspired with a second man, Jacob Seiden, Principal Software Architect at Seventeen O Three Associates, a New York based software company. Police are seeking information regarding the location of Mr. Seiden, and encourage anyone with information of his whereabouts to report it immediately."

"That's it?" Chuck asked.

"Yup." Scott replied.

"Hmm. Not much." Chuck said.

"Gratefully." Scott said, shooting a glance at Vincent.

"I'm sorry about one thing." Diane sighed.

"What's that?" Scott asked.

"I didn't get a picture of BTB in handcuffs." Diane said.

"How did he react?" Vincent asked.

"The police went into his office, and when they came out with him his face was beet red." Diane said in a low voice "He was crying."

Scott and Vincent shared another glance, as each recalled their conversation earlier in the day. They'd been forced into the middle of the thing that BTB had started. They were glad to see him gone.

“Well, it’s getting late.” Chuck said “Sushi anyone?”

“Naa, not me.” Scott said.

Diane shook her head.

“What about you Margret Cho?” he said to Vincent “You gonna leave me hangin?”

“Tide?” Vincent asked. Rising Tide Sushi was a favorite spot a few miles away.

“Tiiiiiide. Alright Vincentè, ma brutha from anotha mutha. Ma sista from anotha mista, ma Margret Cho from anotha ho….”

“Cut that out, or you’re going alone.” Vincent interrupted.

He and Chuck got up, noisily replaced their chairs and said their goodbyes, making their way out of the building.

Scott and Diane sat in silence, not as awkward as it was empty.

“Diane?”

“Scott.”

“Would you like to have dinner with me tonight?”

“Si.”

“Really? Great!”

“It took you long enough.” she giggled.

“I know. It’s work, you know how it is. It’s…” Scott searched for the right word.

“Delicate?” Diane offered.

“Delicate. Yes. Exactly! Delicate!” he shook his head at Diane “That’s what it is, it’s delicate.”

“Yes I think we’ve established that it’s delicate.”

“Yes. Yes I suppose we have.” Scott said feeling somewhat relieved.

“Sooo?” Diane asked “Are we going to eat out of these vending machines? Is that your idea of how to impress a gal?”

“No." he said emphatically, shaking his head a little "No no no no."

He got up and walked over closer to the sandwich machine and tilted his head sideways so he could read the label on a sandwich in the machine “I think you deserve better than…’Tuna Salad with Lettuce and Tomato.’" then in a tone of equivocation, added "Although, it won’t be past its expiration date until this coming Wednesday." he kept his head horizontal and swiveled it to give her a questioning look.

Diane scrunched up her nose and shook her head.

"Alright, then I guess it's off to beautiful downtown Saratoga, lets take a look over by Big Basin Way."

"Now you're talkin'." she said smiling.

As Scott picked up and reassembled his newspaper, he said absentmindedly "I wonder how they found out about BTB."

Diane looked serious, just for a moment, and said "I don't know, it's not a big place. Maybe someone overheard something. You never know." then she turned and left to lock up her desk.

Scott stood in the empty cafeteria for a moment, contemplating if she was saying that she was that someone.

"Enough intrigue for one day…" he boomed "I'm hungry! Let the feast begin!" he made a flourish with his hands to the empty room, turned the corner out of the break room and yelled, knowing he and Diane were the only two left in the building "Diane?"

He heard a distant "Yes?" from her behind the sea of cubicles.

"Loose the pigeons!"

He heard her chuckle.

"Today is the day Diane. The big one's coming. I can feel it in my bones!"

"Today? It's nighttime."

"Inspiration doesn't run on a schedule!"

"Can we eat first?"

"Yes! Sustenance! We shall drink from the finest kegs!" he said, as she passed him, he followed her to the back door and out into the parking lot. He opened the door to his car for her and with a deep bow said "m'lady…" gesturing her to the passenger seat of his Lotus Esprit.

She got in and looked up at him "m'lord…" giving him a royal nod as he gently closed her door.

Scott was suddenly feeling an intense wave of relief, now that the recent problems were behind him. However, the sudden excitement and anticipation he felt about the future possibilities with Diane eclipsed everything as he rounded the car in four long strides, hopped in the driver seat and roared out of the parking lot.

# § Characters §

**Eddie Ferrara:** Connected to the Angelo Cento crew.
**Margret Ferrara:** Eddie's mother.
**Aldo Ferrara:** Eddie's father, and owner of Aldo's pizza.
**Carmella Ferrara:** Eddie's older sister.
**Peter Ferrara:** Eddie's older brother.
**Antonia Stellini:** Eddie's girlfriend.
**Philly Constantine:** Connected to Eddie's crew.
**Vin:** Connected to Eddie's crew.
**Tony '*Tony D.*' Donato:** Connected to Eddies' crew.
**Angelo Cento:** Eddie's *capo*.
**Primo '*Pin*' Pinelli:** Member of the Cento crew.
**Victor Forza, Sr.:** A *capo* predecessor of Angelo Cento and Mario Ruzzi, and father of Eddie's boyhood friend 'Junior' Forza.
**Marie Forza:** Wife of Victor Forza Sr.
**Jimmy '*Knievel*' Leonardo:** Member of Angelo Cento's crew.
**Benny Guomondussonur:** Small time drug dealer.
**Louie:** Owner of Louie's Tavolo da Pranzo in the Bronx, and cousin of Angelo Cento.
**Victor '*Junior*' Forza, Jr.:** Boyhood friend of Eddie's and son of *capo* Victor Forza.
**Carmine '*Buddy*' Ruzzi:** Boyhood friend of Eddie's and the son of Mario Ruzzi.
**Mario Ruzzi:** Member of the Forza crew and father of Buddy Ruzzi.
**De Luca:** Fell to a quick right from Brother Curran.
**Brother Mark Curran**: The principal of Eddie's high school.
**Jerry Havik:** A boyhood friend of Eddie's.
**Armando Navas:** A friend and business associate of Eddie's.
**Ricky Montez:** One half of The Two Rickys, and business associate of Eddie's.
**Jimmy '*Ricky*' Johnson:** The other half of The Two Rickys, and business associate of Eddie's.
**Val:** Part of the gang that killed Buddy Ruzzi.
**Pira:** Part of the gang that killed Buddy Ruzzi.
**Snakes:** The unlucky bastard that actually shot Buddy Ruzzi.
**Pete Oh'Alin:** Owner of the Shore Inn.
**Ruairi Oh'Alin:** Pete's son, and the bartender at Italia!
**Mike Zirella:** Connected to the Cento crew and owner of the clubs Spice and Hi-Class.
**X Cap, Nike Shirt and Gold Chains:** Enforcers at Mike Zirella's Hi-Class bordello.
**Giovanni '*Gio*':** Employed by Mike Zirella to run Hi-Class.
**Mary Elizabeth '*Honey*' Wynn:** Prostitute employed at Hi-Class.
**Jacob Seiden:** Principal Software Architect at Seventeen O Three Associates.
**Richie '*The Prick*' Scala:** Member of the Nicky Trosa crew.
**Carolyn Oh'Alin-Fontana and Dominick Fontana:** the young married couple that Richie Scala killed.

**The Bello Brothers, Hector and Spook:** Leaders of a ruthless drug and prostitution empire in the Bronx.
**Anthony Parisi:** College student victim of the Bello Brothers.
**Salvatore '*Big Sal*' Parisi:** A member of the family and uncle to Anthony Parisi.
**Nicky Trosa:** Richie Scala's *capo*.
**Scott Monson:** Program Manager at technology startup ExchangeVault.
**Andy:** Owner of The Coffee Terrorists coffee shop.
**Martin:** Barista at The Coffee Terrorists.
**Doug:** Manager of the debug team at ExchangeVault.
**Diane West:** Administrative assistant to the CEO at ExchangeVault.
**Barton '*Barry*' '*BTB*' Peale:** Vice President of Sales at ExchangeVault.
**Vincent Ko:** Senior programmer at ExchangeVault.
**Carlos '*Chuck*' Vega:** Programmer at ExchangeVault.
**Michael '*The Fish*' Moretti:** Rival *capo* of Victor Forza, Sr.
**Joe Cuomo:** Member of Moretti's crew.
**Pat Vinci:** Member of Moretti's crew.
**Tommy Fornaio:** the leader of the gang that set up Eddie Ferrara in his early years.
**Tony Bianco:** *Consigliere* in the family during Victor Forza Sr.'s time as *capo*.
**Carmine Mendoza:** Old friend of Victor Forza, Sr.
**John '*Chick*' Fusco:** Son-in-law of the Boss of the family.
**Francesca:** Daughter of the Boss of the family.
**Eliyahu Beretski:** Second owner of Aldo's Pizza.
**Rita Beretski:** Eliyahu's wife, and baker at Aldo's Pizza.
**Regina Beretski:** Eliyahu's daughter; cook and waitress at Aldo's Pizza.
**Mrs. Ayala:** Customer from Fortino's Bakery.
**Jackie Fortino:** Works at Fortino's Bakery. He's not married, it's a sin.
**Matthew '*Zatz*' Barra:** Member of Nicky Trosa's crew and government cooperating witness.
**Ronnie '*The Pope*' Simonetti:** Member of Nicky Trosa's crew.
**Al Cusimano:** Member of Nicky Trosa's crew.
**Crazy John Morozov:** The upside down victim.
**Ray Phillips:** EFT Service Representative at Mediex's bank.
**Suri Poria:** Technical sales representative at ExchangeVault.
**Lynn Jones:** Contact at Parker Content's bank.
**Frank Caforo:** Nicky Trosa's closest cousin.
**Elaine Caforo:** Frank Caforo's wife, runs Plaza Travel.
**Joey '*Bags*' Ross:** Connected to Richie Scala's crew.
**Sammy '*DMV*' Cotti:** Connected to Richie Scala's crew.
**Genaro '*Pipe*' Benvenuto:** Connected to Richie Scala's crew.
**Michael '*Little Mike*' Sullivan:** Connected to Richie Scala's crew.
**Frank Carbone:** Underboss, over *capos* Angelo Cento and Nicky Trosa.

**About the author:** Born and raised in New York City, Nick Apuzzo spent his formative years in the Bronx during the 60's, 70's and 80's. While studying engineering he had the opportunity to work for a large technology company which led to a long career in high-tech engineering and sales, affording him the opportunity to venture out of New York. He currently lives in the San Francisco Bay area of California. This is his first novel.

LaVergne, TN USA
08 July 2010
188837LV00001B/30/P